USA TODAY bestselling and RITA® Award–nominated author **Caitlin Crews** loves writing romance. She teaches her favourite romance novels in creative writing classes at places like UCLA Extension's prestigious Writers' Programme, where she finally gets to utilise the MA and PhD in English Literature she received from the University of York in England. She currently lives in the Pacific Northwest, with her very own hero and too many pets. Visit her at caitlincrews.com.

Canadian **Dani Collins** knew in high school that she wanted to write romance for a living. Twenty-five years later, after marrying her high school sweetheart, having two kids with him, working at several generic office jobs and submitting countless manuscripts, she got The Call. Her first Mills & Boon novel won the Reviewers' Choice Award for Best First in Series from *RT Book Reviews*. She now works in her own office, writing romance.

UNWRAPPING THE INNOCENT'S SECRET

CAITLIN CREWS

BOUND BY THEIR NINE-MONTH SCANDAL

DANI COLLINS

MILLS & BOON

First Published in Great Britain 2019
by Mills & Boon, an imprint of HarperCollins*Publishers*
1 London Bridge Street, London, SE1 9GF

Unwrapping the Innocent's Secret © 2019 by Caitlin Crews

Bound by Their Nine-Month Scandal © 2019 by Dani Collins

ISBN: 978-0-263-27366-3

MIX
Paper from
responsible sources
FSC™ C007454

Printed and bound in Spain
by CPI, Barcelona

UNWRAPPING
THE INNOCENT'S
SECRET

CAITLIN CREWS

To all our wonderful Modern readers—
this one is for you!

CHAPTER ONE

"I BEG YOUR PARDON, sir," his secretary said in the pointedly diffident way that always managed to convey the full range of his feelings.

Pascal Furlani shared them.

And he was not a man who ordinarilyf accepted the existence of feelings, unless they suited him. Or benefited him in some way.

"I have taken the liberty of compiling yet another slate of candidates," Guglielmo continued in that same tone, because he was not the sort of secretary who was afraid to share his opinions, feelings, or thoughts, however he might dress them up. "As the last several met with disfavor."

There was a dig in that, Pascal knew. He stood, not at the window that looked out over one of Rome's wealthiest neighborhoods, but at the glass partition that separated him from the rest of his sleek, modern office. It was the perfect antidote to the fussiness and great weight of Roman history everywhere else in the city.

Pascal knew too well what the three-thousand-year-old city looked like, from its forgotten streets to its most renowned *piazzas*. He knew how it felt to grow up rough and ignored in the shadow of the ruins of former great glories. And what life in this city had made him, the cast-off bastard son of a man who acknowledged only his legitimate issue and turned his back entirely on his mistakes.

He had earned every inch of the sweeping views his office commanded, but he was far prouder of what he'd done inside the walls of The Furlani Company.

Pascal had considered it a decent start when his personal wealth exceeded not only that of his father, but of all his father's legitimate children, too. Combined. He'd achieved that milestone in the first year after the accident.

The accident.

Pascal's lips thinned in inevitable displeasure as his mind tugged him back to the period of his life he most wanted to forget. The one stretch of his life where he'd lost focus. Where he'd come *this close* to forgetting himself completely.

He would never forget that his father had thrown him away like so much trash. He refused to forgive it. He did not hunger for revenge, necessarily—he wanted his life to be its own reckoning. Pascal chose to dominate from afar and show his father precisely as much interest as had been shown to him. And he had not wavered in this purpose since he'd been a small boy—save for that one regrettable winter.

It was not every man who could say that his rise from the ashes was not metaphoric, but entirely literal. The way they always did, Pascal's fingers found the grooves on his jaw that told the tale of the car crash that had left him scarred forever.

He quite liked them. The scars reminded him who he

was and where he'd been, and how close he'd come to walking away from his purpose and ambition for what was, in the end, such a small temptation.

Not that his memories of that time were…small, exactly.

Nonetheless, the office reminded him where he was going. What he'd built with his own hands and force of will. It reinforced his goals. All of them sleek, mon-eyed, and each a pointed jab at the father who had never claimed him and the memory of a lost mother who had left him to his fate with no more than a shrug.

He had no intention of forgetting every last moment of how he'd come to be here.

"If you'll turn your attention to your tablet, sir," came his secretary's voice, excessively placid. Its own pointed jab, as usual. "I have arranged a selection of heiresses for your viewing pleasure, ordered in terms of their social standing."

Pascal turned away from his offices, all that granite and steel that he found so comforting here in the middle of ancient Rome. The building was filled to bursting with his vision. His money. His people acting to bring his dreams to fruition.

It was time for him to take the next step and find a wife.

Whether Pascal *wanted* to be married had little to do with it. A wife would make him look more stable, more settled, which some of the more conservative accounts preferred. A wife would conceivably keep him out of the tabloids, which his board would certainly prefer. And a wife would give Pascal legitimate heirs to his fortune and power.

Pascal would die before he consigned a child of his

to the things he'd suffered, first and foremost being the lack of his father's name.

In addition, getting married would put an end to the mutterings of his board. That Pascal, as a single man with healthy appetites, was an embarrassment to his own company. That Pascal was somehow less trustworthy than other CEOs, imbued as they all were with wives and children, all legitimate and legal.

No one ever mentioned the mistresses and unclaimed bastards on the side, of course. No one ever did.

Pascal dropped his hand from his jaw. Something about his scars—which he knew were faded now to white instead of the angry red they'd been at first—was making him maudlin today.

Welcome to December, a voice inside him said. Snidely.

He knew what time of year it was. And why his thoughts kept returning to the crash and the flames that had very nearly been the end of him. But he had no intention of celebrating that anniversary. He never did.

He eyed his secretary, waiting with obvious impatience, instead.

"What makes you think that this collection of desperate, grasping socialites will be more appealing than the last?" he asked.

"Are we looking for *appealing*, sir? I'm not sure I had that on my list. I was looking more for *suitable*."

Pascal was sure he saw the hint of a smirk on his secretary's face, though the other man knew better than to succumb in full.

"Careful, Guglielmo," he murmured. "Or I may begin to suspect that you do not take this enterprise as seriously as you should."

He walked back to his desk, a massive slab of granite that looked like what it was. A throne and a monument to Pascal's hard-won power and influence. Guglielmo gestured toward the tablet computer that lay in the center, and Pascal checked a sigh as he picked it up and scrolled through the offerings.

Lady this, daughter of Somebody Pedigreed, the toast of this or that finishing school. The daughter of a Chinese philanthropist. Two French girls from separate families that were connected—somewhere back in the deep, dark, tangled roots of their family trees—to ancient kings and queens. An Argentinian heiress, raised on cattle money halfway across the world.

They were all beautiful, in their way. If not classically so, then polished to shine. They were all accomplished, in one way or another. One ran her own charity. One performed the flute with a world-renowned orchestra. Another spent the bulk of her time on humanitarian missions. And not one of them had ever been mentioned in a tabloid newspaper.

Pascal refused to consider anyone with a whiff of paparazzi interest about them or near them, like the California wine heiress who was herself marvelously spotless, but had been best friends since boarding school with a celebrity whose life played out in headlines across the globe. No, thank you. He wanted no scandals. No dark secrets, poised to emerge at the worst possible time. No secrets at all, come to that.

Pascal was a scandal. His whole life had been first a secret, then a shock, trumpeted in headlines of its own. His tawdry, illegitimate birth and his shipping magnate father's steadfast refusal to acknowledge his existence throughout his life might as well have been another set of scars on the other side of his face. He had always felt marked by the circumstances of his birth, his parents' poor choices.

He would always be marked by these things.

His wife, accordingly, had to be without stain.

"You do not look pleased, sir," Guglielmo said drily. "Yet again. I fear I must remind you that an unblemished heiress of reasonable social standing is, in fact, a finite resource. One we may have exhausted." He inclined his head slightly when Pascal glared at him. "Sir."

"I'm meeting with the last of the previous selection of possibilities tonight," Pascal reminded him.

"I made the reservation myself, sir. Moments after you informed me that the meeting you'd had with another woman on that list was, in your words, appalling beyond reason."

"She did not resemble her photograph," Pascal said darkly.

"Sadly, that is part and parcel of the digital dating culture we all now—"

"Guglielmo. She was a sweet-looking, conservatively dressed blonde in the pictures you showed me. She showed up with a blue and pink Mohawk and a sleeve of tattoos. I liked her more that way, if I am honest, but I can hardly parade a punk rock princess in front of my board. If I could, I would."

"The woman you're meeting tonight has a robust social media presence and absolutely no hint of punk rock about her," Guglielmo replied blandly. "I checked myself."

Pascal found his fingers on his scars again. "Perhaps I will be swept away tonight and all of this will prove unnecessary."

"Hope springs eternal," Guglielmo murmured.

After Pascal dismissed him, he didn't launch himself into one of the numerous tasks awaiting his attention. He could see his emails piling up. His message light was blinking. But instead of handling them he found himself sitting at his desk, scowling out at the physical evidence of the empire he'd built. Brick by bloody brick.

Because once again, the only thing in his head was her.

His angel of mercy. His greatest temptation.

The woman who had nearly wrecked him before he'd begun.

It is December, he reminded himself. *This is always how it feels in December. Come the New Year she will fade again, the way she always does.*

His phone rang, snapping him back to reality and far away from that godforsaken northern village in a forgotten valley in the Dolomites. Where he had crashed and burned—literally.

And she had nursed him back to life.

Then had haunted him ever since, for his sins.

Tonight, he vowed as he turned his attention to the tasks awaiting him, he would leave the past where it belonged, and concentrate on the next bright part of his glorious future.

"I think it's important to set very clear boundaries from the start," his date informed him much later that evening. She had arrived late, clearly full of herself in her role as a minor member of the Danish nobility. She had swept into one of the most exclusive restaurants in Rome with her nose in the air, as if Pascal had suggested she meet him at one of those sticky, plastic American fast food restaurants. Her expression had not improved over the course of their initial drinks. "Obviously, the point of any merger is to secure the line."

"The line?"

"I am prepared to commit to an heir and a spare," she told him loftily. "To be commenced and completed within a four-year period. And I think it's best to agree, up front and in writing, that the production of any progeny should be conducted under controlled circumstances."

Pascal was sure he'd had more romantic conversations on industrial sites.

"Is it a production line?" he asked, his voice dry. "A factory of some kind?"

"I already have an excellent fertility specialist, discreet and capable, who can ensure to everyone's satisfaction and all legalities that the correct DNA carries on into the next generation."

Pascal blinked at that. He had had simpering dinners. Overtly sexual ones. Direct, frank approaches. But this was new. It all seemed so…mechanical.

"You are staring at me as if I've said something astonishing," his date said.

"I beg your pardon." Pascal attempted to smile, though he wasn't sure when or if he'd ever felt less charming. "Are you suggesting that we concoct offspring in a laboratory? Rather than go about making them in the more time-honored fashion, favored as it has been for a great many eons already?"

"This is a business arrangement," his chilly date replied, looking, if possible, more severe than before. "I expect you will find your release elsewhere, as will I. Discreetly, of course. I do not hold with scandal."

"Nothing is less scandalous than a sexless marriage, naturally."

A faint suggestion of a line appeared between her perfectly shaped brows. "There's no need to muddy a perfectly functional marriage with that sort of thing, surely."

"You've thought of everything," he replied.

And later, after he had left his date with a curt nod and an insincere promise to have his people contact her, Pascal waved off his driver and walked instead.

Because Rome was its own reward. The city of his birth and his poverty-stricken childhood. The city where he had become a man, by his own estimation, then joined the military to give himself what his mother couldn't and his father would never. Discipline. A life. Even a career. It had seemed such an elegant solution.

Until that night six years ago when he'd followed a reckless whim, on a moody December night very much like this one. It had been raining in Rome. He'd hoped that meant it was snowing in the Dolomites, on the edge of the Alps, and had decided he might as well drive himself up north and learn how to ski.

He laughed a bit at that as he moved through Piazza Navona and its annual Christmas Market that made the crowded square even more filled and frenetic. He dodged the usual stream of tourists and his own countrymen, taking in the night air and already surrendering to the pollution of Christmas that would invade everything until the Epiphany, then thankfully disappear into the clarity of the New Year.

The night was cold and leaning toward dampness. It was the perfect sort of weather to ask himself how he'd ended up with the coldest, most clinical woman

imaginable tonight. Was that really what he was reduced to? A laboratory experiment masquerading as
a marriage?

He knew he needed to marry, but somehow, he had
imagined it would be...less cold-blooded. Warmer. Or
cordial, at the very least.

And he wanted to make his babies his own damned
self. More than that, he had no intention of following
in his father's footsteps in any regard. Once he married, Pascal had no intention of cheating. He was not
planning to have "arrangements" on the side. He wasn't
planning on having an *on the side*, for that matter.

He had no intention of creating another woman like
his mother, so fragile and so lost she couldn't take care
of her own son. And he would never, ever risk the possibility that he might create an illegitimate child of his
own.

The very idea made him sick.

His phone buzzed in his pocket, and he knew it was
Guglielmo, checking in the way he always did after
these excruciating "dates" that were little more than
vetting sessions. Because Pascal persisted in imagining that he could cut through all the nonsense, ask for
exactly what he wanted and then get it. It had worked
in business, why not in marriage?

Pascal didn't answer the call.

There were a million more things that required his
attention, but he couldn't face them just yet. Instead, he
lost himself in the chaotic embrace of the Eternal City.
Rome was a monument, yet Rome was ever-changing.
Rome was a contradiction. Rome was where Pascal felt
alive. It was the place where he had grown to understand that his very existence was an affront to some,

and it was where he finally figured out how to claim that existence and make sense of it.

Walking through Rome had always soothed him. And kept him alive, some dark years. Long nights with his feet, his thoughts and the grand Roman sprawl had made him whole, time and time again.

So there was no reason at all that he should be caught up in memories of a tiny, sleepy village with steep mountains all around and very few people, where he had never been anything but broken.

He stopped by a fountain in a forgotten courtyard, steps from the roar of a busy road. The water tumbled from the pursed lips of an old god made stone, and in the dark, he almost believed he could see her reflection there in the water the way he always did in his head.

Sweet Cecilia, half nurse and half angel. A woman so lovely and so innocent that he had nearly betrayed every vow he'd ever made to himself and stayed up there in all that towering silence.

The very notion was absurd. He was Pascal Furlani. Not for him the pastoral delights, such as they were, of a remote mountain village of interest to absolutely no one unless they happened to either have been there for centuries or were a part of the quiet abbey that had also been there, in one form or another, since right about the dawn of time. Not for him a life forgotten and tucked away like that, out of sight.

She would have taken her vows by now, Pascal assumed, and become a full nun like the others in the order. Or perhaps his last, half-dreamt night there had been her fall from grace. Would she have stayed? Taken her place outside the abbey walls? Perhaps she lived in the village proper now, or off in the fields that dotted the hillsides with some or other farmer. She would be settled now, one way or the other. Committed to her Lord or married to some man, and unrecognizable.

Just as he was.

Pascal was not haunted by the specter of his childhood. He had lived through it, transcended it and moved on. He had mourned his mother's death, then buried her with greater reverence than she had ever shown him. He rarely thought of his father these days, preferring to decimate the old man and his penny-tante shipping concern from afar.

Pascal did not look back. Ever.

Unless it was to her. Cecilia.

His personal ghost.

"Enough," he muttered. He pulled a coin from his pocket, then flipped it to the air, watching as it tumbled into the water before him. He had made his last reckless decision the night he'd chosen to drive like a maniac up into those mountains in search of one of Italy's many ski resorts. He had been on leave from the army and the idea—or some demon—had seized him, which in those days was all Pascal needed. That and a bottle of something strong.

He had never made it to a ski resort. He'd spun out on a mountain pass after making a wrong turn. The clunker of a car he'd been driving—good for absolutely nothing save ejecting him through the windshield with great force—was the only reason he'd lived.

The car had burst into flames, and Pascal would have burned, too, had he not been tossed off into the unforgiving wilderness.

But even the fire was a blessing in disguise. It had alerted the villagers. They'd trooped out in the middle of the dark December night, collected his broken body and had settled him into what passed for the local hospital. The clinic connected to the abbey, where slowly, carefully, the nuns had nursed him back to health.

Pascal had been torn open, broken and out of his mind for weeks. It had taken him longer than that to heal. Then painfully learn how to move again when the casts came off.

And the greatest danger of it all was not the infections he risked or the bones that healed differently than they'd been. It was not his discharge from the military, or the entirely new life he was forced to face—and figure out while lying flat on his back—thanks to the wreckage of the old.

It was the fact that life in that forgotten village felt sweet. Easy. *Good.*

It had been the greatest temptation of his life to simply…remain.

And his favorite nun had been a part of that.

Not quite a nun, he corrected himself now, his hands deep in his pockets as he brooded at the fountain before him. She had been a novice of the order, young and sweet and uncorrupted—until she'd met him.

But when he thought of what happened between them, her cool smiles and soft hands, blooming into that one night of almost unbearable passion that still made his body stir after all these years—he couldn't help but think that she had been the one to do the corrupting.

He was a master of the universe by any reckoning, and yet…here he stood. In a dark, forgotten corner of the greatest city on earth, the world literally at his feet, her face in his memories making the city dim.

It was an outrage. It was unacceptable.

Pascal headed toward his home, three stories of the top of a building that he had refurbished to suit his particular taste. Distinctively modern inside and an appropriately battered, ancient-looking facade.

It was not lost on him that for all intents and purposes, that description could have been about him.

When he reached his building, he didn't go inside. He headed to his garage instead and somehow or another, almost without conscious thought, he found himself in one of his cars. Then heading north. This time he was neither as drunk nor as reckless as he'd been six years ago, but still. A man did not possess a car as fast as his if he did not plan to use it.

He drove for six hours, through what remained of the night and into the dawn. He stopped for breakfast and strong coffee when he reached Verona. When the espresso had revived him sufficiently, he called Guglielmo to tell him where he was.

"And may I ask, sir, why you are a great many kilometers away from the office? May I assume that your meeting last night did not go as well as you hoped?"

"You may assume what you like," Pascal replied.

And as he lingered over another espresso, Pascal had ample time to ask himself what exactly he thought he was doing. The answer came to him after he'd gotten back on the road.

The months he'd spent in the care of that abbey was the only time in his life that he could recall straying so far from who he was, and he'd resented it ever since. Bitterly. Cecilia had been a kind of enchantment. A witch in a nun's habit.

He'd told himself he was well rid of her when he'd

come back down the mountain and remembered himself at last. He'd meant it. He'd gone about creating his company and doing every last thing he'd ever dreamed.

And yet...he couldn't seem to move on. No matter how many empires he built, no matter how much richer he made himself, he was still haunted by her face.

It was high time for an exorcism.

Two hours later he found himself on the same mountain where he'd nearly died six years ago. It was a cold, crisp morning in another December, and he treated the winding mountain road with a great deal more respect than he had back then.

And this time he pulled off to the side of the road when he reached the top, because he could see the village before him.

It looked like a storybook, which only made him more determined to scrape it off whatever passed for his battered soul. It was like a dream in the morning light. Snowcapped mountains all around, and down in the small valley, fields cut by a tumbling river. What passed for the center of town was a clump of old buildings that dated from centuries past. The church stood at one end of the village with the abbey behind it and off to one side, the hospital where he had survived his recovery. He stared at it a long while, aware that his fingers were on his scars again.

Something in him turned over, with a low hum.

He told himself it was sheer horror that a man like him, raised in the middle of one of the most frenetic and sophisticated cities in the world, not to mention the luxurious lifestyle he now enjoyed, should ever have imagined that he could stay here.

Here.

It beggared belief.

He started up the car again, following the road down and around and around, until it reached the valley floor.

Where everything was exactly as he'd left it.

There was no reason that his heart should be clattering about in his chest as he drove the familiar road to the church. He would find the old priest and ask after Cecilia. He would almost surely find such a reunion faintly horrifying, and once he did, he would leave. The truth was, he'd come a very great distance for what he expected to take all of a few moments. He could have—and should have—sent Guglielmo. Or some other underling, who could have reported back on whether Cecilia was still here. For that matter, there had been no earthly reason for him to drive through the night like a man possessed. He could have taken his helicopter and landed it in the field behind the church, the same field he'd stared at week after week after week from his hospital bed.

No wonder he'd become fixated on the novice nun who'd cared for him. There had been nothing else to do. Except, Mother Superior had told him serenely, pray.

Pascal had not prayed then. He considered a prayer for deliverance now instead. Because he had surrendered to this fantasy for absolutely no good reason. This appalling tour through his own nostalgia.

"You might as well get it over with," he growled at himself.

He unfolded himself from the low-slung sports car and stood beside it a moment. It was midmorning now, and though it was a clear day, the wind rushed down from the mountain peaks and sliced straight through him. He was dressed for a sophisticated dinner in Rome, not a trip to the hinterland.

He adjusted the jacket of his bespoke suit with two impatient tugs of his hands, and didn't bother looking around. The village felt deserted. If memory served, what few villagers there were rarely congregated before the afternoon, if then. The nuns had chosen this valley well. It was the perfect spot for silent contemplation.

Pascal walked up the steps to the front door of the church. The weathered door stood open a crack, and he pushed his way inside, and then paused for a moment in the vestibule as he was walloped with memories.

It smelled the same. It looked the same. And it made his head spin as if he'd overindulged again.

What year is this? he asked himself.

The church might not have changed in the past century. But Pascal had changed tremendously since he'd left here. That was what he needed to remember.

He moved into the church proper, his gaze moving from the quiet, empty pews to the candles flickering in the alcoves. He saw no hint of the old, garrulous priest who he recalled so vividly from six years ago. The place was deserted—

But then he heard a noise. He took a few more steps and saw a washer woman on her hands and knees, scrubbing at the floor before the altar with her back to him.

She did not look around as he started down the aisle, and that gave Pascal ample opportunity to remember all the other times he'd done this exact same walk. All the times the priest had encouraged him to look within for a change, rather than continuing to look outside himself.

What is the point of all this power you seek if your heart is empty? the old man had asked him.

What do you know of either power or a heart? Pascal had replied. And he'd laughed.

But Pascal did not think the old man had been kidding. And those sneaky words were one more ghost that he couldn't quite get to leave him alone.

He dropped his gaze from the stained glass in the small nave, and stood there, several feet away from the woman on the floor. He expected her to stop what she was doing, for she must have heard him, but she didn't. Not even when he cleared his throat.

"If I might have a moment of your attention, *signorina*," he said, his voice echoing back at him from all around.

She moved then. She sat back on her knees, and tugged the headphones out of her ears in one smooth motion. And Pascal was caught, somehow, in the smoothness of it.

But then she shifted around to face him, still down there on the stone floor. And everything…stopped.

That face.

Her face.

He'd been seeing it for years.

He knew every millimeter of her heart-shaped face, and the rich brown hair touched with gold that surrounded it. He knew that wide, generous mouth, and the delicate nose.

Most of all, he knew those eyes. Startling violet set above cheekbones made for poetry.

He knew her, his angel of mercy and the ghost that had haunted him for years.

It was Cecilia. His Cecilia.

"My God," he whispered. "It's you."

"It's me," she replied, her voice flat. Hard. And that was when he noticed that those violet eyes of hers were bright on his. And murderous. "And you can't have him."

CHAPTER TWO

CECILIA REGINALD WAS no stranger to fear or disappointment.

It was right there in the name she'd been left with all those years ago when the English lady—her mother, presumably—had stayed in the only *pensione* in the village for the weekend, given a fake name, and then had left her three-year-old behind when she'd run off. Never to return.

Cecilia had always known that she was disposable, though she happily remembered very little of that first, lost life. Just as she'd always known that Pascal Furlani, who had discarded her when she was fully grown and able to recall every painful second of it, would be back.

At first, she had dreamed of his return. Wished for it, fervently, as if he'd disappeared from the village by mistake somehow. Because assuming he did the right thing—and she'd assumed he would then—would have solved her problems in a neat, orderly and time-honored fashion. Because his coming back would have made sense of the wreckage that her neat, orderly life had become in the chaotic wake he'd left behind him.

And because she had imagined herself *in love* with him.

But of course, that was not when he had deigned to tear himself away from his meteoric rise to wealth and prominence and return at long last. Not when she would have greeted his return with nothing short of delight. Instead, he came back now, when she wanted it least. And not only because she no longer believed in such childish notions as *being in love*.

"Who is *him*?" he asked. "And why do you imagine I would wish to *have him*, whatever that means?"

She didn't miss the affront in that deep, rich voice of his she'd done her best to forget. Or try to forget.

Just as she didn't miss the crack of power in it, either. It seared through her like a lightning strike and she added the unpleasant intensity of the sensation to the list of things she blamed him for.

Cecilia knelt there on the floor, her weight back on her heels, and her hands wet from scrubbing the stones. She had to crane her neck back to look up at him. Up and up and up, for he seemed much taller than she remembered him. While she imagined she looked shriveled and ruined and infinitely hardened by the years—because that was how she felt, certainly.

Back then she'd had faith. She'd believed that people were mostly good and life was certain to work out well, one way or another, even for abandoned girls like her.

She'd learned. Oh, how she'd learned.

Cecilia was fairly certain she wore every last lesson right there on her face.

Meanwhile Pascal looked like he'd stepped straight out of the pages of one of those glossy magazines she pretended she didn't know existed and had certainly never scoured, just to see his face. He looked like the lofty, arrogant man he'd gone off to become, leaving her here to handle the mess he'd made. And the man in those magazines bore no resemblance whatsoever to the broken, half-wild creature she'd taken far too much pleasure in nursing back to health.

If there had ever been anything broken in Pascal Furlani, she couldn't see it now. Were it not for the scars on the left side of his jaw that she knew continued down across his chest—though in her memory, they were far more raw and angry than the silver lines she could see today—she would have been hard-pressed to imagine that anything could ever have touched this man at all.

Much less her.

A thought that made her want to throw her bucket of dirty water at him. Preferably so it could damage that overtly resplendent suit he wore with entirely too much unconscious, masculine ease.

God, how she hated him.

The trouble was, it had been easy to scoff at those pictures of him. To tell herself that she was better off without a man who would go to such places, with such people, and dress the way he did when he was photographed. So breathlessly, deliberately fancy, which even she knew cost the kind of money she would never, ever have. Or even be near. The kind of money that was so dizzying she wouldn't *want* to have it. It was corrosive. Cecilia didn't have to live the high life in Rome to understand that.

Her life here had always been simple. Things were more complicated than she'd planned six years ago, but still. Overall, life was *simple*.

And nothing about Pascal Furlani was simple.

Neither was her reaction to him.

Cecilia had forgotten the way he filled a room. That

antiseptic chamber in the clinic. This whole church. Just by standing there in all his state, his black eyes glittering.

The problem was he was so…arresting.

He had changed since he'd left the hospital, where he'd been so rangy and wiry. He'd filled in. He looked solid. *Big.* Strong, everywhere, with the kind of smooth, powerful muscles that quietly boasted of the worship he paid to his own body and the kind of power he could wield.

But Cecilia did not want to think too much about his body.

His dark hair was as she remembered it, cropped close to his head. It only made those glittering black-gold eyes of his all the more mesmerizing. Electric, even, like another lightning strike she had no choice but to endure while it lit her on fire.

He looked like a Roman centurion. His aquiline nose. His sensual lips. Something impassive and stern in the stark lines of him.

And she hated the fact that she knew how he tasted.

"You're not welcome here," she told him as evenly as she could from where she knelt there before him. "I already made that clear to your little spies. You didn't have to come all the way up into the mountains yourself."

He blinked, and made a small pageant out of it.

"I do not have spies, Cecilia."

Her name in that familiar, charged voice of his rolled through her, igniting fires she would have sworn only moments before had been doused forever.

"You can call them whatever you like." She had the urge to get to her feet, but ignored it, because scrambling up from her knees made it far more obvious that she was discomfited by their power differential. And she did not wish to be discomfited by Pascal Furlani. Not any more than she already had been. So she stayed put, meeting his gaze with defiance as if he was the one on the ground. "They said they were on the board of your company. You will forgive me if I assumed that meant they had something to do with you. Or do you really expect me to believe that two visits from you and your minions over the course of three weeks is a random coincidence?"

He didn't appear to move and yet it was like a storm gathered around him. Cecilia was sure that if she looked down, she would see the fine hairs on her arms stand on end.

"Members of my board were here?" His voice was... darker. Midnight thunder.

It took her a moment to process the way he'd said *here.* As if this village where he'd nearly died and had come back to life again was so far beneath him that the very idea that anyone he knew from his fancy boardrooms might visit it appalled him.

Cecilia tried not to grit her teeth. "I will tell you what I told them. You have nothing to do with this place. Or with me. You left. And you don't get to swan back in here now, no matter the reason. I won't allow it."

His dark eyes flashed. "Will you not?"

Something about that question, too silky by half and far more dangerous than it should have been, had Cecilia tossing her sponge into her bucket. With perhaps too much force, she reflected, when water sloshed over the sides.

"What do you want, Pascal?" she demanded.

Through her gritted teeth.

He looked down at her from his irritatingly great height. "I thought I came here to expel old ghosts."

"I don't believe you'd know a ghost if one appeared at the foot of your bed, wreathed in chains and moaning your name."

Again he blinked as if he expected the movement of his eyelids to bring underlings running to serve him. Something that likely occurred with depressing regularity down in Rome.

"You do not believe that you have haunted me these past years, *cara*?" And she couldn't say she cared for the way he used the endearment, either. Like a sharp-edged blade, and he wasn't afraid to cut her. "I cannot say I believe it, either. And yet here I am, when I vowed I would never return."

"I suggest you turn around, return to wherever you came from and uphold your vow."

He did not take her suggestion. Instead, he stayed where he was and studied her for a moment.

"I do not understand why my board would be at all interested in you," he said after what felt like an eternity. Or three. "I've never kept this part of my life a secret. Everyone knows I nearly died in the mountains and it changed me profoundly. I discuss it often enough. Why would they come here now? What could they hope to find here besides an old lover?"

Cecilia could hardly breathe. She couldn't imagine what expression she wore on her face. *An old lover.* Was that what she was to him? Was that all she was?

But she kept her cool, no matter what it cost her, because she had to. *She had to.* She would not react to the tightness in her chest. The shortness in her breath.

Or that wild, betraying tumult in her pulse.

All that she could chalk up to fear, she told herself as Pascal gazed down at her, arrogant and impatient. It was nothing but panic, surely. The strange feeling, too much like some kind of anticipation, she felt that her worst fear was being realized in the extraordinary flesh whether she liked it or not.

She could understand that. It was her other reactions that concerned her more. Most especially that melting low in her belly that told her terrible truths about her true feelings about Pascal's return that she wanted desperately to deny.

She got to her feet then, taking her time. And as she did, she was fiercely glad that she looked like who and what she was: a woman who washed floors for a living. She was nothing like the sorts of pampered women Pascal always had on his arm in the magazine pictures that were burned into her head. Cecilia knew she bore no resemblance to them and never would. She was not elegant. Her jeans were too big, decidedly ripped and horribly stained. She wore a ratty T-shirt beneath the long-sleeve buttoned-up shirt she'd tied off at her waist. Her hair was a disaster, no matter that she'd tied it back with an old scarf.

She expected she looked more or less tragic to a man like him. He was no doubt asking himself how he'd ever lowered himself to touch one such as her. She wondered it herself.

But this was a good thing, she told herself sternly. Because he needed to go away and never come back. And if she disgusted him now, well, she was only what she'd had to become. To survive him. If that got him to leave, great. Whatever worked.

She ignored the small pang that notion gave her.

"I expected you to be wearing a nun's habit," he said, and she opted not to hear the wicked undertone in his voice. Much less…remember the way she'd thrilled to it, once.

"I chose not to become a nun." She did not say, *because of you*.

But his eyes narrowed anyway. "I thought that was your life's ambition. Was it not?"

"People change."

"You seem markedly changed, in fact. One might even say, distinctly hardened."

"I'm no longer a foolish girl easily taken advantage of by traveling soldiers, if that's what you mean."

His head canted to one side, and his black eyes gleamed. "Did I take advantage of you, Cecilia? That's not how I recall it."

She eyed him. "Whether you recall it that way or not, that's how it was."

"Tell me, then, how precisely did I take advantage of you? Was it when you crawled into my hospital bed, threw your leg over me and then rode us both to a mad finish?"

She remembered it as he said it. She remembered everything. The wonder of taking him inside her. The madness, the dizzy whirl. His big hands wrapped around her hips and his intent, ferociously greedy gaze.

No one had ever explained to her that the trouble with temptation was that it felt like coming home, wreathed in light and glory.

That melting sensation grew worse, but she refused to let herself squirm the way she wanted to do.

Because this wasn't about her.

"I always wondered what it would be like to have a conversation like this with you," Cecilia said when she was sure she could manage to sound calm. Faintly bored. And it was not untrue, though as the years passed, the content of the conversation had changed in her head. She'd asked fewer questions. At some point she'd even become magnanimous. She'd practiced it enough in mirrors. "I find it's less productive than I might have imagined. I don't understand why you're here. *I* am not haunted."

Only furious, still and always, but she didn't tell him that. He didn't deserve to know.

"Can it be as simple as catching up with an old friend?" he asked as if he was…reasonable in any way. Palatable.

She made a scoffing sound. "Please. We were never friends."

To her surprise, his mouth curved. "Cecilia. Of course we were."

Something in her chest seemed to stutter to a halt then. Something different from the panic, the heat.

Because she remembered other things, too. Long afternoons when she would sit by his bedside, holding his hand or mopping his brow with a cool cloth. In those early days, when no one had known if he would make it, she'd sung to him. Songs of praise and joy interspersed with silly nursery rhymes and the like, all calculated to soothe.

When he grew stronger, he would tell her stories. He couldn't believe that she had never been to Rome. That she had never been more than a couple of hours out of this valley, for that matter. Or not that she could recall. He painted pictures for her with his words, of ancient ruins interspersed with traffic charging this way and that, sidewalk cafés, beautiful fountains. Later, when she was no longer a novitiate and often found herself up in the middle of the night—either because she was worried about her future, or because sleep was a rarity for a woman in her position—she'd looked up pictures online and found the city he described. In bright detail.

He'd made her feel as if she knew it personally. Sometimes she thought she hated him for that.

"Either way," she said resolutely, "we're not friends now. Do you wish to know how I know we're not? Because friends do not disappear like smoke in the middle of the night, without a word."

She regretted that the moment she said it. This was not about her, not anymore, and if she wanted to tell herself a harsh truth or two, it was possible it never had been. She could have been the field outside his window. The mountains looming about in every direction. She was simply *here*. He was the one who crashed the car, tore himself to pieces and got the luxury of telling dramatic stories about what the experience had taught him in televised interviews.

Not that she planned to admit she'd ever watched them.

Meanwhile, Cecilia was the one who could remember nothing but this valley. This village. The comfort of the abbey walls and the counsel of the women she'd believed would be her sisters one day.

It was true that he had taken all of that away from her. But another truth was that she'd given it to him. And she knew she shouldn't have mentioned that night.

Something she was in no doubt about when his expression changed. His eyes were too hot suddenly.

His mouth was too stern and yet remained entirely too sensual.

Now that she was standing up, she could better appreciate what the years had done for his form. He had always been beautiful, like something carved from soft stone and twisted into that flesh that had healed so slowly. Now he seemed made of granite. His shoulders were so wide. And the excellent tailoring of the suit he wore did absolutely nothing to disguise the fact that his torso was thick with hard, solid muscle.

And somehow she'd expected that because he'd filled out he would be less tall. But he wasn't. She still had to look up at him. And for some reason, even though she was no longer on her knees, it made her feel a little too close to powerless for comfort.

"By all means," he said in that dark, silken way of his. "Let us discuss that night."

And she'd already started down this road. She might as well say all the things she'd been carrying around inside her all these years, or at least the highlights, because she had no intention of having this discussion again.

"What is there to discuss?" she asked. "I fell asleep in your arms. It was the first time I had done something like that, as every other moment we'd had together had been so furtive. Stolen. But not that night. You asked me to stay and I stayed. And when I woke up in the morning, you had left the valley for good." She made a noise that no one could mistake for a laugh. "In case you're wondering, I woke up the way you left me. Naked. With the sun beaming in the windows and Mother Superior standing at the foot of the bed."

Back then she could have read every expression that

moved over his face. Every glint in his eye. But though she could see something shift there today, she couldn't twist it into any kind of sense. And it was stunning, the things that could wallop a person. The ways that grief could sneak into the most surprising crevices and well up there, like tears.

"Is that why you're not a nun?" he asked.

She wondered if he knew what a loaded question that was.

It is not for me to tell you what to do, child, Mother Superior had said when Cecilia's condition became clear. *That is between you and God. But I will tell you this. I have known you since you were delivered to our door. I watched you grow up. And I greeted, with joy, the notion that you might join the sisters here. But the truth is, the order is the only family you've known. I have to ask myself if you truly wish to dedicate yourself to this life, or if what you want most of all is family. And now you will have your own. Do you truly wish to give that up?*

"In the end," Cecilia said now to the man who was a catalyst for both her greatest shame and deepest joy in life, damn him, "I was not a good fit for the order."

"Not a good fit? You'd already been living in that abbey for most of your life. How could you not be perfect for them? Why would they let you walk away?"

She glared at him. "These are all interesting questions. But not from someone who ran off in the middle of the night. If you had questions to ask me, Pascal, you could have asked them then."

"I did not *run off,*" he bit out. And if she wasn't mistaken, there was something like temper in his voice then. Sparking in that black gaze of his. "You must always have known, *cara*, that my destiny was never here."

Her palms stung and she realized she'd curled her hands into fists. She forced herself to unclench her fingers, one by one.

"That became clear once you left. And then failed to return for six years."

"I'm here now."

"And I'm sure that any moment, the heavens will open up and hosannas will rain down upon us all," Cecilia retorted. Archly. "But until that moment, you will forgive me if I am somewhat less enthused."

"The Cecilia I remember would never have spoken to me this way." One of his brows rose. Imperiously. "I remember soft, cool hands. A pretty singing voice. And cheeks that were forever pinkening."

"That girl was an idiot." Cecilia sniffed. "And she died six years ago, when she woke to find herself not at all the person she'd imagined herself to be."

"I don't know what that means."

"Don't you? I thought that I was a moral, upstanding, pure and wholesome individual. A woman who truly wished to dedicate herself to a life of service. But it turned out that I was wicked straight through, shameless enough to flaunt it in the very abbey that raised me, and so foolish that I actually believed that the man who had engineered my fall might stick around to help with a rough landing. Alas. He did not."

His stern mouth looked starker somehow. "I was told that all sins would be forgiven if I were to do what was inevitable, what I would do anyway, and leave."

Cecilia opened her mouth to argue that, but something about the way he said it tugged at her. "What do you mean, you were told?"

But he didn't answer the question. He studied her for a moment, then another, his hand on his jaw.

"You have yet to explain to me what my board members were doing here. Let me guess who it was. An older gentleman, perhaps? Silver hair and beard, a theatrical cane and a penchant for dressing like an uptight Victorian? And his trusty sidekick, the younger man, round and possessed of an overly glossy mustache?"

He had described the two men exactly.

She shrugged. "They didn't leave their names."

"But I can see from your expression that they were the ones who came here. Why?"

"Your story of narrowly escaping death in the Dolomites, and the recovery that allowed you ample time to shore up your scheme to take over the world, is practically a fairy tale told to small children at this point. Everyone has heard it."

"I'm delighted that you have paid such close attention."

"But that's my point," Cecilia said coolly. "No attention was required. The story was everywhere. You're fairly ubiquitous these days, aren't you?"

"If by ubiquitous you mean wealthy and powerful, I accept the description proudly."

"Because that's what matters to you." She couldn't seem to help herself. Because she had to keep poking and poking to make sure that he really was this stranger he'd turned into. That the man she'd thought he was had never been anything but a figment of her own imagination. She had to be *certain*. "Money at all costs. No matter who it hurts."

"Who does it hurt?" His gaze was far too bright. Particularly with his mouth set in that harsh line. "There will always be rich men, Cecilia. Why shouldn't I be one of them?"

"I think the real question is why you're here," she said past the lump in her throat for the man she'd nursed all those weeks. The man she'd believed was different. The man who had never existed, not really. "Because I want to be clear about something, Pascal. We like this valley quiet. Remote. The sisters spend their lives here engaged in quiet contemplation. If they want the bustle of the city, they know how to drive themselves down to Verona. What none of us need or want, villager and nun alike, is whatever scheming Roman nonsense you or your minions brought with you."

"I told you." And his voice was harsher then. "I came here to face a ghost, nothing more."

"I know that ghost is not me. Perhaps the ghost is the man you were, when you were here before. Because if we're being honest, you left *him* that night, too."

He didn't flinch. He didn't reel away from her as if she'd hit him. And yet, somehow, Cecilia had the distinct impression that she'd landed a blow. Possibly with a very sharp knife.

And she would have to spend some time questioning herself later. She would have to try to figure out why, when she'd dreamed of landing blow after blow, each harder than the last, the doing of it made her feel shaken.

"But that is something you can sort out on your own," she said, hoping she didn't sound as off balance as she felt. "It doesn't involve me."

Because if she stood here any longer, she would forget herself. And she already knew what happened when she allowed herself to *forget*, particularly when she was around Pascal. More to the point, her life was different now. She had no desire to change it completely. Not anymore. Not again.

She stepped around him, yanking her bucket off the floor as she went. She headed for the door at the side of the altar that led into the vestry, thinking she could bar herself in the church if necessary. There were hours yet before she was due to pick up Dante and she very much doubted that a man like Pascal would lounge around, waiting. Whatever whim had brought him here would have him bored silly and heading for home before long.

"Cecilia."

And she hated herself, because his voice, her name, stopped her. He still had that power over her. She had the despairing notion he always would.

"I'm going now," she said, glaring at the window up above her. "Whatever you wanted out of this sudden return is your business. But I don't want it. I don't want any part of it."

"You said I couldn't *have him*," he said. "Tell me who he is."

She was staring up at the stained glass before her. And this was the moment of truth, wasn't it? She had tried to call, of course. Once he had started appearing on the news, and in the magazines. She tried to do her duty by him. But she'd never made it past the main switchboard of his company. No matter who she spoke to, and no matter how they promised that someone would get back to her if her claim was found to be worthy, no one ever did.

Three years in, she'd stopped trying.

Since then she'd been certain that given the chance, she would, of course, come clean at the first opportunity.

But she hadn't.

She'd excused the fact she hadn't made the situation clear to his board members. She'd told herself that they didn't deserve to know something Pascal didn't already know himself. But deep down she'd believed that she would never see him again. That this moment would never come.

Now he was here. She had foolishly thrown Dante in his face straight off. Now he'd asked directly.

It was another opportunity to discover who she was, and once more Cecilia was faced with the lowering notion that it was not who she'd thought. Not at all. Because she wanted—more than anything—to lie. To say whatever was necessary to make him let her go. Forget about her. And never, ever, get anywhere near Dante.

She squeezed her eyes shut. She was too aware of her own pulse, pounding in places it normally didn't. She swallowed, not surprised to find her throat was dry.

And then she made herself turn, because she had done harder things than this. Like sit up in a bed in the clinic, without a stitch of clothing on her body, and face Mother Superior directly. Then explain what on earth she was doing there. Or like when she'd started to show, and had been forced to leave the abbey—the only home she'd ever known—and find her own cottage to live in, just her and her growing belly and her eternal shame.

And neither of those things was all that difficult stood next to childbirth.

So she faced him. The man she had loved, hated and lost either way.

And she had no optimism whatsoever that what she was about to tell him would change that.

In fact, she suspected she was about to make it all much worse.

"*He* is your son," she said, her voice echoing in the otherwise empty church. "His name is Dante. He doesn't know you exist. And no, before you ask, I have absolutely no intention of changing that."

CHAPTER THREE

HER WORDS WERE IMPOSSIBLE.

They made no sense, no matter how loudly they echoed in his head.

Pascal thought perhaps he staggered back beneath the weight of all that impossibility, possibly even crumpled to the floor—but of course, he did no such thing. He was frozen into place as surely as if the stones beneath him had made him a statue, staring back at her.

In horror. In confusion.

There must be some mistake, a sliver of rationality deep inside him insisted.

"What did you say?" he managed to ask through a mouth that no longer felt like his own.

Because while he was certain he had heard her perfectly well, no matter how he tried to rearrange those words in his head, they still didn't make sense. They couldn't make sense.

"This isn't something I *want* to tell you," Cecilia said, tilting her chin up in a belligerent sort of way that was one more thing that didn't make sense.

Because the sweet almost-nun he'd known hadn't had the faintest hint of belligerence in her entire body.

Though her body was obviously the last thing in the world he needed to be thinking about just now.

"It's the right thing to do," she was saying. "So. Now you know."

And then, astonishingly, nodded in punctuation. As if the subject was now closed.

"I cannot be understanding you." His voice sounded as little like his own as the words felt in his mouth, and he still couldn't seem to move the way he wanted to. Or at all.

Cecilia sighed as if he was testing her patience, another affront to add to the list. "You have a son, Pascal. And you shouldn't be surprised to hear that. If memory serves, you never spared the slightest thought for any kind of birth control. What did you think would happen?"

It was the sheer insult of that—and the unfairness—that seared through him, hot enough to loosen his paralysis.

"I was recovering from a car accident in a hospital," he gritted out. "When do you imagine I might have nipped out to the shops and found appropriate protection? I assumed you had taken care of it."

"Taken care of it?" She actually laughed, which nearly let Pascal's temper get the better of him. But she didn't seem to notice. Or care if she did. "I was raised in a convent. With real-life, actual nuns. It might surprise you to learn that the finer details of condom use during premarital sex didn't come up much during morning prayers."

Pascal dragged his hands through his hair, though it was cut almost too short to allow it. Unless he was very much mistaken, his hands were actually shaking, something that might have horrified him unto his soul at any other moment. But right now he could hardly do more than note it and move on. It was that or succumb to the high tide swamping him, drowning him, tugging him violently out to sea.

"I cannot have a son," he snapped out, not caring that his words were far too angry for a place like this. Holy and quiet, with the watchful eyes of too many saints upon him—and none of them as sharp as Cecilia's gaze. "I cannot."

Cecilia sniffed. And her remarkable eyes sparked with what he thought was temper, however little that made sense to him.

"And yet you do. But don't worry. He's perfect, and he doesn't need you." The gleam in her eyes intensified, and he felt it like a blow to the center of his chest. "Feel free to run back to your glossy magazines. Your lingerie models. Whatever makes you happy, Pascal. You can pretend we don't exist. The way you've been doing for six years."

"How dare you take that tone with me." His voice was soft, because his fury was so intense he thought it might have singed his vocal cords. The rage and grief in him so hot and blistering he wasn't sure he'd ever speak in a normal voice again. "You never told me you were pregnant."

"How would I have done that?" She fired the question at him, plunking her bucket back down on the stone floor with a loud crash. She even took a step toward him as if she wanted this confrontation to get physical. "The first time I saw you mentioned in the papers, two years had gone by. Before that? You'd just disappeared overnight. The army had discharged you, and even if they hadn't, they weren't about to hand out a forwarding address. What was I supposed to have done?"

"You knew I was from Rome. You knew—"

If he hadn't been close enough to see the pulse in her neck go wild, he might have believed the cold smile she aimed at him meant she wasn't affected by this interaction. But Pascal wasn't sure that knowledge was helpful.

"Right. So you think I should have…what? Wandered up and down the Spanish Steps while heavily pregnant?" she demanded. "Calling out your name? Or better still, climbed atop the Trevi Fountain with a newborn in my arms, demanding that someone in the crowd take me to you? How do think that would have worked?"

That she had a point only made his anguish worse.

How could this have happened? He couldn't accept it. He couldn't believe it. He wanted to tear down this godforsaken church with his hands as if that would change the way she was looking at him. As if it could turn back time.

As if that could save him from the nasty reality that he'd become exactly what he most loathed without knowing it.

"You keep mentioning magazines, which means you clearly saw me in one," he found himself saying as if he could argue the conviction from her face. As if he could make this her fault and make it better, or different, by shrugging off the blame. "You must have known the company existed. That must mean you *could have* contacted me. You obviously chose not to do so."

Her laugh sliced into him. "I called your company repeatedly. Oddly enough, no one took me seriously. Or

I assume they didn't, because it took you all this time to turn up here."

"Whoever else might have turned you away will be dealt with." Though even as he said that, he already knew what had likely happened. Any reports of pregnancies would have been dismissed by Guglielmo as opportunists attempting to cash in on Pascal's success. He would never have dreamed of wasting Pascal's time with empty claims. "But if you had actually turned up on my doorstep, Cecilia, *I* would not have denied you entry."

She actually dared roll her eyes. At him. "That's good to know. Should you impregnate me and leave me behind like so much trash again, I'll be sure to take that tack. I'll gather up whatever children you've abandoned, camp out in your lobby and hope for the best. What could possibly go wrong?"

"What kind of person has a man's child and fails to tell him?" Something cracked wide open inside him, and it was harder and harder to pretend he was *angry* when it went far deeper than that. When it felt like a catastrophic fissure, deep within. "It has been *six years.* Do you have any idea what you've done?"

"I know exactly what I've done, because I've been here the whole time, doing it," she fired back at him, and he had the uneasy notion that she could see that yawning expanse inside him and was aiming straight for it. For him. "You knew where I was. You knew that I was unpardonably naive. You weren't without experience as you made a point of mentioning more than once. Surely you must have known that anytime people have sex, especially without any protection, there's the possibility of exactly this occurring. You never inquired."

"How dare you put this responsibility on me."

"I will not stand here and listen to lectures from the likes of you on *responsibility*, thank you," she bit out. She moved even closer then, and went so far as to jab a finger toward him—very much as if she'd have liked to put out his eye. "You try being a single parent. All the feedings and diaper changes, the crying for no reason and sudden, scary illnesses. Where were you? Not here, handling them."

"I could hardly handle something I didn't know was happening."

She jabbed that finger again, and it occurred to Pascal that she wasn't the least bit intimidated by him. He couldn't recall the last time he'd encountered such a thing. And certainly not from a woman he'd thought was a ghost a few hours ago—and who he remembered as nothing but sweet.

"Don't misunderstand me," she was saying with more than a little ferocity. "There's more joy in it than ought to be possible, or the species would have died out. But what *I'm* talking about is keeping a tiny human alive. What *you're* talking about is your own hurt feelings because you chose to disappear into the ether and it turns out, there are consequences for that. One of them is the child you helped make."

He felt pale with that anguish, mixed liberally with fury. "You dare to speak to me of consequences?"

"I've lived your consequences, Pascal," Cecilia retorted. "An absolutely marvelous little boy has grown into a five-year-old as a consequence of your carelessness. And after trying more than enough times, I didn't keep banging my head against brick walls trying to find a man who didn't leave behind so much as a telephone number. I decided that I was going to focus my attention on raising my son, instead. And did."

"Cecilia—"

"I never expected you to show your face here again," she told him. "I don't expect you to stay now. You're acting as if knowing I was pregnant would have changed something, but I'll let you in on a secret, Pascal. I know full well it wouldn't have. Why don't you spare us both the dramatics and just…go away again?"

Pascal really did stagger then. He had to reach out to keep himself upright, gripping the back of the nearest pew.

As if her certainty that he would abandon his own child no matter the circumstances was almost as grave a betrayal as the fact she'd kept this secret so long.

"I told you," he said, too many memories flooding his brain then. Of the hours she'd spent at his bedside, talking as well as tending to him. All the things he'd told her in return, because his bed in that clinic had felt disconnected to the world. Why not tell a kind stranger every feeling that had ever moved in him? Why not share every story he had inside him? He'd done that and more. How could she imagine that the man who had done so would turn around and leave now? "I told you how I was raised. What it meant to me to be a bastard son to a cruel, unfeeling man… Have you forgotten?"

Her eyes seemed nearly purple then, with what he only hoped was distress. "I didn't forget. But people say all kinds of things when they think their lives might end, then turn around and *live* very differently, when given the chance."

"I told you," Pascal growled. "And you decided to

do this to me anyway. To my child. When you had to know it was the last thing I would ever have allowed."

Whatever distress might have been lurking in her, it disappeared in a flush of temper as her chin tipped up again.

"I stopped caring about what you might or might not allow," she said with a distinct calm that felt like yet another slap when he could barely keep himself together. "Right about the time it became clear to me that you weren't coming back, and that I was really, truly going to have to have our baby all on my own. And then carry on raising him. I considered adoption, you know. Because my plan was to be a nun, not a mother." Her tone was bitter then. "Never a mother."

Something tickled at the back of his mind, about Cecilia's stories about her own childhood, but he thrust it aside. Because she'd actually wanted to…

"You wanted to give up your child—*my* child?"

Once again Pascal couldn't force his mind to process that. He couldn't seem to breathe past it. It was bad enough that he'd come here on a whim to discover that all this time, the woman who'd haunted him through his life in Rome had kept his child a secret from him. But that he could have come back here today, just like this, and never know? Never have the slightest notion what he'd lost?

That fissure inside him widened. And grew teeth.

"Yes, Pascal," she said. Because she had teeth, too. And they seemed to sharpen by the second. "It was never my intention to have a child on my own. Why *wouldn't* I consider adoption?"

Again Pascal ran a hand over his jaw, his scars. Reminding himself that he had survived the impossible before. Surely he would again.

One way or another.

"I suppose you would like me to thank you for choosing motherhood," he said, unable to keep the bitterness from his voice. "I find I cannot quite get there. I want to see him."

He wasn't looking at her as he said that, and it took him a moment to realize she hadn't responded. When he slid his gaze back to hers, she had a considering sort of look on her face. As if she was mulling over a decision as she looked at him.

For the first time it occurred to Pascal that she might very well bar him from seeing the child. *His* child.

How could he be outraged at being denied something he hadn't known he had when he'd driven into this valley? How could he know himself so little?

"I'll show you a photograph," Cecilia replied, her violet eyes glittering with more of that same *consideration*. "I'm certainly not introducing you to him. He's five. As far as he's aware, he doesn't have a father."

Pascal blinked, but once more couldn't really take that in. He felt drunk again, as reckless and out of control as he'd been when he'd driven that car over the side of a mountain. This was like living through that crash again and again. And more, he felt broken into a thousand pieces, the way he had then.

He reminded himself that he was the president and CEO of an international corporation that had made him a billionaire. He laughed off deals that would make other men sweat. He could surely handle one parochial woman and the rest of this…situation.

All he needed to do was stop letting his damned feelings dictate his reactions.

Something he'd thought he'd stamped out years ago. Six years ago, in fact, when he'd received the ultimate wake-up call, had remembered himself and had left.

Cut his own feelings about his father out of this and it was a fairly simple thing. She hadn't been able to track him down. He hadn't looked back. It wasn't even a saga—it was depressingly common.

He cleared his throat. "So you…live here. With him. At the abbey?"

"We have our own cottage," she said. Grudgingly, he thought.

And Pascal felt better now that he'd allowed a bit of reason back into the mix. More like himself and less like the broken man she'd known.

He looked at the bucket beside her. "If you do not live in the abbey, and you are not a nun or even a novitiate any longer, why on earth are you cleaning this church?"

"I clean," she said. And when he stared back at her without comprehension, she lifted her pugilistic little chin again. The expression on her face was challenging, which he should probably stop finding so surprising. "That's what I do. For a living."

"You…clean. For a living. This is how you support yourself?"

"That's what I said."

This time he understood her completely. The words did not bloom into that same dull roar in his head. He felt like himself again, and that allowed him the comfort of the sort of temper he recognized. Not the volcanic, tectonic shift of before—but the sort of laser focus he usually saved for creatures like his father.

Fewer feelings. More fury.

He liked this version of himself much better.

"Are you truly this vindictive?" he asked her, his voice soft with menace and the power he'd fought for—and had no intention of ceding to a fallen nun, thank you. He shifted his position to shove his hands into his pockets and kept his gaze trained on her. "You say you read about me. You knew about the company and claim you called. So there can be no debate about the fact that you know perfectly well that I'm not a poor man. That no matter what else happened, I would never willingly consign my child to be raised in poverty."

Color bloomed in her cheeks, and he had the sense it was the first honest response he'd seen from her. Maybe that was why he reveled in it, like a thirsty man faced with a mountain spring.

Surely there could be no other reason.

"Your child is not being raised in poverty," she snapped. "He doesn't take a private jet to get his shopping done, I grant you, but his life is full. He wants for nothing. And I'm sorry that you think cleaning is beneath you, but luckily, I don't. I make a good living. I take care of myself and my son. Not everybody needs to be rich."

"Not everyone can be rich, it is true. But you happen to be raising the son and heir of a man who is. Several times over."

"Money only buys *things*, Pascal," she said with the dismissiveness of someone who had never lived more or less by their wits in the worst parts of a major city. "It certainly doesn't make a person happy. As anyone who looks at you can tell quite clearly."

"How would you know?" he asked, his tone deadly.

She flushed again. "I make Dante perfectly happy. That's what matters."

"You live in the middle of nowhere, surrounded by nothing but cows and nuns. What kind of life is this for a boy?"

"There was a time when you thought this valley was paradise," she threw at him. "It hasn't changed any. But if you have, there is no need for you to suffer the cows and the nuns a moment more. You can turn around and leave right now."

"I don't think you're understanding me." He sounded almost gentle, he noted, which was at odds with that cold fury inside him. He leaned into it, because it was better than that terrible fissure. "I am Pascal Furlani and we are discussing the sole heir to everything I have built. No son and heir of mine can grow up like this, so far away from everything that matters."

She scowled. "Then it's a lucky thing your name isn't on his birth certificate, isn't it? You don't have to worry yourself about how he's raised."

Pascal couldn't seem to do anything but stay frozen solid where he stood, staring at her as if, were he to focus, he could make this go away. He could turn her into the ghost she should have been, not...*this*. Not mother to another bastard child, but this one his. *His.*

The scandal when it was discovered—because these things were always discovered, as Pascal knew all too well himself—would brand him the worst kind of hypocrite, given he'd never made any secret of his feelings on his own father's behavior. He'd made himself the asterisk forever attached to his father's name. Now he would have his own, and he knew full well the tabloids would have a field day with him.

But the thought of scandal made a different sort of apprehension grip him.

"Did you tell the members of my board about this child?" he demanded.

"I didn't want to tell *you* about this child," she replied furiously, her scowl deepening. "So no, I didn't share the news with two complete strangers marching around the village officiously, asking rude questions."

"But that doesn't mean they couldn't have seen you. Or have asked someone else. Or otherwise figured it out."

"I didn't much care what they did." And now she sounded impatient, which was just one more insult to add to the pile. "Just so long as they left. Which I would also like you to do. Now."

Pascal couldn't let himself think directly about the child. *His* child. His *son*. It was too much. It was so heavy he was convinced it would flatten him—but thinking about his spiteful, grasping board members in possession of this secret he hadn't known he was keeping was different. It was easier to think about what they would do with the information than it was to think about the information itself.

Or that *the information* was a little boy who didn't know he had a father who would never, ever have abandoned him if he'd had the choice.

"This is a disaster," he muttered, more to himself than to her.

But she heard him. Maybe he'd wanted her to hear him.

"Funnily enough, that's what I thought you would say." Her scowl smoothed out and her chin went up as if she was wrapping herself in armor. "As a matter of fact, all of this is happening precisely the way I imagined it would. So why don't we fast-forward to the inevitable end without all of this carrying on that won't get us anywhere?" Her violet eyes flashed as they held his gaze. "Just go. Leave here and return to your money and your life in Rome. No one has to know that you ever came here. Dante and I will muddle along as we always have and you can spend your time however it is you like. No harm, no foul."

And she even waved her hand through the air with a languid indifference that made something in Pascal simply…snap.

One moment he was standing frozen and still in his fury, and the next he had moved toward her. He wrapped his hands around her soft, narrow shoulders, then held her there before him.

Cecilia made a slight startled sound. Her hands came up and she braced her fingers against his abdomen, though she didn't push him away or try to pull back from him. It was as if she was holding her breath, waiting to see what he would do.

But all he did was lower his face so it was directly in hers.

"This is not going to go away," he promised her, a thundering thing in his voice, though he kept it low. Even. "I am not going to go away. I have a son. *A son.* You have made me a father and taken it away from me, and I will never forgive you for either one of those things. But I know now. And nothing will be the same. Do you understand me?"

He expected her to order him to let go of her, which he would do, of course, because he wasn't the animal she seemed to think he was. Even if it wasn't exactly lost on him that even now, even with what he knew, his body was having a far more enthusiastic reaction to the close proximity with the woman who had haunted him all these years. Her shoulders fit perfectly in his palms, as ever.

And the last time he'd been this close to her, it had been a prelude to his mouth on hers. Then the hardest part of him deep inside her melting, clenching heat, making them both ache. Then shatter. Then do it all over again.

"That," she said very distinctly, her violet eyes wide and fixed to his, "is absolutely never happening again."

For the first time since he'd walked into this church, he saw the woman he'd left here six years ago. The one who had always known what he was thinking. The one who had so often been thinking the very same thing.

She certainly was now.

And she had kept this secret from him. She had made him into his worst nightmare. Pascal wanted to crush her. He wanted to cry. He wanted to tear apart this church and rip this whole valley apart with his hands. He wanted to rage hard enough to turn back time, so that he could prevent this tragedy from happening in the first place.

Or, something far more insidious whispered inside him, *so you could stay this time. The way you wanted to back then.*

And that thought was the biggest betrayal of them all.

Because staying here had never been an option, no matter how much he'd wanted it once. And no matter what price it turned out he'd have to pay for going.

Pascal stopped fighting that roar inside him. He surrendered to the yawning thing, rage and grief, fury and need.

He had never forgotten Cecilia Reginald. He had come back here to exorcise her, but now it seemed he would be twined with her forever in the son they'd made.

It was too much.

It was all *too much*.

So he hauled her up onto her toes and brought her even closer to him, then crushed his mouth to hers.

CHAPTER FOUR

HIS KISS WAS MUCH, much worse than she remembered.

It was hotter. Wilder.

Better, something in her cried.

But this time she knew how to kiss him back.

He had taught her. Six years ago he had taught her how to light the world on fire. How to burn so hot and so bright that she hadn't much cared if he was turning her to ash in his wake—she'd wanted only to keep getting too close to the flames.

Cecilia would have sworn that she couldn't remember any of it. A moment ago she'd have been certain that all those memories had been swept away in the trials and joys of motherhood. That it was all dim recollections of warmth and nothing more.

But it turned out, she remembered everything.

She remembered his taste, and the way he cupped the back of her head with one big, hard palm, guiding her where and how he liked. She remembered the wildfire that scared her and excited her in turn, roaring through her and lighting her up. Everywhere.

She remembered how to angle her head. How to move closer. How to press her body against his until she was all fire again. Fire and need, passion and desire.

Kissing him was like traveling back in time.

She remembered her own innocence. How she'd given it to him, and how carefully, how gently, he had taken it and made her sob with joy and wonder.

She remembered the first time he had kissed her, there in that whitewashed room where he'd spent his convalescence. How he'd pressed his lips to hers, smiling as he'd coaxed her. Taught her. Then tempted her beyond endurance.

She had always imagined, before then, that a kiss would take something from her. And over the past six years she'd told herself rather darkly that she'd been all too right about that. But the truth she'd forgotten—or she'd made herself forget—was that his kiss had made her feel…bigger. Better. Brighter and more powerful than she had ever been before. Like some kind of shooting star.

Here, now, was no different.

She could feel herself shooting wild across a dark night sky, lighting up the world with the force of her longing.

He kissed her, and she kissed him back as if she'd been waiting all this time for him to come back. As if she'd *wanted* this. And with every scrape of his tongue against hers, she felt that same light. That heat.

Cecilia did the only thing she could. She poured all her lost hope, all her misery and worry, anxiety and loneliness, into the way she kissed him back. She kissed him with all the pride she'd stored up inside her for the little boy he'd never known. The love and the odd moments of gratitude that Pascal had come into her life and left her the greatest gift, no matter the cost.

Everything he'd missed. Everything she'd wished

for. She kissed him and she kissed him; she poured it all into him, and got passion in return.

Passion and intensity. Greed and delight.

His hands moved, tracing their way down her back as if he was reacquainting himself with her shape. Her strength.

She shifted, her palms moving down the front of his shirt to find him harder. More solid. And even hotter than she'd let herself recall. It wasn't until she found her way to his belt buckle that she remembered where they were.

Not just in this valley, not far from the abbey that had been her childhood home and where she would never, now, be the nun she'd always imagined she would.

More than that, they were standing in the church where she'd learned how to pray.

She was defiling herself all over again.

Cecilia wrenched herself back, tearing her mouth from his and pushing against his wall of a chest with her hands. But he was so much bigger and tougher than he had been six years ago, and she only managed to create about a centimeter of space between them.

Still, it was enough for reality to charge in and horrify her.

"That will never happen again," she managed to say.

She thought he would laugh, or say something arrogant and cutting. But all Pascal did was gaze down at her, an odd expression on his starkly beautiful face.

"I'm not so certain," he said after a moment.

She pushed against him again, and this time he let her go. And she didn't have it in her to explore the reasons why that made her heart clench. She felt the end of the pew behind her and gripped it. As if anchoring herself here could save her. As if she hadn't blasphemed in every possible way.

Again.

When she knew better.

"Thank you for reminding me that the chemistry between us is dangerous and upsetting," she said, and she made herself meet his gaze when it was the last thing she wanted to do. "It leads nowhere I want to go."

"I had convinced myself I'd imagined it," he said. And she might have taken offense at that if he hadn't sounded so…disgruntled. "I told myself I was weak. Out of my head with pain and recovery and healing. That was the only explanation that made sense."

He lifted his hand to his face, but this time, instead of running his fingers over his scars, he ran them over his mouth. Which reminded Cecilia that she could taste him on her tongue.

Damn him. And damn her for surrendering so easily once more.

Pascal was still studying her as if she'd turned into a creature he couldn't name, right there before his eyes. "But it turns out you're more potent than I gave you credit for."

"I do not wish to be potent," Cecilia managed to get out. "And I do not want any credit. What I want is for you to forget me. The way you already have, for years, before you came back here."

That mouth of his twisted. "But that's the trouble, *cara*. I did not forget."

Cecilia hated this. Him. And most of all, herself.

Because she should have been better prepared for something like this. She'd been on edge when those other men had come and sniffed around the abbey asking questions about Pascal Furlani's famous car accident, but she hadn't really believed that Pascal himself would follow. She'd assumed that if he sent anyone else, it would be more emissaries of the officious variety. Attorneys, she'd supposed, to make her sign documents that would renounce any claim to him she might have had. She'd been ready for that. She prepared stinging speeches that she could deliver to his men, making it clear that she wanted nothing from him and never had and never would.

She hadn't expected him.

And she certainly hadn't expected that he would kiss her again.

Because it cut the knees straight out of her argument, not to mention all her prepared rebukes. It reminded her too well of the reasons she'd given up everything she knew for him.

The truth was, it had been years since she could even imagine how it was that she'd allowed a torn-up soldier to turn her from her chosen path so easily. Sometimes she would sit up at night, when Dante was sound asleep and looked angelic, instead of the whirl of holy terror and inexhaustible energy he could be when he was awake. She would gaze at him, allowing herself to feel that flood of maternal love—but still completely unable to understand how it all happened.

How had a person as quiet and contained as she was...do what she did?

Her life had been divided into before Pascal and after him, and the further she got away from those stolen months, the less he seemed real in her memories. There were a thousand stories about the fecklessness of youth, after all. Everyone knew that young girls were easy pickings, and as embarrassing as it might have been for Cecilia to think of herself in that way, that was the story she'd accepted about herself. That was the story she told, when it was necessary to tell it at all, here in a small valley filled with people who had known her since the day she'd arrived here and could tell her story for her. And often did.

It was a hard shock to discover that all she'd done was mute the man.

Because the reality of Pascal was in full, living color. And his kiss was electrifying.

And Cecilia understood that she'd been lying to herself for a long, long time.

She found she didn't know quite how to process any of that.

"This is all irrelevant," she said now. She moved away from him, aware that her body no longer felt like her own. That irritated her almost more than the rest, because it had taken her so long to get it back. There had been Pascal, then Dante, and years before she'd become simply *Cecilia* again. "Feel free to send your lawyers. Do your worst. I can't say I care."

"Lawyers?" He sounded mystified, though she didn't look back at him to see. "What do my lawyers have to do with anything?"

"Rich men are renowned for going to great lengths to make sure they don't have to give away any of their money, for any reason. Call it what you like. I'm not going to fight you."

"I'm not following you." And his voice changed as he said that. Less the man as surprised as she was at the way that kiss had exploded between them and more... dangerous. It sent a shiver down her spine. Because suddenly, she had no trouble imagining him as a leader of men. A captain of his industry in every regard. "Was I planning to give away my money in some capacity?"

"I'm sure you'll have a battalion of documents for me to sign. So you don't have to claim Dante. And so I will never make any kind of claim on you. Whatever. What I'm trying to say is that I expect it."

"Cecilia." Her name was like an oath. "There is no circumstance under which I would knowingly renounce my claim to my own child. Understand this now."

She couldn't help but look back at him then, though she instantly wished she hadn't. There was an intensity in Pascal's black-gold gaze that made her clench her teeth tight to hold back the shudder that threatened to take her over.

But all that did was send all that sensation spiraling down through her body until it lodged low in her belly.

"You say that now." She told herself he couldn't see her reaction to him. That all she had to do was pretend she wasn't having one. "I think it's likely the shock. Once it wears off you'll change your tune. You'll want nothing more than to get back to your preferred life."

"This is what you think of me?" His voice was quiet, but she didn't mistake it for weakness. Not when it seemed to fill the small church, swelling up from the stones at her feet. "You concealed my own child from me for all these years. Now you imagine that having learned of him at last, I will abandon him all over again. This from a woman who spent months sitting at my bedside. Talking to me. Getting to know me in some small way, I would have thought."

That pricked at her. "The man I thought I knew

would never have left the way you did, in the dark of night. With no word."

Pascal didn't move toward her, so there was no reason she should have felt as if he loomed over her, trapping her, when she'd put several pews between them.

"Remind me, whose hurt feelings are at play here?" he asked in that same quiet way that hummed in her, intense and demanding. "Mine, because of the consequences of my actions? Or yours, because you feel slighted by a choice that might have had to do with you, but you must have known full well had nothing to do with the child."

"It doesn't matter whose feelings are hurt," she fired back, stung. And something like terrified that he'd hit on something she hadn't even known was inside her. Was she truly so petty? It made her stomach hurt that she couldn't immediately answer in the negative. "What matters is that I don't intend to allow my child to play victim to your periodic sentimentality."

He let out a harsh sound. "I have no idea what that means."

"You can't possibly want him," Cecilia said, exasperated.

She had the sense of him growing bigger again. Sharper, this time. Like a loaded weapon, pointed straight at her.

"You do not have the slightest idea what it is I want," he said in that same deadly tone. "How can you, when I hardly know myself? You have known about this child's existence for the past six years. I have known about it for thirty minutes. Pray, do not tell me what it is I *want* when I am still reacting to the news that this child exists."

"I don't want Dante to have to pay for it while you sort through your emotions."

"Cecilia. You do not get to decide what and how I feel about any of this. And you certainly will not dictate what I do."

She didn't mistake that for anything but the threat it was.

"This isn't one of your boardrooms, Pascal," she threw at him. "He's *my* child. You don't get to rip open his life unless I say you can, and I say you absolutely can't."

Pascal laughed. But it was not a sound of amusement.

Cecilia felt it like a kick to the gut.

"You should never have kept my son from me all this time, but you did," he told her, his voice as dark as his gaze, and that thunderous expression he wore. "We all get to do what we can get away with, don't we? And now that I know about him, there is nothing that will keep me from him. And you should know that there is very little I can't get away with, *cara*."

"Stop threatening me!" she snapped at him.

He laughed again, and it was not exactly soothing. "I have yet to begin threatening you."

She panicked. There was no other way to put it. She wasn't sure she could feel the top of her head; her lips still throbbed, she could *taste* him and he showed no sign whatsoever of slowing down.

"Who's to say he even is your child?" she heard herself ask as if the stained-glass saints could answer for her. Or help her out of this situation. "Your name is nowhere on his birth certificate. He might as well have been delivered by fairies for all you have to do with it."

Pascal looked wholly unperturbed. "Then you really

will meet my lawyers, when they arrive here *en masse* to demand and perform a DNA test. Do you really want to force me to force this issue? Because I will. Happily."

What Cecilia wanted to do was scream at him. Rail against him until she satisfied all those hurt feelings inside her that he'd pointed out and that she couldn't pretend weren't there any longer. Until she made him pay, somehow, for all these years and all her loneliness and all she'd lost—

But that was about her. And this needed to be about Dante.

"Listen to me," she said, and she didn't care if he could hear all that emotion in her voice. She wanted him to hear it. She wanted him to understand this, if nothing else. "Dante is a happy, healthy little boy. But this is his whole life. This valley. Me, his mother and only parent. He has yet to so much as question me about whether or not he has a father."

"Do you truly expect that to last? You cannot be so naive."

The fact that she had, on some level, expected it to be a non-issue because she wanted it that way struck her as unbearably foolish then. Something more sinister than simply *naive*. It was one more ugly part of herself she would have to pull out and look at closely—but not now. Not where he could witness all the ways he'd knocked her off her foundations today.

"You barreling into his life and claiming him as your child when that is meaningless to him can only hurt him," she made herself say in as steady a voice as she could manage, under the circumstances. "It will confuse him terribly and I don't want that. And if you're serious about wanting to take your place as some kind of father to him, you shouldn't want it, either."

And for a moment the church was quiet. Pascal kept his dark gaze on her, stern and accusatory, but he didn't speak. Cecilia watched a muscle in his lean cheek flex as if he was biting back his own strong emotions.

The light changed outside, sending the colors from the windows dancing over him, and something shuddered through her, too much like foreboding. She knew, like some kind of terrible premonition, that he meant what he said. That he wanted to be a part of his son's life after all. That she had kept a child from a father who would have wanted him, not the careless, reckless liar she'd thought he was.

And that was a possibility she had never prepared herself for.

It made her feel sick.

"Whatever you do," she said, though it felt like a kind of surrender, "I beg you, do not toy with my son's emotions for the sake of your own ego. Please, Pascal."

But when the tension between them roared into a higher gear, she understood that somehow, her plea had made it all worse.

"I can understand that you're not expecting me," he bit out with a furious, exacting note in his voice that sounded to her like pure condemnation. "And I can even understand that you perhaps require some time to prepare him for this. But my patience is finite, Cecilia. And I am not leaving this valley until I not only meet my son, but also claim him—formally—as my own. I'm prepared to stay as long as necessary to make that happen."

Too many things whirled around in her head at once

then. Too many questions—and too much fear. What would happen if he claimed Dante, formally or otherwise? Would they turn into one more modern version of unconnected parents, forever shipping him off from one place to the other? Would Dante grow up without a sense of his own real home—which had always been one of the great comforts of Cecilia's own life? How would she survive a life that included huge swathes of time without her own son?

She wanted no part of any of that. But she gulped down the questions that threatened to bubble over from inside her, because she was terribly afraid they would come out as tears. And that was the final, ultimate humiliation. She wouldn't—couldn't—allow it. It would break her.

And Cecilia refused to let him break her. Not this time. Not again.

"I hope you enjoy camping alfresco, then," she said instead, heading toward the door. "The *pensione* is closed this time of year. And you're certainly not welcome to stay with me."

She shot a look over her shoulder at him when she reached the door, because she was so damnably weak, and something caught at her. Pascal stood where she'd left him, so solitary, and yet so *sure*. As if he were a pillar that held up the world, or at least this church, and could stand like that forever.

He will, something in her whispered, making goose bumps break out all over her skin. *You will never be rid of him again.*

"Alternatively, you can always throw yourself on the mercy of the nuns," she threw at him, hoping her desperation didn't show on her face. Yet somehow sure that it did. "I'm sure they remember you all too well. But no worries. They took vows. If you ask them for sanctuary, I believe they're duty bound to take you in."

With that, Cecilia threw open the door to the vestry and escaped from her past. But she knew, even as she slammed the heavy door behind her and collapsed against it, that it was only temporary.

And there was no one to help her or save her now as it tightened around her throat and pulled tight, like a noose.

CHAPTER FIVE

"WE ARE NOT in the habit of turning away petitioners in need," said Mother Superior, her face as smooth and ageless as it had been six years ago. She could have been fifty or eighty, for all Pascal could tell. There was a canny wisdom in her gaze and a certain scratchy archness in her voice. And the smile she aimed at him made him want to drop to his knees and rededicate himself to a faith he had never felt deeply enough to pronounce in the first place. "Not even those who took advantage of our hospitality once before."

"You are too good," Pascal murmured in reply.

He would sooner rip off his own arms than admit how strange it had seemed to him to walk up to the front door of the abbey. Then wait to be admitted into Mother Superior's presence as if he was any visitor. Not one who had lived here for months and not of his own accord.

Pascal had never intended to return.

Moreover, he had gone to great lengths to deny that he had ever been as helpless or weak as he had been when he'd been stuck here. He liked to touch his scars to remind him that he could overcome any obstacle, but he had stopped permitting himself to remember the details of this particular obstacle. This valley and the stone abbey were a story he told to illustrate both his strength of will and his ability to climb out of any pit.

He'd managed to convince himself that none of it was real.

But the stone building that housed the abbey had stood in this same spot for centuries. It had been a fortress, a castle and a monastery, and it was built to last ten more centuries in much the same forbidding condition. He followed Mother Superior as she glided along the smooth, spotless halls, made somewhat less dim by the lights set into sconces every few meters. He had to double-check that the lights were electric, and not torches. Because otherwise, it could have been any one of the past five centuries.

It was a relief to exit the old part of the abbey and cross into the modern clinic building. And somehow he was not the least bit surprised when the nun led him to the very same chamber where he'd stayed years before. He stopped in the doorway, not sure he was in complete control of himself as he looked around. But nothing had changed. The same whitewashed walls, free of everything save two items that were surely not considered decoration. The crucifix on the wall across from the narrow bed. And above the bed, a Bible verse in a frame.

No wonder he had spent his time staring out the window at the cold fields instead.

"As you can see, we have kept everything just as you left it," Mother Superior said genially, but her gaze was sharp.

"How thoughtful," Pascal managed to say, even as a revolt took place inside him. As if he was doomed to months of confinement if he stepped across the threshold—

But he was not a superstitious man.

And he would not let this absurd attack of malicious nostalgia affect him.

He stepped into the room, reclaiming it. Because the last time he'd been here, he'd been carried inside. In pieces.

It took him a long time to look at the nun. And to get the distinct impression she'd known exactly how hard it was for him to be here.

"Perhaps this time you can concentrate more on the cultivation of inner peace, and less on external stimulation," she said when she had his full attention, her tone dry enough to make a desert weep.

Pascal would not have taken that tone from anyone else, but this was Mother Superior. And Pascal might not consider himself one of the faithful, but he was an Italian man, and therefore entirely too Catholic by definition to fight with a nun. No matter what she did.

Something he was certain Mother Superior knew well.

Once she left him to his uneasy memories, Pascal found himself with nothing to do but sit on the edge of the narrow bed where he'd wasted far too much time already. Most of it fighting pain and wondering if he would ever stand and walk out of this place of his own volition and on his own two feet.

And, he could admit, with a few very brief moments of joy.

All involving Cecilia.

He didn't know what impulse it had been that got him in his car and brought him here. He'd been haunted by her across the years, it was true. But he'd wanted to put that ghost to rest. He never imagined for a moment that she'd been keeping this kind of secret from him.

And it was easier to bluster on about what he wanted and what he planned to do when she was standing there in front of him.

The simple truth was that he had a son. He, Pascal Furlani, had a *son*.

He couldn't quite grasp the wonder of that. And the devastation, so quick on its heels. One chased the other, and he found himself thinking not of the little boy in the center of it, but of himself as a little boy. He had been in the center of a similar storm. And he'd found himself battered about, used as a pawn by his mother, then neglected when her machinations to force his father's hand didn't work.

He would never do that to his own child.

He vowed that to himself, here and now. Whatever happened, he would keep his feelings about what Cecilia had done in a separate compartment entirely. He would make sure that whatever the storms that raged between the two of them, the child would feel none of it. Cecilia claimed he was healthy and happy—well, now, he was healthy, happy and the sole heir to all Pascal had.

He lowered himself to prone position, and lay there, his hands folded on his chest and his eyes on the ceiling. A position he'd assumed in this very bed a thousand times before. He knew that ceiling better than he knew his own face. Every centimeter. Every faint crack or hint of discoloration. He knew how the light crept across the room on sunny days, and how the cold wind made the door rattle.

The abbey was nothing if not an excellent place for

quiet contemplation of the impossible, like the existence of *his son*. Pascal stared at the ceiling and found himself wondering when he had last been somewhere that was this quiet. There were no sounds of traffic. There was no television blaring out the news. He knew there was a bell that rang out the sisters' prayers, but it wasn't ringing. And some days there were the sounds of the women who lived here, but today, the Mother Superior had told him pointedly, was a day of silence.

Pascal could hear his own heartbeat. His breath.

He had only his mobile phone, the laptop he'd left in the car and his own thoughts—which, he had to admit, was a far sight more than the last time he'd lain like this in this same bed, when he'd had only a collection of broken bones and vague assurances that he *might* make a full recovery. *Maybe*.

And this time, when he looked out the window at the cold fields that stretched toward the towering mountains, he knew that somewhere out there was a child. *His* child.

Pascal was trying to picture his son's face when he fell asleep, his body giving up after his night of driving and all the discoveries he'd made once he'd gotten here.

He woke some hours later to the insistent sound of his mobile, and scrubbed a hand over his face as he sat up, took the call and assured his secretary that he had not taken leave of his senses but was not planning to return to the office anytime soon.

His dreams had been strange and tinged with memories of that long-ago accident, which Pascal assumed was par for the course—but still irritated him.

"I will be staying up north," he managed to growl out.

"I beg your pardon?" Guglielmo replied, in mock

horror. Or perhaps, the horror was not so *mock* from a deeply committed urbanite like his secretary, who had once claimed that visiting the ruins of the Roman Forum was as pastoral as he got. "You plan to *stay*? In that valley you claimed was lost in the mists of time? I'm sure I could not have heard you right. You don't mean you have returned to that abbey, do you? You hate that place!"

"Cancel my appointments," Pascal ordered him darkly. "I have things to take care of here that do not require your commentary, Guglielmo."

"This is all very mysterious, sir," his secretary replied, sounding as unfazed as ever, which was why Pascal tolerated his overfamiliarity and occasional small rebellions. "But how long do you intend to rusticate?"

"As long as it takes," Pascal told him.

It was far easier to sound certain that first day. Because he'd driven so far, then woken up in his same old bed—but he was still *him*. He hadn't woken up to discover that the last six years were all a complicated dream and he was still bedridden, weak and a nonentity with nothing to his name but a pretty novitiate who smiled too long when he looked at her.

And it wasn't until he'd ascertained that he had *not* been tossed back in time to that living nightmare that Pascal accepted how deeply he must have feared it.

That didn't sit well, so he concentrated on the present. He was here again, yes, but it wouldn't be for long. He was more than sure. Because how long could it reasonably take?

But one day passed. Then another. Pascal entertained himself with long walks around the village in the mercurial December weather, which he hadn't been able to do the last time he was here. He told himself he was content to inhale the sharp mountain air and feel winter coming in, swept down from those towering heights. He was taking his first holiday since he'd left this village on a Verona-bound bus six years ago, bound and determined to make something of himself with the second chance he'd been given.

Cecilia could take her time. He was fine.

The third day was stormy and cold. Rain pounded down in sheets outside, and being cooped up in a room that had once been his cell did not exactly improve Pascal's mood.

It became harder to convince himself that he was anything remotely resembling *fine*.

It wasn't until the fourth day—when he was storming along the same looping circle through the fields no matter the suggestion of snow in the air—that the door to a cottage set back on the road between the abbey and the village opened, and Cecilia emerged.

"Is this what you are reduced to, Pascal?" she demanded when she'd shut the door behind her and walked out toward the road. Scowling. "Are you stalking me?"

"Perhaps you have forgotten that I was incapable of taking these walks when I was last here," he told her. Perhaps too darkly. "The valley seemed larger when I could only look at it from flat on my back."

"I'm so glad we have your vote of confidence. Perhaps we can use your enthusiasm to scare up more tourism."

He eyed her, dressed similarly to how she'd been in the church. Except, he could tell instantly, those had been her work clothes. Cecilia was at home today, not prepared to clean an ancient building. She wore a dark sweater that looked sturdy and warm on her slender form. Her hair fell to her shoulders and he had the sudden, unwelcome memory of running his fingers through it as she'd lain beneath him. But what struck him most was the way the moody December sky seemed to reflect in her violet eyes, making her seem as unpredictable. Even though she'd come outside without a coat, and stood there, shivering.

But when he looked behind her to the cottage, with smoke coming out of the chimney and windows lit against the brooding afternoon, she stiffened.

"I'm not going to invite you inside," she snapped at him. "You don't get to meet him on your schedule. I thought I made that clear."

"And this is what you want for him?" Pascal waved a hand at the fields, the clouds. "A pretty view? A limitless sky, but no real options? What can he do here besides farm the land or work as staff in the abbey?"

"As he's *five*, we have yet to engage in any hard-hitting conversations about his employment prospects." Her voice was cool. And insulting. "He's more into trucks."

He considered her, and his near-overwhelming urge to get his hands on her. And not because he was angry. That was only a small part of it.

"Thank you," he said in a low voice. "That is the first bit of information about *my son* that you have bothered to give me. Trucks."

She had the grace to flinch at that. And then look away. "People live perfectly happy lives here, as hard as that appears to be for you to understand."

"Maybe so. But why would you deny him the world on the off chance that he will be one of those people?"

"I understand that the simple life doesn't appeal to you," she threw at him, the cold wind tossing her hair about her. She shoved it back and held it off her forehead as she glared at him. "But that speaks more to your snobbery than any lack in it."

Pascal studied her, as she stood there, hair in a mess and clearly cold, with her body between him and her cottage.

As if she could fend him off if he wanted to walk in that door and handle this his way. Right now.

The urge to do exactly that was like a physical pain inside him.

He had dreamed of his little boy's face. He had imagined it.

He supposed this was *longing*, this rough-edged ache that pulsed in him and left him feeling empty.

Behind her the cottage looked warm and cozy. He could see the buttery light from within, and even though it was winter, he could see the remains of summer flowers and the planting that must take place in spring. As if this was a house well loved. It *looked* happy.

Pascal couldn't bear to think about how easily he could have gone home after his date in Rome, slept, then resumed his life. He might never have come here again. He might never have known.

And he didn't know what to call the thing that moved in him then, all teeth and claws and *what-ifs*.

Cecilia stood there before him, her cheeks flushed from the chill and her arms folded across her chest as if to ward off the plummeting temperatures. As if he was the enemy when she was the one who had done this. She was the one who had hidden away here with this secret she'd had no intention of sharing with him.

"I told you I was staying here," he growled at her. "Did you think I would change my mind?"

"Maybe I hoped you would," she replied.

With a bitter flash of honesty that he could have done without.

It was not until he had taken his leave of her—to stomp his spleen into the frozen fields as he tramped around the valley—that he understood why he couldn't quite bring himself to view her as evil. The way he thought he should. On the contrary, something about the way she'd stood up to him—bodily—made his chest ache, and it wasn't until he was back in his stark, monastic chamber that he understood why.

He would have given anything, or everything if asked, to see his mother stand up for him. Even once.

But Marissa Del Guardia had stood for nothing. Not for herself, and certainly not for the child she'd never wanted who had ruined her happiness—something she had no qualm telling him directly. His father had swept in and swept her off her feet as if she was a flower to pick from a garden instead of a waitress in a restaurant he frequented. He'd used her as he liked, then discarded her when she'd fallen pregnant. He had never looked back.

And Marissa's response had been desolation, followed by sleeping pills, and whatever she could find to take the edge off during the day.

Pascal couldn't imagine any circumstance in which she would ever have stirred herself to defend him. He was only surprised she'd actually carried him to term.

He couldn't deny that there was a part of him that liked the fact that his child's mother was prepared to fight off any adversary. Even if that adversary was him.

But by the time a week had dragged by with him marooned in an empty room with only his memories for company and work to dull that noise, Pascal was beginning to lose his famous cool.

It had been educational, to say the least, to discover how much of his business he could handle from afar. It suggested that it wouldn't do him any harm to relax his grip as he had not done since he started. He would need to consider what that meant.

But there was only so much "rusticating" a man could take in the presence of nuns who treated him like an naughty boy, the long shadow of what he'd done here and how he'd left, and the woman who appeared to think she could wait him out and, in effect, steal his child from him all over again.

Pascal wasn't here to address his workaholic tendencies. He was here for his son.

And he'd been ignored as long as he was prepared to take.

So it was almost lowering, really, when he stormed from his room out into the clinic's lobby to find Cecilia waiting for him.

She stood wrapped in a long, camel-colored coat that made her hair gleam and her violet eyes seem fairly purple. She stared at him for a long, solemn moment as if working up to what she meant to say.

"I've been here a week," Pascal pointed out, caring not at all if every person in the clinic beyond was watching and could hear him. "I have sat in my cell and performed my penance. What more can you possibly want from me?"

"That's a dangerous question."

"Shall I beg?" he asked, his voice soft with the menace building in him. They were alone in the foyer for the moment, though he wouldn't have cared if the entire order was lined up around them, singing hymns of praise. "Plead? Or perhaps I should argue my case with a kiss, which seems to be the only time you forget to view me as your enemy? Tell me, which will work? *I want to see my son.*"

He could see her pulse in the hollow of her elegant neck, but it didn't appease him. He didn't care if she was in the grip of the same emotions that buffeted him.

"No such displays are necessary," she said, and this time, he did not attribute the sudden flush in her cheeks to the cold air outside. "I will let you see him."

"You are too kind, Cecilia. Truly."

"That snide tone of voice won't do you any favors," she retorted, her eyes flashing. "I don't have to let you see him at all. And don't get your hopes up. I'm not introducing you to him. Not yet. But as you say, you've been here a week. I expected you to be gone before morning, again. Instead, you stayed and you didn't try to force your way into my cottage."

"I didn't realize I was expected to pass tests," Pascal said icily. "Secret examinations to discover whether or not I'm a decent human being, it appears. I was unaware that was a subject for debate."

"The woman who cares for him while I clean has them running around outside this morning, as it's clear," she said as if he hadn't spoken. But he knew she'd heard him just fine. "You can see him. And before you complain that it isn't enough, you should be aware that my first instinct was to give you nothing at all."

Pascal wasn't sure he could trust himself to speak then, so he said nothing. He merely inclined his head toward the door, and watched as Cecilia wheeled around, then strode out. She looked stiff, her movements jerky— as if her very bones were protesting this.

It only made the dark thing in him solidify.

She kept treating him like he was that wounded soldier who could have died here, forgotten entirely. And he'd let her this whole week because that wounded soldier still lived in him. And because he'd forgotten that, and remembering it again felt like guilt.

But he wasn't the one who had concealed a child for years. Then refused to let her see him.

He followed behind her, thrusting his hands deep into the pockets of his coat as she led him away from the abbey. He could feel her agitation kicking up all around her, so he stayed quiet. She was walking fast and almost ferociously as if she didn't really want to do this. As if she was forcing herself. As if she was afraid that if she slowed down, she wouldn't go through with it.

Pascal didn't really care how this happened, as long as it did.

When they came to the edge of the field on the far side of Cecilia's cottage, she stopped abruptly. There were three children out there, running in circles around a woman. They looked drunk, he thought. As heedless as puppies.

"He's there," Cecilia said, and nodded toward the group. "The one in the middle."

And Pascal stood, stricken, as the two lighter-haired children seemed to fade there before him. Because all he could see was the dark-haired laughing boy between them. He didn't notice his mother or the strange man watching them. He was too busy making circles and shouting out his joy and delight into the cold air.

But Pascal would have recognized him even without Cecilia. Because it was like looking into his own past. It was one of the few photographs he'd ever seen of himself as a child, brought to bright and happy life right there before his eyes.

It took his breath away.

He felt empty and full, and mad with it. Something slammed into him so hard he expected the mountains had come down around them, but nothing moved except the painful kick of his heart against his ribs.

My son.

Dante was sturdy. He ran fast, and joyfully.

He was like a bright light shining there on an otherwise barren field.

He was like a punch, deep into Pascal's gut.

And for a moment Pascal just wanted…everything.

He'd spent a week here, fighting the seduction of this place. This happy, ethereal valley. The peace of it. The ease.

But he couldn't fight the boy in front of him or the woman at his side.

And in an instant it was as if he could suddenly imagine the life he'd left behind when he'd left this place. Her pretty face the first thing he saw in the morning, if he'd stayed. The child they would have raised together. The odd jobs he might have taken, to keep them afloat here. Nothing like the life he had now. He could see it in a long, beautiful sweep of something like memory when it had never happened and couldn't now, and it didn't matter. He wanted it.

God, how he wanted it.

His woman and his little boy and happy, dizzy loops on a cold field.

All the riches in the world, all the power, the revenge on his own father—for a single, piercing moment all of that fell away.

And Pascal had the unsettling notion that he'd side-stepped into a different version of himself, where that fantasy was real. Where he'd never left.

Later he would come up with reasons and rationales. Right here, right now, all he wanted was as much of that everything as he could get, whatever it took.

"Cecilia," he said, turning to look down at her, aware that there must have been some great emotion on his face. He did nothing to hide it. "You must marry me."

CHAPTER SIX

"HE WANTS TO marry me," Cecilia said.

It shocked her how hard it was to get the words out of her mouth. Possibly because saying them out loud gave them weight. It made them real. Particularly here, in the kitchen of the abbey where she had eaten so many meals in her time. And now cleaned it as if it was still her own.

Maybe some part of her thought it was.

Mother Superior sat at the long, communal table fashioned of weathered wood where the sisters gathered, her hands cupped around a steaming-hot mug of tea. Cecilia remembered when her hands had been tough, but smoother. Now they were gnarled with the arthritis she never complained about, and something about looking at those familiar, aged hands with those dangerous words floating in the air between them made Cecilia's chest ache.

"Does this surprise you?" Mother Superior asked. Mildly enough.

But then that serene, decidedly calm tone of voice of hers was one of her superpowers. It made grown men quail before her. It made novitiates tremble. It had made Cecilia cry, more than once.

Today she scowled into the sink she was scrubbing

down, and absolutely did not feel the slightest prickle of unwanted moisture behind her eyes.

"Yes. It astonishes me, in fact." She shook her head as if she could shake away all the competing, complicated feelings that had been clattering around inside her since that moment outside on the field when he'd looked at her with that unsettling, raw expression on his face. Then had said what he'd said. "If I'm honest, I think it offends me."

But that wasn't the right word, either. It had felt like a sucker punch, directly into her gut. She'd been faintly amazed that she hadn't doubled over.

A huge, wild ache had ripped opened wide inside her, a crevice so deep and so wide that she'd been terrified for a moment that she might actually topple off the side of the world and disappear inside it. Her heart had pounded so hard, even high in her throat, she'd been terrified she might get sick.

Instead, she'd turned on her heel and walked away from him on legs gone wobbly, not sure she wouldn't simply crumple into the cold ground. But she had to get away from Pascal. At once. Because she thought that if she didn't, she might pull down the mountains all around them with the force of her reaction.

He'd followed, of course.

And there had been too much noise in her head for her to process the things he'd said. The reasons he'd laid down before her like proof. Or some kind of cold, cut-and-dry temptation that was supposed to speak to her somehow when there was that *ache*.

"I'm not dignifying that with a response," she'd said. When she could manage to speak at all.

"There can be only one response," he'd replied.

She whipped her head around to stare at him, perhaps imagining that she could shame him out there in the fields she knew too well. The wind had cut into her like knives, but his presence was a far deeper wound by far. How could he imagine otherwise? "I will wait for it, Cecilia."

She was well aware that this time, his *waiting* was a threat. That had been two days ago.

"Why should you be offended?" Mother Superior asked in her maddeningly unbothered way that Cecilia knew full well was *meant* to set her teeth on edge. "What we know about Pascal is that he likes to solve his problems in the most direct way possible. We know what happened when he felt lonely here. Dante is the result."

And it was a measure of how agitated Cecilia was about other things that she forgot to react with her usual mix of emotions at that oblique reference to that morning she had woken up to discover Mother Superior at the foot of a bed she shouldn't have been sleeping in and her whole life changed.

"We know what happened when he left here, and launched himself at the world," Mother Superior continued placidly. "And I'm not the least surprised that his return, wherein he learned that he had a son, should lead to this. It solves all of his problems, elegantly."

"I don't wish to be his problem," Cecilia bit out, her eyes on the sink. "Or have anything to do with solving it for him."

Mother Superior laughed that raspy, lusty laugh of hers that served to remind anyone who heard it that she was, in fact, a woman made of flesh and blood like anyone else. No matter how holy she seemed the rest of the time.

"Child, you have been a problem for that man since the moment he woke up after his accident and saw you there at his bedside," she told Cecilia. "Left to his own devices, he would have taken you with him when he left the first time."

It took a moment for the full meaning of those words to penetrate. When they did, Cecilia set down her sponge, carefully. Very, very carefully. Then she took her time turning and wiping her hands on the apron she wore wrapped around her waist. She was not surprised to find Mother Superior's wise, kind gaze level on hers.

Waiting, she could see. But without a shred of trepidation or concern.

"What do you mean by that?" she asked, though her voice shook, and worse, she already thought she knew. Hadn't Pascal himself hinted at this in the church? "What do you mean, *left to his own devices*?"

"You did not join us for Morning Prayer," Mother Superior told her, her calm tone scraping down the length of Cecilia's spine like fingernails. "When I went looking for you, I found you in his room. You were still asleep, but he was not."

"Are you... You're not saying...?"

"I merely asked him what his intentions were," Mother Superior replied, that mild gaze not only steady on hers, but distressingly compassionate. "He was a man recovering from an accident who had clearly become well again. I suspected that meant he would not wish to stay with us, tucked away as we are from the rest of the world. Meanwhile, he'd taken it upon himself to despoil a novitiate. I merely wondered what his plans were."

"His plans," Cecilia repeated as if she couldn't comprehend what the other woman was saying. When she did. Too well. "You asked him *his plans.*"

"I merely wondered if he intended to take you with him when he returned to his life, as I had no doubt at all he would do, because that is what men like him are put on this earth to do."

"That was never something we discussed."

But she didn't know if she was saying that to protect him or herself, because while it was true, it was also true that there had been an understanding between them. Or she never would have participated in her *despoiling*, a word she might have found entertaining in other circumstances. When, for example, her *despoiler* was in distant cities the way he was supposed to be instead of holed up in the abbey clinic *right this moment.*

Cecilia wasn't finding any of this entertaining at all.

And Mother Superior was watching her face as if she could read all of this right there on Cecilia's cheeks. That she likely could only made it worse. "What I know about you, child, is that you are not a casual woman," Mother Superior said. "You never have been. You do not give yourself to anything unless you plan to do so with your whole heart and soul for the remainder of your days. It is what would have made you such an excellent nun, if that had been your path. And it is what makes you such a marvelous mother."

And how was she supposed to summon up any self-righteous indignation now? When she said something like that? This was why Mother Superior terrified everyone who came into contact with her—and they thanked her for it.

"I can't… I mean I don't believe…" Cecilia put her hands to her face then, to cover up all the reading material she was broadcasting around the abbey kitchen. And she couldn't tell if she was trembling, or her hands were trembling, or if the earth beneath her feet was rocking and rolling. "Why did you never tell me this?"

"What would have been the point?" Mother Superior asked as if she was genuinely curious. "He left."

"Yes, but…"

And that ache in her was too big. Too vast. She felt as if she was nothing but earthquakes and aftershocks, and beneath it all, there was only the ash and ruin of her first love. Heartbreak masquerading as anger when what she wanted to feel for Pascal and their past was nothing. Not regret, not fury—nothing at all.

How had she managed to convince herself that she could be indifferent to any part of this, much less Pascal himself?

"Do you want me to tell you that he wavered?" Mother Superior asked when the silence only stretched out between them. "Because he did. He argued, and he was torn. But in the end, he left. And yes, I chose to protect you from that. What difference would it make to you that it was difficult for him?"

"I don't know. But it would have, surely."

Because it made a difference now. It seemed to coil inside her, warming her. And the warmth made her feel steadier. It helped her breathe.

"Would it?" Mother Superior smiled faintly. "First you thought you would rededicate yourself to your faith. And then it turned out you were pregnant, and you had to wrestle with whether or not to keep the baby or give it over to adoption. Would his wavering have helped you learn how to be strong enough to grapple with these decisions?"

"I'm not sure it was your call to make." Cecilia's voice was harsher than she'd intended, and it made her stomach hurt. Because she had never spoken to Mother Superior before like that. Never.

She rather expected the ancient abbey to come tumbling down all around them at her impertinence, but it remained solid. The walls did not so much as shiver in response.

Worse, Mother Superior only smiled a little more deeply.

"I'm not sure it was, either," she replied, which made all the emotion inside Cecilia feel heavier. Thicker. Because it was hard to focus on blame and fury when the other woman wasn't defending herself. "That is my weight to carry. What you must decide is what you plan to do about it now."

Cecilia turned back to the sink, blinking back the obnoxious sting of moisture in her eyes that she told herself was blame and fury in spades, no matter how heavy it felt. It was still a betrayal, and from the least likely source imaginable. It was far too much *emotion*, with nowhere to go. No outlet at all.

Only the seismic shifts inside her.

"I plan to do exactly what I've been doing," she said, and she was proud that her voice didn't shake. And that she wasn't gritting out her words through her teeth. "My life may not be what I planned it to be when I was twenty, but that's not necessarily a bad thing. It's full. I'm proud of it. I don't need him."

"And your son?"

"Dante *certainly* doesn't need him." And she found that she was gritting her teeth after all.

"Does he not?" Mother Superior made a clicking noise with her tongue. "It was my impression that children bloomed in the presence of both their parents, should they have that as an option."

"I had neither parent," Cecilia shot back at her. Or to the bottom of the sink anyway. "And I'm perfectly fine."

"You had an entire abbey, child. You still do."

"And so does Dante."

"Cecilia," Mother Superior said in that particularly gentle way of hers that was nothing but iron beneath. "There's a difference between accepting a circumstance, even thriving in it, when you have no other choice. You have done so admirably. You always have. But Dante has choices you did not. Will you let your personal feelings about his father dictate those choices?"

Cecilia's eyes were blurry now, and she didn't turn back around because she didn't want Mother Superior to see it. Though she suspected the old woman could see straight through her, either way.

"You say that as if I don't know what's best for Dante. As if I don't want what's best for him."

"I know you love that child," Mother Superior said soothingly. "And you have worked so hard to give him what you think you lacked. But Cecilia. I don't think it's ever occurred to you that when your mother left you here, she made certain you would be tended to by an entire order of surrogate mothers."

"Of course that's occurred to me. It's why I wanted to join the order myself."

It was also why she had stayed here even in the darkest hours of her disgrace instead of leaving the valley behind. How could she leave the only family she'd ever known? No matter how disappointed they were in her?

"But she also made certain you would never know the faintest bit of information about your own father," Mother Superior continued. "I flatter myself that the sisters and I have done our best, but we can only be surrogate mothers, aunts and sisters. You may not recall that when you were about seven, all you wanted was a father. And you cried and cried for what could never be."

She'd forgotten that. But she shook her head. "It was a phase. It faded."

"Child. Why would you choose to do to Dante what was forced upon you? Would you not spare him that pain if you could?"

And that was the question that stuck with Cecilia as she finished up her duties in the abbey that day, then took the longer walk home so as to make sure she didn't stray too close to the clinic. It was the question that echoed around inside her when she picked Dante up from her neighbor and gazed down at him with the usual mix of fondness and exasperation as he shouted the events of his day at her. Rapid and loud, the way he always did when he was overexcited—and he was usually overexcited.

She thought about the question all throughout their normal afternoon and evening. She considered it during bath time, when Dante leaped out of the tub and ran in circles around the cottage, laughing maniacally and waving his hands over his head until Cecilia could do nothing but laugh with him.

She read him a story, heard his prayers and tucked him into bed, and when she turned out the light and left him to sleep, she could still hear Mother Superior's calm, measured voice inside her.

She'd forgotten—or she'd tried to forget—how much and how often she'd imagined herself with a real family when she'd been young. Cecilia had loved growing up in the abbey. All the sisters had treated her as their own, a very junior sister or everyone's child, and she had never doubted that she was loved. And by many.

But she wasn't like the other children in the village. All the intricacies of family dynamics were lost on her. And as Mother Superior had said today, she had found it especially trying when she was a little bit older than Dante and entirely too consumed with making sure that she was *normal*. It had been clear to her that she was not, and it had bothered her. How had she forgotten that?

She supposed she'd set so much of it aside when she decided to join the order herself that she'd somehow managed to wipe it all out in her memory.

Or perhaps you wanted to join the order because it tied up the story of your life in a nice, neat bow, a voice inside her suggested archly.

She scowled at herself as she cleaned up the kitchen. Then she went to sit out in the main room of the cottage. It was a pleasant, open space that felt airy and large when it was neither. She curled up in her favorite chair before the fire, where she liked to read or sew, and did neither tonight. Instead, she stared into the flames, able to see nothing at all but Mother Superior's deft, dear hands wrapped around her tea. And that voice of hers, so gentle and so soft, that sat in her like a stone.

Why would you choose to do to Dante what was forced upon you?

Cecilia blew out a long, hard breath, and then made

herself get up again. She crossed back to the kitchen drawer where she'd thrown the bit of paper she'd found thrust beneath her door one morning. It was a mobile number written in a bold, impatient hand and an initial. *P.*

And maybe it was telling that she hadn't tossed it straight into the fire, but she hadn't.

She stared down at the number and that *P* for a long time.

And when she couldn't put it off any longer, she decided she couldn't face a telephone call. She picked up her mobile and texted him instead. Simple and to the point.

This is Cecilia. We need to talk. Can you come to the cottage?

She told herself he would likely take his time replying, but his response came within seconds.

On my way.

And then Cecilia was treated to some more hard truths about herself, because she…dithered.

There was no other word for it. Before she'd texted him, she hadn't given a thought to her appearance, here at the end of a long day cleaning ancient buildings and tending to an active five-year-old. Or her clothes. The moment he replied, she rushed into her bedroom and found herself changing from her usual loose shirt and comfortable lounging pants into a wholly uncharacteristic shift dress she usually wore only to church. And then smoothing her hair and coiling it into a tidy knot at the nape of her neck.

Then she charged back out into the main room and threw herself into a whirlwind tidying session that had her breathing a little too heavily by the time she'd made the place look less like a child's gymnasium and more like an adult's serene living room. Or as close to such a thing as she could get as she was not a billionaire with staff.

That thought kicked her temper back into gear, and she frowned at herself in the reflection of the windows, because why was she trying to *impress* Pascal? Surely she should have gone the other direction and left herself and the cottage as slovenly as possible, the better to drive him away.

But she didn't change her clothes again.

Nor did she empty the basket of Dante's favorite toys across the rug, the better to be crunched painfully underfoot.

And at some point she would have to face what it meant that she wanted so desperately for Pascal to see her, and this home she'd made for their child, at their best. Just as she would have to face the electric charge within her at the notion he was coming here, and her sneaking suspicion that it was not agitation that was so bright inside her.

She was terribly afraid it was pure, undiluted anticipation.

Another betrayal in a day chock full of them.

When his knock came on her front door—a hard, commanding rap—her stomach fluttered about as if it was beset by butterflies and she hated herself. Fully. But she crossed the floor to let him in anyway.

She wrenched open the door, prepared to be icily controlled and cuttingly polite, and caught her breath.

Because she was never prepared.

Pascal stood there, in profile as he stared off toward the lit-up abbey in the darkness. The light from inside the cottage spilled over him, making a meal out of his strong nose and sensual lips. Even his scars seemed to enhance his appeal, silvery across his jaw, then disappearing beneath the collar of the coat he wore.

He took his time turning his head to look at her, and when his eyes met hers, the world began to burn.

Her first and foremost.

"I have raced to your side on command," he said, his voice low and laced with too many dark things she did not wish to understand. Not when she could feel them all, each individual thread and threat, winding around and around inside her. "Never let it be said that I cannot take an order, *cara*. Like a dog."

Cecilia ignored the way that wound its way down her spine, settling worryingly low in her belly with a pulse she wanted to call pain. But it wasn't pain.

It most certainly wasn't pain.

She forced herself to turn her back on him, then led him into the room as if he was as threatening to her as the tottery old priest—even when every alarm inside her shouted that it was exactly the wrong thing to do. That she should never turn her back on a predator like him, no matter how many too-hot memories she had of a time she'd been pretending she'd forgotten.

But she did it, and though her neck prickled, Pascal did not leap upon her with his fangs bared, or any such superstitious nonsense. *Of course he didn't*, she told herself sternly. She waved him to the sofa before the fire, with its newly plumped pillows and a throw folded just so along the back to hide the stains from small, sticky hands. Then she took her favorite chair again, stuck as it was at a convenient angle to the sofa that allowed her to be close yet not in reach.

"No offer of a drink?" he asked as he shrugged out of his heavy coat and tossed it beside him on the sofa. And then he sat, managing to overwhelm the small sofa with the sheer magnitude of his oversize frame and those *shoulders*. Cecilia somehow doubted she would ever look at that sofa quite the same way again. "No *aperitivos* to help us pretend we're civilized?"

"This isn't a social call."

"Not even a few olives. I feel like a savage."

"That is between you and whatever passes for your god, Pascal," she said tightly.

She regretted it the moment she spoke. And then with far more fervor when his stark mouth moved into something far too sharp to be a smile.

"Incivility does not suit you, Cecilia."

"I brought you over here to discuss introducing you to Dante," she said, reminding herself that she needed to stay cool, controlled. No matter how his presence here seemed to suck up all the air in the main room, making it nearly impossible to breathe. "But the more you play little games, the more I second-guess myself on that score."

The hint of amusement on his face was extinguished as surely as if it had never been there, and she detested the fact that she could *feel* it. As if he was doing it *to* her. And that terrible pang of something like panic, urging her to do whatever she could to make it come back.

No, she ordered herself. *This is not about placating him. This is about choosing between right and wrong.*

But he was looking at her as if she was the enemy. "I suggest that you proceed with caution. Do you truly wish to set up a scenario in which we use our child as a bargaining chip between us?"

Cecilia blinked. "That's not what I meant."

"I can't pretend to know what you have been thinking about while you made me sit in that clinic and relive the worst time of my life," he said in the same dark tone, his gaze so hard on hers that she was surprised her skin didn't open beneath the onslaught. "Revenge, I assume. But in between amusing memories of my accident and what it took to survive it, I have been entertaining myself with tales from the worst divorces."

Once again she hadn't seen him coming. A sensation she did not enjoy. "Divorces? What do divorces have to do with our situation?" She tilted her head to one side. "Or is that what passes for your usual leisure reading material?"

"I was studying custody battles," he supplied, and he settled back against the couch. Another man might have looked idle. Pascal did not. "The nastier, the better. And do you know who suffers the most in such scenarios? Not the battling parents."

It was the second time today that someone else had obliquely rebuked her for her selfishness, and Cecilia found it didn't sit well. She was far too flushed. And she wanted to throw the lamp beside her at his head for daring to lecture *her* on parenting, even in a roundabout way.

But she had spent most of her life learning discipline of one sort or another, so she kept herself still.

"You don't think we should use Dante as a bargaining chip, and I agree, of course," she said when she could be certain the lamp would remain where it was. "Perhaps you could also stop trying to use him to manipulate my emotions."

She expected him to argue. Instead, something in his black eyes gleamed gold. He lifted one finger as if to shrug without bothering to expend the energy required. Somehow that small gesture was breathtakingly infuriating.

"Fair enough," he said. Which was even more irritating. Cecilia hadn't expected him to be remotely agreeable—and in fact, she went still when he smiled at her, because she knew better. "But I know about him now. There's no going back from that, no matter how much of a grace period I give you to deal with the reality you already knew. Surely you must understand this."

He was giving *her* a grace period—Cecilia ordered herself to breathe before she exploded. Especially because there was something about the way he gazed at her that made her think an explosion was precisely what he wanted.

"I would prefer not to be threatened by you at every opportunity," she managed to retort. She laced her fingers together in her lap when all he did was raise that dark brow of his, because throwing lamps would not solve the problem. No matter how satisfying it might be in the moment. "I cannot deny Dante access to his father. Just because he hasn't asked about you before now doesn't mean he won't in the future. I suppose I've been in denial about that."

He only watched her, and though he still lounged there on the sofa, she didn't make the mistake of imag-

ining that he was at ease. His entire body was poised.
Alert. As if he might spring into action at the slightest
provocation. She didn't want to speculate what kind of
action that might be.

Cecilia swallowed and found her throat dry. And
forced herself to keep going, even though it was hard,
because this was ultimately about Dante. And there was
nothing she wouldn't do for him. Even this.

"I don't have a father," she said matter-of-factly.
"There's no possibility of my figuring out who he was,
and at this point in my life, I'm not sure I would want
to even if I could." She held his gaze, though it made
her skin feel much too tight. "And I know your experience with your father was no easier."

He didn't laugh, though his dark eyes gleamed. "That
is putting it more politely than he deserves."

She inclined her head and extended her olive branch.
"I don't see any reason why Dante should have to suffer
the things that we did, if we can prevent it."

"This is very noble-minded of you, Cecilia, after all
these years that handily belie that sentiment," Pascal
said, and his tone was so sardonic it seemed to lodge
itself between her ribs like a bullet. "How exactly do
you imagine this high-minded approach to our child's
life will unfold, practically speaking?"

That was certainly not the expression of gratitude
she'd anticipated. Cecilia sat a little bit straighter in
her chair, and frowned at him. "What do you mean?"

"I assume you will oversee the initial introduction,
as it were." Another flick of that finger, a shrug and a
dismissal in one. She wanted to slap at it. "That makes
sense. Perhaps you should take this opportunity to out-
line your ideal visitation schedule."

She felt herself go still as if she'd blundered into a trap in the woods and had only just noticed the steel jaws lying there, primed to slam closed. "If everything goes well, you can come and visit him whenever you like."

"Very generous indeed." His dark eyes glittered. "But you see, I do not understand why you should get to control how much I see the child that you've concealed from me all this time. Perhaps he should come and live with me, and you can come visit him whenever you like." He smiled then, and it was not a pleasant smile. It was all steel and jagged edges. "Behold my generosity."

"I'm his mother!" she snapped at him, not sure if it was fury or fear racing through her then. Both, perhaps. She caught herself. "A child needs his mother."

"A child needs his father, *cara*. Particularly a boy. Everyone knows this."

"Are you threatening to take him away from me?" she asked, throwing it out there because it was the worst thing. And it was better to keep it right there in the light, where she could see it.

Not that seeing *him* in the cheery light of this cottage that had always seemed so safe and happy to her before tonight was doing her any favors.

"I do not make threats." Pascal was still lounging, one arm tossed down the length of the couch's back, his long legs thrust out before him. But his gaze was dark and intense and focused entirely on her. "You have vastly underestimated the seriousness of the situation, I think."

"Of the two people sitting in this room, I'm the one who's been raising a child alone. I don't think it's possible to underestimate that situation."

"I mean me." And she realized for the first time that he wasn't sitting like that because he was pretending to be at ease. He was doing it to keep himself in check. He was doing it to keep his hands to himself, and not on any lamps. Or her. Cecilia felt a terrible chill sweep over her. "You have underestimated *me*, Cecilia."

It occurred to her then, as he looked at her with that same lethal steel she could hear in his voice and see all over his powerful body, that she really didn't know this man at all. The Pascal she remembered had been compelling, magnetic and charming. But the kind of power that emanated from the Pascal sitting before her tonight had been little more than a spark in that man. The Pascal sitting before her had created an empire in his name. He had taken what little he had and made it a force to be reckoned with on the global scale.

She had known a grateful patient in a hospital, alone and conversant with his own near-death experience and the relief that he'd survived it.

This man was fully alive in every sense of the term.

And he'd made himself a king.

Had she ever been in control of this situation? But even as the question flashed through her, he was speaking again.

"I allowed the shock to get to me," he said in that same dark, deliberate way that was far more terrifying than any display of temper or emotion. "I spent the first few days here in some kind of a daze, trying to make sense of this thing. But your refusal to engage with me was actually a favor. I should thank you."

"I was protecting my son."

There was a hint of a curve on that stark mouth of

his, but no more, and she thought it was cynical, at best. Not anything like a smile.

"You can call it what you like. Once I saw the child, so similar to me in every way, everything crystallized."

He actually shrugged then, with his shoulders. That, too, was worse.

"I don't know what you mean by crystallized," she said, aware that she was talking too quickly. Too nervously. "But I do know that I'm not going to—"

"I've heard a great deal about what you will and will not do, Cecilia," Pascal said, a dark storm in him that she could feel all too well even without any rain. "But now it is time for me to tell you what *I* will and will not do."

"Pascal—"

But it was too late.

His expression was raw again, but this time with a fury that scared her all the more because it was controlled.

"I will not relinquish my claim to my child," he told her. "I will not meekly hand over custody of him. You have already stolen six years of his life from me. I can never get it back."

Another shiver sank down her spine, edged with foreboding. She tried to say his name again, but this time nothing came out.

Too late, something inside her warned.

And she had never seen his black gaze as dark as it was then.

"I don't see any particular reason why I shouldn't take him for the next six years, Cecilia," he said, far too calmly. "Just to make it fair."

CHAPTER SEVEN

PASCAL SHOULD PROBABLY not have taken quite so much satisfaction in seeing her pale.

But then, he had never pretended to be a good man. Save the months he'd spent here, that was, when he hadn't known if he would live through it—and even then, only until the end of it. When he proved himself as lost to decency as ever.

"That is never going to happen," Cecilia threw at him through bloodless lips.

Her hands were in fists in her lap, and she was curled toward him as if she imagined she might take a swing at him.

He almost wished she would.

"It will happen if I want it to happen," he told her, pitiless and very, very certain. "I'm a very wealthy man, *cara*. And wealth is power whether you like it or not, even up here in this valley time has forgotten. Do you really think you could best me in court if I did not allow it?"

"Now we're going to court?" Her voice was fainter then, her color even more pale.

And he almost felt sorry for her; he really did. But he had been here too long, with nothing to do but think through all the possibilities—and he'd concluded there was really only one. Only one possible ending to this situation that gave everyone involved what they wanted. Him more than her, perhaps, but then, he hadn't concealed a child from her.

Cecilia hadn't reached the same conclusion yet. But Pascal couldn't say he disliked the opportunity to teach her a lesson as she made her way toward the only possible outcome.

Especially because she still haunted him. Even when he knew what she'd done. Even when she refused to let him meet his own son. None of that seemed to matter when he dreamed of her soft mouth, her honey-colored hair. Those eyes of violet that should not have been possible, and yet were perfectly natural.

She haunted him even now, when she was in the same room, dressed like the date he'd wished he'd had while spending all of that energy looking for an appropriate wife. She didn't look like a cleaner tonight. She was dressed with a simple elegance that made him want to press his mouth to her collarbone, then bury himself inside her, the only way he could take part in that kind of sophisticated poetry.

It had occurred to him at some point over the past few days that he had been unable to find the perfect wife when he'd looked because he'd already met her. He'd asked her to marry him and she'd refused him, but that was just as well, because it had given him time to understand that his reaction to seeing Dante on that field was just that. A reaction.

He had waited. And he had vowed, with every passing day, that she would marry him as he wished. And she would pay.

Over and over again, until he was satisfied.

And Pascal was rarely satisfied.

"I will do anything and everything I have to do," he told her now, with a quiet intensity he could see rocked her. "If I feel compassionate, I suppose I might allow you to fly down to Rome and see him one weekend a month. Perhaps two."

"One weekend a month—" she began, her voice wild.

But she bit off her own words. And swallowed as if her throat hurt, keeping them all inside. Then she blinked rapidly enough that he suspected it was tears of frustration she was trying to keep at bay.

"I asked you to come over here tonight to discuss Dante's best interests," she said after a long moment of keeping herself together. She'd even managed to keep her voice even. "Which I've come to understand included you taking on the role of his father."

"I am his father. There is no role to take on. It is a fact."

"But you don't seem to have any idea about what might be good for him or you wouldn't suggest these things." Another hard, visible swallow. And Pascal found himself fascinated by the telltale pulse in her neck. It told him how agitated she truly was, no matter how calm she might be pretending to be. "Let me remind you that I'm the woman you made all manner of promises to, all of which you broke when you disappeared. I have no reason to assume you won't do the same thing to my child. And instead of giving me the space to work through this—"

"You had six years, Cecilia."

"—you decided to throw your weight around instead."

And by that point, of course, she was no longer quite

so calm. He noted that the color had come back to her cheeks, and her eyes were a violet storm. Her hands were still in fists, though she was still holding them in her lap. She looked well and truly agitated.

Good.

"You have two choices," Pascal told her, his voice implacable. "You can accept the fact that this is out of your hands. You will see the child at my whim, or possibly not at all, as it suits me."

"That's obviously not possible." Her voice shook. "*Of course* that's not possible. What's the other choice?"

"I told you," he said, and he couldn't keep the satisfaction from his voice. Then again, he didn't try very hard. "Marry me. Then you can see him all you like."

She made a soft noise, then shot up from her chair. He had the impression she wanted to launch herself at him, and even braced himself for the impact, but she didn't. Instead, she moved toward the fire, folding her arms across her chest as if she needed to hold herself intact. Pascal stayed where he was, settling back against the couch, and waited for this endgame of his to play itself out.

Or for her to look at him again.

He frowned at his own bizarre sentimentality, but brushed it away when she began to speak—her attention directed at the fire.

"I don't understand why you would wish to marry someone you think so little of," she said, sounding… subdued.

Pascal made a small opera out of a shrug and a sigh to match. "Whatever I might think of you personally, not to mention the questionable choices you've made, you're obviously an excellent mother to my child. He is as you said he was. Healthy, happy."

And if she didn't already know that of course he'd gone and looked at the boy again without her permission, well. Her denial was not his problem. He had kept his distance. And not because he was interested in obeying her dictates—or anyone else's—but because he had no interest in scaring off his own son.

He would wait for his introduction. Then he would do exactly as he pleased.

Cecilia waited as if she expected him to keep talking, then let out a sound that he couldn't quite define when he didn't. "That doesn't explain why you would want to marry me."

He remembered that moment at the side of the field when it had all gotten to him. When he had found himself swamped with a kind of longing he had since dismissed. Because he was Pascal Furlani, not some soft, emotional creature. He had been reacting to the shock, that was all.

It had been a long, long time since anyone had managed to surprise him.

But he had been given a great many days to accustom himself to this new development in his life. He had a son. That was what mattered. And a son deserved a family. So Pascal could marry his son's mother or he could marry someone else—he didn't much care which, but he was going to make Dante a family.

One way or another, he was going to spend his son's first Christmas with a father like the family man his board of directors did not believe he could be.

"I am a deeply unromantic man," he told Cecilia. He waited as she turned slightly so she could look at him again. "My mother spent a great deal of time carrying on about her great love affair. It shadowed the whole of our lives. And as the result of that affair, I can assure you, love had nothing to do with it."

He could see her take that in and consider it.

"So the marriage you're proposing is in name only."

Pascal saw the faint flare of something like hope in her gaze, too.

Maybe that was why he laughed.

Or maybe he was a bastard in more than simple, biological fact.

"I don't need you to be in love with me, if that's what you mean," he said, again enjoying himself more than he should. "And I'm not capable of love myself. I require a wife in any case. I've been searching for one for some time. The trouble was, I did not wish there to be a hint of scandal attached to her."

"I'm the most scandalous woman in this village," Cecilia said. Clearly hoping that would disqualify her from consideration. "I'm obviously not the right choice for a man of your…stature."

That *stature* was not the word she'd meant to use was obvious enough that Pascal almost thought her intended word glimmered in the air between them, like the heat from the fire.

"Your only scandal is me." And when he saw her gaze take on a calculating gleam, he laughed again. "Do not bother to tell me otherwise. According to all sources in and out of the abbey, I was your only mistake. Which makes you perfect for my purposes."

"I feel certain that I want nothing to do with what you call perfection."

"You have a choice, *cara*," he said, drawling a little as he said it. "Never let it be said I am not magnanimous."

She looked like she wanted to strangle him, which should probably not have made him hard in instant, enthusiastic response.

"Yes," she seethed at him. "*Magnanimous* is precisely the word I would have chosen to describe you."

"Should you choose to marry me, you will be doing me a favor," Pascal continued, almost happily. "You will help me to create a charming picture of domesticity to undercut my board of directors' machinations. You've already met a pair of them. They are always scheming against me, and the fact that I'm a single, seemingly unfettered man does not endear me to them. I can't say that I will ever forgive what you have done here, but my gratitude will be no small thing, I trust."

He could have told her that he also wanted Dante to have the family he'd never had. But he didn't.

"Your gratitude," she repeated, her voice flat. "Or, excuse me, your *potential* gratitude is what I am to look forward to."

"Or you can look forward to a weekend a month. Supervised, of course. Noncustodial parents do have a reputation for disappearing with their children, don't they?"

"And what if I don't believe you?" she asked after another long moment. He could see she was fighting to keep her composure. "What if I think you're just trying to intimidate me?"

"Five-year-olds are resilient," he said with the soft ruthlessness that made even the normally cheeky Guglielmo pause and rethink. "It would be *nice* to have you there when I meet him. It would be *nice* to have you set the stage. But it is not necessary, Cecilia. If I were you, I would not forget that."

"Or what?" she demanded, wildly. "You'll just… steal him away to Rome?"

"Yes." His voice was a hard crack in the quiet room. "Without a second thought."

She stared back at him, stricken. And she was his ghost, once upon a time his angel. But he didn't let that soften him. If anything, that he had believed he cared for her all those years ago made the betrayal worse. He stared back at her, relentless.

"Mama?" The small voice came from one of the doors behind Pascal. "I heard voices."

Pascal tensed. He watched Cecilia's face closely. And he was sure he could see her fight back the urge to shoo the child away. To have him hide himself just a little longer, however futile the gesture.

He thought he saw something like despair in her otherworldly eyes, just a flash of it. Just enough to lodge itself inside Pascal like shame.

But then she smiled. Wide and bright as if there had never been anything in her eyes but sweetness and light.

"Come here, baby," she said, and held out her hand. "You have a very special visitor tonight."

Pascal held himself still enough to crack in half as he heard Dante's surprisingly heavy footsteps move across the floor. And then he watched as the small, sturdy boy with rosy cheeks and black hair standing on end came around the side of the couch. He walked toward the fire and took his mother's hand. Then he gazed at Pascal with sleepy eyes.

Sleepy eyes that were black like Pascal's, with a dark

rim around the irises that Pascal suspected, were he any closer, would be the precise violet shade of his mother's.

It was like a heart attack, but it didn't hurt. It simply…seized Pascal where he sat.

He knew this child. He could see the shape of his own face in the smaller face before him. He could see his own mother's nose. And he could see Cecilia, too. And it had never occurred to Pascal before that children were the real ghosts, patchworks of the past made new—yet unlike the haunts of fiction, wholly uninterested in what had gone before them.

Pascal felt struck down, though he knew he still sat in the same position. He felt everything he'd felt on that field and more, because this time, his son was right in front of him. *Looking* at him.

And Pascal had never understood his father or his choices. But here, now, in this huge moment that was happening so quietly and calmly despite the cacophony inside him, he understood the man even less.

Because he knew that he would fight, kill, or die for this little boy with his sleepy eyes and sulky mouth. He would not think twice.

That his father had walked away from *his* son made even less sense to Pascal now.

"Dante," Cecilia said, her voice soft but perfectly cheerful as if this had been her plan all along, and Pascal stopped thinking about that useless, spineless man who shared nothing with him but biology. "This is your father."

The little boy stared. He regarded Pascal solemnly. One beat, another.

"Okay," he said.

Then he yawned, wide enough to crack his jaw,

didn't spare his mother or brand-new father a second glance, and shuffled his way back to his bed.

They married the following week by special license.

Pascal stood at the very altar where he had first discovered the existence of the child who had changed everything. Dante—his *son*, he reminded himself with that same fierce pride that beat in him now like a new heartbeat—stood beside him, looking proud and overtly solemn in his best clothes.

Dante looked up at him, his little face grave. Pascal didn't think it through. He reached down and put his hand on his child's head, something sweet and unexpected blooming in him at the sensation. At the way the curve of his palm fit the crown of Dante's head.

As if they had been crafted to fit together like this, interlocking pieces. Father and son.

He told himself that was why he felt very nearly emotional when the nuns who filled the pews began to sing, a hauntingly lovely song that he realized belatedly was their version of a wedding march.

Then Cecilia appeared at the head of the small church's aisle, and Pascal…stared.

She was unhappy with him. She had made no secret of it in the days between that night when she had finally accepted reality, and now.

"What concerns me is how Dante will handle this," she had said that night, still stiff and unfriendly at the fireplace after the child had gone back to bed. "You've only just sprung the fact that you're his father on him. I'm not sure how a wedding between me and a stranger is going to strike him."

"Children are resilient," Pascal said with great unconcern.

"You know that, do you?" she blazed at him. "With all your experience handling children? Raising them?"

"If I lack experience raising children, Cecilia," he'd replied silken and dangerous, "whose fault is that?"

And she had paled, but she hadn't backed down. "He's more fragile than he looks."

"If children were not resilient, neither you nor I would be here today. And yet here we are."

She had let out a shaky sort of breath. "I don't know that I think we should base anything on your childhood or mine. In fact, I imagine that the wisest course of action is to think about our childhoods and do the precise opposite."

Cecilia had decided that they should tell Dante that they were marrying together. As the united front she insisted they would have to become if any of this was to work. Pascal did not remind her that she was no longer in control of the terms—or anything else. He assumed that must have been obvious to her already.

"And by work," she snapped at him when he arrived the following morning at the appointed time, "I do not mean to your satisfaction. I mean, we have to find a way to make sure this is about Dante. Because it can only be about Dante."

"Whatever else could it be about, Cecilia?" he had asked. Silkily enough that she'd flushed.

But when Dante was told of their plan, he'd grinned. "Do we get to be a family? Everyone else gets to be a family."

"Yes," Cecilia had said, her voice suspiciously rough and her eyes too bright. "We would get to be a family.

We would all live under one roof. But it wouldn't be here. We would have to move down to Rome, where your father lives."

The little boy had seemed far more concerned with the toy truck he was slamming repeatedly into the leg of the sofa then the conversation.

"Paolo's mother told me about Rome," he said matter-of-factly. "She's from there. You can get gelato anytime you want. Not only when the abbey cook makes it."

"And there you have it," Pascal murmured. "Easy."

The look Cecilia had given him then was murderous.

And he was twisted enough to enjoy that, too.

She hadn't objected when Pascal had spent the rest of the intervening days as much with Dante as possible. He walked the boy to his care. And didn't bother to discuss his feelings on the topic of the soon-to-be Signora Furlani spending her days cleaning, because she only had so many days left here. If she wanted to spend them on her hands and knees on unforgiving stone floors, it was nothing to him.

It was on one of those days that she found him in his little cell, tending to the work that was always piling up on his laptop. He heard a faint noise, looked up— and there she was, standing in his doorway with a mop clenched in one hand.

And for a moment it was as if they'd been tossed back in time. He had the oddest notion that if he looked down at himself, he would find all the bandages and wounds he'd had when he'd first come here. As if the accident had only just happened.

As if maybe they could do this over—though he shoved that thought away almost as soon as it formed.

And he knew she was thinking much the same thing

from that stricken, electric look in her beautiful violet eyes.

It was those eyes he'd seen first when he'd surfaced after the surgery that had saved his life. Those eyes that had insinuated themselves somehow into the confusion of his brain in those fuzzy days, and had tempted him to make his way back to the land of the living.

And it was those eyes that slammed into him again now, making a mockery of his assertion that he was only here—and only doing this—for the boy.

But he chose not to analyze that.

"Dante is putting on a good show," she told him after a moment, her hand tight around the mop handle. "But sooner or later this is all going to come crashing down on him. I hope you're prepared for it. He's a headstrong, often maddening, perfect little boy. I doubt very much that your life is set up to accommodate an active five-year-old."

"The beauty of my life, *cara*, is that it is set up to accommodate me. Therefore, whatever it is I wish it to be, it becomes."

"Spoken like a man who has no idea what I'm talking about," she retorted. "And yes," she continued before he could remind her yet again why it was he had no experience in this area, "I know. It's my fault. But you're the one issuing ultimatums, Pascal. Not me."

He knew what she meant was, he was the one who insisted on marrying her, and was holding her child over her head to make sure she did it. Something he supposed he ought to have felt some guilt about. Oddly enough, his conscience was clear.

"The other thing I have, in abundance, is money," Pascal said. And smiled faintly when she rolled her eyes. "I'm not bragging, Cecilia. Do you know what that money buys? Nannies. Tutors. An army of trained staff to make sure his is the best nursery in Italy. Anything and everything that can make this transition as painless as possible for Dante. And for me."

"But not me, of course." She eyed him as he lounged there on the narrow bed, his laptop open before him. Not in a particularly friendly manner. "Are you not concerned with my transition?"

"Not especially."

She ran her tongue over her teeth. "What is it you expect me to do?"

Pascal studied her a moment. "I suppose you could clean my floors if you desired, but my housekeeper would not be best pleased."

Her eyes flashed. "There's no shame in cleaning a floor."

"In general, no," he'd replied. "But we are talking about the wife of Pascal Furlani, not a nameless single mother in a remote mountain village."

And he didn't have the slightest intention of telling her that the way she glared at him made him want to poke at her more, not less.

"There will be certain expectations upon you," he said.

"You mean your expectations."

"Mine, yes, but sadly for you, not only mine." Or he would keep her naked and tied to his bed. He didn't know quite why he didn't say that out loud. But he had to shift to keep that image from making him reveal too much to her. "You have to be outfitted with an appropriate wardrobe, first and foremost. Then I will have to consider the best way to instruct you in how best to move in the society I keep. Appearances, you understand."

"You must be joking." When he only gazed back at her, she scoffed. "It's not as if you're royalty, is it? You're a businessman."

"There are many things I learned the hard way," Pascal said quietly. "If you do not wish to profit from my example, that is all the same to me. You can flail around, making a spectacle of yourself if that is what you wish. I will allow it."

Not that he could actually imagine this woman *flailing* in any capacity.

"Will it embarrass you?" she asked coolly. "Because if so, it holds a certain appeal."

"I can handle the embarrassment," Pascal replied easily. "But can Dante? Children can be so cruel."

And he had allowed himself a smile when she simply stalked off down the hallway, slamming her cleaning tools about with entirely too much force.

Their wedding day could not come soon enough to suit him.

"I thought you would lecture me," he had said to Mother Superior earlier today when he'd seen her after he'd dressed.

"Would that work, do you imagine?" the old woman asked him, that canny gaze of hers on him. "Would you listen?"

"I listened to you last time," he reminded her as they made their way to the church. "Why not again?"

"You listened to your fear, child," she said when they made it to the door. "I was nothing but a catalyst. And I'll thank you to remember, when fear starts whispering in your ear again, that all it made you was alone."

"And very rich," he'd said drily.

"The abbey looks forward to your significant donation," she'd replied tartly.

And Pascal didn't know why he was thinking about an old, interfering nun's pointed remarks at a time like this. When he was standing here in this church and Cecilia was floating toward him like one of those dreams that had chased him through all the years they'd been apart.

She wore a cream-colored gown and a demure veil, but he could still see her.

Once upon a time she had saved him. Then she had betrayed him. Now she would marry him, and he couldn't help thinking that he'd find the balance in it there. In their marriage.

And better still, in the marriage bed.

He had already kissed her far too thoroughly and long in this very same church, and lightning had failed to strike him down. Thoughts of marital congress were hardly likely to bring the walls down around them.

She arrived beside him and he took her hand, and then it was happening.

The priest was quick. The nuns made approving noises.

Pascal said, "I do" loud enough to be heard in that stark white clinic room he never planned to enter again.

Cecilia's vows were more measured, but she said them. She didn't stumble. She didn't pause for effect.

And then it was time for Pascal to lift her veil and smooth it back from her face.

He felt something like rage pound through him, thick and nearly mad, and it took him a moment to realize it wasn't rage at all. It was triumph.

As if this was about her, not the boy.

But he refused to let himself consider that.

He kissed her instead, with all the pent-up passion of the years she had kept his child from him and the days she'd forced him to sit in that clinic as penance. He kissed her deep, and thorough, and he didn't care if he made the watching nuns uncomfortable.

He kissed her until there was no doubt whatsoever that he was claiming what was his.

And when he lifted his head, she looked stunned. Thrown.

That, too, felt like a victory.

Dante ran before them down the aisle toward the door. Pascal took Cecilia's hand and led her after their son, something primitive working its way through him as they moved. His son. His woman.

His family, at last.

"I want you to be very clear about something," his brand-new wife said when they stepped outside into the December morning. It was clear, but very cold.

Cecilia didn't shiver. She kept her gaze on his while Dante ran in a big, looping circle around Pascal's waiting car.

"I am not certain things have ever been more clear, *cara*," he told her. Truthfully.

Her violet eyes met his, then held. She tipped up her chin.

"You forced me to do this," she said, "and I did it. For Dante. But you should know right now that it doesn't matter if you kiss me like that. This marriage will never, ever be consummated."

Pascal laughed.

Then he slid his hand along her pretty face and held

her cheek in the palm of his hand. He met that outraged violet glare and he smiled at her, because he knew this part. He knew how to get what he wanted, and he would. It was what he did.

"My darling wife," he said, enjoying the words as much as the way she trembled—in fury, he was sure, and he liked that, too. He couldn't wait to taste it. "You will beg me."

CHAPTER EIGHT

ROME WAS A SPARKLING, sprawling mess of a too-big city, Cecilia was a wife when she had never planned to marry—much less in such haste and upon command—and there wasn't a single part of this sudden new life she was going to have to find her way through, one way or another, that made any sense to her.

Pascal had driven them down from the mountains, stopping only for the odd meal or the chance to stretch his legs. Or better still, to let Dante wear himself out enough to resume the trip. For her part, Cecilia had changed into a traveling outfit after the ceremony, too aware that it was an outfit her brand-new husband—her *husband*—had picked out for her. She hadn't wanted to wear anything he'd given her, but she also didn't want any of the nuns to know how fraught and strained her brand-new marriage was. Already.

"I don't want you to dress me," she'd told him, scowling over the clothes he'd delivered to her the night before the ceremony. A wedding dress, traveling clothes and a sharp order to leave all her packing to the staff he planned to unleash on the cottage after they left. His staff would take all the personal items and leave behind the furniture. Maybe she'd been mad about that, too. Maybe she was mad about everything. "Like some horrid little doll."

"Thus far I have only provided you with the wardrobe I would prefer you to wear," he'd replied in that dark, stirring way of his. His black-gold eyes had glittered. "Would you like me to dress you, as well? Because that is a different proposition altogether."

She didn't want to think about that.

Or to be more precise, it was all she thought about the last long night she was still herself. She'd tossed and turned and scowled at her ceiling, and none of it had changed a thing. She'd woken up, put on the wedding dress he'd chosen for her and walked down the aisle as ordered.

And now she was Pascal's wife.

The truth was, she didn't want to think too hard or too closely about any part of it. Not the wedding ceremony. Not the fact that she'd left behind the only home she had ever known for a future she could only describe as unknown. And unsettled.

And she certainly did not want to think about that taunt of his *after* the ceremony.

She would not beg him. For anything. Ever.

But even as she thought such things, and meant them, a quick glance toward her new husband—and the way he navigated the roads with confidence and ease—made something deep inside her…quiver.

She busied herself with Dante, who was overexcited and could hardly contain himself over the course of the long drive. There were tears. Tantrums. Too much sugar, not enough videos, and by the time they finally made it all the way into Rome, Pascal was tightlipped and Cecilia was thoroughly frazzled.

But not too frazzled to be a little smug about it.

"Just remember," she told Pascal as they finally got out of the car, there in a garage that was itself almost too fancy for her to take in, "you asked for this."

Pascal only gave her a dark look. Then he picked Dante up—because the boy had finally gone to sleep—and led the way inside. Up a stair and into three full floors of what Pascal called *home*.

Cecilia's first impression had been…overwhelming.

She'd chalked it up to fatigue. All that glittering, all those views, the soaring entry hall that went all the way up to a chandelier the size of her cottage, and all that *stuff* that shrieked its dizzying cost at decibels she didn't think she could truly understand.

The next morning it was even worse.

Because it had been one thing to see magazine spreads of a powerful man in a rich person's clothes. The magazines were filled with such men after all. It was something else again to be steeped in all that power rather than simply reading about it at a remove. To have it wrapped around her, choking her and making her think that she had been very foolish indeed to come here.

All Cecilia had been thinking about when she'd agreed to this was staying close to her child. And that was all that mattered, she told herself sternly that morning as she crept around the huge, hushed apartment that was the largest single residence she'd ever been in. But she should probably also have spared a thought or two for the fact she was a simple woman.

Cecilia's version of a complicated life had included the boundaries of the same small village that was the only home she'd ever known, and the good or bad opinions of the people who lived there with her. And whether she'd lived inside the abbey walls or in a cottage outside the grounds, the abbey that had always been the center of that village had also been her whole world.

You didn't have a choice, she reminded herself tartly. *You had to come here.*

But that didn't make things any better.

She was…dizzy. Whatever the opposite of altitude sickness was. And that feeling didn't go away as the days passed, the darkness of the waning year enlivened only by the signs of Christmas everywhere she looked in her adopted new city.

Pascal had been good to his word. As far as Cecilia could tell, he had employed a literal army of staff to care for Dante's every possible need. Each and every one of whom Dante found fascinating, so as much as Cecilia might have wanted to reclaim her only child's attention, he didn't want to go with her when she sought him out and found him playing, or doing crafts, or practicing scales on the piano that had its own room. He wanted to continue doing what he was doing, in the company of all the new people who he, of course, found far more entertaining and fascinating than his own mother.

"I don't know what you expect me to do with myself now that you've forced me to come here," she had seethed at Pascal one morning several days after they'd arrived, feeling brittle enough that she might break in two. "I am not used to all this idleness."

Pascal had been in the office he used when he was home, starting his day with a stack of financial papers from around the world and a cup of the strong espresso he preferred.

The look he'd given her had seared through her.

"You are in Rome," he'd said, sounding faintly astonished that such a thing needed to be said. Or perhaps that was his innate arrogance. "If you cannot entertain yourself here, Cecilia, you cannot be entertained."

There was no response she could give to that he wouldn't have seen as a challenge she had no intention of meeting, so she'd swallowed it all down. She'd accepted that for the first time in as long as she could remember, she was well and truly left to her own devices.

She'd gone out and lost herself in the ancient streets of the eternal city.

And it was out in the chaotic splendor of three thousand years of human habitation, losing herself on one street only to find her way back on another, that she realized she'd completely forgotten that Christmas was coming.

When normally this was her favorite time of year. The pressing dark, and the bright lights making joy against the night.

She found herself in a café in a bustling *piazza* one late afternoon, with a latte steaming gently at her elbow. It had been a wet day, cloudy and moody, and much too cold. She had left Dante in the capable hands of his caregivers. Who, if she was honest, she quite liked herself. And how could she argue with Pascal's desire that he receive that kind of attentive care when she herself had left him with the neighbor while she worked?

She couldn't. Or she would have, to be more precise, but she didn't quite dare.

There was something about Pascal here, prowling around his natural element, that made Cecilia feel as if she'd lost the ability to keep her feet on the ground.

And not because it was cracking or rolling beneath her the way it felt sometimes, but because he'd taken it.

She blew out a breath as she looked at the bustling *piazza*, and all the Christmas lights and decorations that made it gleam no matter how dark or thick the incoming night. She could see the gleaming trees, done up proud and bright. She could hear the *zampognari* playing the mournful bagpipes, just as the Sicilian family had always claimed was tradition down south.

For a moment she felt very nearly at peace.

The abbey had always felt magical to her this time of year. The sisters had sung carols every morning, and the village itself had done itself up with trees draped in lights, wreaths on the doors and candles flickering in every window.

And suddenly, the fact she wasn't there to see it this year took her breath away.

Cecilia hadn't expected to miss home this much. It felt like a physical pain, wrenching and terrible, that she couldn't simply go outside, walk for five minutes no matter the weather and find herself in the cool, serene embrace of the abbey. That Mother Superior was not on hand for a dry comment, a bit of wisdom, or both.

She was well and truly on her own for the first time in her life, and Cecilia couldn't say she liked it.

Later, when she'd drained her coffee and left the café, she found her way home again through the tangle of streets, packed full of eras and people and cars that roared this way and that and parked in all directions. She only got lost twice, which she thought showed improvement, and found her way into Pascal's rambling three-story showcase of a home, resplendent in its usual state of modern, moneyed serenity. She was informed that her child was currently being fed and would soon after be bathed, before settling down into his evening routine.

They no longer pretended to ask her what she thought about this routine; they simply performed it.

Cecilia felt a surge of temper—or maybe it was fear—wash over her then. This was all part of Pascal's plan; she knew that. He was going out of his way to show her how easily he could keep her son from her, in retaliation. And she was letting it happen. Just standing here, letting him do his worst. She should storm into the middle of Dante's dinnertime, kick out all the staff members and reclaim her own son—

But even though she started across the polished marble of the foyer toward Dante's set of rooms, she stopped.

Because like it or not, Dante was having the time of his life. What right did she have to take something away from him because her feelings were hurt? Or because she felt lonely? Whether she liked it or not, he was the only son and heir of a very, very wealthy man. If this was how wealthy children were raised—and she certainly wouldn't know—who was she to deny him that?

She turned away from the hall that led to her son and headed for the nearest sitting room instead, so she could stare out the window at all the light and madness and *people* that made up the city she still couldn't believe she lived in now. The glass of the window was cold beneath her fingers, but she didn't lift her hand.

It wasn't as if she didn't see her own child. Dante always knew where she was and any of his new aides knew how to contact her if he needed her. She should congratulate herself on having raised such a confident child that he was happy to race around, immersing himself in his new life without giving her a second thought.

She would get there, she told herself. Maybe a little grimly. Somehow, she would find a way to be happy about all of this. For him.

"You look so glum, *cara*," came Pascal's low, insinuating voice from behind her.

As if the prospect amused him.

Cecilia took her time turning. It was early for him to be home, and she hated that she knew anything about his schedule. His routines. Because the real tragedy was that she'd started to anticipate his return every night. She could tell herself that it was because she grew ever more wary of him, and needed to buttress herself against him however possible...

But that wasn't quite true.

She faced him, entirely too aware that she didn't feel any one thing when she looked at him. It was all mixed up together. Guilt and temper, her long-held anger, and beneath it all, that heat he could generate without even seeming to try.

She could still feel that kiss he'd given her on their wedding day. The way he'd claimed her mouth with his and taught her things she didn't want to know about herself, right there in front of the entirety of the church.

"I'm not glum at all," she told him now. "I was merely contemplating, as ever, the fact that you insisted on this marriage. And yet apparently have nothing for me to do here but wander the streets of Rome like a permanent tourist."

He stood in the doorway, still dressed in the sort of exquisitely cut suit he wore to work. And she really would have preferred the remove of a tabloid magazine, because the pages could only show him in two digestible dimensions. There was no way to sense the brooding power he wore. Or how impossible it was to look away from him. Or how she could *feel* him, like a switch flipped deep inside her.

Magazines made it clear he was beautiful. But the truth was, he was dangerous.

Because somehow it had been easier to hate him in the mountains. Here, where she was the one out of place, she found it a far more difficult prospect.

"You are my wife," he told her with that arrogance of his that should have repelled her. That it didn't was her secret shame. "That is your role. And do not kid yourself, it is a job. Do you think you can handle it?"

"Is this where you lecture me on what to wear and which fork to use?" she asked him, her voice like acid to her own ears. "You understand, it's not the comportment classes I object to. It's the teacher."

She didn't know who she had become here, over the course of these strange, confusing days in a city so large she couldn't make sense of it. And she was so completely within the power of this man, she couldn't make sense of herself.

Yet, she had the distinct impression *he* understood her all too well.

A small curve disturbed the stark line of his proud mouth. "I spent a significant amount of my time looking for the perfect wife. My requirements were simple. Poise, grace and aspirational elegance."

Cecilia hated the fact that sounded like a list of her failings.

"I'm a foundling who wanted to become a nun," she told him, the cold glass at her back. And far too much defensiveness in her voice. "A fallen woman who cleaned floors to care for her illegitimate child. There's no poise in that. And very little grace. And if you wanted elegance—well. You were the one who demanded this marriage."

"And here we are," Pascal murmured, moving farther into the room. "Just as I demanded."

The sitting room was one of several such pointless areas in this jaw-droppingly immense place. As far as Cecilia could tell, the point of *so many rooms* in a home like this was to stock them all full of unnecessary things—antiques, art, that piano and whatever else shouted its status simply by existing. Because otherwise, what would be the point of having them? When she started thinking of this apartment like a museum, it made more sense.

But did that make her one more piece in his collection?

"We're well and truly married, Cecilia, in the eyes of God and man," he told her now. "There's no pretending otherwise."

"I wasn't pretending."

"Are you ready to take on your duties in that regard?" He was still smiling. She knew it was a warning. "I warn you, it may require that you spend less time idle and more time welded to my side, more or less."

"That is not appealing," she said crisply.

Pascal's smile widened. "You like it well enough in bed."

And really, she should have seen that coming.

But Cecilia had been going out of her way not to think about the nights here.

Pascal had insisted that she share his bed.

That first night she'd put Dante to bed, claiming he didn't like to sleep in new places. Only to curl up next to him because actually, she was the one who didn't want to sleep in this new place. She'd woken up to find herself being carried through this too-large place in her brand-new husband's arms, and had panicked.

"Calm yourself," he had told her briskly. "I am only carrying you to the marital bed, *cara*. I am not requiring you perform in it."

"I'm perfectly calm," she'd thrown at him, perhaps desperately. And when they'd reached the palatial suite of rooms that Pascal had said were his, it did not exactly relax her to discover that they were now hers, as well. "Put me down."

And she almost said *please*, but that would be begging.

Pascal had laughed, but he'd done what she asked. And she had been bleary-eyed and panicky, and still dressed in the clothes he'd set out for her to wear to travel that day. Clothes she had wanted to hate on principle, but couldn't. Because she had never in her life worn a sweater so soft, so warm. Or trousers that were not only comfortable to sit in for hours on end, but also seemed supernaturally incapable of wrinkling, even all these hours later. Even the shoes he'd provided had somehow managed to be both fashionable *and* comfortable.

Cecilia had looked at herself in too many mirrors today, whether in rest stops or in all the gleaming rooms of Pascal's absurd home, and she hadn't recognized herself at all. She didn't look like a simple woman who wanted to become a nun any longer. And she certainly didn't look like a country woman who cleaned to make her rent.

And the fact that all it took was a change of clothes to make her look like the sort of woman who really might belong in a place like this made her…uneasy.

"I have no intention of begging," she threw at him, because she couldn't say she liked the intent look in his eyes just then.

While she'd been curled around her son as if the child was her security blanket—instead of the other way around—Pascal had clearly showered, if his damp hair was anything to go by. And worse, was standing there before her wearing absolutely nothing but a pair of low-slung trousers.

Absolutely nothing.

"Did I ask you to beg?" he asked mildly. "Tonight?"

And Cecilia felt as if he'd lit her on fire. He was a perfectly formed, mouthwatering specimen of a man. She had thought so years ago—but it was even worse now. His scars tracked down his left side, where he'd sustained the most damage. But now they seemed like so much decoration. Not angry and livid, but simply scars. Markers on the map of his male beauty.

And the truth was, Cecilia wasn't sure she was equipped to handle this.

"Then why did you bring me in here?" she demanded.

"You will sleep in my bed," he told her as pitiless as ever, his black gaze unreadable. "And no, you will not come to my bed fully dressed. I will consider it an insult."

"But Dante—"

"The child will be monitored, naturally. By staff

members paid for the purpose. Should he need you, they will rouse us both at once."

"But—"

"Cecilia." And she truly hated that soft tone of his, because it was Pascal at his most dangerous. And his most implacable. "I did not marry so that I could live apart from my wife."

"You married as a form of blackmail."

"I did not marry you to blackmail you." And she almost believed he meant that, until he shrugged. And that muscled wonder of his chest moved, making her mouth go dry. "But you would do well to remember that this marriage is for my convenience, not yours."

Cecilia was entirely too aware of that. "I have already given you far too much for one lifetime. I'm not giving you anything else."

And he had stood there, that faint smile on his sensual mouth, and something far too knowing in his dark gaze.

"I have already told you what will happen, but let me elaborate."

"Not on my account," she said, but he ignored her.

"You will beg me for my touch, and you will do so sooner rather than later. Believe this, if nothing else."

Then, just when she thought he would put his hands on her and carry her off against her will... Pascal did the exact opposite. He headed away from her instead, toward the vast platform bed that dominated the room they stood in, which she had been doing her level best not to look at.

Cecilia watched, surprised and a little bit put out, as he climbed into the bed and sprawled there, like Roman emperors of old.

"Do you need a nap before you finish threatening me?" she asked. With perhaps a bit too much emotion in her voice.

"I want you in this bed," Pascal told her in a dark tone that made her melt, then burn. "But I'm not going to wrestle you into it. If you go and sleep somewhere else, I will simply come find you, bring you back and set you on your own two feet. Right there. Until you come to your senses and get into bed beside me. The question you should ask yourself, Cecilia, is how tired are you tonight? How many times do you wish to do this?"

"I'm exhausted," she had managed to say. "I don't want to do this at all."

"Then if I were you, I would come to bed. Now. Instead of performing a grand charade that will end the same way no matter what you do."

And Cecilia had believed him. She had walked stiffly from the room, but not to escape him. Only to tend to herself after such a long trip—and the far longer walk down that aisle that she still couldn't believe had happened. She'd washed her face, then changed into the only thing she'd brought with her that bore any resemblance to appropriate sleepwear. It was the slip she'd worn beneath her dress, and it seemed silly to put it on to sleep in.

But the alternative to that was to crawl into Pascal's bed naked.

And that was clearly impossible.

She stalked back out into the bedroom to find Pascal typing something into his phone, looking wholly at ease. She glared at him, but he didn't look up. Still, she was sure she could feel his eyes on her as she skirted the foot of the bed, then stood there for a moment on the opposite side.

Cecilia understood what he was playing at, suddenly. This was the first surrender. He could easily have picked her up and tossed her on the bed. He could have kissed her and made her forget her own name.

But he was making her do this. He was making her do this *to herself.*

She should have turned and run into one of the many other rooms. One of them was bound to have a lock—

But she didn't. She climbed into bed and lay as close to the edge as she could get without toppling off. Rigid and resentful, like a martyr at the pyre.

He turned off the lights not long after, and settled in. Cecilia waited. Every muscle inside her body was tense, prepared for him to reach over, take liberties, go back on his word…

But instead, and in an indecently short span of time that suggested his mind was not similarly preoccupied, she heard his breath go even.

He had fallen asleep.

Leaving her there with her fingers gripping the edge of the bed as if she'd expected to be dragged off somewhere at any moment. Long into the night.

The next morning she'd woken up because she was so deliciously warm she'd thought she might find herself curled up on the surface of the sun.

But it was much worse than that.

She was sprawled out all over Pascal, her legs tangled with his. Her hair all over his chest. Her mouth there against his hard muscles.

Cecilia had sucked in a breath of pure horror, then

threw herself to the side, hoping against hope that he was still—

"You still feel like silk and longing," he told her, his voice rich with sleep, amusement and something far darker that pulsed inside her. "When you beg me, *cara*, I will make you sob. Over and over and over again."

"In your dreams," she'd hissed at him, already scrambling out of the bed and heading for the bathroom suite.

"Please, *cara*." And his gaze was so hungry she nearly tripped. It made her heart pound even as she felt herself melt, then ache low in her belly and between her legs. "My dreams are far more demanding."

Every night since had been the same thing.

If Pascal was home when Cecilia went to bed, he stayed far off on his side. He made no move toward her. And they still ended up in that breathless tangle each morning. If he was out when she went to bed, she would always wake up with a start when he climbed in, sure that *this time* he would trespass over that invisible line that ran down the center of the bed…but he never did.

And it made no difference. They still woke up in a knot.

Cecilia was beginning to understand that her body simply wanted him. And didn't much care how she got him.

Standing there in one of his many salons tricked out in priceless objects, nothing but glass at her back and her uncertain future before her, the last thing Cecilia wanted to feel was breathless. She glared at him.

"No clever response to that?" Pascal asked almost idly. "I'm disappointed."

"Is that part of my punishment? It's not enough that

you force me to sleep in the same bed with you, you must also taunt me about it?"

"I'm not punishing you, *cara*. You would know."

"I can't imagine how an actual punishment would differ from this," she threw back at him.

"For one thing," he replied, too easily, "it will be public as well as private."

But she had been a nun who turned up pregnant. What could he possibly do to her that she hadn't already lived through, more or less happily?

"Public humiliation is hardly good for Dante. Who is supposed to be the point of all this, isn't he? How quickly you forget."

"I forget nothing," he said, and there was a note in his voice that made her neck prickle in warning.

She didn't pretend to understand this man she'd married. There was something about the way he watched her, hungry and angry at once, that unsettled her too deeply. She hurried from the room, determined to reclaim at least some part of Dante's evening routine after all.

Because she needed a touchstone. She needed *something*.

She dismissed his staff, then read him a story, and kissed him as he drifted off to sleep. As if nothing had changed but the size of his bedroom.

And it was then, in the darkness while her little boy dreamed, that she had to accept the truth she'd been wrestling with. Her heart was not the least bit worried about Dante. Not only would he thrive here, and was— there was no doubt in her mind that Pascal loved him.

With the same reckless, heedless and instantaneous devotion that she herself had felt when he'd been tucked there inside her.

Seeing them together…did things to her. Watching the man who so overwhelmed her squat down to talk seriously, yet kindly, with her child—with *their* child—made her feel something like giddy.

And she might have told herself that she had come to Rome to save Dante from him, but she knew tonight that wasn't true. She wasn't afraid, on any level, that Pascal would harm her son.

She was far more concerned that Pascal would harm her instead.

And the following morning she woke up to find him gone. It felt like a premonition come true—a notion she tried to shake off.

"I'm afraid you cannot go out today," the housekeeper told her sorrowfully when she made to leave after her breakfast. "There are paparazzi camped out around the building, and Signor Furlani would prefer you not give them any more ammunition."

"Ammunition?" she queried. Then blinked. "Paparazzi?"

The housekeeper delivered her the stack of morning papers. And there it was. A picture of the two of them together. Their wedding. Pascal leaning into her, his mouth hovering above hers.

And Cecilia hardly recognized herself. She looked… flushed and starry-eyed. Like the silly girl she'd been when she'd first met him.

She hated that the picture existed. Much less that it was now…out there, for the entire world to dissect. It felt like a kind of death. Something far worse than a shaming.

But far worse than being exposed like that herself was the fact that Dante was splashed across all those papers, too.

His sweet face was there in bright color.

Furlani claims his son! one headline screamed.

And then, just beneath it, *thumbs his nose at father once again.*

Just like that, it all became clear.

Cecilia felt as if a truck hit her. She sat in the breakfast room, her ears ringing, feeling sick to her stomach. She read every single article she could find, then pulled out her mobile to look for even more.

And every word she read was like a nail into her heart.

"How did Signor Furlani leave the building this morning?" she asked the housekeeper when she could speak. When the betrayal was an agony inside her instead of wholly incapacitating her.

"Well, *signora*, he took a car. But—"

"Then get me a car," Cecilia demanded.

And that was how she found herself sitting in the backseat of a luxury vehicle she couldn't have named if her life depended on it, hiding behind tinted windows while men with twisted faces pounded their fists and open palms against the sides. This was the pit her husband had thrown their son into. All to score points with his own father.

None of this had been about Dante.

Or about you.

Pascal's offices were done up in low-slung furniture and steel accents. It made her think of the man she'd married. So beautiful and austere on the outside, and nothing but steel and lies within. There was no comfort to be found here. Or in him.

His secretary met her after a short, undignified squabble with his front desk, and led her back through the gleaming maze of offices separated by nothing but panes of glass. He took her directly to the center, where a group of men stood around a long table in yet another glass enclosure.

Cecilia was starting to rethink her urge to come here and tell her husband exactly what she thought of his little games, but it was too late. Because Pascal's secretary knocked twice on the great glass door, then swept it open. And every stuffy, officious man in that room turned to stare at her.

But it was only Pascal's gaze that she felt.

And her husband did not leap from the leather chair where he lounged as if he was at a café, whiling away the day. He did not look the least bit surprised to see her, and in fact, when his gaze met hers and held he looked even more lazy than he had a moment before.

She had the strangest notion that he was the one who felt out of place, always. Even here.

"May I present the woman in question, gentlemen," he drawled as if he'd invited her here. "Cecilia Furlani, in the flesh. Not a publicity stunt as you have accused me. But my wife."

CHAPTER NINE

PASCAL KNEW THAT Cecilia could ruin him, here and now.

All she would have to do was contradict him and the gauzy, romantic story he'd delivered to the papers, filled with smoke and mirrors about the two of them and their son. She could simply open up her mouth and tell the assembled men any story she liked about their marriage—and the real timeline of events. She could tell them who he had been six years ago and how he had left her to have and raise his child on her own. That truth would do the trick with this particular group of hypocrites quite nicely. It would give them all the ammunition they needed to start making noises about *moral questions*.

Even if she didn't wish to tell the truth—even if she decided to editorialize at will—it didn't matter. It would do the same damage. Worse, in this room with too many eyes on them, he couldn't stop her.

They wanted a reason to call him unfit. All she had to do was give them one.

And Pascal couldn't think of any particular reason why she wouldn't go ahead and do just that.

He stared at the face of the woman who had haunted him when she was not in his life, and was something far worse than a ghost now that she was. Ghosts only came out at night. But Cecilia haunted him always. Bright light of day through winter dark, then back again.

How had he imagined it would be different once he'd put his ring on her finger?

He knew why she was here, barging into his office with that furious look on her face. Oh, yes, he knew. He had told her she would beg, and he'd been arrogantly certain that all it would take was one night in his bed. Maybe two.

But he should have known better. He should have understood who Cecilia was. Not the soft, fragile girl he'd met all those years ago and had made into a monument of sweet innocence in his head, but the far tougher and more self-possessed woman who'd stared him down in a church and thrown his fatherhood in his face.

Perhaps the truth was she was both. But either way, Cecilia did not bend.

Meanwhile, Pascal felt as if he might break.

He had told himself it was time to make announcements about his marriage because it was high time he take charge of his unruly board and cut off their favorite line of dissent. It made business sense, he'd assured himself. And it was only a few days to Christmas, which meant the interest in the story would dissipate quickly as everyone turned their attention to their holidays. He'd had the distinct sensation that planting those newspaper stories had been an act of reclaiming himself somehow. Returning to form.

Or maybe, something sly suggested inside him, *you knew exactly what reaction she would have.*

Because despite his best efforts, Pascal was the one who was falling apart, little as he wished to admit that.

He was the one who woke again and again in the night, every time she shifted to get closer to him. She did it in her sleep. He was the one who held her, staring into the dark and wondering what the hell had happened to him. Where was the man who had built his entire life as a shrine to revenge? Where was the Pascal Furlani who would do anything at all—and had, happily—to live his life *at* the father who had always ignored him and pretended he didn't exist?

Most of Pascal's adult life had been an exercise in proving that he did, in fact, exist.

In his father's face, one way or another, in a way that could not be ignored.

And he didn't know how to reconcile that part of him with a man who wanted nothing more than the woman who only suffered his touch while she was asleep to want him while she was awake.

As desperately as he wanted her.

"Your new husband has been telling us romantic stories about the two of you, *signora*," said Pascal's least favorite board member, Carlo Buccio, with his silver hair, fussy beard and the cane he used as a prop. Carlo was forever looking for ways to take more away from Pascal. To render him little more than a figurehead, because that was the thing about power. People always wanted more of it. And better still, they wanted others around them to have less. He and his mustachioed sidekick, Massimo Pugliese, prided themselves on being thorns in Pascal's side.

He recalled, then, that they had also taken a field trip to the mountains. No doubt they were annoyed that their version of Pascal's life hadn't been splashed all over the tabloids first.

"Surely it cannot all have been fairy tales," Massimo chimed in, right on cue.

Pascal could do nothing but watch a series of complicated emotions chase themselves across Cecilia's face. He gritted his teeth as she shifted her condemning glare from him and looked at the rest of the assembled men.

But to his surprise, she laughed.

"Romance and fairy tales in a corporate boardroom?" Cecilia asked lightly. "How inappropriate. Why on earth would such a private matter be discussed at all?"

And something in Pascal hummed a bit at that, amusement and admiration at once, though it hardly wiped away the tension that gripped him.

Because this was no trophy wife, clearly. This was no airheaded little bimbo, whose worth was in the picture she made while hanging on a rich man's arm. Not that Cecilia didn't make a pretty picture, but the glory of his wife, Pascal understood then as he never had before, was that she exuded that same matter-of-fact grace that her Mother Superior did. It wasn't holier than thou. It was the way she held herself and the frankness of her violet gaze. She didn't simper. She didn't avert her eyes. She didn't shrink down with so many male gazes trained upon her.

She stood there in his glass and stone meeting room as a kind of beacon. Of what was right, no matter what.

It was subtle, but effective. There was a mass clearing of throats and shuffling feet, as a room full of powerful men readjusted themselves to what Pascal could only consider the enduring power of the nunnery.

Cecilia might not be a nun. She might not have made it through her novitiate period, thanks to him. But that didn't mean she hadn't been convent-bred—or that she couldn't wield it like a weapon when she chose.

He had been so focused on claiming her that he hadn't stopped to fully appreciate what she brought to the table.

"I was under the seemingly quaint impression that one's private life was just that." And Cecilia might have been standing there as if she was addressing the room, but Pascal had no illusions. He knew that she was speaking directly to him when she said that. She even turned that gaze of hers on him again. *"Private."*

"Privacy is for far less powerful people, *signora*," Massimo said with his patented obsequiousness.

Cecilia merely turned a bland gaze his way. "How powerful is my five-year-old son?"

"Pascal has been filling us in on this…secret relationship of yours," Carlo said, his voice ripe with insinuation.

Pascal tensed even further in his chair at the head of the long table. Because she was clearly not happy with him, and here was her chance to vent her spleen. Here was her chance to get back everything she imagined had been taken from her. All she had to do was tell the story of what had actually happened, with all the bitterness and hurt she'd shown when she'd told the same story to him. These men would twist to suit themselves—and what they wanted to believe, so long as it advanced their position at his expense—and Pascal would have no choice but to go to war. Again.

And he saw the exact moment Cecilia understood that.

She blinked, and he could see her violet gaze turn canny. Considering. She turned it on him, and not for the first time, he wondered what she saw. If he had ever haunted her the way she did him.

He couldn't bear the tension and so he stood to break it, smoothing his hand down the front of his suit. He kept his gaze intent on Cecilia.

And then he waited for her to betray him, the way everyone who had ever vowed to love him had, sooner or later. His mother. His father. Now his wife, who had stood in a church and made her vows, though he'd told himself then that he hadn't believed them.

Because, of course, he'd forced her to that altar. He'd made her take those vows.

But in the dark of night, with her hair a fragrant cloud across his chest and her soft curves pressed into his side, he'd wanted to believe that every word she'd uttered before the priest had been true.

He'd wanted it more than could possibly be wise. Or healthy.

And all of that led here. Where he, a man who had callously betrayed anyone who ventured close to him in turn, waited in a moment that stretched on and on into eternity, for his just deserts.

Lord knew Pascal was full up on just deserts. He'd been choking them down his whole life.

Cecilia's lovely mouth curved, slightly. Her eyes flashed.

And Pascal was already calculating his response. Damage control. Counterattacks. The best way to undercut whatever she was about to say—

"I beg your pardon," Cecilia said, and again her voice was mild in the same way Mother Superior's always was. Kind, almost. And underneath it, absolute steel. It took Pascal a moment to notice she was not looking at him—she was looking at Carlo. "Something that is a secret to you, *signor*, is not necessarily a secret to the people involved. What a strange question. Would you like to share with the room every detail of your private relationships?"

For a moment Pascal couldn't process that.

It wasn't only that she'd taken aim at one of the most notorious philanderers in Rome, whose complicated series of mistresses left him eternally open to tabloid speculation. As did his wife's equally comprehensive selection of lovers, many of whom she paraded beneath Carlo's nose.

He supposed that it wouldn't have mattered whom she'd asked that question. There wasn't a man in this room whose private life could bear the scrutiny. It was only Pascal, who had lacked a wife and had insisted upon a social life over the past few years, who was subject to these patronizing reviews of his intimate relations.

It took a long moment for her question to penetrate, and for him to admire the way Cecilia had done it—so beautifully shifting the conversation away from Pascal.

It took another kick of his heart for him to understand the far more salient point.

She had not betrayed him when she'd had the chance.

She had not betrayed him.

And it was as if the floor dropped away from beneath his feet. As if the world shuddered to a halt and then stood still for a moment. Still and impossibly, confoundingly airless.

He felt tight, everywhere. As if he had exploded, and then had contained each and every shard, binding all the jagged edges inside himself.

He couldn't breathe. He couldn't *think*.

She had not *betrayed him*.

Cecilia turned her gaze back to his, then, and everything else fell away.

There was only this. Those violet eyes filled with temper, sadness, sheer fury and something else he couldn't name.

There was only her, standing there in the clothes he'd bought for her, looking like every dream he'd ever had of the perfect wife.

Because the only dream he'd ever had, in all these years, had been her.

Her. Cecilia.

The only person alive who had not betrayed him at the first opportunity.

The fact that they were still standing here in full view of his entire shark tank full of grasping directors impressed itself upon him, then, as if from a great distance. Pascal moved from the table, distantly amazed that his body still worked. That the explosion that was still rolling through him in the form of aftershocks had not, in fact, taken him out at the knees. That while he might feel every one of those jagged edges, they were not necessarily visible.

His head was spinning. He could feel the thump of his heart, and the tightness in his gut. He expected his hands to be shaking when he reached out to usher Cecilia back through the door, but they weren't.

Somehow they weren't.

He excused himself, and her, or maybe he sang a happy song—he would never know. It was all noise and wonder and *her* inside him.

More than that, he didn't care what any of his board members thought. Not any longer.

He led Cecilia out of the meeting room. And for the first time since he'd built it, Pascal cursed the bright, open office he'd been so proud of before. He led her through a maze of glass and too many eyes, winding his way back to his own office, when all he wanted was privacy. A closed door. A place to hide and figure out what the hell had just happened.

When they reached his office at last, he ignored Guglielmo and motioned for Cecilia to precede him inside. She did, her back in a beautiful straight line as she moved ahead of him, then kept walking across the floor toward the bank of windows.

For a moment he could only stare. Ancient, beautiful Rome outside the glass and his Cecilia within. It made his chest hurt.

"Why did you do that?"

He threw the question at her, his voice a rough, low sort of growl as he closed the door behind him. Then locked it, for safe measure. And he hit the button that darkened the glass all around them, making his walls distinctly opaque and private at last.

But he didn't move from the door.

"A better question is why you did it," she replied, keeping her back to him. "Why would you share pictures of our wedding with the world? Why would you tell them lies about us? And why—" And that was when she turned, her violet eyes dark with that fury again. "Why on earth would you give them pictures of Dante, Pascal?"

And for a blistering moment it was as if he couldn't remember why he'd made the very distinct choices he had. As if all she needed to do was look at him with her otherworldly eyes, and he was lost.

But he refused to accept that. *He refused.*

He opened his mouth to give her his reasons. It wasn't as if he didn't have them, or hadn't suspected he might be called upon to do just that. After all, he had long since made an art out of acting the bastard he knew he was. Biologically and otherwise.

Yet somehow, beneath that steady violet gaze, he found he couldn't do it.

Cecilia had not betrayed him, but he couldn't say the same.

He remembered his own mother then. Wailing on the floor after another rejection from his father.

We are the dirt beneath his feet, Marissa would cry.

Pascal had spent so long exulting in that status, turning it around and making it a virtue, that he'd forgotten the truth of it. He could call it whatever he liked. He could dress it up and use it to his advantage, and he had.

But dirt was still dirt.

He looked at Cecilia, his beautiful wife who had been wholly innocent until she'd met him. And he knew that sooner or later, the longer he kept her with him, all he would do was tarnish her, too.

He would cover her in dirt. Hadn't he already done so?

She had been pure, and he had corrupted her. She had built herself a life after he'd left, putting together the pieces of a fall from grace right there in the abbey where she'd been raised, and making it something beautiful. And he had ruined that, too.

He had forced her into coming with him. Threatened her with the loss of her child.

That was who he was. A man who had never known one of his parents and had suffered for it, and yet had thrown himself wholeheartedly into pressuring the only parent his own son had ever known into doing as he wished. And more, making her believe that he would take the child away from her.

Dirt into dirt. Dirt forever, staining him no matter how exquisitely he dressed these days. Dirt was who he was.

The distance between them seemed far more vast and unconquerable than simply the span of his office floor.

He wished that he'd done something on one of those torturous nights when he'd lain awake, holding her in his arms and wondering how he would keep from breaking. He wished he'd simply turned, set his mouth against her skin, and let it happen.

Where would they be now?

But of course he hadn't done it. Pascal preferred to armor everything, especially if it would have been better to cherish it. If there was a gift that could be given, he could be counted upon to break it first. To make it into a challenge instead.

Because going to one war or another was all he knew how to do.

That and cover any good thing he found in his own brand of dirt and kick it around a few times, just for good measure.

If he was any kind of man at all, he would fall to his knees here and now, and beg her the way he'd told her she would beg him.

If he was something more than a grim monument to a whole life spent avenging himself on a man who stoutly refused to care one way or the other, he would have thanked her.

Loved her. Cherished her.

Just like the vows he'd made himself, there in the only place on this planet where he'd ever briefly toyed with the idea that he could be more than just an angry man. A good one, say. Or simply…whole.

But he couldn't do it.

He couldn't make himself do it.

"I did it because that is who I am," he told her, and his voice sounded like the old man he would become. Bitter. Old. Calcified by his own grim march toward the darkness. "I seek my own ends, Cecilia. Always. I know no other way."

She sucked in a shocked sort of breath as if he'd punched her, so he kept going.

"Nothing and no one is safe," he growled. "I will use you. I will use our child. I will use anything and everything if it serves my purpose. Did you expect something else of a man who threatened you as I have?"

And he braced himself for tears. Temper. It was one thing to stand and deliver his own character assassination. It would be something else again to hear her do it. But he told himself he was prepared.

Because it wasn't as if, no matter what she said, it wouldn't be the truth. She took a few steps toward him, and then stopped, almost as if she hadn't meant to move. He wondered, almost idly, if she would strike him. If he would let her.

But she didn't raise her hands. Instead, Cecilia studied him, for the span of a long, hard breath. Then another.

She took another step toward him, and he couldn't

help himself. He could only admire how quickly and easily she had taken to his new role of hers, however little she'd enjoyed her time in Rome. Even in a temper, as today, she had dressed from the wardrobe he'd provided her. Her honey-colored hair was twisted back into an effortless chignon. It only emphasized her unusual eyes. She wore a wool dress that hugged her lithe curves and a pair of boots in butter-soft leather. She looked simple, yet elegant. She always had.

The only difference now was that the clothes she wore enhanced what was already there, in a way the ragged, torn clothes she'd worn in her role as a cleaner never could.

It was due to his own arrogance that he'd ever imagined she was within his reach.

Accordingly, he stood where he was, ready for anything she might throw at him.

"That's a dark picture you paint," was all she said. "Of a dark and remorseless man, incapable of changing himself for the better."

He couldn't read her expression. Or her voice. He could feel his pulse, rocketing through him too hard. Too fast. "It is an accurate portrait."

"You say that as if I did not already know exactly who you were, Pascal."

His lips thinned at that. "Then I should not have to tell you these things. But I will." He told himself his throat was not dry. He was not too tense. That none of those things were happening to him, because he should have been perfectly calm. "If I were you, Cecilia, I would go."

"Go?"

"Take the child. Leave. You were right all along—this was a mistake."

The words felt to him like a thunderclap. Intense and huge. Impossible to ignore.

And everyone knew that when thunder rumbled, the storm could not be far behind.

"I could do that." But Cecilia's voice was too quiet. Too soft, and yet not weak at all. Steel serenity, and he knew precisely where she'd learned it. Her violet gaze held his. "Or instead, I could beg."

Beg.

The word seemed to take over his head, his chest, *him*. It seemed to pour in from the sprawling, ancient city outside to fill the room. It was in his blood, bruising and powerful.

I could beg, she had said.

And he remembered, again that moment on a frozen field high up in the mountains. He remembered how deeply and fervently he had wanted all the things he knew he couldn't have. Because he had never had them.

His woman. His son.

A family.

I could beg, she'd said.

He knew better. He was Pascal Furlani, not another, softer man. And all he knew how to do was struggle. How to fight. How to punish the world in general and his father in particular for failing him.

But Cecilia *lived*.

She had nursed him back to life, literally. She had given birth to a brand-new life, Dante.

She was life. Love. All the things that Pascal did not dare permit himself to imagine he could ever, ever have—

"This is me begging," she said, her voice musical. Impossible.

And then she made it worse by sinking down onto her knees, right there before him. With all the ease and grace of a dancer or a queen, as if she wasn't the one capitulating.

Or as if, he thought in some kind of a daze, as if surrender cost her nothing.

When he was certain it would destroy him.

"Pascal," she said, her remarkable eyes locked to his. "I want you to make me your wife, in every possible way. I'm begging you to do it. Right now."

And Pascal had been born a lost cause. Accordingly, he'd lost himself for years, as an avocation. He reveled in that dirt, that stain, and had only imagined himself found when he'd nearly died on a distant mountain. Until this woman smiled at him, then nursed him whole.

He was lost in that gaze of hers, violet and sure.

And maybe the truth was that he was already lost. That he had been for six years now, and counting.

So he pulled her to her feet, then swept her into his arms, taking her mouth in a kind of fury.

And lost himself for good.

CHAPTER TEN

CECILIA UNDERSTOOD EVERYTHING in a sweet, sudden rush. A glorious flash of flame and longing, while his mouth moved on hers and remade the world again.

It was all about fear.

She wrapped her arms around him and let him bear her down to the ground, sighing in happiness as he fit that exquisite body of his to the length of hers, proving yet again how well he fit.

How beautifully they had always fit, just like this.

Fear was why she hadn't looked harder for him, when she could have. Fear was what had kept her in the mountains guarding her child, instead of taking the harder, scarier route and facing him six years ago. Five years ago.

Or any day since.

And fear was what had made him do what he'd done. She got that now. Because revenge was what Pascal knew. It was easier. Anger was far more palatable than those hot, confusing mornings when they woke up wound up in each other. If he made her angry, she understood, he could fight her. He could make demands, issue threats.

He could reduce what was happening between

them—what had always been happening between them—to a simple little battle.

But Pascal was not a bully. She knew that like she knew her own heart. It wasn't her weakness he was after, it was her strength. Weakness would have wrecked him. It was her strength that allowed him to treat her like an adversary.

Because adversaries could not be hurt. Adversaries fought.

And if they were fighting, they couldn't be afraid.

Cecilia understood all of it as he kissed her, his mouth hot and wicked and *perfect*. She understood it as she kissed him back with all the fire and need he'd taught her.

Pascal pulled back and stripped himself out of his jacket, his shirt. Cecilia took the opportunity to pull off the dress she wore, leaving her in nothing but a bra, her panties and her boots.

His eyes darkened, and that sensual mouth of his firmed. And he looked at her as if he wanted nothing more than to get his mouth on every last centimeter of her. As if he might die if he didn't do precisely that. Now.

"You kill me," he growled, the sensual menace in his voice making her shudder with *want*. "Every time, you kill me."

His hands were on her, like bright hot flame and searing madness, testing the shape of her breasts and then gripping her hips to haul her toward him again.

And his mouth on hers was a revelation.

So good, so right, that Cecilia understood why she'd been refusing herself the very thing she'd given so freely six years ago. *She was afraid.*

Of what it would do to her. And what it would do to her life. Because the truth was, having sex with Pascal had already changed her entire world once. What would he do this time?

But she already knew. Sex wasn't the danger here. Sex wasn't going to ruin her and wreck her, stalking her across the years until she found him again. Love was.

And the simple truth was, she had never stopped loving Pascal.

She wasn't sure she ever would.

So Cecilia kissed him back, pouring the years they'd been apart into it. The fear and the loneliness, and more than that, all her dreams. All her joy. The flavor of the life she'd lived away from him, and all the secret hopes she hid inside her that this new life they'd started together would bloom despite their best efforts to pretend it was a misery.

She kissed him and she kissed him. And when he got to his feet again, then pulled her up, she followed him blindly. Greedily. He carried her over to the long, low sofa, and lay her down upon it. She watched, breathing too hard, as he kicked off his trousers and the boxer briefs he wore beneath them, then bared himself to her gaze at last.

For a moment she lay there, sprawled out in abandon. She simply looked at him.

Because she could never get enough of *looking* at this man.

His scars, his muscles. All together, the devastating masculine beauty that was Pascal Furlani, the only man she'd ever touched. The only man she'd ever loved.

As far as Cecilia was concerned, the only man there was. Full stop.

His black eyes glittered. His shoulders were wide enough to cling to, forever. Between his legs, the hardest part of him stood tall, proud.

And she loved him.

There was nothing else to understand, but that.

She lifted her hands toward him, and she smiled. "How much begging do I have to do?"

"Take off your bra," he ordered her, his voice a gritty rasp.

Cecilia levered herself up and reached around to obey him, pulling off one cup, then the other. Then she bared her breasts to him, his gaze alone making her nipples pull tight. She let out a shaky sort of breath as sensation washed over her.

"And your panties," he said. His hard mouth curled in one corner, making her shake even more. "But you can leave the boots on."

She didn't know why that struck her as so unbearably delicious, but it did. She hurried to comply, pulling her panties over her hips, then fighting to get them over the leather of her boots.

And when she was done, she was on her feet again, standing before him. On display in a way that should have made her think twice.

But she was thoroughly his. That was what she thought about.

His black eyes burned. His mouth curved even more.

And then he was reaching for her, pulling her close and then lifting her up.

Cecilia held on to his wide, hard shoulders as she crossed her legs around his waist. Then she moaned as he shifted her farther, lifting her up and then holding her there—stretched taught above the hardest part of him at last.

His face was close to hers, drawn into a fiercely sensual mask that made her whole body hurt. In the best possible way.

"Beg me," he whispered.

His expression was raw. His black eyes were lit with a golden need. And Cecilia felt the same inside as if she'd been scraped clean. Hollowed out.

And all that was left was this. *Him.*

This thing that had always been between them, coiled tight and wild and impossible to ignore—though they'd both tried.

Love.

There was no other word for it.

She dug her fingers into his shoulders and she gazed down into his face, taut and hard with the force of that same rampant need that was charging through her, leaving her molten hot and nearly bursting out of her own skin.

"Please, Pascal," she whispered, filled with the exquisite joy of a surrender that felt like a triumph. "Please."

And then he thrust into her, deep.

He impaled her upon him, and for a moment they both froze, swamped with the same wild sensation.

The heat. The sweet, slick perfection.

Home, Cecilia thought. *Love.*

Yes.

And she didn't know which parts of that she'd said out loud.

But then it didn't matter.

Pascal was bringing her back down to the couch again, bracing himself above her as they both adjusted and he slid in even deeper.

Her mouth was in the crook of his neck, and her teeth were at his shoulder.

And he was surging inside her, pounding into her again and again and again as if they would die this way, or die if they didn't, or die and be reborn and do this dance forever, just like this.

Cecilia met him. She was a part of him. She kept her legs wrapped around his hips and met his every thrust.

She remembered the glory of this six years ago. The brief flash of pain, then nothing but need and longing made flesh.

And it was better now. Deeper, harder.

It was too much and not enough. It was everything and yet they strained together for more.

Pascal did something with his hips, making her throw back her head to ride it out. Then he bent his head to take one tight nipple into his mouth, and she was done. She shattered. Her whole body clenched hard around his, then shook.

She shook and shook and shook.

But still he kept going, pounding her through one shivering climax, then straight back into the fire to burn toward another.

Cecilia held on to him for dear life, and she loved him. She cried, she called out his name and she let herself drown in the exquisite flames, the remarkable burn, as it mounted inside her all over again.

But it wasn't until she started to shudder again, her thighs clamping down hard on him, that he finally lost that deep, measured pace that he'd been using to drive her wild.

And for a moment it was all speed and fury, beautiful and deep.

Then Pascal was shattering, too, her name on his lips as he lost himself inside her at last.

And Cecilia thought, with perfect clarity, *this*.

She wanted this. All of this. The storm, beautiful and elemental, that was this man and the passion that had sparked between them from the first. From long before she'd understood what it was that called her to his side in that clinic. She wanted the thunder of the need she felt for him, the lightning that was their passion that felt like its own fury, like pain and sometimes like loss. And the rain that followed, but brought life to the world.

It had brought her their son.

She wanted that storm with everything she had, everything she was. It was worth the price she'd paid. It was worth anything.

She reached up and took Pascal's face between her hands. She felt his scars on one side, the evidence that he could overcome anything. She searched his gaze, black-gold and unfocused, though he slowly focused in on her.

And for a moment it was as if he was new.

As if the rain had washed them both clean, so they could start again.

Cecilia wasn't afraid anymore. Not to beg for what she wanted, and not to set free the things that roared inside her, desperate to get out. And certainly not of the man still lodged so deep inside her, it was hard to remember they were different people.

"I love you," she said, very distinctly. "I love you, Pascal."

The effect on him was instant and electric.

And not good.

His brows clapped together. His eyes flashed. He scowled at her, and then he moved back. He disengaged himself from her body and pulled himself away, a lot as if she'd scalded him.

Cecilia stayed where she was; propping herself up on one elbow she watched him stalk away from her.

It wasn't as if there was any angle on that beautiful body of his that she didn't admire.

She watched him shove a hand through his hair. Then he stood with his hands on his hips, glaring toward his windows as if he could level Rome with the force of his temper. She wasn't surprised when his hand drifted down to stroke the scars on his jaw.

"I love you, Pascal," she said again, so there could be no mistake.

And when he turned back to level that same glare at her, she only smiled. She sat up, but she did absolutely nothing to cover herself. She simply smiled back at him.

And he looked at her as if she'd taken a swing at him.

"I've always loved you," she said as if she was confiding a great secret. "Even when I hated you the most, there was a little part inside me that hoped that you would come back. Because that was what would make it right, no matter what had happened. I just loved you, and I wanted to be with you, even when I would have sworn up and down I didn't. And when you did come back, what terrified me the most was that all that love hadn't gone anywhere. It was just waiting—"

"It is impossible," he told her then, sounding as if he was chewing glass as he spoke. "You must know this."

"Which part?" She watched him stalk over to grab his trousers and wondered if he was having as much trouble concentrating as she was. What with all the nudity in the room. "Because I assure you, it's actually quite easy to love. You just do it."

Pascal didn't say anything. He dressed quickly and quietly, and when she didn't rush to do the same, he lifted one of those dark brows at her direction.

Cecilia sighed, then took her time refastening her bra. She stepped into her panties, pulled them into place, and then she took a very long time indeed to wander over across the office floor and pick up her dress. When she finally shimmied it over her head and back into place, he was gritting his teeth so hard that she was fairly surprised his jaw didn't shatter.

She smiled. Pascal did not.

"I told you that you would beg, and you did," he said darkly. "But I see no reason whatsoever to drag out the rest of this charade. I will have my secretary contact you and you can hammer out the details with him."

"What details?"

"We've already covered this," he said, but though his voice was as commanding as ever, his eyes told a different story. It was as if he was so wounded he'd… gone numb. And had no idea that he was staggering about while missing a limb. "Take Dante. Go back to your mountains. You're safer there."

"I love those mountains," Cecilia said. "I always will. But they're not the only thing I love."

"I heard you." His voice could have cut stone in half,

and she was somewhat surprised she wasn't in pieces herself. "I don't need to hear it again."

But she had decided to stop being afraid. No matter what.

"I want everything, Pascal," she told him. "I want a real marriage. I want a real family. I want a real life. With you."

"And you deserve those things." He sounded stiff, but she could see the torment in his eyes. "But I cannot give them to you."

She made herself laugh. "You're one of the richest, most powerful men in Italy. You can give me whatever you want to give me."

"Cecilia—"

"Think of it. *Real life*, Pascal. No threats, no lies. No secrets. Just us."

And she could see the storm break in him then. She lifted her hand toward him—but he stepped back as if he was afraid that she would tear him in two.

As if she already had.

"I can't be *real*," he threw at her, and her heart broke at the sound of his voice. So ragged. So raw. "I wouldn't know how to begin. I was born broken and I've only gotten worse."

And she wanted to put her hands on him more than she wanted her next breath. She wanted to gather him to her, and soothe him somehow. She wanted to shout at him, shake him.

But she knew he wouldn't let her do any of that.

Instead, she tried to smile. "All you have to do is choose love, Pascal," she told him quietly, but with every bit of truth she knew right there in her voice. "Choose me. Just once."

Six years ago he'd run. And she understood why he had, why he'd believed he had no other choice. But understanding the past didn't change it; it could only—if they were lucky—change the future.

"Just once," she whispered.

But Pascal was shaking his head. And she wanted to scream at him, beg him all over again, but he looked tortured. Ripped apart.

"I can't," he gritted out. And then he stood a little straighter, lifting his head to meet her stricken gaze head-on. "If that means you have to leave me, I understand. I told you. I think you should."

She had been asleep the last time he'd left her. And maybe that had been a kindness after all.

But Cecilia wasn't asleep now.

She thought about the past six years, and how hard she'd fought not just to give Dante a good life, but to also make sure that her own didn't feel like an albatross around her neck. She'd chosen her life, and she'd made it good, with whatever pieces she'd had left after she'd had to leave the abbey.

And as much as she loved this man standing before her, as much as she'd always loved him and always would, she didn't see any reason why she should do any differently now.

She could, she knew. She could back off. She could say something placating, or try to smooth things over. She could continue this half-life she'd been living since she'd come to Rome with him. Wandering about aimlessly half the time, and then living for those moments when she woke up in his arms, and could pretend she was horrified to find herself there.

There were a thousand games that she could play, but she didn't want any of that.

She wanted him, not games.

She wanted their family.

She wanted everything that she'd told him she wanted, but she was greedy. She wanted him to want it, too. She'd grown up with a family of nuns, so she knew her way around a martyr. And she didn't want any of that, either.

She could accept anything. She could make anything work, and had.

But here, now, in this marriage that she could have resisted, but hadn't—all so she could have the pleasure of pretending he'd forced her into it—she was done accepting things. Working with whatever came her way. Making the best of it.

He tasted like everything she'd ever wanted, and that was what she wanted now. *Everything.* Cecilia had no intention of settling for anything less.

"No," she said.

Pascal stared at her in that frozen, arrogant way he had as if he assumed he must have misheard her. Because certainly no one could possibly dare cross him.

"No?" he echoed as if he didn't quite understand.

"I told you what I want." Her voice was distinct and steady. And she held his gaze. "And for once, Pascal, I'm not willing to settle for less. If it's too much for you, I understand. But I'm not running away from anything. If you can't handle this…"

And then her voice cracked, because she wasn't a machine. She was a woman, flesh and blood, and fighting for the man she loved the only way she knew how.

"If you don't know how to fight for us, I can't help you."

"Cecilia—"

"I'm not going anywhere," she told him. "Dante and I are staying put. But I won't stop you if you need to run away, Pascal. *Again*."

Then, before she could change her mind and beg him all over again—and in a whole different way, possibly involving tears—Cecilia turned her back on him.

No matter how much it hurt.

And this time she was the one who walked away.

CHAPTER ELEVEN

PASCAL STOOD THERE for a long, long time after the door closed behind him.

After she'd left him the way he'd told her she should.

He stood there in that office that he'd been so proud of before. The office that represented who he was. All he had. All he was.

But instead of admiring the sharp, modern lines and their juxtaposition with ancient Rome right there outside his window, all he could see was Cecilia.

She was everything he'd ever wanted. Poise. Grace. Elegance.

And somehow, despite all that, she loved him.

She loved him.

How could she possibly love him?

Pascal could feel his heart kicking at him as if it was trying to beat him up from the inside out. He was hardly aware of it when he wheeled around, grabbing his heavy coat on the way out, and muttered something largely incomprehensible to Guglielmo.

He needed to get out. He needed to get away.

He threw himself into the streets, the way he always had.

Rome was his first love. The eternal city—and his

eternal and only salvation. Rome was how he had learned who he was, what he could do. Rome had made him. There had been years Pascal had believed that only the battered old streets of this city knew him at all.

He walked and he walked, chasing the December day toward its brief afternoon. It was two days before Christmas and the weather was raw. Damp and cold. Still, it suited his mood. It matched the tumult within.

He navigated his way over slick stone and around knots of people. It seemed to him as he moved that he could feel the pulse of the city inside him, the whispers of three thousand years of so many lives. Hopes and dreams, loss and grief, all there beneath his feet.

It was as if the stones themselves seem to hum with all the life—and love—that had happened here. Too many times to count. Rome was stories that could never be told, lives tangled together and lost in time. Myths that anyone could recite and smaller, hidden tales no one would ever know. He could hear that humming everywhere. He could feel it shoot straight down his spine.

Then again, he thought as he found himself in a far-off *piazza* lit up with Christmas trees and a festive market, it could as easily be the carolers.

He stood there in a neighborhood he rarely visited, a part of the same grand mosaic of stories lost and found, lived and lost. And though it was not his custom to play the slightest attention to Christmas songs, or Christmas itself if he could avoid it, he found himself listening despite himself as they sang.

Songs of joy. Songs of peace.

Pascal had always preferred to believe they were lies…but the familiar songs didn't feel like a lie this gloomy evening. He did.

And maybe that was why, sometime later, he found himself in a neighborhood he usually preferred to avoid. And worse, standing outside the house he knew well though he had only ever seen it in pictures. There had been some dark years when he had set men on this house, to watch it. To report back. To give him a sense of what it was he fought.

He had sworn to himself that he would never come here himself. Never in person. Not after all those times his mother had come here when Pascal was a child, only to be turned away.

Over and over again as she wept that she was dirt.

Pascal had vowed that he would never allow his father the opportunity to do the same to him.

But it was a short, bitter sort of day, and the long night was already gathering. He looked through the lit-up windows at tidy, unremarkable rooms that indicated the owners were well-off—if not particularly flashy. Even here there were Christmas trees on display and festive decorations that looked as if they were part of a design feature, not the kind of family nostalgia he'd always assumed the people who lived here indulged in.

Mostly because he never would.

And then a man he'd seen in pictures—often in a split frame next to his own face but never in the flesh—walked into the main room and frowned as he looked around as if searching for a mislaid item.

Likely not his discarded son, Pascal thought bitterly. Never *that*.

He wasn't sure what he expected to see. A monster, perhaps. A worthy opponent, certainly. A focal point for everything he'd done and all the ways he'd gloried in rolling around in the dirt just to throw it here.

But all he saw in the bright windows was a shriveled old man. Alone.

And if the look on his face was any guide as he huffed around his little domain, an unhappy one to boot.

Once again Pascal felt as if the ground had been snatched out from beneath his feet, there where he stood in the narrow road as the darkness fell around him and the winter night grew colder.

For the first time—maybe ever, if he was honest—he had to ask himself why he had expended so much energy to build an entire life *at* this sad, tired, mean creature. The life he saw through the windows was so narrow. So small.

And exactly where you're headed, a voice inside him that sounded a lot like hers warned him.

Because all Pascal had done in all this time was make himself small, too.

And it was as if something vast opened up inside him then.

Cecilia.

She was endless. She had walked into his life and nothing had been the same. First, she had brought him to life. Then she had given him the tools to build an empire worthy of her, though it had cost her. And when he'd finally returned to her, haunted by her after all those years, she'd given him a son.

And today she'd told him she loved him, when no one else had ever tried.

She was more than beauty and she was deeper than truth. She was faith. She was hope.

But he'd let her walk away. And he'd come here instead, to watch an old man who had been given the whole of Pascal's lifetime to right a wrong, change his ways, offer a hand across a great divide…and hadn't.

Pascal felt twisted up with the things he didn't know today, but of one thing he was utterly sure. Whatever became of him, he did not want to end up like his father.

All he had to do was open up this death grip of his, let the old man go, and choose. Not to be so small. Not to consign himself to the very same fate. Not to chase the same end the way he'd been doing all this time.

Because Pascal had a child, too.

And Dante was his chance to remake the world. Not to narrow it, choke it with hate, make it hurt and fight and plot revenge.

Dante was his chance to do the opposite. Instead of being the monster his father had been and ever would be, Pascal could be the father he had always wished he'd had.

There was only one way out of the dark and into the light.

All Pascal had to do was finally be man enough to take it.

He turned his back on the house. The man. The father so undeserving of that title. He began to walk, putting distance between him and the street where his mother had wailed to no avail. And as he moved, the dirt from that street that had been on him his whole life fell away, because it had never been his. It belonged where he'd found it.

And as he broke into a run, he knew without a shred of doubt that he would never return.

Pascal ran through the streets of his beloved city. The colors and the sounds, the stories and the songs, all began to blend. All the *piazzas* done up for Christmas, all the people in throngs and gathered in the cafés.

All of them out here in the December dark to bask, together, in the light they made to beat it back.

Hope. Faith.

Pascal finally understood.

He only hoped he wasn't too late.

When he made it to his home at last, he threw himself in through the door, staggering into his foyer. At first he hardly recognized the space, until he realized what she'd done. She'd brought it inside from the streets—the trees all lit up, the chaotic joy of it all. Evergreen trees made bright like a taunt—

Was this what she'd left him to remember her by?

Pascal was sure that she had gone already. That she had ordered the staff to decorate and had packed up Dante, then taken herself off, just as he'd told her to do. Because when he had been offered the choice to stay or leave, he'd left. Six years ago he'd simply left her.

Why shouldn't she do the same?

He shouted for his housekeeper, then shouted for his car—

"I let the housekeeper go tonight," came a voice from behind him. "She has her own family to decorate for."

Pascal turned, slowly. Because he was sure he was imagining it.

But she was there, walking toward him from the hall that led to Dante's suite.

"I just put Dante to bed," Cecilia said quietly when she came to a stop before him, still dressed in the same clothes he'd seen on her—and off her—earlier. "You're shouting loud enough to wake the dead. One small boy will wake a whole lot more easily."

She was still here.

For a moment that was all that he could think about. It was all that mattered.

And as her words penetrated the mad, howling thing inside him, he realized that she clearly wasn't going anywhere—not tonight anyway—if she'd put Dante down to sleep.

He moved toward her, and he felt as if he had the weight of a thousand worlds clinging to each of his limbs as he moved. The world he'd grown up in. The world he'd made.

The world he'd left behind him tonight.

When he reached her, he put his hands on her shoulders as if he needed to assure himself that she was real.

Because he needed her to be real. He needed it more than air.

"Cecilia," he said, because her name was like a song and he'd been trying to get that particular tune out of his head for far too long.

Tonight he'd stopped trying.

And it was time to start singing it instead.

"Pascal," she whispered back, her wide violet eyes solemn.

And then, finally, while the storm raged inside him and his bones ached with the effort, Pascal Furlani sang the only song that mattered.

He surrendered.

He sank down on his knees, took her hands in his and begged.

"Please don't leave me," he said, urgent and low. "I know I've given you no reason to stay, no reason to do anything but hate me. But Cecilia, I can't live without you. I've tried."

She shifted as if she would say something—

But he cut her off, because he couldn't stop now.

"I love you," he told her. "I built empires in your absence, but all I saw was your ghost. You have haunted me since the moment I woke up in pieces and saw you there, smiling. You taught me how to live. To love. To imagine that I could be the kind of man who could do either when I'd never thought I was much of anything but another man's dirt. I don't deserve you. I never will."

"Pascal—"

"Cecilia," he said, a song and a vow, and her—always her, "I need you to stay here. I need to become the man I imagined I was when I was smashed into a million pieces and you alone made me whole. I need to become that man so I can be the husband you deserve. The father Dante deserves. And I am very much afraid that only you can teach me how."

There were tears in the corners of her lovely eyes, and they chased each other down her cheeks as she sank down on her knees so she could be there with him in the sparkling light of so many Christmas trees.

"Pascal," she whispered. "Don't you understand? It's already done. I am your wife. That means you help me. And I help you. And we love each other, forever. That was what we promised."

"I know how to make money," he told her, the intensity in his voice inside him, too. "But what I want is to make you happy. To make our son happy. To make more babies, and make them happy, too."

"I want all of those things," she said. "And I want you happy, too. Pascal, you deserve to be happy."

"I don't deserve you," he managed to say. "I know that much."

Her hands smoothed over his face then. She traced his scars and she held his gaze, and the light he saw in her eyes humbled him. Exalted him.

Made him whole.

"You have hurt me more than I ever thought I could be hurt," she whispered fiercely. "But that could never have been possible if you hadn't also made me the happiest I've ever been. I have to think that that's the point. The hurt and the happiness. All of it wrapped up together. If we do it together, I think that's love."

And then he was kissing her, or she was kissing him. But they were together. And all of this was theirs, that fire, that need. All that brightness they made together, to banish the night, glowed between them.

Pascal began to imagine it always would.

"I promise you," he told her then, his voice as serious as his mouth was hot against hers. "I will never leave you again."

"I will never leave you, either," she replied in the same solemn way as if these were the vows that mattered, here on their knees in Rome with all the Christmas lights to guide them. "We will fight for each other, not against each other."

"You and me, my love," he agreed hoarsely. "That will make all the difference."

For each other, not against. Pascal felt that settle there inside him, deep into his bones.

Choose love, she'd implored him. *Just once.*

And finally, with everything he had and everything he hoped he would be, that was exactly what Pascal did.

He chose Cecilia.

Forever.

CHAPTER TWELVE

THREE YEARS LATER Pascal basked in the sweetness of another perfect Christmas Day.

Up in the mountains the brooding Dolomites stood tall, high above them. He was certain he could feel them there, even in the dark. They had impressed themselves upon him so completely that sometimes he thought he could feel them down in Rome.

He heard a soft sound and turned to see his beautiful wife coming into the room that was lit only by the fire on one side and a tall, gleaming Christmas tree on the other.

He had built her this cottage that was no cottage at all. He had set it outside the small village, up in the foothills, so they could gaze down upon the pretty valley together. The abbey, the church and all those beautiful fields that had been his only entertainment once.

The villagers muttered about rich men and their houses in the hills, but Pascal didn't care if they talked about him beneath their breath as long as they treated his wife as they should. And they did, because Cecilia was theirs no matter the rarefied air she breathed as Signora Furlani. And with every visit, they thawed toward her husband, too.

Pascal would have sworn he didn't care about such

things. He wouldn't have once. But Cecilia cared deeply about the good opinion of the people here—and therefore, Pascal did, too.

There was no limit to the things he would do for her.

"Come," he said now, reaching out his hand. And his Cecilia could still smile at him the way she did now, making his world stop and shudder. "I have built us a fire."

She took his hand and let him draw her close, then lead her over toward the fire.

"Dante told me he was not sleepy at all and would stay up all night, to spite me if necessary," Cecilia confided with a laugh. "But he was out before I turned off the light."

Dante was eight now, filled with his father's stubborn purpose. Pascal anticipated that he would always be the way he was now, prepared to butt heads at the slightest provocation—and also the quickest to apologize and the first to declare his affection. Even thinking of the boy made Pascal smile.

"And Giulia?" Pascal asked, his smile widening as he thought of their headstrong and deeply beloved two-year-old daughter.

"Dead to the world," Cecilia said happily.

Pascal pulled her into his arms, then down onto the rug before the fire. They stretched out together as the flames leaped and danced in the grate. And Cecilia sighed at the way they fit, the way she always did.

Because years might have passed, but the spark between them never took more than the simplest touch to build up into the flames that could still burn them both to ash. And sometimes it took only a look.

Pascal had learned how to work less, but Cecilia worked more. That first year, unable to remain idle, or any kind of ornament, she had started her own charity for orphans and foundlings all over the world.

Sometimes that meant Pascal got to be the trophy on her arm, which he found he greatly enjoyed.

More than that, he found it nothing but entertaining to watch her innate grace up against dedicated sharks like his board members. Or against the inevitable slings and arrows of the mercurial press, who loved them one day then hated them the next.

Cecilia handled them all the same. With that quiet steel of hers that had brought him to his knees once. And always would.

She had made him far better than he deserved to be. And he worked every day to make sure she never regretted her choices.

Last night at midnight mass in the church down on the valet floor, Mother Superior had smiled at him the way she did these days. Fondly. She clasped his hands in her old, gnarled grip, and she'd called him *child*.

Pascal would die before he admitted how much he liked that.

"Fear is always a liar. Love is always the truth," she'd said, that same ring of steel in her kind voice that she'd bequeathed to his wife. "I cannot tell you how it delights me to watch you live that."

"Every day," he'd said, like a new vow. "And always."

Because every day he remembered all those things he'd thought he wanted when he'd stood on the edge of the field that he could see from his windows here on a clear day. When he'd looked at the little boy who didn't know him, running heedless on the frozen grass, and wanted more than he'd ever been given himself.

He remembered the notion he'd had that he was looking at something huge, and how desperately he'd hoped he could find a way to cram it all inside him. To make it work.

God, how he'd wanted it to fit.

Because he hadn't understood then. The things he'd taken for tears were oceans, too massive to be crammed inside him or any one person. There was a vastness that couldn't fit anywhere, and that was the point.

Love grows and grows and grows, he thought as Cecilia lay beside him. It got better all the time. Especially when she tipped her face to his and kissed him.

She smiled against his mouth as he ran his hands along her sides, then over her sweet belly where she'd carried his babies.

And he knew she was keeping another secret. That she would tell him when she was sure, that it was early days yet. But he knew.

He estimated it would be about another seven months before they welcomed another member of the family. But Pascal was happy to take his time unwrapping her secrets, one after the next, until they were like the mountains he could feel out there in the dark. Standing sentry against the passage of time.

Love and hope, ageless and eternal.

Just as they would be to each other. Come what may.

"I love you," Cecilia whispered as she moved against him.

"I love you," he replied.

And it would grow and grow and grow, for the rest of their lives, and on into their children—bright as the light that turned back the night, gleaming on into always, just like Christmas.

* * * * *

BOUND BY THEIR NINE-MONTH SCANDAL

DANI COLLINS

For my wonderful readers.
You make this possible. Thank you!

CHAPTER ONE

PIA MONTERO FEARED her sister-in-law's masquerade ball
would be interminable, and it was, but not for the reason
she had anticipated.

The October evening was cool, but dry. Guests had
embraced the chance to cast off tuxedos and backless
couture for something more exciting. Women twirled in
overblown gowns with bell skirts, elaborate wigs and
feathered headdresses. Men stalked in colorful brocade
jackets with epaulettes and lace cuffs and short pants
with stockings. Some even wore the *traje de luces* of a
bullfighter with horned masks.

The masks were works of art. A few had cat ears and
bird beaks, some covered an entire face, others were part
of a jester hat with bells dangling from the cockscomb.
Some were made from handblown Venetian glass, others were made of lace or satin and adorned with feathers and flowers, beads and sequins.

There were prizes for best costumes, but Pia had chosen to forfeit. She wore an understated gown in indigo
topped with a purple velvet jacket. Her mask was a conservative cat's eye in molded silk painted with musical
notes and roses, ideal for blending in.

She wished now that she'd chosen a full face mask

as she watched a gold-lipped cherry blossom porcelain canvas swirl by. It would have allowed her to hide her thoughts behind a physical mask, rather than having to maintain the aloof expression she had practiced in the mirror at boarding school, back when she'd been hiding hurt feelings over *everything*, most especially being noticed.

Even when girls had stuck up for her back then, saying, "She's shy. Leave her alone," Pia had blushed and burned behind her breastbone, wishing herself into a hole in the ground because someone had looked at her.

Misery did not love company, as it turned out. She'd been lonely her entire childhood, too awkward to make friends and ridiculously smart, which had made her an academic rival, bookish and superior on top of all the rest.

Her saving grace was her bloodline. She came from Spain's aristocracy. Her parents were the Duque and Duquessa of Castellon, her father an innovator in industrial metals who had become a well-respected, elected member of parliament once his sons were old enough to take the reins on what was now a multinational corporation.

Pia was also reasonably attractive—not that she played it up. She eschewed makeup and designer wear, seeing little point in trying to attract a boyfriend when her mother would ultimately assign her a husband.

Which La Reina Montero was trying to do right now, turning a perfectly tolerable evening into something Pia struggled to bear.

"I'd prefer to wait until January, after I've defended my dissertation," Pia said, and braced herself, but it still stung when she received the expected *tsk* of tested tolerance.

Pia's brothers were chemical engineers, both unmarried until they were thirty, but Pia's accelerated study pace and soon-to-be-achieved doctorate only "wasted her best years," according to her mother.

"These things take time," her mother insisted. "Signal your interest. Was that the Estrada heir?"

Please no. Sebastián was decent enough, but he talked nonstop.

"His outgoing nature would balance your introversion. You'll have to work on that so you can host galas like this."

Say it louder, Mother.

"Perhaps if we go into the marquee, we can match names to the silent auction bids." La Reina tilted away her mask, which was mounted on a stick like a lorgnette. "I shouldn't have agreed to anything so childish as a masked ball. Very inconvenient."

"Most people seem to be enjoying themselves," Pia said mildly, noting laughter and noises of surprise as they approached the bustling tent where guests mingled while perusing the fund-raising items.

Ever the observer of animal behavior, especially human, Pia considered why a disguise would instill such high spirits. Was it the nostalgia of youthful play? She wouldn't know. Her childhood had been so rigid as to be a form of conditioned adulthood.

"Poppy is doing well." La Reina acknowledged her new daughter-in-law with reluctant approval as she glanced over the bids for rare vintage wines, antique jewelry, spa packages and VIP tickets to shows on Broadway and London's West End.

Did the masks reduce caution and provoke a willingness to take risks, Pia wondered? Similar to the way social media provided a removal from face-to-face interactions, thereby emboldening people to behave more freely?

Pia certainly felt at liberty to stare more openly. From behind the screen of her mask, she watched a couple debate a bid for a certain item. The woman protested it was too extravagant while the man insisted he loved her and wanted her to have it.

Pia was fascinated by interactions like that. They reminded her of the tenderness and indulgence that existed between her older brothers and their wives. They had both started their marriages in scandal, but had turned them into something meaningful, making her yearn for something like it for herself—as she repaired the family name by way of a low-drama, civilized marriage that was more a contracted merger with a dynasty of equal rank and prestige.

She bit back a sigh. Taking up the mantle of duty wasn't a sacrifice, she assured herself. It was a sensible course of action that benefited everyone, including herself. Her few attempts at dating had been failures, something the perfectionist in her loathed. Love and passion were foreign concepts. She wouldn't recognize either if she tripped over them.

She turned from spying on the couple and ran straight into a man setting down a pencil.

Physically the impact was light. With wistfulness blanketing her, however, the collision felt monumental. Life altering.

His opera cloak opened like dark wings that threatened to engulf her as his hands came up to grasp her upper arms and steady her.

Their masks had caused this, her confused mind quickly deduced. They interfered with peripheral vision. She wasn't clumsy or blind and doubted he was, either. He was too vital and controlled.

She recognized those traits in him instinctively, even though she wasn't usually sensitive to such things. Or sensual either, but she found herself taking in nonvisual elements even more swiftly than the sight of him. The heat of his body radiated around her. The strength in his hands was both gentle and firm. The scent of fresh air and orange blossoms clung to his clothing as though he'd arrived from a long walk through the grove, not from the stale air of a car.

Who was he?

His black tricorn hat had simple white trim. She glanced down to his black-on-black brocade vest over a black shirt, his snug black pants tucked into tall black boots.

A pirate, she thought, and looked back to his porcelain mask, white, blank and angular. It cast a shadow onto his stubbled jaw, his beard as black as the short hair beneath his hat.

She couldn't tell what color his eyes were, but as he looked straight into hers, her pulse shot up with the race of a prey animal. She held that inscrutable stare, arms in his talon-like grip, skin too tight to contain the soar of emotion that rose in her.

Most people skipped past her in favor of more interesting folk, which she preferred. Sustained eye contact was never comfortable, but her mask gave her the confidence to stare back. To stare and stare while her whole body tingled in the most startling and intriguing way.

Sexual attraction? He possessed the attributes that typically drew female interest—height and broad shoulders, a firm physique and a strong jaw. She was stunned to learn she was human enough to react to those signals. In fact, as the seconds ticked by, the fluttering within her grew unbearable.

"Excuse me." Someone spoke behind her, jolting her from her spell.

A woman wanted to place a bid on Poppy's framed, black-and-white photo.

The black satin lining of the man's cloak disappeared as he dropped his hands from her arms. The noise around them rushed back, breaking her ears.

Pia moved out of the way. When she looked back, the man was leaving the tent.

Still trying to catch her breath, she moved to the bidding sheet where he'd left his pencil. She knew all the names on the list and none of those men had ever provoked a reaction like that in her.

At the bottom, in a bold scratch, was a promise to quadruple the final bid. It was signed *Anonymous.*

"How does this work?" Pia pointed to it as her mother finished speaking to someone and caught up to her. Pia's hand was trembling and she quickly tucked it into the folds of her skirt.

"It happens occasionally," her mother dismissed. "When a man wants to purchase something to surprise his wife."

Or didn't want his wife to know at all, Pia surmised. She wasn't a cynic by nature, but nor was she naive about the unsavory side of arranged marriages.

"He'll leave his details with the auctioneer," her mother continued. "It's a risky move that becomes expensive. Other guests will drive up the bid to punish him for securing the item for himself."

"The price one pays, I suppose." Pia's witticism was lost on La Reina.

"This is one of the paintings from the attic," La Reina said. "A modest artist. Deceased, which always helps with value, but not the sort of investment I would expect to inspire such a tactic."

Pia studied the portrait. The young woman's expression was somber. Light fell on the side of her round features, highlighting her youth and vulnerability.

"Do you know who she is?" Pia picked up the card.

"Hanging pictures of family is sentimental." Her mother plucked the card from her hand and set it back on its small easel. "Displaying strangers in your home is gauche."

"The final bid is sewn up," Pia pointed out. "I was merely curious."

"We have other priorities."

A husband. Right. Pia bit back a whimper.

Angelo Navarro nursed a drink as he clocked the rounds of the security detail, picking his moment for the second half of his mission.

He could have sent an agent to bid on the portrait, but along with not trusting anyone else with the task—loose lips and all that—the opportunity to slip onto the estate undetected had been far too tempting.

He hadn't expected such a bombardment of emotions as a result of visiting his birthplace, though. Anger and contempt gripped him; fury and injustice and a thirst for vengeance that burned arid and unquenchable in the pit of his belly.

These people prancing like circus clowns, making grand gestures with extravagant bids to benefit victims of violence, were the same ones who had ignored a young woman's agonizing situation. They hadn't interfered when her child had been taken from her and had continued to revere her persecutors.

Angelo felt no compunction whatsoever at infiltrating this private fund-raiser with the intention of retrieving what his mother had stolen. Or been given. He'd never been clear on how she had obtained the jewelry or exactly which pieces had gone missing. That part didn't matter. He would happily have gone to his grave with the knowledge that she'd fought back in her own way.

However, when this chance to add a fresh blow had arisen, he hadn't been able to resist it.

Did it make him as soulless as his father that he was willing to commit a criminal act to continue her retaliation? So he could show his half brothers how it felt to be toyed with and abandoned to poverty?

Perhaps.

The thought didn't stop him. He casually made his way to the corner of the house, waited for the guard's attention to turn and slipped into the dark beyond.

He came up against a Family Only sign on the first step of the spiral staircase and smirked with irony as he slipped past it to climb to the rooftop patio.

The stairs gave a nostalgically familiar creak as he reached the top—where he discovered someone had arrived ahead of him.

The sound and light from the party were blocked by

the rise of the west wing of the house, casting the space into deep shadow. He could only see a silhouette and the lighter shadow of her mask as she turned from gazing across the moonlit Mediterranean. Even so, he recognized her as the woman who had careened into him as he was bidding on the portrait of his mother.

For one second as he'd steadied her, he had forgotten everything—his thirst to punish, his purpose in coming here. Something in her uninspired costume gave him the impression she didn't belong here any more than he did. That she was hiding in plain sight. His male interest had been so piqued, he had nearly asked her to dance.

"Oh." The lilt in her voice told him she had identified him from their brief encounter as well, which also told him she had found it as profound as he had.

"Were you expecting someone else?" He adjusted his mask to peer harder into the shadows. The rickety bench where his mother used to read to him was gone, replaced by a dark shape that suggested a comfortable, L-shaped sectional.

"I wasn't expecting anyone."

That was good news. On many levels.

"Did you follow me?" she asked.

"No." He would like to think he would have timed things differently if he had known she was up here, but he wasn't sure. Nor was he as dismayed as he ought to have been that she was now an obstacle to his goal.

"Did *you* invite someone to join you?" she asked, vaguely appalled.

He should have said, *Yes*. She sounded so uncomfortable at intruding, she probably would have hurried away, but something in him balked at letting her think he was involved with anyone.

He heard himself say a throaty and inviting, "Not yet."

Her silhouette grew more alert. The air crackled between them.

"Who are you?" Her voice sharpened and her mask tilted as she cocked her head.

It struck him that he couldn't tell her. *Damn.*

"I think the purpose of a night like this is to maintain the mystery."

"And telling me would identify you as the buyer of that portrait you bid on so generously. And anonymously."

"True." The peril he was in began to impact him. She could place him with the painting and here on the rooftop. Maybe she didn't know his name, but there was a chance she could find out.

Dared he linger? Was it worth the risk?

He couldn't tell whether this rooftop patio had been repaved or the old bricks merely pulled up and reset, exposing the hidey-hole he had discovered as a child. He doubted his half brothers had ever found it. If they had, they wouldn't have been so sly in their sale of this estate. There was every chance the new owners had found the treasure, though, and kept the contents without mentioning it. Angelo had very little faith in humanity, particularly those who sat like cream on the top of society without having worked to get there.

He couldn't leave until he knew for sure. He had come this far, and so decided to wait her out.

He joined her at the wall. The last time he'd been here, he'd barely been tall enough to peer over. His distant memory of that time was swept away by the breeze off the water and the woman's voice beside him.

"If you didn't follow me or come to meet someone, why are you here?"

"Curiosity." It wasn't a complete lie. He was definitely intrigued by her. "You?"

"To think."

"About?"

"The nature of happiness. Whether it's a goal worth pursuing when there are no guarantees I'll find it. That it would come at the expense of others if I did."

"Nothing too heavy, then," he drawled. Her hand was close to his on the wall, pale and ringless. "In my experience, happiness is a fleeting thing. A moment. Not a state of being."

"And if a moment is all you have?"

His scalp prickled beneath his hat. He turned his head and tucked his chin, trying to see through the dark and the holes in his mask to read her expression, but it was impossible.

"Regret is also a moment. A choice *not* to seize happiness when it presents itself."

"I *would* regret it if I didn't take a chance," she agreed with a nod of contemplation.

"What kind of chance?"

She let a couple of seconds tick by with crushing silence, then said in a thicker voice, "An overture. Letting my interest in someone be known." Her hand had been curled into a tense fist, but it unfurled, her pinkie finger splaying toward him.

His stomach knotted. "Are you married?"

"No." Through the rush of relief in his ears, he heard her add, "But obligations to do so loom. And I don't want to risk making a fool of myself when I don't know if he's even—"

"He is," he cut in. His chest felt tight and his throat could barely form words. "He's interested."

CHAPTER TWO

PIA'S HEART WAS pounding so hard, she ought to have hammered down the walls around her.

"Do you know who *I* am?" she asked faintly.

"Should I?"

"No." If he did, he would be treating her differently. With kid gloves, because of her family's influence. There would be no intimate questions about whether she was meeting someone or encouragement to act impulsively.

It was enormously refreshing not to carry the weight of history and expectation, which had been the nature of her dilemma when she'd come up here. That ever so brief moment with him in the marquee had sent her into a spiral of doubt about duty to family versus selfish pursuits.

"Are *you* married?" she asked.

"I'm not involved with anyone. But a moment is all I have, too." His velvety timbre was layered with regret.

She kept trying to place his voice, certain she would remember if she'd heard him before.

"I don't even know what I want except not to let this moment pass without…"

"Seizing it?" he suggested.

"Stealing it," she said wryly, finding the idea deeply

seductive. It was the best of both worlds. She could briefly shed mousy, dutiful Pia Montero without giving her up for good. It was *safe*.

"Strangers in the night." He held out a hand as if inviting her to dance.

Her hand went into his even though the music was a distant drone without a discernible tempo.

He was too compelling to resist, though. It wasn't the outfit, either. She understood that some animals were innately dominant. He was one of them and he ought to send her scurrying, but she was too fascinated. She was utterly riveted by him and her reaction to his air of supremacy.

She distantly noted that she would have to tell her mother to find her a good-natured beta male so she wouldn't be so completely overwhelmed by the simple act of being held in a man's arms.

This was biology, she told herself through the fog of her deepening attraction. She was reacting to a chemistry that didn't come from a mix of beakers, but from the scent of pheromones off skin. Receptive male meets receptive female. The pseudoerotic nature of their disguised identities and their clandestine meeting on an unlit rooftop exaggerated the excitement.

But even as her head tried to explain it and dismiss it, her body grew pliant and her feet shifted closer into his sphere. She wasn't acting like herself, but she would never have an encounter like this again, when she could *be* someone else, free of commitment and the constraints of being Pia Montero. When her physical appearance and other shackles of identity were so absent she was nothing but the energy of pure, universal womanhood.

And he was all man.

"I want to kiss you," he said in a voice that rumbled deep in his chest.

Her pulse skipped. It was only a kiss. She wanted to feel his mouth, to *experience* him. "I want that, too."

"Come here."

It was magnetic attraction rather than his arms that pulled her as she followed him into the shadow of the chimney. She couldn't discern his features at all as he slipped his mask up, knocking his hat away.

His arms encircled her and his mouth brushed against her cheek, seeking and finding hers.

An electric current jolted through her at first contact, leaving her tense and waiting when he drew back slightly, his breath catching the way hers had.

She wasn't great at kissing. It was yet another of those human interactions that had eluded her, but as his mouth returned, she discovered she liked it. His lips settled firmly across hers, flooding her with incredible heat, smooth and unhurried. As if they had all the time in the world for stolen kisses.

Her hand found his stubbled cheek and she enjoyed the abrasion against her palm as much as the lazy play of his mouth against hers. He teased her like that a few times, deepening the kiss with incremental degrees until she was parting her lips to catch his, wanting more. Her tongue darted out on instinct, practically begging for more.

With a growl in his throat, he settled into a hot kiss of intense passion, something she recognized with a fresh jolt of surprise and excitement. Then she lost the ability to consider what was happening to her as his strong arms pulled her into a world of pure sensual pleasure. The strength and safety of his embrace was all that held her together as she shuddered under an onslaught of pleasure so intense a helpless noise throbbed in her throat.

"Stop?" he whispered against her lips.

"Never. This is…" *Overwhelming. Glorious. Essential.*

She touched the back of his head, brought him back into the kiss and tried to give him the same sort of pleasure she was receiving. She offered all of herself, completely open to whatever he needed. She had never experienced anything so extraordinary.

He made another noise, this one more unfettered, as though he was slipping loose of whatever sort of control he held himself under—which perversely thrilled her. His hands stroked firmly through the layers of her velvet jacket and full skirt, molding her form, lighting a fire under her skin, sending a heavy ache into her loins.

"I've never felt like this," she told him in a rasp of need, burrowing her hands beneath his cloak, into the heat beneath his vest. She had never been so forward, seeking so compulsively to touch a man, to take in his textures and musculature.

He swore. "Me, either." His hand cupped the back of her neck and his breath pooled hotly against her throat. "But this can't happen." He scraped his teeth against her nape, making her nipples pinch into sharp sensitivity. "I can't start something. I was never here."

"Neither was I," she said with a choke of rusty laughter. "Keep going."

Her greedy hands went down to his butt. She had never done such a thing, never realized that the hard flex of his glutes could offer such a thrill as she squeezed.

He did the same to her, his strength pulling her so close she felt the shape of his erection through his trousers and the velvet of her dress, hard against her belly. Her brain distantly processed his arousal as potentially alarming, but her body fairly melted under a hot flush of desire.

"Yes. Like that," she said in an agonized whisper. She had never been more thrilled by anything in her life.

He muttered something about wrong time and place, but he pressed her beneath him onto the lounger, his cloak falling heavily around them. He kissed across her bare collarbone, whiskers abrading her skin. When his hand sought beneath her, she arched so he could lower her zipper and loosen her bodice.

She was braless and he groaned with gratitude as he cupped her naked breast and lightly scoured her skin with his stubbled cheek before he closed his mouth over her nipple.

Desire was such a knifing ache in her that she swallowed a cry and arched again, unable to get close enough. She struggled against the confines of her skirt, ground herself against the ridge of his erection, yearning for the pressure of him *there*. Between. Where she was damp, her pulse throbbing like a signal.

"This is insane." He lifted his head, looming like a gothic shadow over her, dangerous and fierce—but she wasn't terrified at all.

"It's a memory," she murmured. "A good one."

His breath cascaded across her cheek in a rasp of disbelief. Agreement. He caught her earlobe in his teeth, sending delicious shivers through her whole body.

When he lifted himself again to drag her skirt upward, she bent her knee to help, embracing the chilly air against her naked thigh, excited by the fabric of his trousers as he settled between her legs.

"I don't have anything."

"A condom?" She hadn't thought of that. This was the point when they ought to stop. *She knew that*.

"Are you on anything? I don't have any health issues."

She wasn't, but she had thrown supplies in her clutch this evening, thinking her cycle was due and didn't it always arrive at the least convenient time.

"I'm okay. It's fine." She didn't want to stop. There would never be another moment like this one. She needed him more than she needed air.

His hand cupped her cheek. "Thank you." It was the growl of an animal loosed from a cage and threatening to consume her. His busy mouth went across her jaw and down her throat and back to her breast while she ran her hands over and over the layers of clothing across his back.

When he stroked his broad hand up her thigh, she got her hands beneath his clothing, too; found the hot, smooth skin of his waist and the hollow of his spine. She would have tried to work her hand around to open his belt, but his thumb slid inward to graze over the silk between her legs.

She gasped and went very still.

"No?" He froze.

"Yes." She could barely speak, the yearning in her grew so sharp.

"Mmm…" He did it again and caught her light cries with his kiss, making love to her mouth with his tongue as he teased and caressed and his thumb found its way beneath silk to stroke into slippery heat.

She shuddered as she kissed him back, flagrant and uninhibited, playing her tongue against his, her hands roaming everywhere she could reach. She was trying to convey how much pleasure he was giving her. Trying to reciprocate it.

"You're gorgeous," he told her as he lifted himself just enough to unbuckle and release his fly.

"You can't see me." She searched the dark, trying to make out the shadowed features so close to her own, but there was only the black cutout of his silhouette against the blanket of stars above them.

"I see you." His eyes glittered despite the lack of light, making it seem as though he saw all the way into her soul. "Sensual. Curious. Pensive. And courageous enough to steal what you want." He kissed her with a smile on his lips.

"I'm not courageous at all— *Oh*."

He slid her panties to the side and settled his hot, hard, naked flesh against hers.

She throbbed with anticipation. *Ached*. She knew he was about to ruin her for whatever husband lay in her future, not because he would take her virginity, but because no man would ever make her feel this way again. Elemental and beautiful. *Free*.

"I see power." She let her fingers move through the short, silky strands of his hair, petting this dangerous wolf who could devour her, but held her in thrall instead. "Self-discipline and patience and intelligence."

"I'm none of those things. Not right now." His voice skimmed across her cheek while the crown of him, fierce and hot and hard searched against her damp, untried folds.

"You're perfect," she insisted.

The party was a distant soundtrack, her self-control long thrown away.

She had no regrets as she felt the press of him, the

pinch and sting of his shape forging into her. She didn't even care if she orgasmed. She was thrilled enough by this—the act of finding a lover who pleased her. Of choosing him and by extension choosing herself. It was selfishness in the extreme and a moment of physical connection that would always be hers—something she would reach for to soothe the bleak isolation that would continue to be her constant companion through the rest of her life.

He nibbled at her jaw as he rocked his hips, settling himself fully inside her. "You feel incredible."

"You, too," she murmured, dazed by the intensity of lying with him this way. Clothed and joined, his weight crushing her lower half while his arms cradled her. His scent was a drug, his lips tender and teasing.

On instinct, she sought his mouth, perhaps looking for reassurance, but it turned passionate quickly. It was such a remarkable, glorious feeling to kiss like this while their bodies were locked. She wished they were naked. He was so gloriously, beautifully wonderful.

With a growl, he shifted, braced on an elbow as he withdrew and returned in a slow, testing stroke.

The friction caused an acute stab of pleasure that left ripples of shivery sensations in its wake. She gasped and dug her fingernails into his shoulders, astonished.

He chuckled softly. Roughly.

"That was something, wasn't it? Perhaps we're being spared by the gods. If I had met you any other time, I would chain you to my bed forever," he threatened.

If only...

He moved again, making all of her sing. She clutched at him, trying to make sense of the sensations overtaking her, but it was far too engulfing. She found it impossible to think, only feel. There was a sting and heat and a kind of tension she had never experienced. She wanted to absorb herself into his skin, but there were so many barriers. All she could do was hang on as he cast off restraint and moved with more purpose. Their breaths grew more jagged, each stroke making her fight cries of increasing pleasure.

She didn't know how to communicate to him how dazzling and wonderful this was except to allow animal instinct to overtake her. She licked his throat and offered her hips for the driving force of his. She stroked her hands beneath his shirt against his lower back, encouraging his rough possession while she brazenly sucked at his bottom lip.

And just when she thought she couldn't rise one more degree of arousal, couldn't take one more second of this onslaught of sensation, nature took over again and her climax swept her up into the heavens above them.

He stiffened, tightened his grip on her and stopped breathing exactly as she did. Then he shuddered and ragged cries sounded against her neck while she opened her mouth in a silent scream, all of her world shattering around her, leaving her destroyed, never to be the same again.

Angelo touched a kiss to the top of her spine as he finished zipping her dress.

She let her hair fall and adjusted her mask as she turned to offer her mouth to his.

He took a final, lingering taste of her, trying to memorize the exact plump shape of her lips with the sweep of his tongue. When he drew back, he searched through the faint light cast by the party on the far side of the house, aware that he would spend the rest of his life looking for this pointed chin, that wide mouth and elegant forehead framed by this fall of dark hair.

Against his better judgment, he almost asked for her name, but she spoke first.

"We should get back." There was a creak of misery in her voice. She caught at his hand and pressed his knuckles to the hot pulse in her throat. "Thank you."

"Thank *you*."

It was an impossible situation. He wasn't supposed to be here. And much as he was enthralled by her sexually, he didn't know if he could trust her. It was best to leave this as a torrid, dream-like encounter.

"I'll go first and distract the guards. They won't be alarmed I've been up here."

"Because you're a woman?" Females could be treacherous. His grandmother had been one of the cruelest. But the guards might be tempted to frisk him if they caught him leaving a private area. He appreciated her giving him a clear path of escape.

"Until we meet again," he said as he adjusted his mask and hat.

"In another life," she said with a melancholy pang in her voice, turning away to begin her descent.

With one ear cocked for voices or a return of her footsteps, he moved into the corner of the patio. He flicked on his cell phone for light and noted that, aside from a thorough cleaning of the moss that took root every winter, the new owners had left the bricks exactly as he remembered them. He only had to move a planter of dormant flowers to expose the familiar, hexagonal brick beneath. He pried it up with the blade of his pocketknife and shone a light in to check for vermin or prevent a nasty spider bite.

The space was dry and empty—except for the tobacco tin. He drew it out and opened it long enough to see the glitter of jewels and the head of a small plastic wolf—one of his own treasures tucked away so his brothers wouldn't steal it, melt it, or otherwise use it to torment him.

In the distance, the music stopped. A male voice said something about costume judging.

With a well-practiced move, Angelo smoothly set the brick back into place. He slid the tin into the pocket of his cloak as he straightened.

Moments later, as he slipped down the stairs and past the sign that read Family Only, his brain quit replaying the most exquisite lovemaking of his life and made the connection.

The guards wouldn't be alarmed at her presence in a private area *because she was family.*

He swallowed an imprecation and waited to look at his phone until he had melted past the party perimeter and hiked through the orange grove to his car. It took two swipes to bring up a photo of the new owner of the estate, Rico Montero. Another swipe and there was Rico's sister, Pia.

Angelo knew that pillowy bottom lip. Intimately. He knew how her vanilla skin tasted. The silk of her hair against his brow still tickled him with sensual memory.

His lover wasn't a cast-off mistress of a playboy or a daughter of a businessman trying to elevate her circumstances. Her forlorn, *It's a memory. A good one* had made him think she lived some sort of deprived existence, but how rough could her life be?

He knew women could be in an abusive situation without it being apparent to the world, but Pia held a lot of aces. She earned dividends from the family corporation run by her brothers, lived in a small but elegant house in a very exclusive neighborhood. Her social media page was covered in photos of exotic landscapes.

She came from a family exactly like Angelo's father and brothers—titled and entitled. Angelo already knew the Montero brothers' scandalous affairs with vulnerable women, a PA and a housemaid, had been papered over with quickie marriages, the Duque's political career and the family's positions of power and wealth left unscathed.

As for Pia, her fine-boned features were even more patrician and elegant without the mask. She was photographed at the occasional gala, her smiles unapproachable, her poses as deliberately nonchalant as a fashion model showing off a runway gown.

That lissome figure had been delightfully supple. He experienced a latent pulse of heat recalling the feel of her writhing beneath him, but she wasn't his type. He preferred bubbly, outgoing women with real jobs. Ones whose motives and interest in him were crystal clear. He had learned the hard way that his wealth made him a target for the decidedly mercenary members of either sex.

He threw his phone onto the passenger seat and pulled away, disgusted with himself for giving in to impulse with someone so *wrong*.

It wasn't the snobbery of an upstart toward the bastion of old money or the petulance of being shut out of that privileged life and therefore wanting to tear it down. His contempt went far deeper. Someone must have known what had gone on in that cottage on the Gomez estate all those years ago, but they had chosen to ignore it. They had continued associating with monsters, enabling Angelo's father and brothers to enjoy a level of status they had no right to. His father should have been jailed and, when the old baron died, Angelo should have received a portion of his estate.

Despite being fourteen and away at boarding school, still grieving his mother's suicide, Angelo had been abandoned and turned onto the street. Angelo was convinced his brothers had deliberately burned down his mother's cottage, both for the insurance money and to prevent him returning to live there.

Angelo had scrambled to survive and if his brothers had left him to make his new life, he might have left them to living their old one. Instead, when they realized a cache of jewelry was missing, they had come after Angelo, accusing him and his mother of theft.

Given the way Angelo had been living, his brothers had believed him when he'd said he didn't have anything but the shirt on his back, but they had been convinced he knew where the jewelry was hidden.

As he proved tonight, Angelo had had a very good idea where his mother had buried the treasure, but no amount of being knocked around or intimidated had got that secret out of him. Instead, he had bit his split lip and resolved to destroy them, no matter how long it took.

Angelo could have come forward as the baron's bastard anytime in the last decade and a half, demanding his share of their father's estate through legal channels. Aside from having no desire to acknowledge that half of his DNA, it would have been expensive. Until the last few years, he hadn't been able to afford that sort of fight. It also would have turned his mother's anguish into nothing more than sordid muckraking in the press. He couldn't do that to her memory.

Besides, he had perversely enjoyed his brothers' fruitless search. If they had ever managed to unearth the jewels, he would have staked his claim. It was, after all, compensation his mother had taken with the knowledge she would never be left anything by Angelo's father beyond the use of a run-down cottage.

As far as Angelo was concerned, this tin of jewelry was his inheritance, fair and square.

He might have let his brothers go to their graves thinking the fortune well and truly lost if the masquerade ball hadn't presented such a perfect opportunity to collect it. If they hadn't sold the estate in such an underhanded deal and put his mother up for auction as if they were philanthropists for doing so…

They made him sick.

As he reached the field where his helicopter waited and climbed aboard with the weight of the tin in the pocket of his cloak, he considered when and how he would reveal to them that he did indeed possess what his mother had taken.

He wanted them in the weakest possible position, fully on the ropes, when he dealt this blow. Currently, they were still living off the proceeds of selling the estate to Rico Montero. Those funds would run out quickly, given Darius's gambling habits and Tomas's recent divorce. When they began to look hungry, Angelo would tip his hand.

It would drive them crazy. They would want to stake a claim, but doing so would force them to admit their family connection. They would have to admit how Angelo had come to exist and how his mother had got her hands on these diamonds and pearls.

Angelo would enjoy seeing them twist and turn against each other when that happened.

Like every nearly perfect caper, however, there was one witness who could blow the whole thing apart. Pia Montero.

She could place Angelo on the estate this evening. *If* she discovered who he was.

CHAPTER THREE

Six weeks later...

"WOULD YOU EXCUSE me a moment?" Pia said to her mother and Sebastián.

She didn't wait for her mother's permission or even glance to read what was likely an expression of disapproval. Her mother probably thought she was giving in to nerves, but Pia didn't care. She rose abruptly from the table and hurried to the toilet, where she lost every bite of the lunch she'd just eaten.

What on earth?

She wrung out a cloth and dabbed the perspiration from her wan face, shocked at the violence of her sudden illness. She'd been feeling odd all week, thinking she might be coming down with something, but she wasn't running a fever. She wouldn't dare accuse her mother's chef of anything less than using the freshest ingredients.

That left one obvious explanation before she went down the road of blood panels for exotic diseases.

But it was impossible. Her cycle had arrived the day after the masquerade ball. That ought to mean she wasn't pregnant. However, she realized with another roll of her tender stomach, she hadn't had a period since.

She couldn't be pregnant. *Couldn't*. Her mother's top tier, preferred choice for Pia's husband was in the dining room *right now*.

Think, she commanded her rattled brain, but she was too shaken and confused to even recall the dates and count the weeks properly.

She would put off reacting until she'd had it confirmed, she resolved. And she would take a test immediately.

She fought her composure back into place and returned to the dining room, but didn't retake her seat.

"I'm very sorry, Mother. I'm not feeling well and have to go home. May I call you later in the week to try this again, Sebastián?"

"Let me drive you home." He rose and set aside his napkin.

"I wouldn't want to impose. Mother's driver collected me. I'll have him run me back."

"Not at all. Thank you for lunch, La Reina. I look forward to seeing you again soon."

Pia's mother offered a meaningless smile and tilted her cheek for his air-kiss, but her glance toward Pia warned that a lecture would be forthcoming.

Moments later, Pia was beside Sebastián in his sports car.

Through lunch they had established that they both enjoyed scuba diving and beachcombing. He mostly worked out of Madrid, but had holidayed as a child in Valencia and would love to settle in this area once he was raising a family. His mother bred show dogs and he had taken a runt out of pity. He admitted to shamelessly spoiling it, which had made her mother smile stiffly while Pia had experienced a weak ray of optimism. Perhaps they could have a successful marriage after all.

"I'm very sorry," she apologized again. "I've been fighting something all week and should have canceled."

"In sickness and in health, right?" His bold calling out of today's less than subtle agenda made her stomach roil all over again. She couldn't lead him on if she was carrying another man's child.

"Sebastián, I think we should slow down."

He took his foot off the accelerator, instantly alert. "Oh, you mean—" He glanced at her, then made an abrupt turn into the parking lot of a mechanic's garage. "Did I say something to offend you?"

"Not at all. But something has come up that makes me think it's best if we put off discussions until the new year."

She tried for a polite smile and a poker face, but the longer he searched her expression, the more culpable she felt. She had to look away.

He cleared his throat, then spoke carefully. "It may surprise you to hear there are very few circumstances that would put me off what we're contemplating."

She licked her numb lips. "You don't realize how serious this circumstance might be."

"I think I do." He sounded so grave, so sure, she closed her eyes in dread.

Was it obvious? Would rumors circulate before she'd had a chance to confirm it? To discover the identity of the father and tell him?

For the first time since she was a child, her eyes grew hot and her throat swelled with the urge to cry.

"My family wants this alliance quite badly, Pia. I'm not without a checkered past that you would have to accept. Offering solutions and protection to one another is the point of this sort of partnership. Please talk to me about anything you view as an impediment to our moving forward. I'm quite sure I can accommodate you."

She wanted to goggle at him, unable to believe he would be willing to take on another man's child, but he reached across and squeezed her hand with reassurance.

She swallowed and found a faint smile. "Let me call you later in the week, after I've had time to think some things through."

"Of course."

He took her home, but she only stayed long enough to double-check her dates and call her sister-in-law.

An hour later, she was halfway up the coast. She stopped at a village market and bought an off-the-shelf pregnancy test, took it into a service station restroom and sat in her car a long time afterward, absorbing the fact that she was carrying a baby.

The baby of a man she didn't know. At all.

She was a smart, responsible woman. How could she have been so careless?

She didn't let herself dwell on the fact that both her brothers had been through this. That maybe some dark and desperate part of her had sabotaged herself into this position, hoping to find a version of the happiness Cesar and Rico had both found.

That sort of thinking was beyond illogical. It was self-destructive.

And genuinely impossible when she didn't even know her lover's name.

But that was why she wanted to see Poppy.

She put her car in Drive and returned to the scene of the crime.

* * *

Half an hour of mutual admiration with her two-year-old niece restored a little of Pia's equilibrium.

Despite the circumstances, she looked forward to motherhood, she realized with a small bubble of optimism. She wouldn't be a distant, coldly practical woman like her mother, even though she already knew La Reina would judge her harshly for showing affection toward her child. She scolded Sorcha and Poppy for it often and Pia could still hear her mother rebuking her own nanny for hugging her.

Don't spoil her. She'll become dependent.

Yes, it must have been the early hugs, not the lack of them thereafter that had turned Pia into the withdrawn, insecure, social-phobic person that she was.

"Will you go with Nanny while I talk to your *mamà*?" Pia asked Lily.

Lily gave Pia's neck a fierce hug and said, "I yuv you," in English, bringing tears to Pia's eyes as the small girl waved bye-bye on her way out the door.

She would have that soon—someone who would say those words and mean it, every day.

"I think I got some good ones," Poppy said, setting aside her camera as they entered the lounge. "Thank you. I'm making an album for Rico for Christmas. I don't know what else to get the man who has everything."

Pia's brother Rico had been in a bad place after his brief first marriage had ended in tragedy. Then he had discovered that Poppy had had his daughter in secret. Since locating them, he'd become more like the brother Pia recollected from her earliest years, before he left for school; the one who was patient and protective, willing to sit with an arm around her so she felt safe as she watched an evil witch in a children's movie.

"Coffee? Wine?" Poppy offered.

Pia faltered as she realized she was off alcohol and likely coffee, as well. Good thing she had barely touched what her mother had served.

"I came from lunch at Mother's. Nothing for now, thank you."

"Did she say something about the auction? Is that why you're here?" Poppy winced as she sat. "When you said you wanted to ask me about it, I thought you wanted the auctioneer's card." She picked it up from a side table. "Am I in trouble?"

"No. But I would like that, if you don't mind." Pia pocketed the card. "No, Mother is quite pleased you broke records on the fund-raising, even if she doesn't agree with your methods."

"Because of the painting," Poppy said heavily, shoulders slumping.

"I meant the costumes. Mother thinks that sort of thing is a gimmick. What are you talking about? Which painting?"

"The one from the attic. The young woman. She's the reason I raised so much. The bidder paid a ridiculous sum."

"I remember it. Who bought it?" She held her breath.

"That's the trouble. I don't *know*."

"The auctioneer didn't tell you?"

"Wouldn't," Poppy said flatly. "I *tried*. The previous owners were upset and wanted to know."

"Baron Gomez?"

"And his brother, yes. Do you know them?"

"Only vaguely by reputation." Not a good one. The

family had fallen on hard times after the previous baron's death. One brother was a womanizer, the other a gambler. Neither was particularly adept at business. Both were too old to be her mystery man and too young to have fathered him. "Why were they upset?"

"Good question! They sold us the property as is, with all sorts of furniture and other items left behind. When I found the painting in the attic, I thought it was rather good so I called the family as a courtesy, to be sure they wouldn't mind my auctioning it for the fund-raiser."

"Did they say who she was?"

"Their stepsister, the daughter of their father's second wife. She lived in a cottage at the corner of the property. It burned down after she died. She must have passed at a young age. She looks about fifteen in the portrait and it was painted thirty years ago. In any case, the new baron struck me as rather callous when he laughed and said, 'Sure, see what you can get for her.'"

"Was he at the ball?"

"They declined the invitation. But he asked me to note that he had donated the painting."

Pia wanted to roll her eyes at the man's "generosity," but was too well-bred.

"I should have told Rico that something felt off, but I thought I was being sensitive."

"Why? What happened?"

"The painting went for a hundred thousand euros! Someone quadrupled the final bid to ensure they would get it."

Pia hadn't known it had gone for *that* much. "What was the painting assessed at?"

"Five hundred euros."

"I see." She didn't. At all. But it was nice to know her baby's father had a generous streak.

"I *know.* I wanted to thank him personally, but the auctioneer said the purchaser specifically requested I send my thank-you to the Gomez family for donating it and that I should tell them how much I got for it. Your mother said it was crass to mention the figure, but that since it was such a substantial donation I should honor his wishes." Poppy's eyes went wide again. "Huge mistake."

"Why?"

"For starters, I don't think the Gomez family would have let me sell it if they'd realized I would get that sort of money for it. First the younger one, Darius, called me and went *crazy.* He was swearing and making threats, trying to get me to tell him who bought the painting. He wouldn't believe I didn't know. I was upset and told Rico. He called the older one and tore *such* a strip off him. My Spanish vocabulary was deeply enriched, let me tell you." Poppy was making light of it, but Pia could tell she was still unsettled.

"I wonder if the purchaser knew what kind of hornet's nest he was stirring up," Pia said, even though she instinctively knew he must have. The man she'd met had seemed extremely sure of himself.

"I'm quite sure I was pushed into the middle of a battlefield. When Rico hung up, he asked if someone named Angelo Navarro had been on the guest list. I guess that was the name of the person the Gomez brothers suspected was behind the purchase. I checked and he wasn't on it, but anyone could have placed that bid on his behalf."

I was never here.

A cold prickle left all the hairs on Pia's body standing on end.

"Angelo Navarro," she murmured. "Do you know who he is?"

"Rico did some research. He's a tech billionaire who came up *very* recently. Quite predatory. He's targeting the Gomez interests… 'Picking off the low-hanging fruit,' Rico said. Rico told your mother's assistant to bar all of them from any future events. I didn't realize there was a central registry for offenders." Poppy chuckled dryly.

"Sorcha set it up when she was Cesar's PA," Pia recalled, trying to hide her shock and alarm. "It's the kiss of death." A firmly closed door by the Monteros was a firmly closed door against the social and financial advantages that came from circulating in Spain's wealthiest circles.

Pia had presumed that her baby's father had been an invited guest to the ball and therefore had been vetted for casual association. Given his willingness to pay so much for the painting, he had to be wealthy. That meant he might not be her mother's first choice, but he was of suitable rank and standing that he would be accepted despite the unconventional circumstances.

Instead, he was an outsider who'd just been blacklisted.

"So what are you auctioning?" Poppy asked.

"Pardon? Oh." Pia wasn't one to lie. She rarely got herself into a situation where it was necessary, only the occasional prevarication over whether a meal had been enjoyed or a dress suited. "I have a few art pieces I want to place in their next catalog," she hedged. "My life will change as my academic career ends."

As she sat with her upturned hands stacked in her lap, cupping the air where her belly would swell in a few months, she debated whether to confide fully in Poppy. Poppy had been in nearly this exact position when she'd been pregnant with Lily.

But Pia had learned a long time ago that whining about a problem didn't solve it. Obstacles weren't to be mentioned until she had formulated a plan to overcome them—at which point her solution would be critiqued for merit and edited as necessary.

She wanted to cry, but rose instead.

"It's growing late. I'd rather not drive in the dark. Would you mind not mentioning to Mother that I came out today? I cut our lunch short, said I wasn't feeling well."

"The lunch with…?" Poppy gave a little sigh as she rose. "Pia, I don't want to speak out of turn, but are you sure an arranged marriage is right for you? Look at your brothers."

Pia couldn't help her small snort of irony.

"Please don't take offense, Poppy, but yes. Look at them. When Cesar married Sorcha, he threw over a long-standing agreement that would have paid a family debt." That relationship was in tatters and so was the one from Rico's first marriage, not that she had the poor taste to mention it, but everything Rico should have gained from that marriage had since been lost when it was discovered he had had Lily with Poppy.

Poppy paled anyway, forcing Pia to do something completely uncharacteristic and reach out to squeeze Poppy's arm.

"I consider both of you dear friends. Your children are a gift," Pia told her sincerely. "I'm pleased my brothers are in fulfilling relationships, but you've seen enough of our family's inner workings to understand the expectations placed upon all of us. On me to be the last bastion of rational behavior. I *have* to make a good marriage or brand the Monteros as impulsive and inconstant forever."

"You're expected to pay the price for our happiness?" Poppy asked. "That's not fair. Or rational."

"Perhaps not." But she wasn't supposed to bring further detriments to the table, either. "I'm not like my brothers, Poppy. I'm not built to go against the grain." One wild night notwithstanding.

"Women never are," Poppy said with a spark of defiance. "I didn't tell Rico about Lily for a lot of reasons, but deep down I know fear was the biggest thing that held me back. This…?" She waved at the mansion she had restored with impeccable taste. "Fitting into your world has been hard and terrifying and I know I'm making mistakes every single day. But it's worth pushing myself to be more than I ever imagined I could be to have what I have with Rico. My only regret is that I didn't tell him sooner, so we could have been happier sooner."

Pia forced a careless laugh. "Happiness is fleeting, Poppy." Where had she heard that before?

"I mean that we could have been together sooner. In love sooner. Which makes us happy." Poppy frowned with concern. "I know you weren't raised to expect a marriage based on love, but it is possible to find it, Pia. Do you want to be married to someone else when you do?"

"Food for thought," Pia said to end a discussion that

was a lot more complex than Poppy realized. "I'll see you at Christmas."

But she drove home with white knuckles, mind churning over words that had struck particularly deep.

My only regret is that I didn't tell him sooner.

CHAPTER FOUR

ANGELO HAD READ the note so many times in the three days since he'd received it that he'd memorized it. Nevertheless, he read it again.

> Señor Navarro,
> We met at my brother's gala in mid-October. Would you have time for a brief conversation?
> If your preference is the same as you stated at our previous meeting, I will respect your wishes and you won't hear from me again.
> My contact details are below.
> Sincerely,
> Pia Montero, MSc.

No hint of the passion that had exploded between them. In fact, if he were to pick up this card from a desk or mantel, he wouldn't have any sense that something intimate had occurred between the parties concerned. It came off as a desire to reopen a business discussion, little more.

Which made him suspicious. Was she trying to draw him out? How closely linked was she to Tomas and Darius? Had she confirmed to them that Angelo had been on the former Gomez estate that night?

Angelo had no doubt that was how she'd learned his name. His brothers had thought they could disrespect and discard his mother one more time, but Angelo had ensured their disregard backfired.

He glanced at the painting of his mother. Freshly cleaned and newly framed, it hung over the safe that held the jewelry he had recovered. He had thought the portrait lost in the cottage fire. He would have paid any amount for it, but what made its acquisition truly priceless was the fact his brothers hadn't received a penny from his purchase. Given what he'd heard from the auction house, they were incensed they hadn't thought to extort him for it themselves.

As far as they knew, however, an agent had obtained it for him. They had no proof he'd been at the estate in person.

Unless Pia had said something.

This sudden communication from her could be a trick to force his admission that he'd been there that night.

Given that possibility, Angelo had taken the precaution of having her properly investigated, but there was little in the report that he hadn't read online.

Her age or educational history had to be misstated. Only a genius could earn a master's degree in environmental science before she'd turned twenty-one, after a double major in biology and chemistry and a minor in sociology. Three short years later, she was about to defend a dissertation analyzing polymer deterioration on barnacles and bivalves.

That was tomorrow, Angelo noted with a glance at his calendar icon.

This report wasn't telling him what he really wanted

to know: Why was she contacting him *now*? Had it taken her that long to find him?

Even more salient, why had she made love with a stranger that night? *That* question had been driving him mad.

Some people enjoyed conquests. Angelo's father and brother, for instance. He would normally think her targeting him had been a move from a fortune hunter, but aside from her own healthy coffers, he couldn't fathom how she had known he would meet her on that rooftop.

She had compromised him once he was there, though. The fact he'd given in to impulse and dallied with her, putting himself in real danger of being caught with his pants down, made her a weakness he should avoid.

He still didn't understand why he'd been so compelled by her. The high of his caper? The erotic circumstances of intimacy with a stranger? The sexy feel of his costume?

He sneered at himself and went back to scrolling through the report, finally seeing something new—speculation that she was in the early phases of finding a husband. Only *titled* bachelors with fortunes and impeccable reputations need apply.

Angelo pushed away from his desk, glad his damned brothers weren't on the shortlist, but it still disgusted him. If she was shopping for a husband, this card of hers wasn't an invitation to rekindle things. She *had* to be working with his brothers.

Nauseated, he picked up the note and studied her clean, level script. It would be easy to send word that she was mistaken; they had never met.

If she was operating on their behalf, however, it was exactly the closing of ranks and exertion of influence that had allowed his father to victimize his mother without consequence. He wouldn't let any of them get away with that again.

He messaged his pilot to ready his jet for Valencia.

Over the years, Pia had taken classes in public speaking and presenting. She had even gritted her teeth through an improvisation class to learn how to roll with the unexpected. Nothing had fully extinguished her discomfort in speaking to a group, but she had developed coping techniques, like picking out one or two unthreatening faces and pretending the rest didn't exist.

As for presenting and defending her material, her expertise in that had been honed during every family dinner from the moment she had joined her parents in their dining room at eleven. Speak clearly. Make her point in as few words as possible. Back up her position with supporting facts when required. Emotions proved nothing. Move on.

Since she didn't expect her audience to consist of more than the committee, the chair, her mentor and a few fellow students monitoring the procedure as they prepared for their own defense, she presented her dissertation in a small conference room off the university's faculty lounge.

After she attached her laptop to the projector, the chair introduced her.

"Thank you." She began her prepared remarks with a surface smile toward the committee and swept it around the room to find her two receptive faces.

Oh Dios.

Since visiting Poppy last week, Pia had quietly and obsessively researched Angelo Navarro. He claimed to be Spanish born, but had spent several years in America and now had homes around the globe. His childhood remained a mystery, but the story of how he'd made his recent fortune was everywhere.

After a few years in low-level jobs setting up video game equipment, he had hustled his way into promoting championships. That had led to partnering with tech entrepreneurs and gaming nerds to develop microprocessors for faster gaming. One of those patented chips had made its way into all the top smartphones and, three years ago, his team had accidentally created another chip that was now revolutionizing artificial intelligence.

He'd since begun offering high-speed cloud services that were expanding faster than a cumulonimbus on a humid summer's day and held untold reserves in cryptocurrencies. He probably buried gold bullion on his private tropical islands, too.

Pia had studied his photo, comparing it to her memories of a shadowed visage and a stubbled jawline beneath the edge of a mask, but in person he was even more fallen-angel-beautiful. His black hair gleamed. His eyes were utterly mesmerizing with their aquamarine color, crystal clear and piercing as he stared back at her, smug at having taken her so unaware.

She didn't need visual proof this was her mystery lover. She *felt* him. Felt the impact of being in his presence. Her heart hammered like a dull ax behind her breastbone—once, twice, three times. The careful tending of her diet to hold morning sickness at bay threatened to have been for naught.

Her falter lasted only those few heartbeats while she accepted that she was on a ship that had struck an iceberg. The galley was on fire and sharks were circling in the water. Panic was not an option. *Roll with it*.

She accepted the premise. This wasn't what she had expected or planned, but she wouldn't give him the satisfaction of rattling her. She made him one of her points of contact, using this opportunity to show herself as confident and knowledgeable because, in this narrow milieu, she was. She found a smile and made her purpose clear to everyone in the room as she began working through her presentation.

She compartmentalized, pulling a steel curtain across the messy gush of emotions that would need every type of mop, bandage and stitches later, when she was in a position to let down her guard and process what was happening.

The hour went by quickly. Suddenly she was shaking hands with the committee, having earned a doctorate and a grade of Excellent. She should expect a *cum laude* distinction, one informed her on the sly.

"I imagine your father will be very proud," her mentor said. "I would have thought your whole family would turn out for this."

Pia didn't mention that her father, a PhD himself, had a copy of her dissertation and would provide notes over Christmas with the expectation that she would incorporate them before final publication.

"They were tied up," Pia murmured as a tingle like radiant heat accosted the right side of her body.

He hadn't been wearing that cologne at the ball, but she recognized his scent all the same. Her throat flexed with the effort of maintaining her screen of calm as she turned to face him.

"Señor Navarro," she said, offering her hand.

"Angelo," he corrected. His clasp sent electricity through to her nerve endings as he took the liberty of greeting her with, "Pia."

"Thank you for coming," she said, desperately pretending they were strangers when all she could think about was how his weight had pressed her into the cushions while her entire being had seemed to fly.

"An informative talk." His eyes dazzled, yet pinned her in place. There was an air of aggression about him. Hostility even, in the way he had appeared like this, when she had literally been on the defensive. He seemed ready for a fight.

She had almost hoped he would leave her hanging after her note. She could have raised their baby with a clear conscience that she had tried to reach out while facing no interference from this unknown quantity.

As for what would happen if he did get in touch? She had tried to be realistic in her expectations, but Poppy had stuck a few delusions in her head. They seemed even more ridiculous as she faced such a daunting conversation with him. How had she even found the courage to say such frank things that night, let alone *do* the things they'd done? Wicked, intimate, carnal things that caused a blush to singe up from her throat into her cheeks.

"I need a moment," she said, voice straining.

She had already declined invitations for drinks, fearful her avoidance of a glass of champagne would make her condition obvious. She only had to say a last goodbye to the committee and, "Thank you again, but I must take this meeting."

Moments later, trembling inwardly, she led Angelo into the small office off the lab where she had worked the last three years when not in the field. She had already packed her things into a small cardboard box that sat on the chair. She was shifting from academic work to motherhood and marriage. That was all that was left of her former life.

Angelo seemed to eat up all the air as he closed the door behind him and looked at the empty bulletin board, the box of tissues and the well-used filing cabinet.

Pia started to move the box, but he said, "I'll stand."

He was taller than her, which made him well over six feet because she had the family's genetic disposition toward above average height. His air of watchfulness was intimidating, too, especially when he trained his laser-blue eyes on her again.

"Your card was very cryptic," he said.

She had spent a long time composing it, wondering why he had sneaked into the ball when he could easily have afforded the plate fee. At the time, she had thought his reason for being on the rooftop was exactly as he had explained it—curiosity. She had many more questions now, but didn't ask them yet. There was every chance she would never see him again after she told him why she had reached out.

Memories of their intimacy that night accosted her daily. It was top of mind now, which put her at a further disadvantage. Her only recourse was to do what she always did when she was uncomfortable—hide behind a curtain of reserve and speak her piece as matter-of-factly as possible.

"I'll come straight to the point." She hitched her hip on the edge of her desk and set her clammy palms together, affecting indifference while fighting to keep a quaver from her voice.

"I'm pregnant. It's yours."

* * *

Angelo took it like the sucker punch it was. He jerked his head back in reflex and physically rocked on his heels to recover his equilibrium.

"*That's* the reason you tracked me down?" What about his brothers?

"It seemed a significant enough reason to. And I know what you're going to say." Her lashes swept down and her mouth tightened. "I take full responsibility. I had what I thought was my cycle the next morning so I didn't consider taking any precautions. Feel free to mock my extensive education in biology."

The silence ticked out for a full minute as he absorbed news that changed his life. All he could wonder was why he wasn't *more* shocked.

Probably because he'd had sex without protection, same as she had. He didn't need anything but adolescent whispers to know this was exactly the consequence he had risked that night. Only an adolescent would behave that recklessly and *not* expect this outcome. He wasn't a teenager. He had known the risk he was taking and he'd done it anyway.

He didn't let himself ponder why.

He did try to manufacture skepticism and searched for reasons to be suspicious, but he couldn't even scrape up anger. They'd both been rash. This was the result.

"Who else knows?"

Her amber eyes flashed up, appalled. "No one." As if the thought of anyone knowing was far too compromising to admit.

He ignored the sting of that and tried very hard to imagine how she could have known he would be at the ball that night, let alone got to the rooftop ahead of him.

How could she have tricked him into unprotected sex so she could present him with this outcome, all in league with his brothers?

While managing to look hideously ashamed of it?

"It's been confirmed?"

"I have the result from the doctor's blood test." She started to reach for her purse, but he flicked a hand to indicate proof was unnecessary.

"I believe you." Given her discomfiture and the effort she'd made in tracking him down, he didn't think she would have told him unless she was sure it was his.

"I'm keeping it," she stated, voice cool. "I felt you should know, but this doesn't obligate you. I'm more than capable of supporting myself and the baby."

He searched her aloof veneer for the woman whose sexuality had been so tuned to his own they'd made a baby within minutes of meeting each other. Where was the goddess who'd set the bar so high he hadn't looked at another woman since?

"You're free to walk away if that's your preference." She glanced toward the door in what smacked of a dismissal.

"You think I would turn my back on my child?" That annoyed him. *His* progeny would never be something shameful to be shipped away to a penal colony of a boarding school, never recognized or provided for.

Her brows lifted with surprise. "Given our no-strings agreement, I anticipated your interest would be low to nonexistent."

"You anticipated wrong." His harsh tone made her stiffen, but she offered a jerky nod of acknowledgment.

"Very well. I suggest a trust. I'm in the fortunate position of being able to offer the child a comfortable upbringing without prevailing on you. It's really about what you consider a fair arrangement for the long term."

"Prevail," he insisted, his attention caught by her use of *the*. Not *our* child or even *my* child. *The* child. "I want and expect to be fully involved," he stated without equivocation.

"I see." Another blink as she absorbed that, cheeks hollow. "Well, we have time to discuss exactly how that will look. My wish is that we remain as discreet as possible while we work that out."

"You don't want anyone to know I fathered your child?" He wasn't shocked. She was a pedigree show dog caught in heat by an abandoned mongrel. He deliberately cultivated the image of a low-rank plebeian on an upwardly mobile trend as he infiltrated the establishment. All the better to annoy his noble brothers, but, "Why tell me at all if you want it to be our little secret?"

"I considered not telling you," she admitted frankly. Damn she was cool, perched so still on the edge of the desk, projecting patient tolerance of his presence before her. "But both of my brothers learned belatedly that they had children. I extrapolated that you might also feel cheated if such news came to light well after the fact. By being open with you, I expect we can make adjustments to accommodate our joint participation in the child's life while mitigating otherwise-damaging rumors."

There was the *the* again. He choked on a humorless laugh. "You sound like you're still pointing at data and graphs. Speak like a human."

She sat taller, her chin coming up, but there was a flash of irritation in her gaze that he found very satisfying. It meant he was getting under her skin.

"I'm too smart to be in this position. So are you. It

serves both of us to keep this as simple and quiet as possible."

"Consenting adults have affairs. Sometimes they slip up. This news won't hurt either of us." In fact, in the back of his brain, he was seeing how this new connection to the upper echelon of society could play out very much in his favor. Maybe that was her concern? "Are you trying to sideline me because of who I am? You don't want to be associated with me? Is that it?"

"I don't know who you are, do I?" she shot back. "I know your name. I know you sneak into parties to which you aren't invited, place wild bids on innocuous items, then lurk in private areas like a cat burglar, seducing strangers you catch unawares. Would you like to explain *any* of that?"

He narrowed his eyes. "I was under the impression the seduction was a mutual agreement."

She looked away and briefly touched the back of her neck before clasping her hands in her lap again. "It was," she allowed. "But it was impulsive and irresponsible."

"What happened to 'no regrets'?" What had happened to that introspective, intriguing woman he'd been so compelled to hold and touch and possess? He really had been on some kind of daredevil high that night. She *definitely* wasn't his type.

"Regret comes from wishing for a different outcome from the one you face," she said flatly. "The truth is, why you were there and who you are doesn't change the fact that I chose to behave in a way that will reflect badly on my family. I can't undo that, but for their sake, I intend to do everything possible to cast this in as least damaging a light as possible."

She really didn't know about his connection to the

Gomez family. She couldn't, or she would be hysterical right now.

As he was processing whether that was a good or bad thing, comprehension of what she was really saying dawned. With it came a flush of incendiary heat.

"You're getting married anyway." He was instantly and inexplicably furious.

She stilled, asking cautiously, "How do you know about that?"

"I know a lot of things." He didn't have a clue what was happening, not to himself or her. He moved forward on reflex until his knuckles were on the hard desktop on either side of her hips, the tip of his nose a hair's breadth from hers. "I'm not letting a stranger raise my baby."

"I can't help the state of our relationship, can I?" She set a hand on his chest, but didn't push him away. Her hand lifted slightly from his shirt, as if she found him too hot to touch. She wasn't as unaffected as she was trying to appear. Her breasts rose and fell unsteadily. Her eyes were huge, her pupils big enough to eclipse her golden irises.

"You know what I mean. I want my child, Pia. Full access, every single day."

It was fascinating to watch the burst of emotion behind her eyes, the light flush of pink beneath her skin while she fought to maintain her unaffected expression.

"Until July, I'm the only one with access. I suggest you take that time to reflect on whatever reasons you had for not wanting it known you were at my brother's that night. When you can react less emotionally, we can resume this discussion."

He was starting to see how she used fifty-dollar

words to put distance between herself and others, but he didn't back off one iota.

"You're carrying my heir. My *blood*. I will not walk away. Not now, not ever."

His words had an effect. He was close enough to see how deep they struck, causing both a spark of something that might have been gladness, but it was swallowed by her flinch of anguish.

"Angelo." It was the voice he'd heard on a darkened rooftop, ringing with *want-but-can't-have*. Her fingers curled into his shirt. "I told you that night I have obligations. They're due sooner than this baby."

From the moment he'd seen her in the conference room, he had itched to get her like this, close enough to feel the heat beneath the frost that encased her.

"You have obligations to me now."

She shook her head, but her pleading eyes slid to his mouth.

As he recognized the craving in her gaze, he experienced a rush of pure, carnal lust. Exactly the same spell that had gripped him that night. Her lips were right there, parted and shiny. Her breath moved across his own in shaken pants.

He wasn't the martyr she seemed determined to be. He gave them what they both wanted, cupped the side of her neck and took her mouth with his, reveling in the blast of heat and hunger. Lightning and craving hit him like whiskey. Her unique flavor and satin textures were all he would ever need in this lifetime.

She softened with surrender, exactly as she had that night, feeding his swell of powerful greed.

He held back nothing as he ravaged her mouth, slaking weeks of thirst. Her mouth moved under his, melting and clinging. Her arm went around his neck, pulling him down even as he firmed his arms around her, pulling her off the desk to stand against him.

She was on tiptoe, her body long and taut against his, exactly as he wanted her. This was what he had been looking for in his online searches. This tactile sensation of silk shifting against heat, a slender back and the small, firm lobe of her butt cheek in his hand; the crush of her breasts to his chest and her thick hair in his fist, the citrus scent and the tentative greeting of her tongue when he claimed her mouth with a sweep of his.

A sudden thump against the window had him jerking his head up, his arms shifting to form a protective shelter around her.

Outside, a young man stooped to pick up a yellow disk and laughed as he walked away, thumbing toward the window as he called out, "People are making out in there."

Pia made a noise of anguish and slid out of his arms, took two steps away and kept her back to the window. She hung her face in her hands. "Did he recognize me?"

"What if he did? We were only kissing."

She shot him a stark look and he had to agree. Given the pace of their last kiss, they would have been making love very soon. His body was starving to have her beneath him. He was tense and aching, restless as an animal on the hunt. Twitching like a creature with the scent of his mate in his nostrils.

"We can't do this." She plucked a fawn-colored overcoat off a hook.

"Not here," he agreed, taking the coat.

She hesitated, then let him hold it for her. She shrugged

into it as though pulling on her composure, the sensual woman of moments ago gone.

What the hell?

She gathered her purse and started to shoulder a laptop bag. He lifted the cushioned strap off her shoulder and dragged it free of her arm, partly out of chivalry, partly to catch the shift of awareness that flickered in her eyes before she lowered her lashes and stepped away.

Interesting.

He looped the bag onto his own shoulder, then brushed aside her attempt to pick up the cardboard box. He glanced at the contents: notebooks and screen cleaner, a nameplate and a framed certificate of her master's degree. He realized she was permanently vacating this office and he was suddenly reminded why.

"We should go for dinner. To celebrate."

"Celebrate?" She was so taken aback that she stumbled in retreat.

Amusement gathered across his cheekbones. "Your doctorate," he clarified, adding dryly, "The baby, too, I suppose."

He hadn't fully processed her pregnancy. He would become a father next summer. Was it cause for champagne? It wasn't cause for anything less, he decided.

"We don't celebrate things like that," she said stiffly, buttoning her overcoat. "Today was a completion point in exercising my academic potential, nothing more. Given this pregnancy wasn't planned, I wouldn't call it an achievement of remarkable note, either."

Wow. Was she really made of ice or was her indifference a defense mechanism?

He pressed his hand over the seam of the door before she could open it.

She released the knob and pivoted to face him, lifting her chin. She was a nice height. He wanted to kiss her again. Press her into that door and make love to her against it. Drain the tension from both of them so they could talk without every word feeling like a grenade lobbing sexual anticipation.

He resisted. He didn't even brush away the strand of hair caught on her eyelashes even though his fingertips tingled in anticipation of her warm, downy skin.

"This baby is a remarkable enough achievement that I won't let another man take credit for it." It was vow and warning combined. "*I* will be Papà. No one else. So you and I will celebrate our engagement."

She displayed no reaction beyond a tremble of her eyelids and a fade of color from her smooth complexion and soft pink lips. After a long, tense moment she swallowed.

"How long have you known who I was?" she asked.

"I guessed your identity before I was off the property."

"And you waited until *I* found *you* before you came to see me. Until I told you I was pregnant before you asked me to dinner. I bring more to a marriage than a womb, Angelo. I expect my future husband to want and value *me*. So, no," she said firmly. Frigidly. "I will not marry you."

"Oh, *querida*, you're right that you don't know me. You shouldn't have revealed your deepest fear." He enjoyed the subtle confusion of latent desire and wariness that came over her as he bent his elbow, looming as though he would kiss her again. "Marry me or I'll go straight to the press with a tell-all."

CHAPTER FIVE

DEALING WITH THIS man was like having a slippery grip on a slingshot aimed into her own face. He unsettled her. Worse, his kiss had completely undermined the control she needed to project. She was doing her best to pretend she'd already forgotten it, but he was *impossible*.

She would love to go home and regroup, but there was no telling if he was serious about spilling their story or not.

"Dinner it is, then." It was a basic negotiation tactic she had learned from dealing with her parents. Concede to something minor to buy time to work on her counter-argument. "Where shall I meet you?"

"We'll go in your car. I had my driver drop me."

Her hatchback was perfectly serviceable for carrying rain gear and collection buckets to beaches. It achieved great mileage, was comfortable on long treks and slipped easily into four-wheel drive on a muddy track.

Apparently Angelo expected something sleeker and sexier. He looked at her with disbelief. "This is your car?"

She beeped the fob to prove it.

He stole the key and adjusted her seat as he climbed behind the wheel.

With Angelo's attention on traffic, she brooded on

the fact he had known who she was all this time and hadn't bothered to get in touch. His indifference hurt to the point her insides felt raw.

Her brothers were so happy, so irrevocably in love, she had allowed herself to entertain, just for a brief second, that she might trip into something like it for herself, even though she knew it was unrealistic, especially with a man she barely knew.

After days of mulling it over, however, she had decided to risk learning whether she and Angelo had anything beyond lust between them.

The lust was in full force. She was still reeling from their kiss. And his bold personality was as overwhelming as she had recalled.

She, however, had hardly proved herself to be a thrill a minute, droning on with her dissertation and having to be told to "talk like a human." She had shown herself to be as boring as every man had ever judged her to be, so it was hardly a shock that he wasn't interested in anything but the baby and perhaps another quickie if she was going to be easy about it.

She felt stupid for imagining he had been searching for her and might have welcomed the arrival of her card. It wasn't like her to be naive and romantic. Life was a lot less hurtful when she kept her expectations low, calculated odds and formulated logical steps to achieve her goals. Investing hope and yearning for emotional regard only courted crushing disappointment. *She knew that*.

Which was what she was experiencing right now, her heart sitting under a thorny weight as she revisited his marriage proposal based solely on the fact she was pregnant with his child.

She had never expected to marry for love, but she

did expect to be a full partner with her husband. She brought wealth, reputation, intelligence and practicality to a relationship. She was well-groomed, articulate, and spoke several languages. She might not enjoy being the center of attention, but she could lead a team, run a household and organize the hell out of just about anything. She was a decent sketch artist and played guitar on beaches if someone else wanted to sing.

Sensible, gallant Sebastián would appreciate all of that and bring his own quiet strengths and runt puppies to the relationship.

While unpredictable, Angelo was all threats and demands and brain-erasing passion.

She hadn't expected that. Not the kiss or the conflagration that had engulfed her the night of the ball.

Having given in to that once was causing a huge detour in her carefully mapped life. She couldn't let him shake her off her footing any more than he already had.

Yet here she was, in the passenger seat of her own car, arriving where he had driven her. He handed her keys to a valet outside a newly built beachfront hotel with old-world wedding cake architecture.

She scraped herself together and asked facetiously, "This is your home?"

"I bought the chain last year and keep a suite in each of them."

The *one* time she resorted to sarcasm and all she got out of it was his *gotcha* smirk for her trouble.

"I thought your focus was electronics," she said in a not so subtle, *I know things, too* way.

"I've reached a level of success that forces me to diversify."

Find places to park his money, he meant. She tried not

to be impressed. She came from money, but his story was the sort of rags-to-riches tale she couldn't help admire.

"We're going for dinner, aren't we?" she asked as he steered her from the entrance to the restaurant and toward the elevators.

"You led me to believe you didn't want us to be spotted together."

Moments later, he let her into a tower penthouse decorated in muted tones of gray and ivory. There was a full galley kitchen, a master and a smaller bedroom, a dining area, a workspace and a lounge. Two-story windows overlooked a beach populated with pale, English travelers seeking winter sun.

Pia stood at the windows and linked her fingers casually when she actually wanted to clutch her elbows and hug herself. She didn't enjoy confrontation, but she knew how to frame a dispute and debate it calmly and constructively.

"Marriage isn't possible, Angelo. Let's take that off the table and discuss how to make shared custody work." She hadn't even begun to imagine that possibility.

"It won't. We're marrying."

Apparently he was less versed in "discussing." She bit back a sigh.

"If you think threatening a scandal will coerce me, you're wrong. I'd prefer to avoid one, but we are an extremely formidable family." She knew her parents would support her in every outward way. She would just have to suffer the rest of her life with the unrelenting knowledge that they'd *had* to. "You'll fare better working with us, rather than against us, trust me."

"First of all, I don't. Trust you, I mean." He came to

stand next to her, hands pushed loosely into his trouser pockets, shoulders relaxed.

She had a feeling he genuinely was at ease while she was only pretending to be.

"Secondly, if you think threats of ruin will scare *me*, you're wrong. Not because I think I'm impervious, but because I'm not afraid to lose everything I own to get something if I want it badly enough." He turned his head. He was both laughing at her and deadly serious. "Can you and your formidable family say the same?"

Her stomach lurched. "There are no winners in war."

"Then don't start one."

She looked back toward the horizon, mind racing while her body tingled with awareness of his. "I didn't think one moment would risk my freedom," she said, voice steady even though she was caught somewhere between disbelief and despair.

"Marrying a man your mother chooses for you is freedom?"

"Marrying you because you decree it certainly isn't," she shot back.

"I want to marry so our child will have immediate access to both its parents. What is your vision of parenthood? An army of nannies and off to boarding school the moment you can?" he guessed scathingly.

"No." It came out reflexively because it was the last thing she would do to her child, not after having experienced exactly that mass production approach to child rearing. "The child won't go away to school until he or she is old enough to make an informed decision about the benefits and drawbacks." She would be hands-on, hugging and steadying and probably smothering, but she would work on not being too helicptery.

"Why do you say it like that? 'The child.' Why isn't it *our* baby?"

"He or she is not an object we own. Further, if I say 'my' baby, it implies that I'm excluding you from the decision-making process. If I say 'our' it implies we're a couple. 'The' is a neutral acknowledgment that *the* child is a person in his or her own right for whom we are charged with making decisions that affect his or her entire life."

He shook his head in bemusement. "You can take the scientist out of the lab…"

His chide shouldn't have felt like such an indictment, but it did. She refused to flinch, though, only said, "I don't plan on experimenting on *any* child, particularly my own. Marriage to a stranger comes with too many uncontrolled variables. There is little stigma these days in having unmarried or separated parents so I see no compelling reason to marry."

"Every relationship requires time to get to know the other person. Those variables can be identified and labeled and filed into one of your folders however you see fit. The only reason I will accept for you refusing to marry is that you are in love with someone else. Are you?" His voice took on a lethal note that made her stomach wobble.

"No. But I'm not in love with you, either."

"Yet," he shot back with a wicked grin.

Her heart lurched and she looked away, fearful he would read into her physical infatuation and maybe even glimpse how reluctantly fascinated she still was with him, standing there countering her arguments in sabre-like flourishes of sharp and steely words. She couldn't marry that!

Yet every night since meeting him, she had gone to sleep wondering about him, imagining things having gone a different way. Wishing. Yearning.

It was a passing phase. *Por favor, Dios.*

"Love is largely a romantic notion. I'm not a romantic." She wasn't allowed to be.

"I noticed," he said pithily.

She hid her flinch.

"The only reason you're balking at marriage is because your parents expect you to marry a milquetoast from a 'good' family with old money. I happen to be a reverse snob who feels nothing but disdain for those who inherit their wealth instead of earning it. But I'm willing to overlook that flaw in you."

So magnanimous.

"Remind me to show you what I've earned from my patents in biofuels and recycling of recovered plastics." She showed him what disdain looked like. Her mother's blithe smile, right here, on her face. "My parents expect me to marry someone with an unblemished background who complements our business interests, yes. *I* expect to marry someone who shares my values and supports my aspirations, whether that be motherhood or scientific research."

She didn't know where that last bit had come from. She had resigned herself to giving up that part of her life and contributing to the betterment of mankind through—*blech*—charity galas and the patronage of scientists who were allowed to pursue their passion.

"I don't care how many microscopes you buy as long as you're there when *our child* gets a ribbon at school. Which reminds me. Why weren't any of your family at your thing today?" He waved a hand toward the dusk closing in beyond the windows. "A PhD is a big deal, isn't it?"

"Not in my family." It was more the price of membership. "It's something we're capable of, so we do it."

"Everyone in your family has a doctorate? Attained at twenty-four?"

"My father was twenty-five." She looked at her nails. "My brothers were both twenty-six." And yes, she had pushed herself to squeak hers in before her birthday next month. It was the bargain she'd struck with her mother, to get it finished early so she could marry before her eggs went stale. She was quite proud of the accomplishment, but knew better than to expect a fanfare for it. It was enough to know privately that she had done better than everyone else.

"Your mother…?"

"Married a scientist so she doesn't have to be one."

"Ah. But you'd like to continue to be one."

"Yes," she said with growing certainty. "I've allocated the next few years to marriage and starting a family—"

"Such an overachiever, getting it all done in one day."

Hilarious.

"I should probably disclose, I don't possess a sense of humor. Dare I hope it's a flaw that is a deal breaker?"

His mouth twitched. "I'm just as happy laughing *at* as *with*."

She looked away, refusing to smile, even though she kind of wanted to sputter out a chuckle. The stakes were far too high, though.

"What's *your* vision of marriage, Angelo?" she asked, bracing herself as she pointed out, "You've had an hour to process this. I can't believe you're really prepared to marry a stranger."

"Believe it," he said implacably. "My father was garbage. He gave me twenty-three chromosomes and a lot of bad memories. I'll do better by my own child. A *lot* better. Full disclosure," he mocked, "I have a blemished background. Flaws you *will* have to overlook."

"What kind of blemish?" she asked warily.

Once again he gave her a look that was so penetrating it made her feel encased in ice, unable to move. After a charged moment, his expression changed from severe to dismissive. He contemplated the horizon.

"We'll discuss it another time."

Frustrated, she demanded, "When? After we're married?"

She hadn't meant to speak of it as though it was a fait accompli. She rubbed away the shiver his austere look had lifted on her arms.

"Look, I accept that you want to be a good father. For the baby's sake, I'm pleased. That still doesn't mean we should marry."

"Live together then? I'm not hung up on making it official."

"Oh? Why didn't you say so? I'll marry as planned and you can come live with us. One big happy family."

"You're right. Your sense of humor needs work."

"I wasn't joking."

"I'm a man with an open mind, Pia, but my tastes don't run to ménage."

"I'm still seeing a solution, not a problem."

"Let me spell it out. I'm possessive. Any man who lives with us will be skimming the pool. You and I will share one bed."

"Optimistic, too."

"You don't want to sleep with me?" He hitched his shoulder against the window so he was facing her.

"Not something you hear often?" she inquired with a lift of her brows that she hoped conveyed disinterest.

"Not often, no. When I do, I accept it as the truth. Today…"

"Why would I lie?"

"I don't know." He studied her.

It took everything in her to hold his gaze and keep her uneasiness from reflecting in her face.

"How many contenders were there?" he finally asked.

"For what?"

"Paternity."

"Excuse me?" She was pretty sure she was insulted.

"You were right when you said we're both too smart to be in this position. The excitement of the moment got the better of us. I accept that. But in the cool light of day, you slipped up again and didn't visit a doctor for a precaution. Given your extensive education, you are *way* too smart to make such a simple miscalculation."

She didn't know where he was going with this, but she felt as though he was peeling layers off her as he did it. She wanted to run, but she had to stand there and act completely bored.

"So?"

"You're smart, but you're not experienced." He spoke in a tone of dawning realization.

"In what way?" Her stomach flipped over as she attempted to maintain her laissez-faire attitude. "The use of birth control? You're right. It hasn't come up."

"No? Why's that?" He had a look on his face that was both amused and bemused, as if he knew the answer while she still didn't understand the question.

"Because I haven't had to use it before." Obviously.

"Because you were a virgin," he concluded. He was smiling. Laughing at her. *Dios*, no.

"Why is that relevant?" she asked, as mortified heat climbed her cheeks.

"Because even with my vast experience, I usually know a woman more than ten minutes before I'm making babies with her. I *always* know her name."

The air seemed to crackle and snap between them.

She clenched her teeth, not enjoying hearing about those legions of other women and refusing to examine why. "How many babies do you have?"

"Just the one." He nodded at her middle.

He seemed to take the opportunity to track his gaze all over her sage-green jacket and its matching skirt. She had chosen the knit skirt because it was comfortable while the jacket's turned-up collar lent her an air of polished authority.

He took in the rest while he was down there, skimming his gaze to her snakeskin pumps and back to the bronze lace of her camisole between the lapels of her closed jacket, then finally up to her eyes.

He hadn't even touched her, but she felt restless and lethargic and self-destructive. Ready to abandon sense and propriety all over again.

It was all the reason she needed to reject him. He was far too dangerous, undermining her with a look. She couldn't live her entire life with that!

"You understand this baby has been conceived?" she asked frostily. "No further action is required."

He chuckled softly. "The question on the table is whether you *want* to."

"I've answered. I said, no thank you."

"Because you want to sleep with the overbred nob your mother has chosen."

Put that way, she dreaded it, but, "When the alternative is someone who casts aside modesty or decorum, I struggle to see the strength in your argument."

"I usually have enough decency not to have sex in public, but neither of us showed much decorum or restraint, did we? You gave up your *virginity*. It's very rare for couples to react the way we do, you know."

"Current levels of overpopulation lead me to believe lust is fairly common," she murmured with another examination of her nails.

"Not this kind of lust. It's extraordinary. Do you need another sample?"

His hand started to come up and she dropped her own, jerking back a step beyond his reach.

He scratched his cheek as he chuckled. "So jumpy."

She smoothed her embarrassed irritation from her brow. "Deep emotions, such as lust, are detrimental to a comfortable life. Destructive, even. As we've demonstrated."

"The damage is done, *querida*."

"So let's not compound it."

"Agreed." He straightened off the window. "Let's not bring anyone else into this child's life that doesn't need to be here."

"Certain people, like my family, are already in my life. They will be affected."

"What are they going to do? Disown you?" His pitiless gaze dismissed them either way.

Her chest constricted. No, her parents wouldn't yell or reject her, but she would lose her chance to win their approval. For once.

Was that what she was holding out for? As that unpleasant truth slapped her, she knew that Angelo had won. Their baby had won. She was no longer the child. She was the parent and it was time to give up the fantasy of earning her parents' affection and show the sort of concern and unconditional love that she'd longed for all her life.

Damn it.

"My mother will need to be informed," she said with defeat. "Immediately."

"I'll go with you," Angelo said as she exchanged a few brief texts with her parents and announced she would visit their home on the way to her own.

"It's not necessary." Pia dropped her phone back into her purse.

"It is." Angelo didn't need approval from her parents. From anyone, for that matter, but the influence her parents exerted over her shouldn't be underestimated.

Pia was such a mystery. Coldly analytical, then flaring hot. Fascinating, but frustrating.

She moved to the mirror in the hall and set her purse on the table as she searched through it. "My parents are aware of your name in relation to the painting. They'll want to know your motives. How you came to be at the ball."

"Tell them you invited me."

"I don't lie to them."

"Then tell them you had no idea who I was and made love with me anyway." He shrugged it off, sidestepping what she was really asking.

He would have to tell her eventually, but he would wait until she couldn't back out of their marriage. That was partly tactical, partly selfish. He wanted his revenge on his brothers and it would carry so much more flavor if he was marrying up. Marrying spectacularly well, in fact.

But his ever-present aversion to dredging up his mother's situation rose in him. He never discussed her with anyone, ashamed to admit what he was. He carried a lot of guilt, too. His very existence had contributed to her agony. He had burdened her and ultimately let her down. He hadn't seen her suicide coming, but should have. He hadn't had many resources at the time, but he should have done something. In his heart, he was convinced he could have stopped her had he been there.

Pia pensively refreshed her lipstick, casting him a look with her reflection.

"Is this the sort of marriage we'll have? One where we keep secrets? Because I was prepared to start mine to Sebastián by telling him I was pregnant with another man's child. The least you could tell me is how I come to be refusing him." She began pulling the pins from her hair.

"Never say that name to me again," he suggested pleasantly, moving to stand behind her in the mirror.

He picked out a few pins himself, concentrating on releasing the twist without causing her any discomfort.

She held very still, eyes downcast, her exposed nape begging for the press of his lips. He combed his fingers through the mass, watched the play of light through the silken strands, enjoying the smooth caress between his fingers.

"I don't know what sort of marriage we'll have," he admitted. "Marrying and starting a family has not been on my radar. I spent most of my life rootless, my own security tenuous. Until a few years ago, I was in no position to support anyone but myself. When I finally began making money, it was buckets of it. I had to pivot to defend against a different kind of predator, not the kind who eat the weak, but the kind who challenge the strong."

He let his hands rest on her shoulders and lightly dug his thumbs into the tendons at the base of her neck. Like magic, the stiff, aloof expression on her face melted. She closed her eyes and her expression grew so sensually blissful, he nearly picked her up and carried her to his bed.

But he had to make her understand.

"Mistrust is ingrained in me. I don't know yet if you're friend or foe, Pia. I certainly have no illusions that your parents will be on my side."

Her eyes opened, the shadows in them difficult to interpret.

"I only know that you're carrying my child. That our child will need you. That makes you as much my responsibility as the baby is."

"So you don't trust me, but I'm supposed to trust you?" she asked huskily. "Even if you keep secrets?"

He smiled. "Your intelligence is one of your most attractive qualities. Do you know that?"

"Almost as high a compliment as having a great personality." She brushed his hands off her shoulders and moved away.

"I meant it as a compliment. Why compliment your looks when your beauty is obvious." Even when she was walking away. Her skirt was a hip-hugging knit that caressed her backside and thighs every time she moved. He'd been admiring it all afternoon.

She stood in the middle of the room, hand on her middle, expression tight, face pale. "We should go."

"Nausea?" Now he wanted to tuck her into his bed and cuddle her.

"It comes and goes. I have biscuits in the car that help."

"When do you see the doctor next? Any concerns?"

"None. Everything is normal. I have an appointment in the new year."

"I'll come." He was already looking forward to it.

"If you like." The chill was back. So annoying, but he soon learned she came by it honestly.

Marble floors gleamed beneath a chandelier of icicle-like crystals as they entered the Montero villa. A wide staircase led to a gallery where stark, contemporary art decorated the walls.

The butler directed them into a showpiece of a parlor, the sort of room Angelo had glimpsed as a child, but had been held back from entering by his mother's tense hand on his arm, her voice sharp with caution. It was not a place he had been welcome and, judging by the expressions on the Duque and Duquessa's faces, he was no more welcome today.

"Navarro," her mother repeated, glancing sharply between them.

"Pia's plus one at the ball," Angelo lied smoothly so Pia wouldn't have to. "I trust my generous donation made up for concealing our relationship."

"Relationship." La Reina's tone dropped to subarctic levels. "How did you meet? The university? I don't believe I'm familiar with your family."

"No?" Angelo countered, thinking La Reina had

probably been marrying Javier about the time his grandmother had become his father's second wife. But he couldn't think about the dirty secrets from his past. Not now when he needed to be on the top of his game.

"Nemesis Tech," Javier identified as he shook Angelo's hand with a solid grip. "I've read of your developments with integrated photonics. The first light-based microchip to be commercially viable."

"The reason smartphones can do so many things at once without bursting into flames," Pia translated for her mother.

"My team gets all the credit," Angelo said smoothly. "I only backed the winning horse." And flogged it to any manufacturer with money, from smart toasters to NASA.

"Technology," her mother said with a tolerant smile as they all sat. "Perhaps an introduction to Cesar would be prudent." La Reina sent that to Pia in a not so subtle query as to why her daughter had brought a stranger into their home on short notice. One who had not defined his use of the word *relationship*.

"Introductions to the rest of the family will happen in due course." Pia was utterly composed, hands folded in her lap, voice lacking inflection, face unreadable. Much as she'd been when she had kicked him in the gonads with her news. "I'm pregnant. Angelo is the father. We'll marry as quickly as possible."

The ensuing silence was so profound that the click of the door broke it like a gunshot. The butler came up against the charged air as though he had hit a noxious cloud. He persevered through it to bring Pia's requested cranberry mocktini and Angelo's glass of Javier's private label brandy.

"Dinner as scheduled, *señora*?" the butler murmured as he set the drinks.

"Push it back until I inform you." La Reina waited until the door had been closed again. Her color hadn't risen. Her voice hadn't changed. She only prompted, "Javier?"

"The Estrada merger was an ideal fit for the fuel cell innovations Cesar is pursuing. Microprocessing is a different direction entirely."

Sebastián again? Angelo wondered if they realized he could buy that fool's enterprise a dozen times over and his next generation chip wasn't even on the market yet.

"Rico enjoys the challenge of a pivot." Pia spoke as though they were discussing the purchase of a car or some other innocuous detail. "Cesar will find ways to capitalize. Both of them have dealt with the unexpected before."

"They have," her mother agreed.

Another profound silence. Pia stacked her white hands. Her mother sipped her frosted glass of white wine.

"I understand the social ramifications," Pia said, spine never faltering from its finishing school posture. "We'll marry as quietly as possible. Remove to a honeymoon somewhere unobtrusive and return after the holiday party season dies down."

"I never agreed to that," Angelo cut in.

"To marriage? Then we put Sebastián off for a year," La Reina said to Pia, apparently enjoying a quick pivot herself. "It's only fair to his future heir that there be clear distinction. You'll go away, as you do, and we'll work out a suitable arrangement with…" She gave Angelo a disdainful nod.

His scalp nearly came off. "I didn't agree to some furtive, backroom ceremony that implies we have something to be ashamed of. We'll marry with a proper wedding where everyone we know is invited."

These people really knew how to allow a silence to do their talking. He looked from Pia's downcast lashes, to La Reina's pointedly raised brows, to Javier's disinterested sip of his brandy.

"Are you embarrassed that your daughter is pregnant by me?" Angelo asked Javier. It was a double-barreled question, one the older man neatly brushed aside.

"The children and the family's social standing are La Reina's bailiwick."

"Is that a yes or a no?" Angelo asked with more antagonism.

"Angelo." Pia's clammy hand touched his.

"When one is drawing the wrong sort of attention, one ought to mitigate the damage," La Reina said in a chilly voice. "Take control of the conversation and lower the tone, for instance."

He barked out a humorless laugh.

"Am I speaking too plainly? My child is not something indecent to be swept under the rug." A bastard. A stain. The product of a crime. No one was saying it, but he heard the labels from his past and felt each one like the whip of a belt.

"Keeping a low profile will benefit all of us, including the baby," Pia said.

"If you act like we've done something wrong, people are going to believe we have. No." He rose, too angry to sit here like one of these overcivilized relics clutching their pearls. "Speed up the timetable if you'd rather not be showing in our photos," he told Pia. "The sooner the better works for me, but we are giving this wedding every bit as much fanfare as you would with one of those interchangeable grooms on your mother's list. We'll announce our engagement with a press release *tomorrow*."

"Have you thought this through, Pia?" her mother asked as if he hadn't spoken. "Faustina's parents are backing your father's challenger because of Rico's situation with Poppy. This reinforces accusations that Monteros lack moral fortitude."

"Maybe they do," Angelo interjected. "Given you don't want to recognize your own grandchild."

"I didn't say we wouldn't recognize the child. Of course the child will be a Monetero." La Reina sent a small frown of affront toward her daughter. "Pia."

The word was a signal of some kind. Pia stood.

"Angelo and I will iron out the details in private, but I wanted you to be informed. We won't stay for dinner. Thank you for seeing us."

Angelo was no stranger to being shunned and insulted and run off like a mangy cur. He didn't intend to hang around for more of the same, but he was astounded that Pia allowed herself to be dismissed like some panhandler daring to come to the door.

"Will you take me home or shall I ask Mother's driver?" Pia asked him, her face a blank mask.

Angelo shot one last glower at her parents. "I'll take you home."

CHAPTER SIX

"IT'S BEEN A long day. I don't want to go back to the hotel," Pia said when Angelo ignored her direction to turn into her street.

"We're not going to the hotel." He still sounded furious.

She bit back a whimper of helplessness, one limp, cold hand cradled in the other. It really had been a long day. She wasn't up to further confrontations. Nevertheless, she tried to explain. "That wasn't shame they were expressing."

"The hell it wasn't."

"It was damage control."

"Yes, your father's election prospects. *Quelle surprise.*"

"It's not about votes. Not the way you think. My father is actually a good politician. He's extremely well-read, believes in science and facts and weighs the costs and benefits very objectively. He's never swayed by special interests or emotional pleas and certainly not by suitcases full of cash, only by sound reasoning. It's in the country's best interest that he retains his seat. That becomes more challenging when his children are having babies out of wedlock every other year."

"*You're* ashamed," he accused.

"I'm embarrassed that I showed a lack of self-discipline." And that she had embraced longing and hope and other nonsensical ideals that weren't based in logic. Soon she would advertise that bad judgment on the big screen that her belly would become. "I failed to live up to expectations. No one enjoys failing."

"You failed to stand up for our *child*."

His words, his tone, caused a spasming clench across her chest. Guilt. Anguish. Resignation. It was so intense, she had to take a moment to breathe through it.

How did she explain there was no point in growing indignant with them? Demanding feelings when there were none?

He turned into a private airfield. A stab of panic struck.

"Where are you going?" Was he so angry that he was leaving her? She couldn't blame him, but the profound sense of abandonment that gripped her as she faced him climbing onto a jet and disappearing was nearly more than she could bear.

"*We* are going to my home."

She opened her mouth, but he was jamming the car into Park and flinging himself from it, handing her car fob to someone with instructions to drive it to her home.

Stunned, she didn't move until Angelo came around to open her door.

"I don't have any luggage." That wasn't entirely true. She kept a clean pair of jeans and a warm pullover in the back seat for weather changes in the field.

"We'll manage." He jerked his head at the waiting jet.

"Angelo." She sought to reason with him, but he cut her off.

"What the hell do you have to stay here for? They didn't congratulate you on our baby or your doctorate or your forthcoming marriage. They don't care about you so why would you want to do *anything* they tell you to do?"

Tears slammed into her eyes. She fought them back, fought back the clawing sensation in her throat and the sick nausea that roiled in her belly.

The sad fact was, these weren't tears because her parents overlooked her accomplishments or disapproved of her choice in a husband. This was a deeper anguish that aligned directly with the rejection he was feeling on behalf of their child.

She knew that injured anger so well. It hurt her that he was experiencing it. Hurt her that their baby might one day see it and feel it.

She looked at the jet, thought about how many times she had done exactly this—jumped on an airplane yet never quite managed to outrun this ache. Or had anyone chase her and tell her she was missed.

For once, however, she wouldn't be alone in her pain.

She cleared her throat and asked that her laptop and other effects be transferred aboard. She waited until they were in the air, after they'd been served a light bisque with puff pastry and Angelo seemed marginally less incensed, to try to explain.

"My parents are not emotional people. They will never be happy about this baby because they aren't capable of it. If you expect an effusive expression of joy from them in response to anything, you will be sorely disappointed." She had had to learn that lesson over and over. It still hurt, but it remained true. "On the other hand, they aren't specifically *un*happy, either. What you witnessed was resistance to a course correction."

"Something I've witnessed twice today," he said darkly.

She fought letting him see how stricken she was to be

likened to her mother, which only made her more like La Reina, she supposed.

"One doesn't achieve a goal by giving in the minute an obstacle is encountered," Pia said, her voice empty of the defensiveness squeezing her in a vise. "I had no idea how you would react to this. Of course I tried to preserve the life I had planned for myself. That's very natural and human."

His snort disparaged the bunch of them as any such thing.

"How will your family react?" she asked stiffly.

He flinched and turned his profile away. "I don't have any."

Given what he had told her of his father and his childhood, she had wondered. This was obviously a raw topic for him so she didn't go digging around, only ate the last morsel of lobster in her bowl.

"Mine may not be the most demonstrative family, but we are loyal. What you saw as sweeping under a rug, my mother saw as a genuine effort to shield the entire family from adverse consequences. *I* would prefer to marry in private," she added.

"I stand by my response. Ducking attention implies we have something to hide." He sounded immovable.

She realized her phone was blowing up. "Did we just come into range or something?"

"The pilot has turned on the Wi-Fi, yes."

She looked at the numerous texts and missed calls from her brothers, the notifications from the family lawyer, her mother's assistant, the family's PR manager and—*Really, Mother?*—Sebastián.

"Who is it?" Angelo asked with a frown.

"Everyone." She quit scrolling and considered turning it off, but Poppy rang through with a face call. Pia made the split-second decision to accept so she could test the temperature with her brothers.

"Why didn't you *tell* me when you were here? I'm pregnant, *too*," Poppy said.

"What?" Pia's brief soar of excitement fell away. "Are you crying?"

"Yes." Poppy laughed and wiped her eyes. "I had to ask Rico to put Lily to bed. She doesn't understand that you can cry from being happy and hormonal, but I totally broke down when he told me. I'm *so* happy. And I don't want to steal her thunder, but I would bet any money Sorcha is pregnant, too. I haven't seen her take so much as a nip of alcohol in weeks. This is so *perfect*, Pia."

It really wasn't, but Pia was pleased by Poppy's reaction. She congratulated her on her own pregnancy, then had to ask, "Is Rico upset with me?"

"Of course not. He's worried. But thrilled," Poppy hurried to clarify. "He's been on the phone to Cesar a few times. They want to talk to you. And Angelo." Poppy gave her a look that accused her of holding back.

Pia smiled weakly. "It's been a long day. Tell Rico I'll call tomorrow, after Angelo and I have had time to make a few decisions." She signed off.

"I like her," Angelo commented.

"I would challenge anyone not to," Pia said mildly, hiding the stab of jealousy that struck like a bolt of lightning out of nowhere.

They finished their meal and Angelo noted it was still early enough in California to call his lawyer there.

Pia closed her eyes, wishing she had been able to ask Poppy if she still thought telling her baby's father was the right thing to do. She wanted to ask how to cope with the conflict of being happy about the baby, but overwhelmed by how it was changing her life at a pace she couldn't adapt to. How to make things work with the father when she didn't know what sort of person he was or what he wanted from her.

Was she a fool to put any trust in him at all?

She didn't realize she had fallen asleep until she woke at the sound of her name.

A warm, blanketing sensation of well-being surrounded her as she dragged herself back to consciousness. She only realized as she picked up her head that she was tucked beneath Angelo's arm, her head pillowed in the hollow of his shoulder.

His other hand fell away from caressing her cheek to wake her.

"We can sleep in the stateroom if you're too tired to go to the house, but it's only ten minutes from here."

She nodded dumbly and gathered herself, asking as they disembarked, "This is your island?"

"It's often reported that I bought the whole island, but that's inaccurate. I own the largest property and I purchased several of the more modest homes for my staff because I often prefer to be alone in the house. But there are many holiday homes here. There's a busy village in the harbor and a variety of tourist accommodation."

A handful of staff welcomed them into the massive villa—maids and security, a butler and one of Angelo's personal assistants. The butler showed her around a modern mansion decorated in bone white and natural stone. The lounge was sunken off the dining area and the exterior walls were glass panels that opened onto the pool surround. The water glowed pale blue in the night and the pool was so big, there was a bridge to an island within its shallows. Three potted palm trees and a bistro table with tall stools sat upon it.

Beyond that, the wide stretch of white sand glowed in the moonlight. The shape of a cabana, a boathouse and a private dock were outlined in fairy lights.

"This is beautiful."

"One of my business partners, a security specialist, told me about it. He and his wife live on the other end of the island. You'll meet her tomorrow. I asked her to take our photo for the press release."

"You have a rooftop patio like Rico's," she noted as she turned to study the side of the house that faced the water. It was all flowing lines, elegantly placed lanterns and recessed stairways.

"Would you like to see it?"

It was dark and the wind off the water chilly. She hugged herself, mouth dry as she considered what had happened on the last rooftop. What was wrong with her that she wanted to do that again? She didn't know him much better at all.

At her silence, he let a slow smile form on his face until he was so wickedly beautiful, her stomach wobbled. He took her hand and she didn't balk as he led her through the house.

When they reached the top of the stairs, he motioned at an open door to a spare bedroom. "What do you need for your research lab? Concrete walls or just an office space?"

"I—" She was so surprised, her tongue tangled. One way or another, pursuing science had always been an uphill battle. Her father set high standards; her mother thought it a distraction. Sexism was rampant and her studies often took her to remote places that were a challenge in themselves.

She didn't know how to compute that Angelo would simply take her at her word that she wanted to continue to work and try to facilitate that for her. "I haven't given it much thought."

"Let me know," he said, and led her into the stadium that was the master bedroom—which further disconcerted her.

She tugged to free her hand.

"The lady knows what she wants." He spun to face her.

"I really don't." She folded her arms, taking in the cool blues of the bedding in the soft light cast by the two lamps on the nightstands.

"The access to the rooftop patio is off this balcony." The humor in his eyes told her he was teasing her. "Stay here or go up, either way we're in trouble." He held out his hand.

She didn't move, only glanced toward an archway into what looked to be a master bath of epic proportions. There was a cozy conversation area in the nook and a desk near the door to the balcony. Her laptop bag had been left on the rolling chair.

"Do you really expect me to sleep with you here tonight?" she asked with disbelief. "We've known each other two days."

He sent a pointed glance to the clock that read twelve-oh-seven.

"Technically three." He pushed his hands in his pockets, seeming all the more imposing in the intimate golden light. He angled his head to regard her. "I don't 'expect' sex. I anticipate it."

How did he send all these swirls and eddies into her middle with just a few words and a sexy smile?

"It doesn't have to be tonight." He stepped closer and slowly swept his fingers down her hair, the caress so startling and so powerful that she caught her breath. He left his fist resting on her shoulder clutching a swathe. His thumb grazed the edge of her jaw. "Why so nervous? We've done it before."

"Not with the lights on."

He threw back his head and laughed. "We'll start with only one." He nodded at the night table. "Work up to it."

She hated that he mocked her, made her feel so inept. She knew she wasn't the best at interpersonal relationships. Her upbringing had been a wasteland, her shyness crippling. In the last few years, while most people her age had been clubbing, she'd been immersed in school, partly as self-defense, partly for the sense of accomplishment before she devoted herself to motherhood.

The one time she had acted her age with an impulsive hookup, she'd blown her life to smithereens.

While he remained completely self-possessed.

"I don't know who I was that night," she said with as much dignity as she could muster. "I wasn't me. I believed that you didn't know who I was and that I would never have to face you again. I didn't expect to reckon with the way I behaved. Now I'm forced to and it's not comfortable."

His hand shifted to gently pick up her chin and coax her to look into his sobered expression.

"There was nothing wrong with the way we behaved. Yes, we could have been more responsible, but sex is normal. Actually, our sex was exceptional in the best possible way," he allowed. "*I* don't feel embarrassed by it."

She doubted he was ever embarrassed, he was so confident.

"You don't understand," she murmured. How could he? He hadn't been raised to believe that corporeal yearnings were to be ignored and overcome in favor of rational decision-making.

"I'm not going to pretend I don't want to make love to you. I do." He set his hands on her hips, his touch heavy and possessive and stirring her without even trying. "If you don't want to, I'll survive." His thumbs pressed with tension into her pelvic bones while his mouth curled into a wry smile. "But you're right that we need to get to know one another. That won't happen living in separate quarters of the house. I want to share a room and a bed, if not our bodies."

What about talking? She didn't have much skill or practice at expressing her feelings verbally, though. She had never been allowed to acknowledge them and work through them.

As for the physical… He had held her closer when they had danced that night, but she was experiencing the same pull now as she had experienced then, without the magic of moonlight and music and disguises. She was baffled by her reaction. She set her hand on his chest, maybe distantly thinking to give herself some space to think, but her fingers splayed to take in as much firm muscle as she could. She could feel his heartbeat and it chipped away at any attempt at rational thought.

He moved his hands to her waist, his touch a caress. An invitation to move closer. She stiffened slightly as tingles of pleasure wafted through her.

He lifted his hands off her so only the heat radiating from his palms touched her. "No?"

She wavered. She had spent her life drowning in a dry sea and his touch was a lifeline so compelling and welcome, so powerful, that she yearned for him, but she didn't know how to tell him she wanted him to touch her. It felt like a weakness to need it so badly.

Her body spoke for her, flowing without conscious volition. Her hand slid up behind his neck while her other arm reached to encircle his waist. She closed her eyes, not wanting to see how he reacted, only pressed herself to his front and lifted her mouth in offering.

His mouth landed on hers, sending a ball of heat into her middle while his arms closed across her back, pressing the air from her lungs. Maybe she forgot to breathe. She didn't care. She only wanted this. The uncivilized taste of him and the way her muscles quivered in response.

When he dragged his head up, she whimpered in protest.

"Open your eyes." His hand cradled her jaw, oddly tender when he was holding her in such a hard clasp, but maybe he was holding her up.

She blinked her eyes open, watched him slowly smile at whatever dazed sensuality was clouding her gaze. It was so intimate that her eyes grew wet. She could barely stand it, but couldn't look away. Her blood pounded in a primal, painful beat.

"I wanted to see that," he whispered. "What I do to you."

"It's too much."

"But you'll come to my bed anyway."

"I will," she capitulated, and gasped as he swept her up. Two steps later, he set her on the mattress.

He came down with her, his mouth swooping to possess hers again, ravenous. She tried to keep up, unable to pull apart the sensations that bombarded her. A whisking touch, a tender nibble and the abrasion of his cheek as he went after her neck. The sudden skim of his fingers against her thigh would have been more shocking if she hadn't somehow pulled his shirt free and was mindlessly brushing her palms across his bare back.

His muscular body, hard as iron, half pinned her, and his eyes filled with shifts and flashes when he pulled back enough to look at her again.

Fascinated, she watched his face as he lifted and found the catch that belted her jacket. Slowly he worked the buckle free and opened the front, settling beside her as he revealed her bronze camisole with its matching bra beneath.

"This is what I wanted time for that night." He flattened his hand on her stomach, shifting hot-cool silk across her torso, bending to nuzzle where lace met quivering skin. "To undress you."

He tugged at a sleeve and she pulled her arm free, then draped it across his shoulders, fingertips seeking the heat beneath his collar at the back of his neck.

She learned the difference between expecting and anticipating as she offered her other sleeve only to have him kiss the inside of her wrist, settle his mouth over hers in a way that drugged her into a mindless state and then, when she was trembling, he finally pulled her other arm free.

Hardly anyone had ever seen her this naked and only her jacket was gone. It wasn't just the lack of clothing that was revealing so much as the way her stomach quivered and her nipples pressed against the cups of her bra, and how her hips angled into him the way leaves of a plant sought the sun. Her desire rose so fiercely that she dampened silk he couldn't see and bit her lip against a groan of erotic suffering.

He was killing her, looking at her, biting against lace, slipping a strap down her shoulder, lifting to watch the slither of silk as he drew it up and away.

The way he ate up every inch of skin he exposed bolstered yet destroyed her. And the way he roamed his hand across her, from hip to the underwire of her bra, back down to her navel, then up to trace the swell of her breast against the edge of the cup, turned her inside out.

He began to devour her, stubble scuffing her chest while he teasingly bit at her nipples through the bra before he trailed his tongue where his fingertips had been and delved behind the cup to flick at her nipple.

She made a keening noise and his hand hardened on her hip, urging her to withstand his teasing until he finally took pity on her and released her bra, helping her remove it. He returned to lave and nuzzle and suck, driving her so mad that she hitched her ankle around his and tried to insinuate herself beneath him.

He growled and scraped his mouth down her center, making her abs jump at the flick of his tongue into her navel. He groaned in pleasured satisfaction as he reached the waistband of her skirt and discovered it stretched easily to slide down her hips.

He set kisses on one hip then the other, and kept sliding down with a whisper of his body moving against the covers. As he revealed her panties, he trailed kisses down her thigh, making her melt. Making her burn.

"Angelo," she gasped, shaking with arousal.

"I want you naked this time." The skirt was tossed

to the floor. "Completely naked. So all you feel is me." He began inching the lace down her thighs.

She pressed her legs together, trying to ease the aching between them, then met his gaze as he patiently waited for her to bite her lip, then relax to let him peel off the lace panties.

He rose onto his knees and tossed them away. Then he dragged at his own clothing, movements efficient, gaze traveling over her as he stood to remove his pants.

The wanting in her was back to being that wild, reckless thing that had gripped her the night of the ball. Voices of caution and shyness were drowned out by imperatives of an earthier nature. She wanted his weight. His hard heat moving inside her. His firm hands steadying her. His mouth ravaging hers.

She held up her arms, inviting him back.

He set one knee on the mattress, one hand on the inside of her thigh, asking her to make space for him. But as she hesitantly opened her legs, he pressed for a wide space and settled low between her thighs, like a lazy jungle cat. He made a noise somewhere between a growl and purr as he warmed her intimate flesh with a hot breath that made her sob. Then he leisurely tasted her.

She couldn't speak. Couldn't process this much pleasure delivered in such an intimate fashion. Couldn't understand how he made her feel fragile and feral at once. Greedy and flagrant and willing to give herself up to him completely. But the pleasure he wrenched from her was magnificent. Unstoppable.

"Angelo!" she cried as her climax lashed her, devastating her so she was nothing but panting ash.

He peeled her fist from his hair and bit the inside of her thigh, shocking her buzzing nerve endings back to life.

The animal craving to mate had her fully in its grip now. Her *mate* had her fully in his grip as he rose over her and thrust deeply, pressing a keening cry from her. She closed her legs around him, clinging on in a small battle of strength as he thrust with muted power.

The act grew wild as he scraped his teeth against her neck and she dug her fingernails into his buttocks, urging him to shed what control he retained. She wanted all of him. All of his heat and greedy hunger. All his strength. All his craving and all of the roaring beast within him.

Her vision paled and her breaths were nothing but jagged, helpless soughs, pleading for the crisis. They crested in the same moment, the world making one glorious, silent rotation as they were held on that beautiful precipice. Then the universe exploded into colors and streaks of joy and every molecule in her body caught fire as she slowly fell back to earth.

CHAPTER SEVEN

ANGELO HAD THOUGHT he knew what he wanted—to burn past Pia's layer of reserve and remind her how they had ended up in this situation. Along the way, he expected her to quit acting like she was better than him. Then he would issue a press release announcing he was hitching his common bag of bones to one of the aristocracy's privileged princesses, dragging all of them down a peg. The photo of Pia wearing some of the stolen jewelry would be an especially insolent nose-thumbing to his brothers.

He hadn't expected his hunger for Pia to be outright insatiable. They had made love three times through the night, the third time when she woke him at dawn by sliding languorously against him. Her sleepy mouth had painted a path across his chest to tease his nipple. How was he supposed to resist that? As they'd rolled into each other and twined their limbs, he'd been hard and she'd been slick and ready. Their joining had been natural and lazy and so sweet his teeth still ached.

He wanted to be smug, he really did. Physically, she was an easy conquest, but damned if he wasn't easier. He had taken her apart and she had destroyed him right back, then managed to look very wan and delicate over breakfast, stirring protective instincts he hadn't known he possessed. She was avoiding eye contact and blushing and obviously so self-conscious about losing her inhibitions, he couldn't help but caress a knee here and kiss the inside of her wrist there and reach across to slide a tendril of hair behind her ear.

"Is that your journal?" he teased, not sure if he should be flattered or worried that she might be recording her thoughts and impressions of his performance last night.

"It's a data log of my pregnancy." She frowned as if that ought to be obvious.

No casual food diary for Dr. Pia Montero. She proceeded to show him how she ruthlessly recorded caloric intake and nutrition, her morning weight and hours of sleep, physical measurements, the supplements she was taking, type and duration of exercise, and general notes on symptoms, physical and mental, including what time they occurred.

"Why?" He estimated this would take an hour of her day for the next thirty-plus weeks.

"I'm a willing subject. Why wouldn't I make an effort to contribute knowledge and understanding of a condition that affects the majority of women, directly or indirectly, at least once in her lifetime?" She blinked owlishly behind a pair of glasses that were provoking serious librarian fantasies in him.

"Aren't you turning it into more work than pregnancy already is?"

"Recording my observations relaxes me."

Did she realize how much she revealed with that remark? He could have asked what she could possibly be nervous about, but she was so earnest as she noted every detail of their baby's life as it formed within her that he found himself suppressing a rueful grin. Especially because she wasn't doing it to impress him or anyone else, but for womankind in general. He couldn't mock her for that.

Which made his own goal of highlighting the farce that was her noble birth seem petty and misguided.

He clung to his ambition until he began setting out the jewelry on his desk, when his desire for retaliation began to be smothered beneath a wave of revulsion.

"Family heirlooms?" She scanned the ostentatious pieces. Most were reflective of late twentieth-century indulgence. Intricate pendants hung from thick chains of yellow gold. Layered pearl necklaces were bedecked with amethysts and emeralds.

"This reminds me of the royal engagement ring." She touched a pair of blue sapphire earrings surrounded by white diamonds.

Angelo had to resist pulling her hand away, as though she were a child reaching out to touch a hot stove.

In the height of his anger after leaving her parents' home, he had coldly calculated that he would dress Pia in the extravagant white diamond choker with the matching bracelet. It was a notable piece that some elderly contemporary of his grandmother's might glimpse and recall, causing the first stir of rumors. Definitely his brothers would recognize it. He had planned an ambiguous headline saying something about the secrecy of their relationship coming to light—one that would incite panic that a darker family secret was about to be revealed.

But the thought of these blood diamonds touching the smooth, fragrant skin he had tasted and stroked through the night sent an oily sensation into the pit of his gut. *No.* Just, *no.*

"I don't wear jewelry as a rule." Pia eyed the enormous, pear-shaped diamond in a platinum setting. Sprays of diamonds came off either side. Her impassive expression was the furthest thing from covetous. "Rings and bracelets get in the way when I'm reaching into tide pools and necklaces get caught on the microscope. I appreciate that these have special meaning to you. I'll wear something for the photo if you insist, but I've never been one to adorn myself. I'm hideously practical that way."

"I'm glad you hate it," he said flatly.

"I didn't say that!"

"Excuse me, Angelo. The stylist is here," his PA leaned in to say. "And Mrs. Killian."

"Call the jeweler in the village," he instructed. "Ask him to bring his engagement rings. Immediately."

"Yes, sir."

"Angelo—"

"It's fine," he said abruptly, not examining whether his veering from his plan was a sign of weakness or principle. "Melodie." He greeted his neighbor and introduced the highly sought-after photographer to Pia, then waved at the jewelry he'd left on his desk. "I have a second assignment for you. Photograph these for an auction catalog."

He tipped the empty tin so his toy wolf and race car fell into his palm with a wrapped hard candy his mother had sneaked to him twenty-five years ago. He had wanted to save it for a special occasion, but hadn't been able to get back to the rooftop to retrieve it. It went into his pants pocket with the toys before he swept all the ill-gotten jewelry back into the tin.

"Oh. Where…?" Melodie was startled as she accepted

the heavy tin. She looked to Pia, who pasted on her most inscrutable smile.

"Your house is Fort Knox," Angelo reminded Melodie. Her husband had wired this one and was probably the only person on earth who could break in and steal that box if he wanted it. "Take it to your studio and get to it as your time allows."

Pia was utterly perplexed by Angelo's behavior. One minute he'd been her indulgent lover, touching her across the breakfast table in casual affection that soothed the constant ache of emptiness inside her. She had needed that reassurance after a night of completely immersing herself in the pleasure he gave her. She felt stripped raw by their passion. The winter sun stung her scorching skin and gave her no place to hide as he looked at her with a knowing, wicked grin.

She had buried her nose in her notebook, right back to boarding school, using research and reporting as a place to hide.

Then he'd brought her into his office, "To find something to wear."

He said nothing about the portrait that hung behind his desk. The canvas had been gorgeously restored so the subject was hauntingly pretty and maybe even familiar?

She hadn't had time to compare his mature, masculine features to the soft, youthful feminine ones. He had distracted her by producing a fortune in jewels jumbled together in a cheap tin. He poured them out as if spilling marbles on a play rug.

What she had said had been true. She found jewelry more of an encumbrance than something she enjoyed wearing, but the pieces had also been very—she cringed inwardly—flamboyant. Not just a statement of wealth, but a tacky neon sign declaring it.

She hadn't meant to reject it, though. Being in any sort of intimate relationship was new to her and she walked a tightrope of wanting to preserve her sense of self while maintaining some of the closeness they'd found through lovemaking. They would have a much better foundation for communication and understanding if he wasn't keeping secrets from her, but she wound up feeling she was the one who had damaged their delicate bond when he swept everything away and ordered the jeweler to bring a different selection.

Now he was marching around the house with Melodie, discussing where they should take their engagement photo, providing no opportunity to reestablish their connection.

He decided on the lounge and Melodie began setting up her equipment.

Pia followed Angelo to the guest room where the stylist excitedly pulled selections that were nothing like Pia's usual earth tones.

"She's right," Angelo said as the woman held a dress to her front. "That blue brings out your eyes and makes your skin look like honey."

Flustered by what sounded like an effusive compliment, Pia tried on the sleeveless dress. The circular neck strap that formed the collar lent an air of sophistication while her bare shoulders kept it feminine.

Since the rest were even sexier and more attention grabbing, she accepted the blue and sat for her hair and makeup. She only endured this level of fussing for the occasional gala, but always insisted on a light hand.

"A natural look, I understand," the stylist assured her.

"You hardly need anything. I wish I could duplicate this glow of love with cosmetics. It's all a woman needs."

A shrink of panic pulled a chill into her center. There's no *love*, Pia wanted to protest. How could there be? This was the glow of a sexually satisfying night. Pregnancy, perhaps. Regardless of what it was, Pia didn't want it on display. Her emotions and self-worth and composure were delicate crystals in a snowflake, not the cast-iron reinforcements that most people possessed. She needed to protect herself at all times.

As the woman worked, however, her reflection grew more limpid and vulnerable, leaving her devoid of her usual shields. No dull colors, no bare face with glasses. No pinned-up hair and accoutrements like clipboards and notebooks. Her boring life typically left its stamp on her, but today she wore a flush of sensuality. Rather than the sophisticated, straightened hair she usually preferred when forced to dress up, the stylist had exaggerated her soft waves so the mass bounced as she walked.

"We're in luck—*I'm* in luck." Angelo's voice changed as the sound of her heels drew his attention. He straightened, very handsome in a bespoke dark blue suit, his tie not yet on. His rakish, casual air was in full force.

At his approving tone, everyone looked at her.

Melodie was at her tripod and the jeweler stood at the dining table, setting out rings on a black velvet swatch. Two of the servants hovered, Angelo's PA lifted her face from her tablet and the stylist came out behind Pia to agree enthusiastically with Angelo.

"Doesn't she make a beautiful bride-to-be?" the stylist gushed.

Everyone applauded.

Pia wanted to *die*.

It took every one of her twenty-four years of struggling to overcome her bashfulness to smile distantly and hold up her chin as she crossed what felt like a mile of hot coals to reach Angelo.

"You look stunning." The warmth in his smile evaporated when she only offered a deliberately absent, "*Gracias*."

Angelo introduced the jeweler, who had recently been to New York and had brought back a fresh selection for the well-heeled travelers who vacationed on the island.

"I thought this one? The setting wouldn't catch on anything," Angelo said impassively, offering a platinum-set, emerald cut diamond. It had to be three carats, but was remarkably understated despite the trapezoid cut diamonds on either side. The band was lightly brushed to give it a frost-kissed finish.

Pia looked at the ring and saw water in all its phases, from ice to glimmer to mist. Mostly, she was knocked off her feet that Angelo had heard what she'd said and was trying to find something that would work for her.

"Or this?" Angelo started to reach for another, but Pia couldn't take her eyes off the first ring. The last time she had experienced such a covetous desire for an object, she'd been looking at a two-man deep-dive submarine.

"I like this one."

He threaded it on her finger and, when it fit perfectly, another cheer went up.

A fresh flush of being too conspicuous and unguarded came over her. She tried to fight it, but Angelo surprised her with a kiss. His fingertip touched her chin, tilting up her mouth. In a smooth move, he captured her lips, casually flipping her into memories of the night they had shared. His other hand skimmed lightly across her bare shoulder, finding the exposed skin in a tickling caress as he gently brought her in closer.

No, she realized belatedly. She was the one who moved into him, trapping her own hands between them in her need to be closer while he warmed the back of her shoulder with his palm. Her fingertips reached to his jaw, begging him to stay close enough to allow her to continue devouring his lips while sensations tugged in her middle and her knees became liquid.

Distantly she heard a click and there was a flash behind her closed eyes. Melodie murmured, "That was the one, mark my words." The stylist tittered.

Pia blinked her eyes open and saw the flare of satisfaction in Angelo's, as though he had deliberately provoked her clingy reaction.

The magnitude of the moment struck her. She was *marrying* this man. Having his *child*. She would be under his power *forever*.

Shaken, she did everything she could to recover her composure, drawing back and smoothing a hand down her dress only to see a hard light come into his gaze.

Pia pretended she wasn't bothered and went through the motions for the rest of the shoot. All the photos were nice, but Angelo decisively chose, "The kiss."

The image on the back of Melodie's camera might as well have been a compromising nude. Pia was clearly in the throes of passion, encouraging the slant of Angelo's mouth over hers with reaching fingers while her ring caught the sunlight.

"The one with my hand on your shoulder is more elegant, don't you think?"

"For the eighteen hundreds, sure," Angelo mocked.

"I adore this," Melodie said of the kiss. "You look

like one of those timeless cinema couples from a classic black-and-white film."

"Keep the color," Angelo said, and insisted Melodie transfer it to him immediately, without working any editing magic. Within minutes, he had forwarded the photo to his publicity company.

Twenty minutes later, Pia's phone was making more noise than a popcorn popper. Colleagues, acquaintances, former students and fellow scientists wished her well. Social invitations began pouring in from every corner in ill-disguised attempts to be invited to the wedding.

She didn't have much chance to respond. The wedding planner arrived and details were decided on the fly because, according to Angelo, "We want to marry within the month."

Pia did prefer to marry before her pregnancy began to show, which gave them until mid-January. They wouldn't announce she was expecting until after the three-month scan, but her head whirled at the scale of wedding Angelo wanted in less than four weeks.

"A thousand?" Pia snapped her head around when he said it. "Mother's assistant said five hundred."

"That was her estimate for how many she would invite. I'll have the same."

A thousand people. They might as well be televising the event while performing it naked on a beach.

She reminded herself that the half dozen pairs of eyes in his lounge this afternoon had been excruciating. It could be *ten* thousand at this point and it would be the same torture.

As the day pressed on, she did what she always did when the spotlight turned on her and scorched her to the center of her soul. She focused on creating order and maintaining her posture and manners. She spoke in a clear voice and approached everything with a rational, objective view.

She also pretended this wasn't *her* wedding. It was one of her mother's galas that needed an appropriate theme for decor and menu. She didn't let herself care whether her bouquet was roses or calla lilies because if she concerned herself with small details, she would work herself into a panic attack over the fact she would eventually have to stand in front of *a thousand people* and reveal that Angelo could make her knees weak simply by looking into her eyes.

Finally, Angelo dismissed everyone.

Exhausted, Pia made a point of shaking hands and saying goodbye to each person, then told Angelo flatly, "I'm going to change."

She needed to regroup.

Angelo couldn't believe what an ice queen he was marrying.

He should probably be grateful she had shut down somewhere between the stylist and the engagement ring. When he'd looked up as she entered, he'd been kicked in the stomach by how genuinely lovely she was. Speechless. Close to stammering.

She had walked across the room with such a standoffish expression, however, he'd become freshly annoyed. Insulted, even. She acted as though everyone around her was here to serve her and not worth a sincere smile or a personal word.

At least she liked the ring he had chosen, which had leaped out at him as somehow perfect. Subtle, yet with glints of fire. Mesmerizing and more complex the longer he stared at it.

Kissing her had been an impulse. A power move, maybe. He had wanted to force the thaw, and he had, but she'd nearly burned up any thought in his head except a desire to take her back to bed. Hell, if they hadn't been surrounded, he would have had her on the dining table.

Melodie's voice had yanked him back to reality.

Just as quickly, Pia had put on her lady-of-the-manor act and things had deteriorated from there. The photo shoot had turned into a parody of old sepia photos and when the eager-to-please wedding planner had invited Pia to describe her dream wedding, she had pretty much recoiled.

"Stay with tradition wherever possible. Many of these decisions can be fielded by my mother's personal assistant."

Her mother's *assistant*. Apparently, Angelo *was* being swapped into position like an outfielder midgame. If things were different, that would give him pause as to whether he wanted to marry her, but they had a baby on the way. He went ahead with the announcement.

Which prompted hundreds of texts and emails.

He left many of those to his own assistant, but sent a quick note to his team, reassuring them nothing would change and promising to speak to them soon.

Pia might answer to her parents and their staid ideas of tradition, but Angelo had his team of gamers, misfits all of them, but who were as genuine and generous as the ones who had taken him in so many years ago. They earned disgusting amounts of money, but they were kids and they had been knocked off guard by his news.

Angelo paid back his karma by looking after them as best he could.

If he had thought Pia would provide a maternal influence for them, he would be sorely disappointed. She was so freaking detached. That remark about guests, for instance. Maybe she knew he was being perverse, determined to invite as many guests as her mother, down to the exact number. Even so, she was acting as though she was planning a funeral, not their wedding.

She faltered as she realized he was following her into the bedroom.

"I want to change, too. I hate suits." He didn't hate them that much now that he could afford them and had them tailored to fit like a second skin.

"Try heels," she muttered, and turned her back, gathering her hair to offer her zipper.

He almost asked if that was what had put such a sour look on her face, but as he lowered the zip, he revealed the black lace beneath.

"Strapless. I wondered what you were wearing." He traced the band of the bra to the hook and eye closure.

She moved away, into the closet. He toed off his shoes and opened his belt, tugging it free as he followed her.

She was buttoning one of his black shirts over her delightfully pretty black underwear, shoes abandoned beside the dress on the floor.

"May I?" she belatedly asked, rolling a sleeve up her delicate wrist.

"Hell, yes, you may." He eyed her legs. "I may refuse to buy you any clothes of your own." He meant it.

"I'll buy them myself." She walked out of the closet.

He bit back a curse.

"Stop playing mind games. If you're angry, say so. I

won't chase you around this house begging you to tell me what's wrong."

"I'm not angry." She came back into the closet, brushing by him in the doorway. "I don't even know how to play mind games." She yanked open a drawer, slammed it, opened another.

"What, then? Why are you acting like I've got a gun to your head? Are you really that embarrassed to marry me?"

"I never said that." She paused, seeming genuinely surprised, but still cross. Her color was high.

"You're treating our wedding planner the way I treat my doctor when he tells me to turn my head and cough."

"I was perfectly civil!" she cried with a complete lack of civility. She went back to slamming through drawers. "I don't like being the center of attention. I hate it. Loathe it. There are no words ugly enough for how much I despise being stared at. The fact that you're standing there watching me melt down because I can't find my pants is my own personal nightmare and I hate myself for being this way, but I *am*."

She stopped, eyes welling, cheeks flushed, arms folded over her shuddering breasts.

Angelo reached out and dragged her jeans off a hanger where they hung in plain sight at eye level. "See, if you had asked my thoughtful and efficient staff…"

She grabbed them and shoved her legs into them, giving a little hop to snug her bottom into the seat. She might have sniffed, but it could have been the sound of the zip.

"I hated the idea of a big wedding when I thought I'd be marrying someone *normal*. Someone unremarkable. Like me." She gathered up the tails of the shirt and knotted them with shaking hands. "I *want* a hole-and-corner wedding and photos that are so boring no one even looks at them. I don't want photos that make me look like—"

She started to brush by him but he leaned to block the doorway, one shoulder against the casing, arms folded, trapping her into continuing this conversation.

"Like what?"

She hugged herself, brow crinkled. "Like I feel," she admitted in a strained voice.

The house could have exploded and he would have stayed in this timeless bubble with her, every word ringing with impact.

"How do you feel?" he asked.

"I don't know! I've never been allowed to feel, have I?" She flicked at her hair so it wasn't in her eyes. "Like my toddler nephew. Confused. Irrational. Like I should be able to make sense of this. Make order from the chaos, but I don't have any control over what's happening to me or how I feel about it. I don't like being—"

"Human?" he suggested dryly.

"It's never been encouraged," she said flatly. "You saw what they're like."

Her parents were definitely part of the problem, not the solution, but it was more than that. He saw the real issue now and wondered how he hadn't seen it sooner. The way she fell back on what she knew when her confidence flagged, how she used her big words to distance people and kept that aloof smile on her face. She was exactly like almost every gaming nerd he'd ever met—introverted and quiet and preferring to live in an alternate universe because participating in the real world was such a burden for her.

"You're shy," he accused.

She took a breath as though his words had struck somewhere tender.

"I am," she admitted miserably. "I always have been. Literally painfully shy. I feel the hurt inside me when people look at me. I hate that I have to work so hard to be as confident as…" She waved. "As all those people out there who talk like old friends when they've only met each other today."

"And right now? With me?"

"Like I have a pin in me, right here." She pointed to her chest. "Like there's a knife twisting, making each breath burn." She clenched her eyes shut, blinking at the ceiling to fight back her tears. "I wasn't supposed to have *any* feelings, especially bad ones. I certainly wasn't supposed to blush and cry and hide. I was supposed to get over it. Become a society maven who holds court over the masses the way my mother does. A fashion icon. A belle of the ball. Instead, it's a good thing she's incapable of disappointment because I am her greatest achievement in that regard."

"That's a lot of self-hatred. Maybe lighten up on yourself."

"I can't! You just accused me of treating the wedding planner like a molester. You told me to act like a human. Like I'm some kind of robot. I know I'm bad at this, Angelo. I've tried to learn how to get past it. Nothing works." She scowled, but he saw the flex of anguish beneath.

"Is that why you bury yourself in research?"

"Tried to, but girls aren't allowed to like science in my family," she grumbled. "I hated dresses until my brother told me about silkworms, then it gave me something interesting to think about when I had to wear one.

And yes, pursuing my doctorate made for a convenient argument against being rushed into marriage. It was a great excuse to avoid a lot of mindless socializing, but I like it, too."

"You really are as efficient as you are intelligent." He wasn't being sarcastic. He was impressed. He had street smarts that wouldn't quit, but academically he'd been more of a skater, capable of better grades, but only finishing the American high school equivalency at night school when he was in his early twenties. Even then, he had only done as much work as necessary to pass.

"It's also the only way I've ever been able to connect meaningfully with my family. My father especially, but my brothers, as well. I've always been a detriment on a social level, but I held up the Montero reputation in scholarly circles. Advanced it even, which my mother appreciates. To a point."

"Does your father?"

She didn't say anything. After a moment, she sighed. "My father isn't equipped to appreciate gestures. I wonder sometimes if he felt like I did as a child, or if he's on a spectrum of some kind. He's a genius and he genuinely doesn't care about social niceties. Somewhere along the line, he concluded very logically that a lack of diplomacy would hold him back so he married my mother to take care of that for him. She never talks about her childhood. I only know there was a title and little else, which means she holds very tightly to the life they've built together."

"And sacrificing her daughter in order to maintain that life is justified?" He clenched his teeth with repulsion.

"She doesn't see it that way. She thinks she was finding me the sort of partner she has, one who has worked with her to build a life that benefits all of us. I'm part of that team, Angelo. I had one job—to reset the family reputation. And I completely fell apart. The worst part is, all this distress and guilt I'm wallowing in? Completely useless. They don't care that I feel sick about it. *They're* not happy or sad or anxious or furious. They're *inconvenienced*." She flung out a hand, trembling all over. "They'll get over it while I'll live the rest of my life with this grating knowledge that I let them down. Now you want me to be some sort of princess bride and I'm going to fail at that, too."

"No, you won't. Come here." He had to hold her, she was shaking so badly. He moved into the closet and gathered her into his arms, cradling her against his chest, soothing her trembling body with a gentle massage of her back and petting her silky hair. "Cry if you need to."

She rubbed her face into his chest as she shook her head. "I never cry."

Because she wasn't allowed to? Hell, he had shed a tear the first time he'd had four figures in his bank account. Last night, as he had held her soft, naked body against him, he'd let his hand rest on her stomach and his throat had closed up. His chest was tight listening to her struggle right now.

She held on to him at least, trusting and warm, letting him rub her spine and try to comfort her.

"I won't make you be something you're not. I promise you," he said into her hair.

"But that's the problem," she groaned. "I *agree* with you. I don't want our baby to look back and think I was embarrassed. I want him or her to feel loved."

He drew in a sharp breath, stunned by how deeply her

words pierced his heart. His lips against her hair turned into a kiss of gratitude.

"Thank you for that," he said, profoundly moved. "I was treated like blasphemy. Sent to boarding school so I wouldn't be seen or heard. I *need* this baby to be welcomed and accepted."

"I do, too." She lifted her face, mouth quivering. "I mean, beneath all the angst of planning a wedding and photos and distress at how my parents reacted, I'm really excited." She blinked matted lashes. "Insanely excited."

"Me, too." He cupped her jaw, such tenderness welling in him that he could hardly breathe.

She melted into him and he had to let his mouth settle over her unsteady smile.

Her clothes quickly wound up on the floor next to his, but she didn't seem to mind having to search again later.

CHAPTER EIGHT

THEIR PHOTO WENT VIRAL.

"I don't understand," Pia said, trying not to have heart palpitations two days later as they were traveling back to Valencia. "How are we still trending? Are you *that* famous?"

"In the gaming community, I'm afraid so," he said dryly.

"Because of your chip? My father invented one of the first lightweight, scratch-resistant metals for laptops. No one is excited in *that* community."

"Before our chip, I was one of the public faces in gaming, promoting championships and color commentating."

"I read that in your bio when I first looked you up." She frowned, still confused by this. "You really run tournaments like any other sport industry? Why would people enjoy watching other people play video games?"

"The same reason people who play beer league football also like to watch the World Cup. They follow players' careers and enjoy watching great plays by their favorite teams. They root for them to win."

She shook her head. "I don't follow sports. I may never fully comprehend that mindset. Why are your fans so suspicious of my motives?" *Gold digger. Outsider.* She threw her phone down. "Are you a gamer? How did you become involved in it?"

"Chance." He set aside his own phone as their flight attendant brought their breakfast. "I stumbled into one of the early e-sport tournaments by answering an ad to help move equipment. I connected with a player who had flown in from America to work the event hoping to find a sponsor, but he was terrible at networking. Didn't like to take the initiative. I got us a meeting that wasn't successful, but it went well enough that when he heard I was homeless, he offered his sofa if I could get myself to LA. His house should have been condemned, but I worked on a freighter for a month, then worked under the table to help with rent. On my days off, I figured out how the promotion side of gaming works. When you're hungry, you hustle. I was starving."

She blinked. "Why were you homeless? Was this after you left boarding school?"

His face blanked, perhaps regretting he had shared so much. "My tuition was halted when I was fourteen."

"Why?"

"My mother died. My father's family no longer saw a need to maintain my upkeep."

"And cut you off at *fourteen*?" Her teen years had been agonizing and lonely, but at least she'd had a roof over her head.

She glanced at her phone where other comments had ranged from comparing her to a scantily clad female ninja character in a particular game to questioning whether she "deserved" to become part of Angelo's beloved team.

"No wonder they idolize you for what you've made of yourself. You're very inspirational."

"In an industry of introverts, an extrovert is king," he drawled. "I'm inviting my team to our engagement party. They'll hate it as much as you will."

"I won't hate it," she protested, even though she already hated it a little, mostly because it had ruffled so many feathers.

Angelo was fixated on having their party tonight, but her parents had already been committed to another function elsewhere. It would be bad form for La Reina not only to back out, but to host a competing event, even if it was for her daughter. Angelo had booked it at his hotel and suggested her parents come by when time allowed.

That had still left her mother in the position of backing out of their own social event because they couldn't possibly be anywhere but at their daughter's engagement. Pia had tried shifting Angelo on the date, but he'd been adamant. At the last moment, Cesar and Sorcha had swooped in to insist they host the party at their home. It was a strategy straight from the Montero playbook, taking back home court advantage.

Pia's parents had had to withdraw from the other affair, something at which her father was supposed to have presented an award. That was bad enough, but they weren't the only ones jumping ship in favor of the far more exclusive event up the coast. If anyone held more social sway in the country than La Reina Montero, it was her son's wife, Sorcha. Dignitaries attended for the chance to rub shoulders with the Duque and Duquessa, while young professionals, jet-setters and the fashionably elite wouldn't miss a chance to mingle with the Montero heir.

Pia had quit reading her texts. She didn't know who she was causing to be snubbed and didn't care, too busy with her own concerns. Along with the multitude of calls and emails with her own accountant and the family lawyers and PR team, she was working with her stylist to curate her wardrobe for the events they faced through the holiday season and into her wedding in mid-January. She was trying to be nicer to the wedding planner, but the young woman was underfoot at every turn with questions and samples and suggestions.

Finding a wedding dress on short notice had meant calling in a favor with a friend of Sorcha's in Italy. Her poor designer had had to swear a blood oath to keep Pia's pregnancy under wraps until such time as they wanted to announce it, and Pia still hadn't settled on a dress for tonight.

Then there was the act of moving from the gorgeous little house her maternal aunt had bequeathed to her to the island mansion where an interior designer was already asking about nursery furniture.

"Of course you should keep this house if you want to," Angelo said as he wandered the rooms of her home, taking in the earthy tones and comfortable furniture. "It will give us our own space when we come to visit your family. You'll have to convert one of these rooms to a nursery, though."

"Oh dear Lord," Pia whimpered.

Angelo chuckled as he kissed her forehead. "Why don't you nap before we have to dress and leave for your brother's?"

"I have so much to do." She could barely face it, though.

"I'll wake you before I leave for my meeting," he

promised, nudging her into the bedroom, where he draped a blanket over her.

She should have known he was lying.

Two hours later, the jangle of the landline woke her. Few people used it beyond her family or the occasional call from the grocer. She answered in time to hear her housekeeper on the extension telling the caller she wasn't available and offer to take a message.

"I'm here," Pia said. "Who's calling?"

"This is Tomas Gomez, Señorita Montero. Do you know who I am?"

"I'll take it," Pia said, sitting up. The phone clicked as her housekeeper hung up. "I believe my brother Rico now owns an estate that previously belonged to your family."

"That's right. It was in our family for generations. Do you know why Angelo was on the estate the night of the masked ball?"

"W-was he?" She instinctively played dumb, mostly because she was so surprised to receive this call.

"He was there for more than the painting, Pia. But you already know that, don't you? Were you helping him?"

Her skin crawled at his use of her name, but she couldn't seem to hang up the phone. "In what way? I don't know what you're talking about."

"The jewelry. Did you help him retrieve it?"

She caught her breath loudly enough he must have heard it.

"Where is it? Can you get it?"

"It's in the possession of a security company." She said it out of instinctive fear he would break in here looking for the treasure if she wasn't frank about it. "Why are you talking to me about this, rather than Angelo?"

"Don't you want to know that your fiancé is a thief? A con artist? It's no accident he booked your engagement party for the night your parents were scheduled to attend an event where *I* will receive some well-deserved recognition for my philanthropy. That's what kind of man he is. He's trying to buy respectability by attaching himself to you while nursing an old grudge against people he knows are better than he is. Your mother would be horrified if she knew the truth of his background. Not that I'll say anything. If you can get me the jewels?"

She shuddered at his sly tone. Tomas was no better than the kind of man he was describing. She distantly heard the front door.

"He's coming." She hung up.

Her skin was clammy, her mind whirling. Had Angelo known who she was that night? Had he followed her to the rooftop and purposely seduced her to put her in this position of having to marry him? Why had he been there? For the painting, yes, but something else? Something on the rooftop? A tin full of jewelry, perhaps?

The door opened and her intended entered. His charming, "*Querida,*" rang falsely. "What's wrong?" He frowned.

"You said you would wake me," she mumbled, not having to pretend a scattered mind as she rose, head aching and spinning. "I need to get ready."

Despite her aversion to shining brightly, Pia wore a silver dress covered in tinsel-like beadwork. It scooped across the tops of her breasts and ended midthigh. Her feet were in some sort of glass slippers that completed the icicle look.

He smiled darkly in the back of the car, beginning to enjoy the private knowledge that he alone knew how easily she melted under his kiss or caress.

"We have time," he pointed out, glancing at the closed privacy screen.

It was an hour to her brother's villa and, he discovered to his consternation, he longed quite badly to touch her. This afternoon's meeting with her brothers had been tense, their contempt for him undisguised. He ached to fill his hands with her, catch her cries of pleasure in his mouth and reaffirm that she belonged to him. She'd seemed befuddled and distracted when he arrived home, but now...

"Come here," he invited.

"I had a call while you were out," she said in a hollow voice. "From Tomas Gomez. He asked about the jewelry."

For a wallflower, she excelled at delivering a surprise crosscut that snapped a jaw. A nest of snakes came alive in his belly.

"What did you tell him?"

"That you left them with a security company. That's what Melodie's husband is, isn't he? A security expert?"

Top in his field, globally.

"So you confirmed to Tomas that I had the jewels." A call to Pia had been inevitable, he supposed. The scumbags wouldn't confront *him* if they could unsettle a woman or turn her against him.

"He asked if I helped you retrieve them," she continued in that empty voice. "Did I?"

A metallic taste filled his mouth. "Inadvertently," he admitted.

"On the rooftop." Her voice developed a pang that

made him feel as though she was slipping through his fingers. "That's why you seduced me."

"Our lovemaking just happened, Pia."

"Did it? He said you're using me to climb society's ladder. You knew who I was!"

"I have my own society. I don't need yours," he spat, even as panic dug talons into him. "Don't listen to that piece of garbage. He's a liar." *Don't side with him.*

"He called *you* a liar. And a thief."

"It takes one to know one," he muttered. White-hot anger grew into a spiked ball inside him, too painful to contain. "But I've never lied to you."

"Only hidden the truth."

"Do you *want* the truth?"

"I don't know. Will it make me an accessory to whatever crimes you've committed? My brother bought the Gomez villa *and its contents*. If you took something more than the painting you purchased, you were stealing."

"I didn't steal anything. I retrieved something my mother left for me. I retrieved my *mother*."

She snapped her head around to look at him. "Not the girl in the painting. She's too young."

"Her name is Angelica. It's the only image I have of her. She was the daughter of the baron's second wife from her first marriage and yes, she was far too young to be a mother. *My* mother." Despite a lifetime of damming up the truth behind shame and anger, the toxic words spilled out of him in a torrent. "The accusation is that she took the jewelry from her mother's bedroom," he said, his voice low and gritty and brimming with three decades of helpless hatred. "I am quite certain it was all brought to her by my father, since it was kept in the safe in his office. He spent time with my mother when his wife, my grandmother, had gone out for the day."

Pia covered her mouth, eyes wide with horror.

"I suppose I'm lucky I wasn't thrown into a river or given away when she had me. At *fifteen*. I had six years with her in that moldy little cottage before they sent me to that prison they called a boarding school. I barely saw her after that. Don't ask me why she stayed. To ensure my tuition was paid, I imagine. Maybe she felt too damned fragile to fight for a better life. All I know is that she killed herself shortly after my father died, well aware she would be turned onto the street otherwise. *I* was."

Angelo's acrid fury clouded the darkened back seat of the car.

Pia was speechless, utterly unable to form thoughts into words she was so anguished on his mother's behalf. Pia was overwhelmed and frightened by her pregnancy and she was an adult with resources. She had a support system and her baby's father was beside her in this journey, putting her down for naps when she was too overtired to see the sense in it.

"Did your grandmother know?" she managed to gasp.

"Of course she did. Everyone in the family knew. They also knew which side their bread was buttered on, so they let it go on."

"That's horrific." She couldn't grasp it. It was too awful.

"It is. And if my half brothers want the jewels back, they can damned well acknowledge how my mother came by them, not call my future wife and tell her I *stole* them. They can admit I'm as entitled as they are to a share in the family fortune."

"But you could… I mean, wouldn't a DNA test—"

"I could insist on a test," he said, cutting her off with a biting tone. "This isn't about proving our relationship any more than it is about the money. I hate that I carry any trace of their tainted blood. They can have the damned name and title. Protecting that is why her *own mother* allowed her to be abused. No, I'm quite content to remain an ugly family secret, but I won't let them continue to enjoy the life they lead when it came at her expense. I'm taking it apart brick by brick."

"Why can't you…?" She balked even as she started to say it.

"Tell the world what happened? Put my mother on trial in the court of public opinion? My brothers will claim she instigated what happened to her. That's what kind of people they are. My poor, upstanding, blameless father, a grown man, was helpless against a teenage seductress. Who are *your* parents going to believe, Pia? The bastard with a grudge? Or one of their own?"

They would distance themselves as much as possible, she suspected. Her entire body went cold.

"I wish you had told me sooner," she said, projecting to the ramifications if this came out.

"When?" he demanded. "While we were two strangers having our tête-à-tête on the rooftop? When you were informing me that we'd conceived a child? Or do you mean before we publicly attached ourselves with the engagement photo? Frightened to be associated with me now, Pia?"

She looked guiltily to the window, heart clenching at his scathing tone.

"There's still time to back out." His gritty voice dared her to try. "I'll make it very uncomfortable for you if you do."

She glanced back to see him sitting with his clenched fists on his thighs, his profile cast in iron. How comfortable would he make it for her to continue forward and marry him, she wondered hysterically? Especially if the truth came out?

There might as well have been a wall of ice between them the rest of the drive. She didn't know how to reach past it and wasn't sure she wanted to. When he had asked her to trust him that first night, she hadn't expected anything of this magnitude. She felt tricked, especially when he was speaking so ruthlessly about going through with their marriage. He was hardly motivated by any genuine feeling toward her, was he?

Her angst made her smile all the more strained when they arrived at Cesar's mansion to find Rico and Poppy were already there along with her parents. The rest of the guests weren't due for an hour, but Sorcha had wanted a chance to break the ice and get to know Angelo.

"Pia, would you be a love and pop up to say goodnight to the boys?" Sorcha entreated while she was removing her coat. "Enrique found a shell the other day. He's convinced you're the only one who can identify it." She took hold of Angelo's arm. "You, however, look like a man who might be up for sampling my stock of Irish whiskey. Can I tempt you?"

Pia was dying for a moment to collect her thoughts and the children always restored her. "I'll join you shortly," she promised Angelo, and veered up the stairs.

She had only been with her nephews for five short minutes, however, when Cesar came in.

"Tía is expected downstairs," he told the boys in a gentle but firm voice, his affectionate stroke of his older son's hair softening the blow.

"We'll have a proper visit soon," she promised them.

"Christmas," Enrique whispered with a grin of anticipation.

"Exactly." Pia couldn't help cupping his little face and kissing his forehead. She did the same to Mateo and blew another kiss at them as she left.

Cesar stopped her turning down the hall toward the stairs, opening the door to the playroom across the hall and waving her in with an imperious look.

"Oh, I see. It wasn't the boys who wanted to see me." Why was that such a kick in the chest?

"They always want to see you, but so did I." Cesar swung the door mostly closed.

Pia crossed a loomed mat imprinted with a town of roadways and buildings, stopped at the indoor slide and turned to face her brother, arms folded. Defensive? Absolutely. It was bad enough she hadn't brought home someone from the preapproved list of bachelors. Her groom's backstory was even more shocking than any of them imagined and she was pregnant by him. Which meant she'd had *sex*.

It didn't matter that Cesar had been in this position himself. His role had been the other side and he'd never been as sensitive about having his private business strewn about, probably because he was secure in his place in the family and the world.

What made this confrontation particularly difficult, however, was the fact that she liked her brothers. Their marrying wonderful women had certainly helped her feel closer to them, but Cesar especially was the person she most hated to disappoint. He had suffered betrayals from other quarters and once his trust was lost, it was never regained.

She braced herself for his rebuke.

"You don't have to marry him," he said flatly. "Ignore whatever Mother has said about how things look. *I* will always look after you."

She was too shocked to react. They never spoke from the heart. The most sentimental thing he'd ever said to her was his sincere thanks for her presence at his wedding because it had meant so much to Sorcha.

This conversation instantly became uncomfortable. She reflexively pointed out the obvious. "I've been living independently for five years. I can take care of myself."

"Clearly," he said, which was a rebuke, but a gentle one.

"Lovely glass house you live in," she retorted.

"It is," he agreed, nodding with gravity. "Which is why I'm telling you to do what's right for *you*. I will back you up with Mother, support you in any and every way you need. How well do you even know this man, Pia?" Now he sounded like the clichéd big brother. "The gaps in his background report make me suspicious."

"You had him investigated?"

Cesar snorted. "If you think he doesn't have a hundred-page dossier on every single one of us, you really do need someone to start looking after you."

Maybe she did, because her first thought went to how badly it would hurt Angelo to have his mother's pain uncovered by some paid snoop, then subsequently held up as a blight on his character. That poor young girl had been in an untenable situation. She had given birth to a baby she shouldn't have conceived and loved him enough to protect and provide for him the only way she could. Pia's heart fractured thinking of her.

"His lawyers are sharks," Cesar continued. "Negotiations have been heated."

"*Our* lawyers are sharks," she dismissed. She'd been copied on everything and thought it was going as well as it could, given both sides had proprietary interests to protect.

"How long have you known him? Are you in love? Don't tie yourself to him because you think you have to. I want to hear it from *you* that this is what you want."

She parted her lips, but discovered it was only to draw in a deep sigh.

Still time to back out, she heard Angelo saying. Those words had hurt because he hadn't tried to convince her to stay with him. He had threatened to make her life difficult if she didn't. One more indication his desire to marry wasn't about her at all. No matter how great the sex, he was marrying her for the baby and possibly other, darker motives.

The irony was, his devotion to their child carried tremendous weight with her.

"He wants this baby, Cesar. In a way that—" She cut herself off, unwilling to go down the road of their father's shortcomings. There was no point.

Cesar got there anyway. "That's why you have to do what's right for you," he said gently. "I didn't have the power to make things better for you when we were young. I do now. *You* do. Say the word and I will end this engagement right now."

What could she say? That she *wanted* to marry a man who had stolen something that technically belonged to Rico? That she wanted a husband whose history could come to light and throw a shadow over all of them? That she hoped whatever scandal arose, it would blow over before their child was old enough to understand any of it and would never be harmed by it?

"Pia?" he prompted.

"Tell me something, Cesar." She had to clear the huskiness from her throat before she continued. "Do you blame Sorcha for the fact her father had two families? That she was part of the illegitimate one?"

"Of course not," he snapped. "Her father's behavior had nothing to do with her."

"Will you please remember that if anyone talks to you about Angelo?"

"What are you saying? Forewarned is forearmed. Tell me everything."

"It's not mine to tell," she said as the door swung inward, silent on its hinges.

Angelo stood there, one shoulder negligently braced against the jamb.

She knew immediately he'd been there long enough to hear her comparison of his circumstance to Sorcha's, maybe more.

Keeping his gaze locked with Pia's, he said to Cesar, "Your wife does not have a promising career on the magician's circuit. Her attempt at misdirection was blatant and obvious." He held out his hand to Pia. "She is, however, an extremely charming hostess. I don't wish to be rude. Shall we rejoin our party, *querida*?"

She knew her acquiescence would be agreement to more than a party. The engagement would proceed. The wedding would happen. Chips would fall as they may.

Cesar was wrong. She didn't have the power here. Her baby did. And she genuinely believed Angelo would love their child. Maybe some hidden part of her even saw that as potential he might one day love *her*.

She moved to set her hand in his and they went back downstairs.

CHAPTER NINE

THEIR ENGAGEMENT EVENING went quite well, all things considered. Angelo hadn't meant to tell Pia the truth so baldly, driving it between them like a wedge. Maybe he'd had to do it with anger in order to get it out and brace himself for what he expected would be a rejection.

Her family's maneuverings, allowing her to slip away for an intervention from big brother, hadn't surprised him one bit. He had accepted a whiskey and told himself he would be better off if she broke their engagement. He had no desire to become part of this stuck-up family and suffer their judgment for the rest of his life. He didn't want to stare into her eyes across the breakfast table every morning and see—

With a choke, he'd set aside his drink and went looking for her, leaving a surprised pause behind him.

He had arrived at the cracked door in time to hear her brother's script spoken exactly on cue. Pia quite easily could have spilled everything Angelo had revealed to protect her own family from future scandal, but she hadn't. She had shielded his mother in the only way she could, by maintaining her privacy.

That kindness nearly broke him. He had kept her hand in his the rest of the night, doing everything he could to ease her tension as they made the rounds with guests. When they made love that night, it had been with something new between them—the first strands of trust.

But it was immediately put to the test.

Now that Tomas and Darius knew Angelo had the jewels, their campaign to discredit him began in earnest. Rumormongering online suggested everything from accusations of child labor to tax evasion. Paparazzi began tailing them and a woman he'd never met claimed to be pregnant with his child.

Angelo took sensible steps. He had Pia's housekeeper change the phone number and instructed her staff to screen all communications. His security team upgraded the alarm system on her house, a pair of guards began to shadow them when they went out, and another pair remotely monitored for suspicious activity.

None of that could protect them from the whispers and snide asides that followed them into cocktail parties and benefits. Much of the animosity was pure snobbery couched as concern for Pia.

"He's American, isn't he?" he overheard a woman ask Pia in an outraged whisper, because *that* was a crime.

"Spanish," Pia said evenly. "America is where his head office is located. He has a home in California."

"Are you moving there? Because if he isn't part of *this* life, how will he fit in? I mean, have an affair. *Look* at him. But I can't see you *marrying* him."

"Is that a regret for the wedding? I'll let Mother know."

The woman's face had dropped and Angelo had seized the opportunity to draw Pia onto the dance floor, taking dark satisfaction in giving the woman no time to rephrase after Pia's cutthroat response.

Pia's mother was concerned that RSVPs weren't coming in thick and fast, though. It was another indicator that people were dragging their feet as they debated taking sides. So far, Angelo wasn't winning.

Pia wasn't winning, either. He'd thrust her smack in the middle of his war. Perhaps that should have prompted an apology from him, but he was so disgusted by her crowd's desire to turn on what they perceived to be an outsider, he could only bite out, "Hypocrites."

They had just arrived at a hotel ballroom to be informed by a greeter they weren't on the list.

Angelo's brothers were keeping a low profile, probably not even here, but that was what made this worse. They were getting the word out that Angelo was *persona non grata* and it was working.

"This is exactly what happened to my mother," Angelo said as they stepped away from the entrance to a nearby alcove. "Any friends she might have made in her early years disappeared, not standing by her at all. They preferred to suck onto my father like lampreys and continue to benefit from his influence. They're still doing it. How can you want to be counted among these blue-blooded parasites?"

"I don't," Pia said stiffly. "You know my feelings on parties. These weeks of making appearances, providing nothing but fodder for gossip, have been hell. I'm here for *you*."

"For your parents, you mean," he shot back. "And your father's delicate reputation."

"If you and I slink off, never to be seen or heard from again, my parents will be better than fine. My mother would prefer our notoriety die a quick and permanent death. No, I'm dragging myself through all of this for you. I don't agree with your methods, but I do agree that people are backing the wrong horse. Even more, this is about how our child will be accepted in the future. That starts with us staking our right to be here now."

She had pulled out her phone and was scrolling through her contacts as they spoke. She tapped out a text, throwing her phone back into her clutch.

"Who was that?"

"Someone who had better remember the numerous alibis her cerebral roommate provided in a desperate effort to fit in."

"To hell with that." Her words about their child had struck home. He took her hand and glared down the greeter as he drew Pia into the party. If this crowd thought they could ostracize him, they could try saying it to his face.

Inside, the decor marked the year change with balloons and streamers. Champagne cascaded down a pyramid of glasses. Hundreds of vintage clocks littered the ballroom, meant to be taken home as swag. A chanteuse presided over a dance floor, crooning a modern pop tune, but she was barely audible over the din of convivial guests.

The chattering voices slowly petered off as heads turned to stare, leaving the breathy singer sounding overloud. She was a professional, however, and didn't miss a beat as she transitioned into a rendition of something from a film soundtrack.

Pia, however, wasn't as unaffected. She dug her nails into the back of his hand.

Angelo was genuinely sorry to put her on the spot this way, but he would be damned if he would back out now.

"As usual, *mi sirenita*, your beauty is turning heads." He lifted her hand to kiss her knuckles.

In the last few weeks, she had begun embracing bolder colors and styles. Tonight, she was stunning in an aqua gown with a mermaid skirt that inspired his endearment.

Predictably, a composed Mona Lisa smile was her only response.

"You have a nerve," a man said, weaving forward through the crowd.

Darius. Angelo recognized him with a lurch in his chest. Drunk and mean, as usual.

Angelo felt both sickened and murderous. He was fourteen and helpless again, yet mature and powerful and cold-bloodedly willing to fight this man to the death.

He instinctively tried to draw Pia behind him, but she set her cool hand over his knuckles and wiggled her fingers, drawing his attention to the fact he was crushing her hand in his grip. His lungs burned and he would have shoved forward to confront Darius, but a scantily clad redhead emerged from the crowd.

"Pia!" She waved off the security guard who had been about to put his hand on Angelo's shoulder. There really would have been bloodshed if he'd managed it.

"I'm so glad you could come!" The woman air-kissed Pia's pale cheeks. "You all know Pia Montero," she announced to the crowd at large. "One of my dearest friends from my misspent youth. Don't say a *word* about our exploits," she warned Pia with a girlish laugh. "And this is your infamous fiancé." She batted her lashes at Angelo. "We've been hearing *so* much about you. Please let me introduce you around."

* * *

As hideous evenings went, this one took the prize, but Pia recognized a turning point when she stood on one, mostly because it twisted her stomach into knots.

This had been the most blatant attempt to snub them yet, and she'd had to gather every shred of courage she possessed to tackle it. She had hated leaning on one of the very connections Angelo found so contemptuous, but it had *worked*. Much to her astonishment. She rarely reached out to any of her acquaintances, especially young women from boarding school. They might as well have been a different species, she'd had so little in common with them.

But along with understanding how difficult it would be to come back from any sort of retreat, she had wanted to make Angelo see that not everything in her family's titled life was a false front for dark acts. Maybe this wasn't "their" type of people, but that didn't make every single person here a terrible one.

Of course, there were definitely some awful examples, she noted with an inward groan as a drunk staggered up and poked his finger into Angelo's ruffled tuxedo shirt.

"You—"

Angelo grabbed the man's hand in what looked like a warm, thumb-grabbing handshake that drew the man in close. Only Pia saw that he squeezed tightly enough his knuckles went white and so did the man's face. Angelo used his other hand to grip the man's bent arm. His thumb dug into the soft flesh above his elbow as he said, "Darius," through gritted teeth.

Dios mio. She saw the resemblance, but only vaguely. Any good looks Darius had once possessed had been sacrificed on the altar of poor life choices.

"Angelo," she murmured, affecting a calm smile as she glanced around.

Most people had lost interest in them now that they'd been introduced as the latest celebrity couple. A few stared unabashedly, though.

"You black sheep bastard. You knew where it was all along," Darius choked.

"I know where it is now. Shall I tell the auction house you'd like a catalog? So you can purchase what you've wanted to get your filthy hands on for so long? Proceeds will go to a charity for pregnant teenagers. A worthy cause you'll want to support, I'm sure."

Darius snorted dismissively only to stiffen and make a strangled noise, telling Pia that Angelo had exerted an extra pulse of pressure.

"I'm reporting this to the police," Darius threatened, voice straining with agony. "Theft. Assault."

"You go right ahead," Angelo said, staring with dead eyes into his brother's. "You tell your story. I'll tell mine."

"You're proving what an animal you are."

"Keep pushing me, Darius. See what happens."

Sweat broke in beads on Darius's upper lip.

"You don't look well, *hermano*. Go home," Angelo advised in a voice that raised the hair on the back of Pia's neck. "Never let me see you again."

He released him and Darius staggered away.

Angelo gave his hands a quick wipe on his thighs.

Pia pasted on her most unruffled smile and took his hand, leading him onto the dance floor. It was the last thing she wanted to do. They were both stiff and unco-ordinated as he took her in his arms. She felt the clash of his heart battering in his rib cage through the layers

of their clothes. Her own heart was falling down a per-
petual flight of stairs, but she hid it with a stock expression of serenity.

Concern for Angelo had her scanning his granite features. He was a million miles away, his mind in some
dark place that prevented him from finding the beat in
the music and dancing as smoothly as he usually did.

When it came to physical contact, she usually let
him initiate it. She only ever felt comfortable touching
him freely when they were in bed, naked and entwined,
shields on the floor with their clothes.

She slid light fingers against the side of his neck,
though, caressing to get his attention.

"It's a worthy cause," she said. "I didn't know that
was what you were doing with the proceeds. I think any
mother would be proud of a son who was doing everything he could to right such a wrong done to her. I'm
very sorry I will never meet her."

"Me, too," he said, drawing her in tighter with a firm
touch that crashed her into his taut frame. He was still
gripped by rage.

She let her head settle onto his shoulder, wholly un-
familiar with trying to offer comfort, but she ignored
the music and the lively people surrounding them. She
slipped her arms around his waist and tried to radiate
strength and acceptance. Tried to heal him in some small
way.

After a few moments, his hold on her changed. His
hands moved across her back, settling her more securely
against him. The tension gripping him eased. His lips
touched her temple.

"Thank you," he murmured.

She wasn't sure what she'd done, but she closed her

eyes, pleased to have helped him in some small way, hoping with all her heart he was finding the closure he needed.

For the first time, they didn't make love when they came home. Granted, it was well past midnight. Pia barely bothered to remove her makeup, while Angelo insisted he needed a shower. She didn't remember him coming to bed. She fell asleep hard and fast, but they made love in the morning.

He rose so abruptly afterward, however, she was compelled to ask, "Is everything all right?"

"Of course." He stood there in all his naked glory, the flush of their lovemaking fading on his chest. His abdominal muscles were stacked and tense, though, his jaw shadowed by midnight stubble, his gaze flinty. "Thank you for having my back last night. Every night, lately. I hadn't realized, but now I do."

"Of course. That's what marriage is for."

"Is it?" His inscrutable gaze didn't waver from hers, making her self-conscious.

"From what I can tell." Her shrug nearly caused the sheet to slip. She wasn't sure why she was hiding behind it, but she felt awfully insecure despite their scorching connection moments ago.

He seemed very far away. Distant and watchful and displeased.

"I've judged my parents' loveless marriage more harshly than it deserves, I think," she said pensively, reevaluating something she'd only ever seen as coldly practical and lacking in personal regard. "There's value in a dedicated partnership where you can trust in the other and lean on their strength. You can become more than the sum of the parts. That's a relationship worth pursuing, I think."

He snorted, incredibly intimidating as he drilled her with his unwavering gaze. "You're still willing to marry me?"

Her heart leaped in alarm. He wanted to back out? Because he'd achieved acceptance? He didn't want her after all?

"Knowing what a black sheep bastard I am?" he continued.

"Don't," she murmured, recoiling at the depth of angry hurt that coated his tone.

"How are *you* going to balance *that* out?" He sounded both appalled and tortured. "How will you compensate for it? You can't. And they may yet force it to light, Pia."

"I don't know how I'll react." She curled her fingers into the edge of the sheet, her toes into the mattress. "But it won't change my commitment to you and our marriage. Not if we're both faithful and sincerely trying to make a life together."

He didn't seem particularly appeased. His jaw pulsed as he ground his teeth, his brooding gaze cast into the middle distance.

"We don't have to discuss any of this unless it becomes necessary." It was a cowardly avoidance of a hard subject, but she was terrified that the tentative bond they'd formed was disintegrating. It wasn't strong enough to withstand hard examination.

His cheek ticked and he nodded once, jerkily, and went to dress.

She slipped into the shower. She could have invited him to join her and wished she had, but she didn't know how to extend herself that way. It felt weak to want to touch him when they'd just been physically close.

She was afraid of rejection—that was the real issue. It didn't help that Angelo remained withdrawn and she didn't know how to bridge that gap.

At least their New Year's Eve appearance clinched their position as the couple to support. Acceptances to their wedding poured in.

Pia couldn't say she was relieved exactly, but for the sake of everyone involved she was thankful they had overcome whatever hurdle Angelo's brothers had posed.

Which freed her up to panic about the new life upon which she was embarking.

Angelo had spent the last weeks making inroads into the society that should have been his by birthright. Now she would take her place next to him on his turf, a global stage focused on the technology sector. She would have to become what she had always felt would make her a square peg in a round hole—the wife of a powerful man.

Angelo willingly stayed in her home in Valencia while they rode out these turbulent weeks into their shotgun wedding, but after their honeymoon in Australia, he intended to take her to America until her third trimester reduced her ability to travel. They would return to Spain until the baby was born, after which he expected they would divide their time between a handful of his preferred homes.

Along with learning the ropes of motherhood, which Pia looked forward to, she would continue decorating his arm and joining him at networking events. She would have to begin entertaining. Host *functions*.

So even though Angelo frowned with concern when

she reported the final number was nine hundred and fifty guests, and said, "It's only one day," she knew it wasn't. It was a daunting lifetime of feeling isolated in a crowd.

"What have you done in the past to cope?" he asked, seeing something in her expression that made him set aside the tablet he was working on.

"Mostly I ran away," she joked, trying to dismiss her character deficiency even though he wasn't teasing or mocking her for it.

"What do you mean?"

"Well, they were legitimate field studies, but I might have left early for them." She looked at her nails. "Or stayed longer than strictly necessary. Or collected data for other researchers."

For the first time in days, he seemed to relax as he tilted a look at her that was both empathetic and indulgent. "Would you feel more comfortable holding a clipboard than a bouquet? Because I'm open to it."

She wrinkled her nose. "I'll try imagining it while I'm walking down the aisle. Maybe it will help."

"What have you decided with regards to research?" He pulled his earbuds out completely and left them atop his tablet, giving her his full attention. That always disconcerted her, but made her insides squirm today when she was trying to hide how disheartened she felt at the life she faced.

"I don't know that I'll have time to pursue any." She set aside her own tablet and the calendar that was being synced to his. Eaten up and overwhelmed.

"Because of the baby?"

"And your work. I'm looking at all these events you have scheduled and now your assistant is asking if I want to take an active role in some of your charities. That's the sort of thing my mother always did and—"

"You are not your mother," he cut in. "There are only a handful of events where your presence is important to me. I'll mark them and the rest are up to you. My people have done all my organizing until this point and can continue to do so. Our baby won't be as accommodating, though," he said wryly.

"I know," she said on a little sigh. "Fieldwork is out for several years, so I might as well take on charity work."

"We'll travel with you." He shrugged.

She choked out a dismissive laugh.

He frowned. "I'll help as much as possible from day one, Pia. That's why I want us to be a family. I realize it won't be easy to carve out time in the beginning, but I don't expect you to sacrifice that brain of yours to my photo ops. Is there something you can work on in the short term that's more piecemeal and can be done from home?"

She hesitated, rather stunned by his attitude. "This is weird for me. I've always had to work really hard to justify *wanting* to study. Mother thought it was a waste of time since she expected me to live a role like hers once I was married. I made a strong case for at least getting my doctorate, but my father and brothers have always questioned my interest in biology. The family business is alloys so they thought I should follow in their footsteps. Even when I fund from my own pocket, some professor is always quick to weigh in on whether my pursuit has merit or tell me my time and money could be better spent elsewhere. It's exhausting."

"Do I need to put on a cardigan and throw a research

fund-raiser to get your idea approved? I can do that. I can talk just about anyone into just about anything."

She'd noticed. She told him things she'd never told anyone.

"I've been contributing some of my data to a pregnancy study," she admitted. "It's a surprisingly under-studied area. Women are considered to be vulnerable in this state, physically and mentally." She dismissed that with a roll of her eyes. "Obviously, we're not a testing ground for new drugs, but there are a lot of things that aren't known. I've been thinking about how to structure a few studies of my own—"

"Done. What do you need?"

"More pregnant women?" she suggested tartly, suppressing an astonished chuckle that he was so quick and unquestioning in his support.

He came to take her chin in a light pinch. "I will proceed with caution on producing more of those. I'm discovering they can be quite a handful. If there was some decent data warning of the real danger they pose, we men might show some restraint in making them."

"Oh, good luck with that," she sputtered.

"You're right." His teeth flashed in a grin of humor. "As if we'll read when we could put our time to better use." He winked. His irises shone with the warmth of a summer sky and he was so blindingly handsome in that moment that she caught her breath and thought, *Oh.*

This was why they called it falling. Her head swam and her feet couldn't feel the floor. The world tilted and her heart flipped and wind rushed in her ears. When his mouth touched hers, such a soaring joy gripped her, she thought she would burst.

* * *

That lightness carried her into her wedding day, putting secretive smiles on her sisters-in-law's faces as they fussed around her with the rest of the bridal party. Her stylist kept going on about the romance of the day and how there was so much "love in the air."

They know, Pia thought, desperately trying to hide her tender new feelings because the sense of exposure was so intense. And she didn't know how Angelo felt. Was he growing to care for her, too? Or was his support of her all part of a play they were enacting for the benefit of their child?

She dearly wished for a moment of privacy to collect herself, but solitude was the only luxury this wedding didn't afford her. She had to hide her insecurities behind a calm smile as she was harnessed into her mikado silk A-line gown and took the weight of her veil, covered in thousands of seed pearls, as it was draped over her hair.

Pia wasn't convinced she was worthy of romantic love anyway. Sorcha and Poppy, yes. They were warm and outgoing, witty and quick to laugh. They were so easy to adore—it was no wonder Pia's staid brothers had fallen head over heels.

Pia didn't even know where to start in making herself emotionally appealing. Whatever good qualities she had cultivated had never swayed her parents toward words or demonstrations of love. Even loving friendships were built on confidences, something she found difficult because the things she valued had rarely been valued by others. Her niece and nephews loved her, which felt like a miracle, but Pia didn't let it go to her head. Such well-loved children were factories for the recycling of it, pouring out adoration for anyone who brought them a toy or took them into the garden for an hour.

As for Angelo, she had shared more with him than anyone in her life, quite possibly revealing as many reasons *not* to love her. Who wanted a wife who fought tears because her wedding day felt like too big an ordeal to face? One who would rather wear woolen socks and rubber rain gear than a gown worth a quarter million euros?

The moment arrived and her father appeared to escort her. He looked flawless and handsome and said a polite, "You look lovely."

Pia waited an extra, agonizing second, hoping for something… Maybe that clichéd remark that he didn't want to lose her? That he was proud of her? That he forgave her for getting pregnant and forcing this wedding to the wrong man?

"Are you ready?"

The urge to cry lurched harder in her throat.

Love was impossible to force; she *knew* that. She also knew that longing for it made the lack of it even more painful. She couldn't pin her dreams on Angelo falling for her. Couldn't do that to herself and continue to suffer this ache the rest of her life.

She swallowed back her tears and let her father guide her to the top of the aisle.

The music changed and the guests stood and turned to watch her procession. She wanted to cling to her father's arm, but forced herself to hold to the pace he set and smile and breathe.

Her gaze snagged on Angelo's as she moved toward him. His attention flickered to her bouquet and she could practically hear his voice in her head. *Nice clipboard.*

She wanted to laugh, then. Laugh and cry and run up to hug him. The rest of the congregation fell away and no one existed in this cavernous church but the two of them as she came to a halt before him.

She was lucky, so lucky, to have him. Lucky to have passion and a devoted father for her child. It was all she truly needed.

It would have to be, because it was all they had.

Their special day was paved with rice and rose petals, but Angelo felt like the fraud he was.

His first dalliance with Pia had been just that, a pleasurable encounter that had been as pure as something that earthy and erotic could be. It had been free of ulterior motives, at least.

Then, when her pregnancy pulled them into a forced engagement, he hadn't cared what sort of uproar his appearance in her life might cause. In fact, he had embraced making waves in her patrician pond.

He hadn't cared because he hadn't *cared*. Now he was realizing how much his presence in her life was costing her. The greater the stakes became, the more it bothered him. He sure as hell wouldn't have allowed Darius anywhere near her if he could have avoided it.

He kept trying to forget that night even as moments from it flashed into his memory—the snubbing at the door, Darius's punishing truth that Angelo would never be anything but the ill-begotten bastard he was.

Pia's revelation that she was putting herself through this trial *for him*. Yes, their end goal was the best life for their child, but he could spirit her and their baby to America and skip all this nonsense if they had to. He'd been ready to quit Europe altogether that evening. He was neither beholden nor sentimentally attached to his birthplace. He lived on the island in the Med because the climate suited him.

Pia, antisocial science nerd that she was, had an inner badass, though. One who came to the fore when she decided she wanted something. She had kept him at the party until midnight when he would have happily left minutes after his confrontation with Darius. She had circulated with her hand tucked firmly into his, smoothing any lasting rough edges, cementing their position as a power couple well above whatever basement level of hell his brothers might have slithered back into.

Much as Angelo was loath to care about such a puerile victory, it meant something to him that Pia had refused to give up on getting it for him. He was still stunned. Moved.

But somehow, in the crashing of his old world into his new one, his shell of anger had been shaken, crumbling enough to expose the shame beneath. Shame that leaked into a bigger stain as he realized he was pulling an innocent—no, two innocents—into the mire of his origin story.

He had gone to bed that night convinced he should break things off with her. Of course, he'd made love to her the very next morning, before they were properly awake. Her soft, questing hands and receptive scent had got to him the way she always did.

Trying to leave after that would have been the height of callousness. He couldn't bring himself to do it anyway. Every time he tried to set some boundaries between them, she did some small thing he found charming and disarming or revealed a hidden tidbit about herself that roused the protector in him. He kept wondering who would keep the vagaries of life from knocking her around if he wasn't there to shield her?

He was becoming dependent on her in his own way, which was equally concerning. He liked her. She made him laugh and made him feel strong and necessary and powerful. She made him think and believe he was a better man than he was.

His palms were sweating as she walked down the aisle toward him, conscience heavy with the knowledge he was binding her to disgrace purely to feed this craving in him to have her by his side. Always.

The churn of cement in his gut didn't stop until they were pronounced husband and wife. Even then, he had to wonder how long it would take such a brilliant mind to realize she'd made a terrible mistake.

CHAPTER TEN

GIVEN THEIR RUSHED SCHEDULE, they had held their wedding midweek, the day before Pia's twelve-week scan. Her specialist appointment was the last thing on her calendar before she had two solid weeks of nothing to do, but she would have given up a kidney to stay in bed this morning.

"I should have canceled it," Angelo said when she yawned again, shivering with the force of it. "Or moved it to a later time."

"No." She fought another yawn. "Let's get this done and start our honeymoon. I'm looking forward to it."

He left a beat of silence for her to hear her own words. "Again, I wanted to stay in bed."

Now she was blushing, but she was pleased he was the teasing lover she saw so rarely these days. The car pulled into the underground entrance to the clinic and the interior of the car went into shadow. Seconds later Angelo slid out. He reached to help her, all humor gone from his expression as they hurried inside, hoping not to be spotted.

Speculation was rife that this was the reason for their rushed wedding, so she wasn't sure why they bothered. Twenty minutes later, they were reassured everything was fine. They could make their announcement and end all this secrecy.

She barely heard, too awestruck by the grayscale image with the fluttering heartbeat. She felt her hand grasped and squeezed. She dragged her gaze away and saw Angelo's eyes were damp as he fixated on the screen.

He met her gaze and his expression turned indescribably tender. He used his knuckle to brush away a tear on her cheek that she hadn't realized had brimmed and spilled over.

"I don't know why I'm so overcome," she said with a crooked smile. "It's biology. This is how reproduction happens."

"You're making us a little miracle." He caressed her jaw and looked back at the screen.

She looked back as well, hoping he was right.

Angelo rarely took vacations and knew this one would be a memory he would recall as one of the best times in his life. In fact, he was hoarding as many small moments as he could, making a point of enjoying the simplicity of his wife feeling for a dry bathing suit, failing to find one and seeking a new one from a drawer. She wore only a sarong, hair loose so she was an exotic island maiden. They were castaways in paradise and he never wanted to be rescued.

She stepped her bare feet into black bikini bottoms, pulled them up then loosened and dropped her sarong. She closed a strapless, neon pink top across her breasts, ran a finger around the edges, gave a jiggle and a wiggle and moved to the mirror. Frowned.

"I'm gaining weight!"

If she had gained a full kilo since telling him she was pregnant, he would be shocked, but there was a lovely ripeness to her figure that made his palms itch. The tug in the flesh between his thighs shouldn't have happened. They'd been in that bed only minutes ago. This entire vacation was nothing but combing beaches, snorkeling and making love. Lather, rinse, repeat. Quite literally, he thought with a private smirk, thinking of the shower they'd taken before their most recent nap.

"I believe you're supposed to gain weight." He went across to stand behind her, hands finding the waist that might be a fraction thicker, but the changes were happening so gradually, he couldn't see it. He kissed her shoulder. "You're beautiful."

She turned in profile, eyed her abdomen. "The baby won't care if I'm fat."

He bit back agreeing or mentioning that he wouldn't, either. Only a very stupid man offered an opinion on weight.

"I want to hold our baby," she murmured, settling a hand beneath her navel. "It's what I'm looking forward to the most. The comfort and affection of holding someone."

"Hello?" he teased, pulling her arms around him before wrapping his arms around her.

She made a face as she came into contact with the damp bathing suit he hadn't been afraid to pull on. "You know what I mean."

"I don't. Explain it."

"My parents weren't demonstrative. I've always felt... I don't know. Lonesome, I guess. Needing affection."

"Even now?"

"Maybe not *right* now," she murmured, leaning

against him, cheek nestling into his shoulder. "I wish we could stay here forever. Everything will change in a few days."

He couldn't refute that. He had the same sense of being in a bubble with thinning walls. It couldn't sustain this height of positive pressure and would burst any second.

His hands moved on her, trying to hold as much of her as possible against him. It was desire, the passion that always gripped him when he touched her, but it was more. He wanted to seal this connection they'd found, clamp it so tightly it became a part of him and could never be torn apart.

The need put urgency into the kiss he dropped on her mouth, but something else twined through him. A determination to hold on to what they had. Play it out. Make it last.

So even though the luscious sound in her throat told him she was instantly receptive and eager, he gentled the stroke of his hands. She ran her open mouth up his neck and caught hungrily at him, and even though he was hard and ready and so desperate to be joined with her he might have begged if she commanded it, he took his time. He cupped her face and slowed their kiss and let it deepen until she was trembling against him.

He pressed soft kisses to soft skin, soothed her with long plays of his hands across her bare skin, giving both of them ample opportunity to enjoy the sizzle, allowing anticipation to build to a screaming pitch before he found the next plane of silken skin to worship.

He melted his beautiful ice princess inch by inch, waiting until her arms were heavy around his neck, her knees weak, before he eased her onto the mattress and stripped their minuscule bits of clothing.

Then he joined her. Kissed her. Cruised his mouth everywhere, tasting strawberry nipples and vanilla skin and the honey between her thighs. Her fist gripped his hair and her knee curled up and, because giving her pleasure gave him so much pleasure, he lazily swept her over the cliff into the smashing waves of orgasm.

Her cries of release sent the demons of desire into a frenzy within him, but he lashed them down, forced himself to patience, not allowing himself to rise over and thrust into her no matter how damp he was with perspiration or how badly he shook with craving.

He pressed kisses against her thighs and her calves and rolled her onto her stomach so he could lick the indent of her spine and pool his breath between her shoulder blades.

She shivered and squirmed and gasped, "What are you doing to me?"

"I'm making love to you." He wasn't sure if he said it or thought it, but it was all that was in his head. Sexual desire, but also a yearning to caress and please, explore and taste. Possess and give.

He combed his fingers into her hair, lifting it away from her neck so he could suck delicately against her nape. He bit lightly against her dampened skin so gooseflesh peppered her and she shuddered and groaned and lifted her hips with invitation.

He caressed her with his whole body, loving the feel of her beneath him like this. His erection nestled in the crease of her buttocks. Her thighs parted at his lightest touch, allowing him to stray his touch into her damp center where she called to him so inexorably.

Her movements beneath him drove him mad and still he only gathered her beneath him, stilling her so he could keep her right here. His. Forever.

"I want to touch you," she pleaded.

He drew back and she rolled into his arms, making him shake with relief and desire as her breasts, soft and supple, were crushed against his chest. Her nipples were hard points, her thigh downy as she stroked it against his hip. Her scent was all over him, clouding like an aphrodisiac, leaving him drugged and high.

"I love touching you like this," she confessed, hands roaming across the naked planes of his chest and hips, his thighs and buttocks and then—her confidence in bed had come a long way—to cup between his thighs. She purred as she weighed and shaped him, making him grit his teeth to hold on to his control.

As she guided him to the place he most wanted to be, he almost mourned the foreplay, wanting more time to claim every glorious cell of her body, but he was taken over by the animal that needed its mate. He settled atop her and sank into her with a ragged groan. The world opened before him. Pia was his world. All of her was his.

And this, the slow pump of his hips, stoking more pleasure than any man had a right to, was everything he ever needed.

As Pia's heart rate slowed, she reminded herself that climax released a host of chemicals in the brain. This sense of security and eye-dampening closeness was as biologically normal as her sensitive nipples and weight gain.

Love also caused those same symptoms. Or so she'd heard.

Was that what this was? This emotional dependence

and sensation that she would split in half from the joy wanting to burst from within her, just because his weight pinned her and his skin was still damp with perspiration?

She was beginning to fear it was, and she didn't know what to do about it. Tell him? What if he didn't care? What if he didn't return her feelings?

Her haze of satisfaction and rumination was broken by his ringtone.

"I told you we had to get out of here before that happened." His sexy rasp tickled her ear.

"Mmm... My fault for falling under you."

His smile flashed as his heavy arm left off caressing her shoulder and the blanketing warmth of him rolled away.

Definitely love, she thought, as that brief smile struck like sunshine in her heart.

He was maintaining a light work schedule, all but a few key ringtones set to ignore.

"Killian," he said as he frowned at the screen. "I have to take it."

Roman Killian was the husband of their engagement photographer, Melodie, but he also owned and ran the global company that provided all of Angelo's security needs.

Pia heard Killian's voice as clearly as Angelo's.

"Arson," Killian stated bluntly. "Brazen and designed for maximum damage. All the staff had gone to their own homes so there are no injuries. They have the suspect. Darius Gomez. He claims to be your brother."

Pia sat up with alarm, fingers searching for the edge of a sheet as she scanned to the glass doors leading onto the private beach of their luxury villa.

"Keep it as quiet as you can, but prosecute to the full

extent of the law," Angelo ordered. "Not an ounce of le-
niency. Add whatever security my staff requires to feel
safe while they clean up."

Any lingering warmth from their lovemaking was
gone. His tone was hard and sharp as jagged glass, shear-
ing off her buzz of gratification.

"Now we find out," he said gruffly as he ended the
call and tossed his phone onto the mattress between them
as though throwing down a gauntlet.

"Find out what?"

"How you'll react. I'll release my side ahead of any
lies they try to concoct." Her lover was gone and here
was the brute who gave no quarter to those who had
wronged him. Who stared unwaveringly into her eyes
and dared her to try to talk him out of the action he intended to take.

Her heart stuttered in her chest and she tried to swallow, but her throat was too dry. She wanted to stop him
to spare him whatever suffering was coming, but stopping him was futile, she could tell. The only other thing
she could do was wall up her own emotions to allow
room for his.

She nodded jerkily. "I'll call Rico. He needs to know
first."

They went straight back to Spain, rather than going to
California.

Pia had a very difficult conversation with her brother
while Angelo was barking orders into his own phone.

"You should have told me the minute you knew he'd
been here uninvited. Do you know how they behaved toward Poppy?" Rico had never spoken to her so harshly.

"Angelo is not one of them." She would *not* allow that

comparison. Ever. "Look," she tried in a more concilia-
tory tone. "I understand why you're angry, but it wasn't
my story to tell."

"Now it is? When everything is going to hell in a
handcart? He didn't even have the mettle to tell me himself?"

"I wanted to do it—"

Rico hung up on her before she could explain.

She didn't mention Rico's reaction to Angelo. He was
moving beyond damage control into aggressor. His press
release dropped while they were in the air and he had
a news conference scheduled immediately after they
landed. He not only didn't ask her to stand at his side
for it, he sent her to her mother's.

"I want to be with you," she argued.

"No, you don't."

She caught her breath, hearing it as an accusation
until he added, "I want to know you're insulated from
any further acts of aggression. Darius is in custody, but
that doesn't mean Tomas won't try something."

Now she would be worried sick about him, standing
at a podium like a target, but he was in crisis mode. She
didn't add to his concerns by arguing. She did what she
had always done when there were bigger problems to
solve. She stepped out of the way.

Going to her parents' house was no picnic. Her father
was in Madrid, which made little difference aside from
the fact her mother commented, "I suppose he'll have
to hold a press conference of his own."

Pia felt rather helpless. "Angelo didn't mean for this
to happen, Mother."

"Didn't he?" La Reina asked with a blithe look. "He
seems to have been seeking blood this whole time.

Why on earth did he insist on that pageant of a wedding otherwise?"

Pia never talked back to her mother, not in an outburst of emotion, but she cried, "That was for our baby! You were on board with a big wedding, too."

"Pia." Her mother's tone dripped with condescension. "That was not the wedding I envisioned for you. This is not the marriage. Especially now."

"Well, he's the husband I wanted," she spat back, shaking at the confrontation while her mother only gave her a faint frown.

"Are you able to take hold of your emotions and discuss damage control?" La Reina stirred cream into her tea, the clatter of her spoon jangling Pia's nerves.

The man she loved, really, truly, deeply loved, was going through hell. Pia wanted to cry and rage and throw a tantrum, she was so upset for him, but the one thing her mother had taught her was to shove aside that sort of reaction and think logically about what could be done on a practical level.

Dragging in a deep breath, she found her composure and firmly pressed it over her shredded control. "Of course," she insisted.

"Do you have any influence over him at all?"

She almost lost it again, but managed to hang on to a civil tone. "He is entitled to his outrage, Mother. Were you aware of what his mother was going through when it happened?"

"I barely knew them," she dismissed. "There was a rumor the stepdaughter had been with the gardener's son and that's why she wasn't out in society. Until this press release, I believed the news reports that she had died after a brief illness."

"Doesn't it sicken you that the truth has been covered up? Or are you only upset that we've been attached to it?"

"Why *are* we attached to it, Pia? You've never been promiscuous. Have you heard any of the statements he's made? He loathes what we represent. He is not Poppy or Sorcha, coming into our lives through honest fallibility and with an earnest desire to be one of us. He targeted you. All of this has been orchestrated for maximum damage to more than his brothers. He's trying to take down the aristocracy."

"That's not true." She didn't explain that Angelo hadn't known who she was that first night. Her family still thought they'd been dating in private before the masquerade ball. "His mother was treated horribly," Pia continued fervently. "If he married me to champion her, I can live with that." Mostly. Of course she wanted her marriage to be more than that, but at least it was an altruistic motive, not the calculating one her mother was suggesting.

"You continue to possess an unfortunate streak of compassion." Her mother sighed. "If he wanted help with his battle over his mother, he should have gone about it differently, not seduced you into his scandal. He manipulated you into helping him achieve influence. Now he's swinging a scythe with the Montero name on it."

She shook her head, but her mother was sowing a seed of doubt.

"This isn't justice he's seeking, it's vengeance," her mother continued. "You understand he's been buying up his brothers' debts? Placing liens on their properties? Buying stocks in a hostile takeover to force them out? His aim is to ruin them, Pia."

"So?" Maybe it was a vigilante move, but she didn't blame him for his ruthless tactics.

"You're too smart to allow yourself to be used."

Pia wished she could claim Angelo had married her because he loved her, not that her mother would see any value in such a declaration, but Pia would. No such words had passed their lips, however. And now, all kinds of doubts were prickling to life inside her.

"Do you insist on staying married to him?" her mother asked stiffly.

"Yes." She wished her voice had come out stronger.

Her mother's mouth pinched. "Very well. Let's find our best path forward."

Utterly drained, Pia was trying to recover with the cool weight of a lavender eye pillow across her brow. A chamomile tea steeped on the table beside her, but she'd chosen to rest in the front parlor so she would greet Angelo the moment he turned up.

She was snapped out of her doze by the chirp of brakes. Raised voices caused a commotion in the courtyard. It sounded like Angelo and Rico.

She stood up too quickly and had to grasp at the back of the sofa to catch her balance as her head swam. As soon as she was steady, she hurried out the front doors.

Angelo had arrived in a car she didn't recognize, and Rico had parked behind him on the circular drive. They were standing between the bumpers, car doors open, locked in a heated exchange.

"It's my *house*," Rico spat. "My wife spent the last year turning it into a *home*. How dare you jeopardize that?"

"Rico!" Pia trotted down the steps, afraid they would

come to blows. "What's wrong? What happened?" She inserted herself between them.

"His brothers are trying to renege on their sale of the estate," Rico barked. "Because he's making a claim on their proceeds from it. And because *he* stole property they left there. Thanks to *you*," Rico added in a sideswipe at her.

"I took what belonged to my mother. Her share of the family fortune, bequeathed to me." Angelo took Pia's shoulders to set her aside as he tried to step forward into combat.

Pia slapped her hand onto his chest, keeping him from advancing, but the ire in him nearly bowled her over.

"Make them a settlement for it. Make this go away," Rico demanded, gaze locked with Angelo's.

"I don't want it to go away. I want them to rot in hell. If you don't think they should, you can rot there with them."

"At the expense of my wife and children?" Rico was outraged.

"Angelo, please," Pia begged, as caught between them emotionally as she was physically. "Please calm down and let's discuss this rationally."

"Oh, there's a surprise, coming from you." He brushed her off him, taking a step back so the verbal and physical rejection was equally devastating. "Let's be rational then," he said to Rico with scathing sarcasm. "You bought that estate at a bargain price in a backroom deal. *You* pay the settlement they want."

"Angelo."

She was genuinely shocked and appalled at the vindictiveness spewing out of him. Distantly she understood that he must have been through a lot today, but her mother's comments seemed to hold more water as she saw how much thirst for punishment was in him.

"That's not fair. Listen, I'm not saying your brothers are innocent, but don't confuse their crimes with your father's. Should they be held to account for his actions? Do you want our child judged on the way you're behaving? That means you have to pay for your father's crimes, too. Don't be like them," she pleaded. "Stop this cycle of hatred."

"Why? Because it's inconvenient for *you*? So you can go on living in your damned ivory tower, ignoring what my mother went through? You're all the damned same! Of all the women on all the rooftops, I had to get the one who thinks preserving this—" he flung a hand toward the villa "—is more important than common decency."

"Who the hell are you to talk about decency after the way you targeted her to pursue a vendetta?" Rico demanded.

Angelo choked out a humorless laugh, his gaze careening into her own.

As their gazes caught and clashed, his stare hardened. He seemed to search into her soul, seeing all the insecurities and doubts her mother had planted inside her. Now Rico was making the same accusation and Pia knew she shouldn't give those charges any weight, but she was looking for reassurance in Angelo's expression and seeing only a flinch of angry contempt.

And a flash of hurt that was so profound it speared her like a paralyzing poisoned dart.

"Angelo." Her lips were numb as she moved jerkily forward to set a hand on his arm.

He pulled away, his profile cast in iron.

"Angelo, I love you," she whispered, voice faint because she had never said the words before. Her throat was nothing but sandpaper, her chest a broken shell. She didn't know how to offer her heart when it was such a tender, thin-skinned little thing. It was new and delicate as butterfly wings, beating in her cupped hands.

"Don't." His head went back in recoil. "Even if it were true, how long would it last?"

Even if it were true? His rejection of her feelings was so shockingly *typical*, it knocked the breath clean out of her.

"I'm never going to be one of you. I don't *want* to be."

"I'm not one of them, either. You know I'm not," she choked, stricken that he would lump her in with those horrid people who'd failed to ask questions and had turned a blind eye, leaving his mother to her suffering.

"No, you're special, Pia. You are. Far better than I deserve." His gaze came back, resolute. "You know it. Your family knows it. *I've* always known my illegitimate hands shouldn't be handling the fine china. You deserve better than me, Pia. You genuinely do." His voice became agonizingly gentle even as he dismissed every tender moment that had bound them together. "I can't bring you down with me. It's only going to get worse. Turns out money does not buy respectability." His eyes were shadowed with futility. "Best to end it here and now, before I do any more damage."

When he turned away, she lifted a hand, feet rooted with shock. She didn't realize he was getting into the car and leaving until the engine started and he pulled away.

Then her breastbone fractured and her throat strangled on a tormented, "*No*—" but he was already shooting through the gate and gone.

"He's right. You're better off without him," Rico said,

grasping her arm, trying to hug her. "We'll look after you. And the baby."

Ice formed around her, stiffening her joints, making her brother's attempt to comfort her an awkward, unwelcome embrace. She wanted Angelo to hold her and look after her and their baby. She couldn't breathe. She had laid herself bare to the man she loved and he'd left.

No one would ever love her. *Ever.*

"I'll take you inside," Rico said.

"No." Pia withdrew into her protective casing the way one of her beloved hermit crabs cringed back into its borrowed shell. She would need a bigger one to hold this amount of heartbreak. She didn't know how she would carry the weight of it, but that was another day's job.

"Go home to Poppy," she managed to say. "She'll be worried. I'll sell my house to pay your legal bills. You won't lose your home."

"Don't be ridiculous."

"It makes perfect sense," she said with one of her well-practiced expressions of cool reason. The profound loneliness washing over her was as familiar as returning to a big, empty house. "This was my error in judgment. Let me make amends."

CHAPTER ELEVEN

FROM THE MOMENT Angelo had been forced to release his mother's story, he'd been in agony. All his helpless, furious guilt at being unable to help her, or prevent her early death, had risen up to turn him on a spit of fire.

He hadn't wanted Pia anywhere near the ugliness of his news conference. The fresh accusations and blatant lies Tomas had told, trying to absolve Darius from his crime along with their father, had made him sick.

And ashamed. He was so damned ashamed to have one single drop of their blood in him. Even more chagrined that he wanted his wife by his side while he was standing knee-deep in family closet filth.

He'd had the strength to insulate her from the brunt of negative attention they'd been forced to endure, but after weathering that first blast, he had wanted only one thing. To get back to Pia. To crawl into the bubble of calm she always provided—not that he believed all his problems would disappear, but they would be bearable, he'd thought, if he could only hold her.

Rico had caught up to him in the courtyard before he'd even climbed from his car. Of course Tomas was going after the house, claiming some sort of conspiracy between them to defraud him of the jewelry. Angelo's brothers were grasping at any straw within reach.

Angelo hadn't been at his rational best. Nothing in him had wanted to give an inch to anyone. When Pia had tried to reason with him, he hadn't been able to see through his haze. What he had glimpsed, however, had been a harrowing doubt in her eyes. Justified qualms over why he had married her.

Her lack of faith in him had nearly cut him in half, but what did he expect? That she would take the side of someone his brothers were calling an "abomination"?

When she had then claimed to love him, he hadn't been able to take it in. Hadn't been able to accept it, given the ugliness he had brought into her life by forcing their marriage. There *had* been a part of him that had seized the chance to marry her because of her name. He *had* wanted vengeance above anything else.

He didn't deserve to be loved for any of that.

Stop the cycle of hatred, she had said, and he had realized how twisted he had become. If he kept it up, he would be no better than the darkness he had come from.

Angelo reached the airfield in a daze, feeling as though he was bleeding out and had to do something, anything, to stanch the flow. He called his lawyer as he climbed aboard his jet.

"Tell Tomas to stop going after Rico's house. I'll put the proceeds from the sale of the jewelry into a trust until ownership is established." Tomas would accept the deal since his attempt to rewrite the estate sale would be expensive and he had even less chance of winning that than he did in proving the jewelry was his.

"The *señora* isn't traveling with us?" the attendant asked.

"No." He was going back to view the damage at the house. "Double," he ordered as his customary scotch was poured.

He brooded and drank until he landed. Then he walked through a house with a corner blown out where he and Pia had sat for their engagement photo. Plastic sheets hung over the space. The open plan interior had been stripped down to subfloor and studs, but there were still scorch marks on the ceiling.

The rest of the house was intact. Angelo went up to the room where Pia had joined him for only a few short days, but the whole villa felt imbued with her presence. He instantly knew he wouldn't be able to sleep in that bed without her. Wouldn't be able to live here without thinking of her every minute of every day.

He would think of her regardless, no matter where he ended up.

How was he going to live without her? Without their baby?

He nearly went to his knees as he realized what he had done. Pushing her away had been the right thing to do, though. Hadn't it?

Eyes wet, breath rattling in his chest, he left the room and was drawn into the next one, the nursery. Sea-green walls were decorated with shells and seahorses and tropical fish. The crib was assembled with a mobile of starfish dangling over one end.

All of this had been chosen by Pia. He had watched her browse and light up with quiet glee as she found the different items and sent links to their decorator.

She loved their baby—he knew she did—yet he hadn't believed her when she had spoken the words to him. He'd still been seeing the stark guilt in her expression when her brother had hurled his accusations. Angelo knew what they all thought of him. He had been reeling and devastated that his wife believed any of it.

How could she love him *and* doubt him?

What did he expect, though? He hadn't been completely honest with her. He hadn't admitted to his own love, even though it was such a force in him he was pulsing in agony at being apart from her.

He hadn't allowed himself to say it or acknowledge it or even fully feel it because, deep down, he'd been convinced he wasn't good enough for her. He had been biding his time until she realized it and rejected him. He had *expected* to lose her.

She had promised that if his truth came to light, it wouldn't change her commitment to him or their marriage, but he hadn't given her a chance to prove that she would stand by him. In fact, he'd sent her to her mother's, then thrown her declaration of love back in her face. And left her. Like a fool.

"Pia," he groaned with anguish.

He couldn't stay here. There was a giant hole in the side of his house and a bigger one in his heart.

Two days later, Angelo sought out Rico at the Montero corporate headquarters.

He had told Pia once that he was willing to risk all that he had for something he wanted badly enough. That included his pride, but his wife and child were worth it.

He was shown into Cesar's office, where both brothers stood in solidarity, Cesar behind the massive mahogany desk, Rico beside it.

Angelo eschewed handshakes and the empty chair in favor of stating his business.

"Tomas and Darius have been neutralized. Not like that," he added with swift, arid sarcasm when two pairs of brows shot up. "In exchange for them signing a binding promise not to talk to the press, I have agreed to let them keep what they have left. If they step out of line, I will finish them and make no apologies for it. You caught me on a bad day," he said to Rico. "I am capable of rational behavior."

"Tell your wife. She wants to sell her house to finance my legal bill."

"That's ridiculous. No," Angelo dismissed the idea. "Invoice me for any inconveniences you've suffered."

"I will," Cesar said bluntly. "Including the prenup negotiations and the wedding. You could have saved us a lot of time, money and trouble."

Cesar's words were a kick to the chest, but Angelo managed to stay on his feet. "We're staying married."

"You're not taking another round out of her. Do you understand how sensitive she is?" Cesar set his knuckles on his desk. "How cruel it was to target her like that?"

"I didn't target her! I didn't know who she wa—" He cut himself off, angry with himself for saying too much, but Rico swore in comprehension.

"When you made that remark about the rooftop the other day, I didn't want to believe it. Are you telling me you two only met that night? That you—"

"I am not discussing our private life with you," Angelo said firmly, pointing a finger in warning. He personally didn't care one iota. His sense of modesty was very low. Pia, however? "Do *you* understand how sensitive your sister is? How *shy*? How *smart*? Don't stand here and act concerned about her when she's out there earning doctorates two years before you did and you can't even be bothered to show up and give her a round of applause."

Rico lost some of his bluster. He sent a disgruntled look toward Cesar.

"Poppy wanted to organize something. Lily got sick and it slipped our mind."

"Sorcha called Mother to set up a lunch. You'd think she pitched overthrowing the government." Cesar straightened off his desk and sighed. He folded his arms as he regarded Angelo. "I'm smart enough to know how smart my sister is, yes. I've asked her to join our research team several times. She's always preferred fieldwork and biology, but I hoped once the baby was born, she might finally consider my offer more seriously."

"*Did* you get her pregnant on purpose?" Rico demanded.

"Wow." Angelo tilted him an affronted glare. "Delightful as Pia's family has turned out to be, *no*, I didn't resort to time-tested methods to become a member. You could bowl tenpins with those balls, asking a question like that when you didn't plan *your* family."

Rico narrowed his eyes while Cesar deadpanned, "I've seen them. Five pins, tops."

Madre de Dios.

"I married Pia because we're expecting a baby. Because I want to be a better father than I had." Angelo had briefly lost sight of that, but never would again. "I'm staying married to her because I'm in love with her. That means, for her sake, we're going to learn to play nice." He drew a small circle in the air. "I thought cleaning up my mess with my brothers was a good start. Now, you have a pleasant evening, gentlemen. Convey my regards to your infinitely more charming wives."

"Same," Rico shot at his back.

Angelo had texted Pia while he was on the island, telling her the security team had deemed it safe to move back into her home. He checked there first, but the housekeeper said she had packed a bag and left instructions to ready the house for sale.

Angelo reversed that order and presumed Pia had decided to stay at her mother's.

He went there and was informed that Pia had left two days ago for her own house. When he expressed his dissatisfaction with that information, he was forced to wait twenty minutes before La Reina deigned to see him.

He gave her the report he'd given her sons. "Aside from lingering speculation in the press, which should die off fairly quickly, this should all be over."

"Thank you for informing me." With a smile of pressed civility, she rose.

"Your staff tells me Pia isn't here," he said, preventing her from leaving. "She's not in her home and not answering my texts."

"That's to be expected."

"What do you mean?" Angelo bristled, suspecting she was deliberately punishing him, but he couldn't read anything malicious in her expression. No enjoyment of his frustration, only a vague puzzlement with his continued presence.

"I mean that she does this. She travels out of range, thereby taking a few days to respond to messages. It's something you should expect of her as common behavior."

"So you don't know where she went? Aren't you concerned?"

"She's a grown adult. She makes her own schedule."

"She's pregnant."

"She's not foolish." Her mouth twitched slightly as if she heard the irony in her own words, given her daughter's choice in husband. "Do you have reason to believe there would be a medical issue?"

"No, but…" Angelo clenched his teeth, wondering how Pia had withstood a lifetime of this stonewalling. "Did she—" He could barely bring himself to ask. "Is she avoiding me? Seeking a legal separation?"

La Reina frowned. "I should think you'd be the first to know that, not me."

"So she didn't say anything like that to you?"

La Reina rang for her assistant and asked with exaggerated patience, "Do we know where my daughter is?"

Clearly "we" didn't.

"A research trip, *señora*," was the unhelpful answer.

"There you are. She'll turn up when she's finished her fieldwork," La Reina said.

"Where did she go? When is she coming back?" Angelo asked the assistant.

"I'm sorry. I don't have that information, *señor*. She books her own travel."

Frustrated, he returned to her home and went into her office to see if he could figure out where she'd gone. Why had she left without telling anyone where she was going? It didn't portend well and left a sick knot in his gut.

It made him think she really was fine with ending their marriage so she could go back to the life she'd led before.

He had a quick peek at her social media profiles, half thinking he would approach some of the people he'd met during their goodwill tour before their wedding. He quickly realized none of them were on there. Her friend list consisted of her immediate family and her privacy settings were locked down. Her only public content was the photographs he'd once thought proved she lived a globe-trotting life in exotic locations.

Now he knew her better, which cast a fresh light on the remoteness in her snapshots. While they'd been in Australia, he'd taken several photos of her, and she'd said, "I'm usually alone and I hate taking selfies so I'm never in my photos."

Until this moment, he hadn't heard the deep loneliness in that statement. Now he saw it clearly in the beautiful places she visited without having anyone with her to share her experience.

He looked more closely at her home office. Every wall was covered in bookshelves. Three of the nonfiction titles were written by her—where the hell had those come from? Why had she never mentioned that she understood economics well enough to write investment strategies for non-professionals?

There were dozens of textbooks on a range of subjects, a handful of self-help tomes on public speaking and networking, two shelves of dog-eared romance novels and a shelf stuffed to the gills with journals. They were all neatly labeled with dates.

He took one out at random and saw nothing but numbers and dates and Latin names. So much information gathered and filtered through that sharp brain of hers, distilled and shared on her terms.

Because she found human interactions so difficult? Or because she had no one with whom to share her discoveries?

His heart truly began to ache, then. She had admitted to feeling lonely most of her life. He'd seen how she struggled to connect. All this time, he'd feared that she would never feel anything genuine toward him when maybe all he'd had to do was let her know how much she meant to him. How much he loved her.

He loved her and missed her and not knowing where she'd gone was torture.

But finding her turned out to be as simple as checking their joint credit card statement. The Faroe Islands. Where the hell was that?

He called his pilot and was soon headed in the direction of Iceland.

Over a lifetime of nursing loneliness and scorn, Pia had discovered there was a strangely comforting symmetry in being physically miserable when she was emotionally miserable.

There was also something reassuring in returning to familiar routines. She set her trusty, well-worn, gel cushion on a suitable rock, propped her journal on her crooked knee while balancing an umbrella with the same hand and used her free hand to begin making notes on the colony of seals below her.

The wind blew the rain into her face and onto her page, but that was why she wore a rubber coat and used pencil instead of ink. The damp sank into her bones, but she had brought a cushion and a thermos of hot tea as consolation. The man she loved would never love her, but that was why she was here. Even forsaken souls could be useful to humanity if they didn't mind a little tedium and isolation.

The bark of the seals and rush of the waves drowned out the sound of footsteps until the boots appeared in her peripheral vision.

She gasped and looked up, telling herself it was a local who had tramped out to ask her what she was doing, but she already knew it was Angelo. Her body knew it before her eyes confirmed it.

He scanned the small harbor below, but looked at her as she tilted the umbrella back so she could see him. His brows pulled into a frown.

"What are you doing?"

"Working."

"I thought you wanted to set up a pregnancy study?"

She glanced down, almost saying that what she studied only mattered to her and she was beginning to think she didn't matter to anyone.

She slanted the umbrella over herself again. "I told you I like to collect data when I need to think."

"You could have told me where you were going."

"You didn't tell me where *you* were going."

"Touché." Beside her, she saw his hand give a restive flex. "I went to the island. The house is a mess, but the nursery looks good. It should all be repaired and ready for us by the time the baby arrives."

"Us?" She bobbled the umbrella and her nerveless fingers nearly shot the pencil across the pebbly ground. "You and the baby?"

"All of us."

"You ended our marriage, Angelo. You *left*." Her chest locked up and she could only blindly stare at the chop of white beards on the gray scroll of waves. She had come away because she couldn't face that he'd abandoned her so unceremoniously.

"You said you wouldn't let my past change your commitment to our marriage."

"It didn't."

His hand caught the fabric of her umbrella and shoved it back so he could see her. Rain had soaked into his hair and was running down his face. The spitting drops peppered her face as she looked up at him.

"Then why are you here?" he growled.

"You said we were over. I needed to feel like myself again. To do something I know how to do well instead of…" *Faking it. Banging into walls. Falling in love and failing at marriage.*

"I was worried about you."

"The baby is fine. I spoke to the doctor before I came away. She said it was okay to come."

"I was worried about *you*."

"No one ever worries about me." She tried to shove her umbrella back into place.

He didn't let her. "*I* worry about you."

"The baby—"

"*You*," he nearly shouted.

She was so startled, she let go of the handle. He lost his own grip and the umbrella tumbled away in the wind.

Pia didn't move, only tugged her woolen hat more firmly onto her head.

"I'm still one of the blue bloods you love to hate," she reminded him.

"You're the only blue blood I can stand," he muttered. "My own included. Hopefully our baby will have more of yours than mine."

"You'll love it either way?"

"I will." His tortured gaze shifted to the water. "I can't change what I am, Pia. Sometimes I hate myself for existing. For causing so much pain to someone I loved."

"I can't speak for her, Angelo, but it sounds like she loved you exactly as you were, despite the blood you carry. That blood doesn't change how I feel about you or how I'll feel about our baby."

"How do you feel about me?"

Her eyes welled. She looked down at the page that was growing soaked.

"Do you want to hear how I feel? Angry," he said, sounding incensed. "I'm angry on your behalf. I hate that your father doesn't see how special you are and that your mother values her wealth and standing over the suffering she causes you."

"It doesn't—"

"Don't say it doesn't matter. It matters. *You* matter, Pia. You matter to me. But I understand that she won't change. Neither of them will. I didn't mean to make you cry."

She dug up a tissue and he crouched to catch her eyes with his own.

"Your turn. Tell me how you feel," he commanded.

"Grateful." It was a cowardly admission. A small, easy one because she didn't have the courage to make a bigger one. It was true, though. "No matter what happens between us, I will always be grateful you gave me someone who will love me as I am."

His expression altered. Torment seemed to grip him. "Pia, I'm that person. *I* love you exactly as you are."

Her heart lurched and she felt so dizzy, she nearly fell off the rock. "You can't."

"Of course I can. That's why I left. I couldn't stand that I was doing it again, hurting someone I loved. It was terrible logic because I wound up hurting you anyway. I'm looking forward to you preventing me from being so stupid again."

"But I'm not…lovable."

"Of course you are. You're funny and smart and kind and sensitive. Sexy as *hell*. Brave."

"See, you're lying."

"Modest. Very beautiful, although I know you don't care about that. Curious and warm."

"Robotic."

"Introspective. Affectionate." He touched her knee where her jeans were soaked through.

She was starting to shiver, but not from the cold. She couldn't hold her mouth steady. "Why are you saying all this?" He was inspiring such a depth of hope, but she was so afraid to believe.

"Because I love you." His expression became very grave while her heart teetered and rolled. "I could not have gone through this without you, Pia. I couldn't have faced my past and moved beyond it. I would have let it destroy me if I hadn't been falling in love with you this whole time. I wouldn't be capable of love if you weren't here, inspiring it in me."

"I don't know what to say to that."

"Tell me you love me. Please." His used the backs of his fingers to gather the raindrops dripping off her jaw. He swiped his hand on his wet jeans. "I promise you I will believe you this time."

"That word doesn't seem like enough for the way I feel. It doesn't seem like it matches all those wonderful things you just said. You're—"

He cupped her jaw with his damp palm and his wet thumb silenced her lips.

"You don't care about my past. That's all that matters to me."

Her chin crinkled under the line of his thumb while

her insides were nothing but trapped birds flittering every which way.

"It can't be this easy after it was so h-hard." Her throat was tight, her voice a mere squeak. "For so l-long."

"It won't always be easy, *mi amor*," he said with tender understanding. "Sometimes I will tell you to come in out of the rain and you'll make me stand here and count chickens with you. Other times I'll punish you by making you dress up in designer gowns and talk to strangers."

"And you'll still love me despite my petulant sighs?"

"I will love you *because* of them. Because they will remind me you're there for my sake, not for designer gowns. It's inevitable that we argue over the small nonsense of life, but it won't compare to the harmony I feel waking next to you or holding your hand in mine."

He took hers now, made a tiny adjustment to her rings. Brought her hand to his lips and kissed her trembling fingers.

"I want to build a life with you, Pia. Not one that seeks vengeance. One that fosters love. I need you in my life, every day, helping me do that."

"I wanted this so badly and I've been trying so hard not to hope for it. It hurt so much when I was convinced it couldn't come true. Now I'm afraid I'm going to wake up and find out I really am dreaming."

He bit her knuckle hard enough to threaten pain.

"Ouch! Hey." She scowled, trying to snatch her hand away in reaction.

He grinned and kept her hand in his as he stood. He gave a gentle tug. "Can we get out of the rain?"

She glanced at her ruined notebook, pages curled and turning to pulp.

"I'll buy you a bowl of soup," he coaxed. "We can talk about a foundation to address the effects of climate change on marine mammals or…" He scanned the beach. "What are you doing here?"

"Do you really want to know?" She was embarrassed, but trusted him enough to know that when he laughed at her, it would be in the kindest way possible. "I named them several years ago. I check on them when I'm feeling blue. I like to see who is hooking up with whom and count the new babies."

His valiant struggle to keep a straight face was love in its purest form.

"I also have a colony of penguins and some polar bears I like to track." She rubbed her nose where rain was dripping and causing a tickle. "A pod of whales. Way too many dolphins, but they're so playful and cute."

"I'm excited to hear all about them," he assured her with a solemn nod. "Soup?"

She rose, gave a little shrug to knock the worst of the gathered rain off her coat.

"Or we could go to my hotel room," she suggested. "Warm up in the shower before we dry off and go to bed. Maybe not talk much at all for a while."

"Then order room service? See, this is why I love being married to a woman who is smarter than me." He helped her gather her things, then stood with her in the rain a moment longer. Long enough to kiss her senseless.

With his arm firm around her, he drew her from the empty beach into their shared future.

EPILOGUE

Eighteen months later...

"CAN WE HOLD JELLY?" Lily asked, one arm curled trustingly around her Tío Cesar's neck while he clasped her affectionately against his chest.

Angelo had a very difficult time denying his nieces and nephews anything, particularly sweet Lily with her high voice and innocently batted lashes and her hilarious shortening of Angelica's name to Jelly.

Tío Cesar was another story. Angelo enjoyed a good-natured trashy relationship with his wife's brothers, well developed over the year since they'd all had their litter of newborns and he'd partnered with them on an alloy for a gaming console they were jointly developing.

"You're shameless," he said to Cesar, nodding at Lily, who coaxed with a wave of her free arm, entreating her younger cousin to join them.

"I like to connect with my nieces. That's how one keeps the title Favorite Uncle. Pro tip," Cesar advised in a facetious drawl.

Fighting words. Angelo narrowed his eyes. "Wait until *your* daughter's birthday." He would spoil her enough for a lifetime.

"*Please*, Jelly?" Lily begged. "Tío Cesar wants to read us a book."

Angelica peeked from where she had her face buried in Angelo's neck. She wasn't particularly shy, but she made strange with her uncles sometimes, mostly because she didn't see them as often as she saw Poppy and Sorcha and the children.

She had also just woken from her nap to a lot of people and attention, not that they were making a big deal out of her first birthday. Pia had invited her brothers and their families to spend the weekend at their island home because it was the middle of the summer and they all enjoyed an excuse to spend time together. The grandparents had chosen not to make the journey for something so frivolous, which kept it to a laid-back gathering where the children could be as boisterous as they liked.

"Want to cuddle with Lily and Tío?" Angelo asked his daughter.

"Maybe Brenna will join us," Cesar said of his daughter, noting the little firecracker was working up to fight her brother, Mateo, to the death over a pool noodle.

"You on that, Rico?" Angelo mocked as Angelica went to Cesar and Rico waded into the dispute, his year-old son naked on his hip.

"Tío!" Enrique called from the diving board. "Watch me flip."

"Where are the women? How did we get outnumbered? Ah, Memo," Rico muttered as a wet stain appeared on his shirt. "I knew that would happen. Here." He handed his son to Angelo.

Angelo diapered his nephew while Rico caught Brenna back from chasing her brother down the stairs into deeper water. He plopped Brenna with her father and the girls, then threw off his stained shirt and cannonballed into the pool to soak the boys.

"I told you they'd have everything under control," Sorcha said as the women appeared with trays of food and drink. Memo went to Poppy, then pointed at his father in the pool so she took him across to hand him in to Rico.

"I'm insulted there was any doubt in us." Angelo scooped Pia close and stage-whispered, "Thank God you got here when you did."

She chuckled and looped her arms around his waist, gazing over the convivial chaos of their pool party. "This is nice."

"It is."

"Okay," Poppy said, coming back to uncork a bottle of wine. "I've been very excited for this day. Our first vintage and everyone is weaned, right? We girls finally get to split a bottle of wine?"

Pia wrinkled her nose and looked at Angelo. They had suspected they wouldn't be able to keep it under wraps a full three months.

"Really?" Poppy asked with shock, catching their look while bright tears came into her eyes.

"We didn't mean to," Pia admitted sheepishly. "It just happened."

"Oh, we know how it 'just happens,'" Sorcha teased.

"Too true," Poppy said, coming to hug both of them. "That's wonderful news. Congratulations."

Much later, when Angelo was lying replete next to his wife, her damp body relaxed against his, he said, "Do you remember our honeymoon?"

"I think we were just there," she said on a luxurious

sigh and a slither of her naked skin against his own. She settled her head more comfortably on his shoulder.

He smiled into the dark. "That's what I meant. I remember thinking I had to memorize it because I might never be that happy again, but I am. Often."

"A wise person once told me that happiness is fleeting, not a state of being."

"He might not have been as smart as the woman he was talking to."

She brought her thigh up to rest across his stomach. Her face turned into his skin as she kissed above his heart. "For the record, after much dedicated research, I have concluded that happiness is a goal worth pursuing."

"Hypothesis proven?"

"Beyond a shadow of a doubt."

* * * * *

MILLS & BOON

Coming next month

THE GREEK'S SURPRISE CHRISTMAS BRIDE
Lynne Graham

'I have a proposition that you may wish to consider.'

'Did Isidore mention that I'm in need of money?' Letty had to force herself to ask, her creamy skin turning pink with self-consciousness.

'Your grandfather asked you to call him Isidore?' Leo remarked in surprise.

'Oh, he didn't invite me to call him anything,' Letty parried with rueful amusement. 'To be frank, he didn't want to acknowledge the relationship.'

'That must've been a disappointment,' Leo commented wryly.

'Not really. I wasn't expecting a miracle but, considering that my father never paid any child support, it's not as though I've cost that side of my family anything over the years,' she responded quietly. 'My mother has always been very independent but right now that's not possible for her, so I've had to step in...'

'Which is where I enter the equation from your point of view,' Leo incised. 'Your grandfather wants to amalgamate his shipping firm with mine and retire, leaving me in charge. For me, the price of that valuable alliance is that I marry you.'

A pin-drop silence fell.

'You would have to marry *me* to get his shipping business?' Letty exclaimed in disbelief. 'I've never heard anything so outrageous in my life! I knew he was an out-of-date old codger, but I didn't realise he was *insane*!'

'Then I must be insane too,' Leo acknowledged smoothly. 'Because I am willing to agree to that deal, although I also have more pressing reasons for being currently in need of a wife...'

Letty felt disorientated and bewildered. 'You *need* a wife?' she almost whispered, wondering why there wasn't a stampede of eager women pushing her out of their path to reach him and then suppressing that weird and frivolous thought, irritated by her lapse in concentration.

'Six months ago, my sister and her husband died in a car crash. I am attempting to raise their four children. I need a wife to help me with that task,' Leo spelt out succinctly.

'*Four...*children?' Letty gasped in consternation.

'Aged five and under.' Leo decided to give her all the bad news at once. 'The baby was a newborn, who was premature at birth. Ben and Anastasia were on the way to pick him up and finally bring him home from the hospital when they were killed.'

In the stretching heavy silence, Letty blinked in shock. 'How tragic...'

'Yes, but rather more tragic for their children, with only me to fall back on. They need a mother figure, someone who's there more often. I work long hours and I travel as well. The set-up that I have at the moment is not working well enough for them.'

Letty shrugged a slight fatalistic shoulder. 'So, you make sacrifices. You change your lifestyle.'

'I have already done that. Bringing in a wife to share the responsibility makes better sense,' Leo declared in a tone of finality as though only he could give an opinion in that field.

'And you and my grandfather, who doesn't really *want* to be my grandfather,' Letty suggested with a rueful curve to her soft mouth, 'somehow reached the conclusion that *I* could be that wife?'

Continue reading
THE GREEK'S SURPRISE CHRISTMAS BRIDE
Lynne Graham

Available next month
www.millsandboon.co.uk

COMING SOON!

We really hope you enjoyed reading this book. If you're looking for more romance, be sure to head to the shops when new books are available on

Thursday 28th November

To see which titles are coming soon, please visit
millsandboon.co.uk/nextmonth

LET'S TALK

Romance

For exclusive extracts, competitions
and special offers, find us online:

 f facebook.com/millsandboon

🐦 @MillsandBoon

📷 @MillsandBoonUK

Get in touch on 01413 063232

For all the latest titles coming soon, visit
millsandboon.co.uk/nextmonth

MILLS & BOON

THE HEART OF ROMANCE

A ROMANCE FOR EVERY KIND OF READER

MODERN

Prepare to be swept off your feet by sophisticated, sexy and seductive heroes, in some of the world's most glamourous romantic locations, where power and passion collide.
8 stories per month.

HISTORICAL

Escape with historical heroes from time gone by. Whether passion is for wicked Regency Rakes, muscled Vikings or r Highlanders, awaken the romance of the past.
6 stories per month.

MEDICAL

Set your pulse racing with dedicated, delectable doctors in high-pressure world of medicine, where emotions run hig passion, comfort and love are the best medicine.
6 stories per month.

True Love

Celebrate true love with tender stories of heartfelt romand the rush of falling in love to the joy a new baby can bring, focus on the emotional heart of a relationship.
8 stories per month.

Desire

Indulge in secrets and scandal, intense drama and plenty of hot action with powerful and passionate heroes who have wealth, status, good looks…everything but the right woman
6 stories per month.

HEROES

Experience all the excitement of a gripping thriller, with a romance at its heart. Resourceful, true-to-life women and s fearless men face danger and desire - a killer combination!
8 stories per month.

DARE

Sensual love stories featuring smart, sassy heroines you'd w best friend, and compelling intense heroes who are worthy
4 stories per month.

To see which titles are coming soon, please visit

millsandboon.co.uk/nextmonth